The MANNEQUIN QUEEN

The Mannequin Queen
Copyright © 2025 K.N. Fitzwater. All rights reserved.

4 Horsemen
Publications, Inc.

Published By: 4 Horsemen Publications, Inc.

4 Horsemen Publications, Inc.
PO Box 417
Sylva, NC 28779
4horsemenpublications.com
info@4horsemenpublications.com

Cover & Typesetting by Autumn Skye
Edited by Kris Cotter

All rights to the work within are reserved to the author and publisher. No part of this publication may be reproduced, stored in a retrieval system, or transmitted in any form or by any means, electronic, mechanical, photocopying, recording, scanning, or otherwise, except as permitted under Section 107 or 108 of the 1976 International Copyright Act, without prior written permission except in brief quotations embodied in critical articles and reviews. Please contact either the Publisher or Author to gain permission.

All characters, organizations, and events portrayed in this novel are either products of the author's imagination or are used fictitiously.

All brands, quotes, and cited work respectfully belongs to the original rights holders and bear no affiliation to the authors or publisher.

Library of Congress Control Number: 2025949794

Paperback ISBN-13: 979-8-8232-1033-1
Hardcover ISBN-13: 979-8-8232-1034-8
Ebook ISBN-13: 979-8-8232-1035-5

Dedication

This book is dedicated to found families,
adoptive families,
and parents who love and support their
children no matter who they are.
Continue to shine your light for a brighter future.

Table of Contents

Act 1
- ✦ Chapter 1...1
- ✦ Chapter 2...12
- ✦ Chapter 3...24
- ✦ Chapter 4...35
- ✦ Chapter 5...47
- ✦ Chapter 6...58

Act 2
- ✦ Chapter 7...73
- ✦ Chapter 8...88
- ✦ Chapter 9...101
- ✦ Chapter 10..115
- ✦ Chapter 11..129

Act 3
- ✦ Chapter 12..145
- ✦ Chapter 13..155
- ✦ Chapter 14..167
- ✦ Chapter 15..179
- ✦ Chapter 16..192
- ✦ Chapter 17..203

Act 4
- ✦ Chapter 18 217
- ✦ Chapter 19 231
- ✦ Chapter 20 244
- ✦ Chapter 21 258
- ✦ Chapter 22 271

Act 5
- ✦ Chapter 23 289
- ✦ Chapter 24 300
- ✦ Chapter 25 313
- ✦ Chapter 26 324
- ✦ Chapter 27 336
- ✦ Chapter 28 346

Book Club Questions 359
Glossary And Translations 363
Author Bio 367

Act I

The snow falls in the box
Hissing its white noise
A sharp-suited man saunters
All in stark color

"*You're about to enter into another world*
"*A world full of sand, magic, and monsters*
"*A world where the Old Gods are dead, and the dead live again*
"*Join me to unearth a forgotten legacy*

"*As we enter the Twi—*"
The image collapse
It hisses in its white noise
It never stops snowing

Chapter 1

HEWN

JOSIAH WAS BORN YESTERDAY, FULLY FORMED AND hairy. A dwarf newly hewn, as the term was told, would have all the musculature and nerves of any stout adult, but with the wide wonder of a child taking in the world around him. And his eyes were quite wide in this world he emerged into.

For one, it was smooth. The walls, ceiling, floor, were flatter than slate with no etched markings of the skilled maker. For another, it was all metal. Leagues and leagues of shiny alloy stretching onward. Josiah had been walking down this everlasting tunnel for his first whole day, wondering about its making. For he knew the purpose of his own making.

All dwarves were hewn from the stone for a singular purpose: To know.

To know all of the world, as much as they could. Of the civilizations that lived in it. Of the food. Of its people. What they know to be true and the lies they told themselves to sleep at night. That was why the dwarves were made small, hairy, and with an archaic accent: So all will embrace them wherever they traveled. Once they know as much as they could obtain, they are called back into the living stone. For that is their true home and family—the mountain that birthed them.

Josiah's purpose was more finite. He was to know what this strange place was—this place of steel. For that was what he had been treading upon. Steel pressed and shaped not by flesh, but cut with fire and screwed into place by something beyond understanding. But he must understand; he must know. Otherwise, he wouldn't be able to return to the stone.

Thus, Josiah traipsed on and on, peering at diversions such as broken glass that once sheltered rooms of tables and chairs. The hall ended with a door. There was no handle, and it was as smooth as the walls it was framed in. There was a square relief on the wall next to it, with numerous slits that formed a circle.

Curiouser and curiouser, thought Josiah, as his broad fingers brushed against the device.

He recalled from the living stone that this was once called a speaker. But is this something that receives speech or gave it?

"'Ello?" He spoke into the cold device.

The only response was his voice echoing in the hollow hall that stretched behind him.

O, of course! I must consider the recipient of this query. How inconsiderate I am.

"'Ello, computer."

A *sh-chk* sounded, and the door lowered before him in its vertical slot. A massive void stretched before him.

Chk.

Chk.

Chk.

One by one, the conical lights illuminated from the expansive ceiling to reveal highways of metal platforms that crisscrossed each other at different elevations, all upheld by metal cords as thick as his bare arms. Below, a red glow of light. Gears from beyond his sight clicked and whirred. The platforms started moving. Some of them rose and fell; some of them rotated around.

Enamored by the display, Josiah stepped forward. The moment he crossed the threshold, the door slammed shut.

"Test subject 479240 has been acquired," stated a serene voice that sounded too smooth to Josiah's ears. "Test 7099 shall commence in 5... 4... 3... 2..."

A horn blared, and the ground shook. The dust falling on his bare shoulders led Josiah to look up. The ceiling parted to allow rows of perfectly cut metal blades shaped like shark's teeth. They whirred in place, feeding the chains that held the platforms into its vicious mouth.

While as alarming as this situation was, Josiah wasn't troubled by it. All dwarves knew that when the world rocks, you roll. Thus, Josiah couched low, tucking hard against his legs, and rolled like a boulder off a cliff. He slammed against every steel platform on his way. When stalled, he simply shifted his mass and barreled over the edge. On and on, he made his descent, not caring about the wreckage he made on his way down, until at last he dropped to the bottom.

There, a single sliver of a podium stood with a red button that shone. Josiah unraveled himself, then clasped his broad hands behind his rugged, back and investigated the contraption. There were no indentions or etchings. It was made of the same material as all that surrounded him save for the button. It was of an unnatural make that imitated glass. Regardless, he found nothing else and pressed it.

A horn blared overhead. The destructive grinder ceased its roar.

"Congratulations. Test 7099 has been completed by a margin of 15 seconds. Test subject 479240 shall be integrated to the menagerie."

Menagerie? A collection of monsters? Josiah wondered. *What sort of monsters are these?*

Josiah found his answer soon enough. A door slid down nearby to reveal a doll. Life-sized for human standards, with eerily pristine porcelain skin—untarnished by the trails of life. Equally unsettling was the figure and face, a perfect golden ratio was set on its frame as if it was done by a master sculptor. No paint or clothes were adorned to mask the feminine stature bearing before him. No emotion came from its mold-press mask for a face. No humanity despite its appearance of one.

Incredible, he thought.

Then it moved.

Faster than anyone should, it ambled toward him as the gears within its chassis whirred. It was joined by another perfect copy. They maneuvered to flank Josiah on both sides and pointed their perfect, slender fingers at him. Those fingers flipped backward on their joints to reveal four-barrel chambers.

Josiah held out his palms. "Wait, where am I? What is this place?"

"Designation?" their voice box rattled.

"Yes? Yes! What is this designation?"

"Silo 51."

Josiah nodded slowly, then tucked and rolled between their legs. He knew he wouldn't be able to survive them. But if he was going to die, he'd do it on living stone. Josiah barreled down the hall, knocking down all these perfect dolls standing at dainty attention. Soon, he came to a wall with exposed sandstone. Blood was scrawled on it by a finger, trying to spell out something in a language he couldn't read.

Josiah unrolled and touched the earth and felt the pull. The call to go home. He pressed the palm hard and willed the stone to know what he knew. When he removed his hand, the words 15 OLIS were hewn.

The sound of gears grinding drew near. Solemnly, he turned to face his attackers. Blank symmetrical, oval faces stared down at him with empty, plastered eyes, silent as ever. Four-barrel guns fired manufactured bullets, piercing into his flesh. The pain was quick, for he felt the call home.

Josiah melted back into the stone. Taking the etched words with him.

"Test subject 479240 has been deleted," boomed the calm voice from earlier. "Please obtain test subject 479241 for testing."

"479241...

"479241...

"*Would you like to taste them, 479241?*" *the voice cooed.*

It was the voice of his master. Sweet and patient like an Anglorian viper. They were in the capital's bazaar, passing by hawkers wearing stylized shackles about their necks and wrists. He forgot why they were there in the first place, the memory eroded from decades of disuse. But he knew he had stopped dead in his tracks because of the strange fruit hanging high above them.

No, not fruit, he must remind himself. They were infants. Babes taken from screaming enslaved mothers for this season's culling. Here they hung in rows, like freshly washed clothes, battered and fried to crispy tenderness. For all of his youth, he and those that lived in Bazzuu's high court dined on such succulence, for the Djinnasi lords couldn't partake in the bounty of the earth, his master included.

The Djinnasi Lord of Air bowed his gem-adorned head demurely to the merchant, his long flaxen hair shifting in the ever-present wind. Once given, he turned to face him. Oh, how he tried to forget his pretty face painted with a pearlescent base and dotted artistically with crystals. How his delicate stained lips parted as he gave an encouraging sound as he handed him one.

There on a disposable linen was a child's severed forearm, hewn from the joint.

"Aww, 479241, you don't like it?"

The merchant behind his master quaked. He could lose his livelihood if he decided the food was poorly made. Or worse, have him killed for attempted poison. For that was one of the many duties of jhasin, along with dancing and lovemaking.

"I ... don't feel well," he fibbed.

Oh, how his master's delicate thin eyebrows raised, "Not feeling well, my coquette? Is it the dress?"

The dress did itch and was sweltering hot. Like all jhasins, he was to be dressed up and dressed down as his master saw fit. They were not born of the womb, but from the Djinnasi's accursed magic and with no assigned gender. It would've been a gift if he wasn't forced to lose his sense of identity along with it. Today, he was supposed to be a Lolita, a revisit of the historical fashion craze that captivated the attention of his master.

"Yes," he murmured backed then.

"Tsk, that's a shame. Strip."

He froze. He glanced at the merchant, who mouthed to him, please. Everyone around them was beginning to take notice. His master's smile straightened into a flat line. He knew better than to let it become a frown.

So, he handed the morsel back to him and undid all of his ribbons and unbuttoned every button. He pulled off every frilly *garment until at last he slipped out of his petticoat. There he stood in his naked androgynous glory. Bald without the curlicue wig and bonnet. Silver whorls graced his skin to enhance and detract features according to the silver model. A doll for everyone's pleasure. Branded with his numbers on the inside of his forearm.*

"Feel better?" his master asked.

He nodded.

"Good, now open up and tell me what you think."

Defeated, he opened his young mouth as he craned his head back. Keeping his eyes skyward as the fatty skin was pushed onto his tongue. Hanging bloated bodies swayed in the lazy wind, causing the hooks to creak against the chain.

"Aramis…

"Aramis…

"Aramis?"

A gentle touch on his arm was enough to break the nightmare.

Aramis, shuddered awake. He was in a busy bazaar but this time in Amaveriel's new market street. Escorted not by his childhood master, but by his beloved friend, Sister Rhyllae—a sister of the Morning Lord. Her head, adorned in a yellow hijab of her order, tilted to one side. Her soft brown eyes were scanning his face in worry.

"Aramis, what's wrong?" she asked. "Is it the chicken?"

Chicken?

Aramis looked up again. Hanging on hooks creaking in the wind were chickens, freshly battered and fried. Sister Rhyllae stood there, in her palms were strips of samples given by the food merchant, who was nervously wringing his hands. Glancing around, he could tell everyone was beginning to take notice of the scene. The air was hot and itchy.

Aramis fled, weaving between gawkers and homemakers alike. To go somewhere—anywhere—from prying eyes. A narrow slip of an alleyway caught his eye. He cut off an ox pulling a cart to duck in there. The noise deadened as he ambled down the alley. Finally, when he was sure he could find some measure of peace, Aramis leaned his back against the wall and slid down to sit.

Aramis Feres.

A name he chose for himself when he finally escaped that hellish capital of Bazzuuport. A name taken from the forbidden manuscripts of ancient times. He wanted to be as brave and clever as those men of foil. More than anything, he wanted to be a man. A man not by physique, but of his own name and making. That was why he traveled far in the desert of Ioun and dunked himself in the mystical spring waters of Zemzem. Yet, for of all its powers, it couldn't remove the branding.

He lifted his right sleeve and found the damning numbers imprinted on his skin: 479241. Aramis rubbed his callus thumb back and forth on it, watching how the ink moved with his brown flesh when pressed. To his credit, the edges managed to blur over the years, one of the few benefits of old age setting in. How long could he live now that he'd entered his fifties? Jhasin were luxury items made to take the toll the Djinnasi lords put them through, yet they were routinely discarded at the sweet age of sixteen. No one knew when they truly expired. Perhaps, Aramis had forty more years? Maybe well beyond what normal humans could achieve. Would he still be able to move like now, run and jump on demand, or would he become infirm like the venerable elders of this city? Would Sister Rhyllae be forced to take care of him by then?

Rhyllae!

Aramis shut his eyes and leaned his head against the wall. In his haste, he left her high and dry. He looked back at the end of the alleyway and found her standing there.

She was not angry, thank goodness. The priestess slowly lowered her shawl about her shoulders, allowing her curls to fluff out about her half-elven ears. Aramis unhooked his cloak and laid it on the ground next to him. Without a word, she accepted the seat.

"It wasn't the chicken." Aramis broke the silence, his words spilling out. "It was the wind. How the metal creak with the heat, I—"

Sister Rhyllae put her hand on his knee, ceasing his ramblings. The ring of tourmalines he'd given her depicted the sun rising over the horizon. To see it still on her finger gave him a small measure of comfort.

"We went through a lot of changes, lately," Sister Rhyllae said. "It's not unusual for someone with your past experience to have relapses. It's nothing to be ashamed of."

Aramis scoffed. "Tell that to the vendors."

"Then, tell me."

He grimaced. *Can I? Can I tell her the madhouse I once called normal?*

Aramis laid his hand on top of hers and looked into her freckled face, searching for any hesitation, any chink in her stalwart armor. Yet, the more he looked, the more he found love in those golden-flecked brown eyes of hers.

"It was my old slave master, again," he began. He recounted the vile memory with the whole truth, not by sight alone, but his thoughts and what he felt.

Though he could see colors of emotion flitting across her expression, she didn't stop him. It was like the early years of their friendship: no longer strangers, yet eager to learn more. A well of healing like the spring waters of Zemzem.

Back then, it was him divulging his past and her taking it in. It took a while to crack her sanctum shell to find out about her past and allow the roles to reverse. Strange how in recent times the roles flipped back once again.

"I had to do it, Rhyllae," Aramis said, more for himself than for her. "If I didn't, that merchant would've been killed, and another would've continued the chain. All of those vendors were slaves ordered to sell by their master's bidding. All of us nothing more than links."

She gave a gentle squeeze on his knee. "You sought out to break that chain, later. Not for only yourself, but for them. For all of us."

"Why am I remembering it now? Why can't the past stay buried?"

The Morning sister hummed and nodded as she gave it some thought. At last she said, "Perhaps, because the past shouldn't be forgotten. When my sisters and I bury the dead, we have to make sure all wounds were healed."

Aramis arched his eyebrows at her.

"Not physically, but spiritually. Otherwise, they come back, worse than before."

"Zombies, skeletons, and the like?"

Sister Rhyllae nodded.

Aramis grunted in awe and stared straight ahead. Would he ever find such peace when his time is up? Or would he come back from the shifting sands of Ioun to seek mortal flesh? Like Bagheera in M'thealquilôk when she was transformed by Tellezard's wicked spell. Like all of the fallen Jessenters two moons past. Would he, like them, rise to the call of the doppelgänger queen, who he'd once called lover?

"*Me'qora*," Rhyllae called out to him, both hands on his. "That won't be your fate."

Aramis's silver eyes refocused, steelier than ever. "Then you have to bury me deep."

She opened her mouth to counterargue and stopped to glance at the wall across from them. Aramis's hand went to the hilt of his twin blades, but stopped short of unsheathing them. There, on the wall, cracks formed before their very eyes. Bits and pieces crumbled away to reveal the words: SILO 51.

Chapter 2

CIRCLE OF THE OWLS

THE COOKIE CRUMBLED THE MOMENT DIDO TOOK a bite.

Ah, what a shame, the satyr mage thought. *Not enough butter.*

But the treasurer couldn't fault poor McGruffin' on such a thing. The whole city was still recovering from the doppelgänger's destruction, and trade from the pirates wouldn't happen until closer to Shab-e Yalda, the locals' winter celebration. Butter was simply too precious of a commodity, even to honored guests.

"'Ere we are," came McGruffin', an elderly dwarf, as he rounded the corner. Laid across his sinewy arms was a flat, rectangular, wooden case.

In her enthusiasm, the satyr slurped down some of the red tea in her cup, both dwarven made, clearing the crumbs left on her palate. Following after McGruffin' was Drake, his loving moon-elf partner, bringing a tray of savory chicken samosas. His white hair, braided in intricate detail, shone brightly as much as his teeth against his black skin.

"Yes," Drake crooned. "Let us see this legacy called dwarven-fine craftmanship."

McGruffin' snorted as he set the case before Dido. "The legacy is not of the dwarves, but of the Mountain Mother 'erself, ye lout."

"So long as you remember I'm your only 'lout'." Then Drake gave the gray-haired dwarf a peck on his temple before he distributed the welcomed treats.

Dido quickly tucked the pastry in her cheek to stifle her giggle as McGruffin's cheeks took a rosy turn. His thick mustache fluttered as he cough and cleared his throat. His broad fingers delicately unhooked the golden latch and pried open the case. Dido nearly choked from the sight.

On the silken bed were twin silver daggers. The handles were slender and wide as the blades they housed. Depictions of dancing desert foxes encased the paracord of elvish linen, leaving all the outer edges as smooth as marbled glaze on a cake. The blades themselves look exquisitely like feathers with no notches. It was a beautiful set of hardened, silver alloy to be sure! But that wasn't what had Dido gagging from excitement. Those streaks in the blade weren't for ornamental design.

Her fingers jumbled through her carpet purse in haste until they acquired her trusty jeweler's eye. Dido stood on top of the chair with her giddy hooves, placed her glasses on top of her head, and leaned her whole body over the table. Scanning through the lenses for that telltale gleam while holding her round spectacles up high.

"They... they can't be," Dido said.

"Aye, lassie, they are." McGruffin' chest swelled with proud.

"Diamonds! You suspended diamonds in the alloy?!"

"It's ta least I can do for the hero of Amaveriel."

"The least?!" Dido fell back on her seat, a palm on one of her ram-shaped horns. The impact knocked the glasses back on her nose. "What more could you have done?!"

"Well, it's not magically enhanced, as per instruction might I add. It wouldn't hurt to 'ave some sort of electrical conduit innit. Or, perhaps a poison capsule, released upon impact, hmm? Or perhaps—"

"—Or perhaps I'll pay you for the services rendered. At least, the first installment." How would Dido explain it all to General Korzha, she hadn't figured it out.

The dwarf eyed Drake as Dido once again dug around in her purse. He gave an encouraging tilt of his head as if to say, 'well, go on now'. McGruffin' pouted, yet he was met more eyeball dancing and head swiveling from the dark-skin beauty. The interaction wasn't lost on the satyr. Hopeful rosy eyes affixed upon him.

"Baaaappphhffine!" he exclaimed. "I'll waive ta fee."

"Really? Oh, the Jessenters thank you—"

"Now wait just a dern minute! I meant the diamonds are free, ye fancy-pansy, fae-happy, two-time swindler. I goot to keep a roof o'er me head, cover me hubby's luxurious lifestyle, put food on me table, maintain the running costs of me business..."

On and on he went, even as Dido shelled out the dinars on the table. He stopped when Dido placed the last coin on the polished wood. Tentative silence filled the room as McGruffin' checked each one for any fae-trickery. No offense was given of course. Most business practitioners don't always state the type of coin that should be tender, and fae tend to give temporary coins. The Faerie culture didn't approve of rampant capitalism and relied instead on bargains and oaths. Dido knew ahead of time that this dwarf was quite thorough in his dealings of her kind. Not that Dido would dare do such a thing, of course! It's too much work for such a simple trick. And she would rather stay with neighbors that would trust her than be run out of town for her folly.

"650 dinars all accounted for." McGruffin' shook her hand. "Thank you for your timely payment."

Dido gave another shake and bowed her head. "The Jessenters are happy to do business with you."

Out in the salty midnight air, Dido donned her coat as Drake waited with the prize. The moon was in the shadow of the scorpion, auspicious for those who seek out quarrels. For a satyr who has no desire for further drama in her busy schedule, Dido couldn't tarry any longer.

"The diamonds were a gift from my people," Drake confessed as he handed her the precious daggers. "Tell the Silver Fox, '*way elyamamen theliads argo'nim.*' Shuka un, my lady."

He then ended the conversation by touching two fingers on his lips, then to his forehead, and arched them downward as he bowed. Dido's mouth dropped as she mimed his goodbye. Hardly leaving from the tiny porch where she stood as the door latched shut.

The Silver Fox, the moniker the locals gave to Aramis Feres. Legend had it, he not only freed the slaves from the terrors of Bazzuuport, but also integrated them throughout the tribes of Ioun, the moon elves included. He took on all their woes, from settling disputes to scavenging a flower that cured an ill child. Aramis dwelled in the desert until his last grand theft from the Djinnasi lords. With that, he guided those refugees across the entire length of the desert nation to the fabled city of Amaveriel, earning another name: shepherd of the desert. Ever since then, he'd 'retired' and lived here for well over two decades.

It wasn't the idea of forgetting that shocked Dido from such a gift. No. Elves still lived a lengthy life of several centuries, with a few lucky enough to hit the millennial age. No, the shock was due to the Silver Fox's reputation.

Unlike those he freed, Aramis never integrated well to city life. He fell deep into black market schemes and racked up charges beyond accounting. From what Sister Rhyllae had told the little satyr, what redeemed him was when he unearthed a trafficking ring sending some of the freed people back into slavery. Aramis showed no mercy and slaughtered them all. The thought of it made Dido shiver, and she pulled her coat closer to her body as she walked down the sandy streets.

To his credit, Aramis never denied the crimes he had committed under Pondo Rhum and didn't resist when pressed into serving the Jessenters. That was how he ended up helping the rebels these past years and had been a valuable asset ever since. Without him, they wouldn't be able to secure the much-needed funds from all the tomes and dungeons that proliferated across these lands. And without him, none would be able to defeat the dangerous doppelgänger that blew up their base and half of the abbey.

Perhaps, therein lay the change of the public's perception. Even the general was willing to pay a handsome sum for the daggers she carried. In fact, Korzha wanted to do it in person, but was convening with the new Mother Superior, Myrrh, still negotiating to further enlist the Morning Lord priestesses to provide more extensive medical assistance to their cause. Sister Rhyllae was a willing volunteer, surely there could be more. Though, Dido could understand the hesitation; there would be no guarantee the priestess on loan would survive the hardships they faced.

The thoughts swirled in Dido's mind as she clip-clopped down the hushed night of Amaveriel, taking the twists and turns of its convoluted streets. She didn't know where Aramis haunted, ever on a constant move for these past two moons. Still, he's the only jhasin living here, and since they were beings created by magic, all she had to do was pinpoint the magical 'scent' of his trail.

Dido took the final turn and stopped cold.

The claustrophobic buildings opened up to a square lot of dust and stacked stones on pallets. A few yards before her cloven feet was the gaping maw of the exposed pyro ducts that riddled underneath the city of Amaveriel. This was the old market. The rebel base was housed underneath these very streets and was destroyed, causing the buildings above to cave in. The Elders had quarantined off this route for the danger of further collapse as they slowly relocated every stone to the abbey for reconstruction.

They have yet to fill in the holes, Dido noted as she walked down the barren street. Stacks of limestone towered over her like ziggurat temples of yore.

Then something fell on her head. Claws dug into her scarf, ripping into her hair. In her panic, Dido willed herself away, transporting a meter from her intruder. Her curls bounced around her horns, free of the strangle hold.

It was an owl. That much Dido can see. Waist-high of the average human, like her, and cloaked in a dark hooded cape about their neck. It landed silent as the grave, her patchwork scarf tangled in one of its talons.

"<So, the gifts were not lost upon you,>" it hooted in the Fae tongue. Oh, how long had it been since she heard anyone utter the Faerie language.

"<Who sent you?>" Dido asked, the tremor in her voice exaggerated by the echoes bouncing around them.

The owl narrowed their eyes at her. "<Come now, surely your time here with these mortals hasn't softened your mind.>"

There was no denying who sent them. The Bramble Court never forgot any slight upon them, no matter how minor. Dido settled the parcel on the ground while keeping her eyes on them, then waved her hands to the side as she slowly rose up.

"<As I recall,>" Dido said back in the Fae tongue, "<I'm on vacation. The records should reflect those terms.>"

"<As I recall, sister of the grove, I'm no bureaucrat for you to squabble at.>" In a blink, they unsheathed their rapier from under their wing, proportioned to their avian size. "<My name is Avarice Novoskya, and your life is forfeit.>"

Dido wanted to say more, explain more, but it was too late. Avarice took two steps forward, their cape fluttering in the change of wind, and then disappeared.

Crab biscuits.

She should've known by this locale alone they would pull such a trick. There's no sand here to alert their whereabouts, and the air is too dry for any spontaneous rain magic. Dido would have to cast a detection spell and quick.

"<By the twinkle of the stars, let thy light glisten upon the shadows surrounding me.>"

In a wink, all the shadows were spotted with specks of starlight. They looked like miniature lakes mirroring the night sky above. Dido's rosy-red eyes scanned for any movement. Her fingers extended in an L-shape as she spun around.

From her peripheral, a starry amoeba slunk into view, too close for comfort. A flash of metal and all Dido knew was her left hand had been impaled by iron. The cry leaped from her gut. Terror surged through her core. She wasn't going to be slain. Oh no. She'll be maimed prick by pinprick.

Dido brought her right hand to bear on their amorphous face, symbols flashing from her fingertips. "*Invinctus!*" Golden sparks shot out from her palm right into them.

Avarice shrilled like no other owl ever did. Dido took no pleasure as they screeched, feathers clutching their face as they stumble backward.

She ran, leaving the wooden case and the avian assassin behind. The satyr mage needed copious amounts of water if she was going to tango with this bird. The closer to the docks, the better. Teleportation would take too much energy, and she needed plenty to spare against this mage assassin.

Instead, she produced her gnarled and twisted medlar wand and tapped on her hocks. "*Brže, brže.*"

All of the silent doors and windows blurred past her as Dido sprinted south. At last, she could taste the sea spray in the air. Lilted laughter drifted from perfumed halls with red lanterns. It couldn't be helped; most of the port was meant to shelter and comfort sailors who survived long voyages. Perhaps she should do the same, for the wind in her sails had diminished. Surely someone would be able to shelter this satyr from her doom.

Dido took a turn and stumbled into a terracotta-filled alley. Nestled in between stacks of pottery were crates of clay and wildflowers that managed to take hold. The little satyr plopped herself down next to a bell jar ready for the kiln, counting her breaths as they slow down.

A feather drifted down in front of her nose.

Nervously, Dido's gaze drifted skyward. Looming overhead from the roof was Avarice. The feathers around their face were singed and starting to molt. Dido jumped up from her seat, hopping from one jug to another with her skillful goat legs. She cringed as she heard the pottery shatter behind her. She'd repay the damages if she was not dead.

Out on the other side of the alley, Dido spun around to pull off another spell.

She didn't.

The moment she halted her cloven hooves, the owl barreled right into her. Dido felt a thousand needles stabbing right into her as she fell back to the stone floor. Wings buffeted her face as the onslaught continued.

Then it relented.

Clunk.

Clunk.

Clunk.

Came the sound of wooden soles walking down the stone pier. Dido turned her head; her right horn knocked against the floor as she did so. There was a young woman garbed in an expensive silk robe. The painted moon peeked from the stylized clouds gracing the skirt and hem of her floor-length square sleeves. The robe was all bound in a houndstooth gray sash, secured into a sparrow bow, with a golden phoenix brooch secured in the middle.

"My, my, my," the stranger said. "What do we have here, a hunter with their quarry?"

Her red paper umbrella hid her face, but Dido recognized the telltale lilt in her voice. The esteemed lady of dance, Tsuki.

No, thought Dido. *Don't come over here. Run. Run, you damn fool!*

Yet, the maiden drooped her umbrella, revealing a perfectly round bun, enhanced by a stream of bellflowers and chimes. Her eyes gleamed as her painted red lips curled into a smirk. "It is untoward to have such clandestine affairs out in the open twilight, isn't it?" Tsuki closed the umbrella shut.

"Only a fool would stand in the way of the hunter's catch." Avarice harked back as they readied their needle.

"Oh, a fool, am I?" Tsuki pressed her delicate fingers on her chest. "I guess it takes one to know one. Otherwise, you would've fled to hide your disgrace of being caught by the sight of another. Isn't that the Circle of the Owls protocol?" With the same hand, the *maiko* tapped at the side of her nose, before waggling it in the air.

Dido felt Avarice's talons tighten upon her flesh. Thoughts spun in Dido's head from what Tsuki said.

How does she know? What connections does she have that allow her to know such things?

"But since I'm a fellow fool," Tsuki said, "I will give you a chance to exeunt with what little honor you have left. *Kudasai.*"

Avarice did leave her body and flew toward Tsuki, who was still smiling against all odds. The owl brought their rapier to bear in flight. Dido's heart raced, her eyes fixed on the sight. Then a shield, of all things, smacked right into the owl. A poof of feathers exploded from whence they were. Avarice sailed with the metal disc over the pier and out of sight.

"The lady said, 'please,'" said a woman with a brassy voice. *Dawn!*

The tousled, blonde lesbian ran up to Tsuki, a fellow member of the Jessenters and a dear friend of Dido's. The martyr red sash tied about her waist flapped in the wind as she drew her gladius blade. Her unbuttoned blouse showed perspiration trickling down between her cleavage toward her naval.

A dark shadow flew over the pier. Avarice readied their fine rapier as they descended. They landed between the two women for a moment before speeding at the dancer.

Tsuki deftly weaved away from their barbs. Then Avarice lunged. The maiden sidestepped the blow and let her fan be pierced instead. In a blink, the *maiko* twisted the fan and disarmed the owl of their needle.

Dawn attempted to stab Avarice from behind, but the crafty owl dove between her legs and landed a few feet from the two. With a cry from their beak, their sword zipped free from Tsuki's clutches. The foil flipped over, and Avarice plucked it out of the air as they raced for another bout.

Focus, Dido told herself. *Now is your chance.*

She turned her face toward the starry heavens above, willing herself to ignore the reigniting sound of steel and feathers. By will alone, she forced the surrounding air to polarize. Without it, there'd be no medium for the magic to channel.

"For sooth I have witness," Dido chanted.

"In darkest blaze

"The spark from heavenly oil

"Presented before me..."

There!

A prickle of static coursed her body and fur, an energetic thrill palpable on her tongue. Yet, she paused in her chanting, for there was another soul present. On the roof across from the way, Aramis stood, cloaked against the increasing wind. His silver eyes pierced the night. He crouched by the edge and held a silver dagger.

He found them! Dido's heart leaped into her throat.

Aramis gave her a knowing nod and tossed the dagger up to hold it by its blade. He meant for the blade to be a magical foci. With that encouragement, Dido continued. Thunder clapped in anticipation.

"Let the fools fall in line

"Of the magical divide

"Between false gods
"And mortals divine!"

With her finger's point, Aramis let loose the silver blade, and Dido trailed her finger along with it. Oh, how it streaked in the sky like a meteor scraping the horizon. It landed true in the chest of Avarice, who was in the air, with their wings spread above Dawn and Tsuki's defensive postures.

"Lightning Strike!" Dido let loose the final words, and it was met in kind.

The clouds parted ways as a rush of plasma clapped through them. Tsuki opened her umbrella over the two of them as it came screaming down. The lightning arced into the embedded silver dagger, and all turned into a flash of white. When they all opened their eyes, they found a charred corpse and the silver gleam of a blade.

It's finally over.

Dido then let exhaustion close her eyes, not caring if she may never wake from its solace.

Chapter 3

SEIZE THE SUN

WHEN DIDO AWOKE, IT WAS WITH THE SUN ON her face and hymnal melodies in her ears. She was swaddled in a blanket with a six-pointed flower embroidered on it. She was laid out on a makeshift hammock in a garden, sheltered by the fragrant branches of a tea olive tree. There was a statue of a lady kneeling with an empty plate, overlooking a cluster of roses, freshly trimmed of the spent blooms. Next to her, in this quaint setup, was General Korzha. Tall and narrow compared to many who dwelled here, the exiled Töskan had resorted to sitting on a large pile of embroidered pillows on the grass, splaying his long legs neatly by the length of her bedding. In his long fingers was a leather-bound book with a white barren tree emblazoned on the cover.

"...And the ship went out into the High Sea and passed on into the West." Korzha read out loud, clearly absorbed with the material.

Dido relaxed her shoulders and leaned back into the hammock. Of course she would be in the abbey's protective cloister, out in central garden, no less. They expanded, from what she could tell, beyond the west wing with more alliums and a donated persimmon sapling, adding to the agricultural projects under their tentative care. Sister Rhyllae told her weeks ago the Elders had approved a hospice center closer to the heart of Amaveriel, making it more accessible in the years to come. But that was not for another season.

"Dear me, you didn't read the entire trilogy while I was recuperating, did you?" Dido finally piped up.

His icy blue eyes flickered over the leather binding from surprise, then fluttered back to the book.

"No," he drew out the word. "I merely picked up from where I left off. Which was, for your information, chapter five. When the king finally met the steward and the land began to heal."

"That long?!"

"Yes, and I am sorry to say, you missed breakfast entirely."

Dido groaned. "How awful. Now I must languish here with an unhappy stomach as the cooks busy themselves with a hearty lunch for the whole cloister. There won't be a smattering of turmeric or a nibble of nutmeg until all prayers are said and done."

"Why, you're more hobbit than satyr than I took you for."

"Hardly," Dido said as she straightened out the hem of the blanket on her goatish lap. "I knew that the moment I wake up, you'll interrogate me incessantly with all the wild questions swimming in your head. I would rather be peppered by them with roasted peppers and olives content in my gullet."

Korzha rolled his eyes and lifted a plate from his side. A half-torn piece of bread, a lump of *jibneh baida*, a salty cheese common in these parts, and half-shriveled prunes adorned the dish. Dido made a pleasant gasp when placed before her; then her eyes queried him.

Korzha waved his left hand. "Fear not, I had my proper fill of sausage and mash."

Satisfied, Dido tucked in as he finished the rest of the passage. When he uttered the line, "Well I'm back, he said," the general closed the volume shut. He tucked it under his arm and gave her a once over.

"You're not on vacation, are you," he stated.

"No," Dido admitted reluctantly. "Not outside of official filings, that is. Truth be told, all of Summer had fled from the grove now. Has been for several decades. There are no green leaves on the trees anymore. The court is all dreary and stale, despite the pumpkins everywhere. Suffice to say, almost all the Fae hail the Bramble Queen. And I ... well ... it's too much of a change for me. 'I needed a holiday. A long one,' if I'm to quote that book of yours."

"Thus, you falsify their documents to appease wondering eyes and escaped out into the blue world."

"Until those slavers captured me, yes. All this time, I feared I would be poached by cruel-hearted humans and those dastardly Djinnasi lords if I ever revealed my magic. But I never suspected the Bramble Queen would use the Court of the Owls against me. Maybe I have been foolish to be afraid for so long."

"Indeed. I learned long ago that our minds could ensnare us with deadlier traps than our mortal foes. It is a poison many had drunk to savor its deceptive flavor."

"I hope you weren't disappointed in me for such failings."

"On the contrary, I find you commendable to continue your duties despite it wrecking your nerves. I wish more could do the same."

Dido smiled and leaned back against the hammock to look up at the clear blue sky.

"Knowing your skillful accounting," came Korzha's brisk voice, "I'm surprised how quick they found out. I suppose all truth wills out in the end. And your oath?"

Dido sighed and took off her glasses to rub the bridge of her broad nose. "The oath of mine to the Jessenters remains the same. For your concern," she said with a point of her glasses, "it was made to the organization, not to your predecessor. So long the organization lives, I am indebted to the cause."

Korzha's lips quirked into a smile. "And we, in turn, are indebted to you. Not by your magical prowess alone, but your zeitgeist of organizational acuity."

Dido laughed. "You're saying that because I hold the key to the backstock of rum."

He returned a chuckle in kind. Then Korzha placed his hand on hers and gently shook it. "Rest, now. The ritual for those blades can wait when you're sufficiently healed."

She forgot how tall six foot was when he stood up and stretched out his lanky body. His graying blonde hair scraping against the blossoms of the tree.

"Hang on now, mister." Dido called out to him when he collected his doublet. Her arms crossed over her chest. "What about you?"

"Me? Ah, yes, the meeting." His face soured from the thought of it. "I must await for further approval."

"Approval? Whatever for?"

For a while he didn't say a word as he buttoned up. His jaw tightened as his eyes clouded with thought, a telltale sign of his inner fury.

Dido pressed on, "The request wouldn't tax them too much on their resources, surely. One healer alone can tend to a single unit, and we can provide the supplies they need."

"The approval is not upon us. It's on whether the new Mother Superior is worthy of the station she offices. That judgement lies with the Baba herself."

Much had changed since the last time Sister Rhyllae was in the Mother Superior's office. The lonely oppressive desk at the end of the room was joined by other desks, adorned with flowers and newly minted stationery. In between them and her was a low table surrounded by sitting cushions. Stacks of various tomes and scrolls were dispersed upon its surface. The left and right walls were still filled with volumes, but in the midst of reorganization. She heard Sister Ruel petitioned to improve their library system. It seemed the Mother Superior let her take a crack at it here first. Behind them all were the windows arching ever skyward, free of glass and the second floor that blocked it. The room was filled with the song of the city bustle. The fresh breeze tantalized her face with the spices from the open market. After being tucked away in the new hospice wing for days, the scent was uplifting.

"Sister Rhyllae, thank you for coming on such short notice," Mother Superior Myrrh called out to her.

Gone were her sunset colors of her old station. Here, Myrrh was adorned with a golden tapestry robe that fell from her shoulders, with the sleeves slit open at the elbow to allow her arms to do the necessary work. Her neck and arms were covered, of course, by a cream-colored cloth that ruched from the seams, creating a warm contrast to her dark skin. Upon her head was the new habit style. The front of the headdress was embellished with the seven rays of the rising sun and shaped in a peak akin to the northern rooftops she heard so much about. The yellow shawl was pinned and draped away from the Mother Superior's face and fell gracefully down her back, the edges embroidered in the same fashion as the robe. It was still shocking to see the neat and tidy chignon at the back of her nape. The headdress option was extended to all mothers and sisters, though Rhyllae was still hesitant to forgo her habitual style. Raised in the Abbey from infanthood, she considered Amaveriel, and the desert it dwell in, home. Though it was a small thing to fuss over, Rhyllae couldn't find it in her heart to erase the culture that supported her.

Sister Rhyllae bowed before her mothers and once more before the Mother Superior.

"Leave us," Myrrh said.

Uh oh, Rhyllae couldn't help but think as the mothers nod and leave. They smiled at her as they passed, but she couldn't discern whether it was genuine or forced politeness. Rhyllae instead tried to discern the meaning of it on Myrrh's face, but the dark beauty was as mysterious as the famous sphinx of legend.

"I heard you have been attending to our ailing sisters. How are they faring?" the Superior asked her.

"Poorly," Sister Rhyllae admitted with downcast eyes. Part of her felt guilty taking a market stroll yesterday, but everyone, including Aramis, insisted she needed a break. "The symptoms were common enough to speak of dysentery, though where and how they encountered such foul waters, I couldn't figure out. That's not to mention the other complications from their bones failing. It's as if the marrow gave up, no matter how hard I tried to encourage it. I have, of course, jasper to spare and have been encouraging our sisters to use them daily. But it was as if we're—"

"—we're swimming up a torrential river." The Mother Superior walked around her desk. There, a slender leather-bound book with a faded ribbon down the middle. The handwriting was poor and, strange enough, made of some sort of graphite.

"Yes," Rhyllae said. "Some of them lost clumps of hair. Worse, there are those bleeding from the inside out. From … everywhere."

The Mother Superior said not a word as she donned stark white reading gloves. With considerable care, she flipped to a page and presented it to Rhyllae for her to read. It was a journal of a lay sister, that much she could tell, and in elvish script, back when the standard unifying language was put to use.

> "…We're swimming up a torrential river," Sister Rhyllae read out loud. "With no end in sight. Flesh burnt and broiled as if touched by pestilence's rotten hand. All hair had been shorn in clumps as a bird would molt. The bowels raged with blood and sickness as if to evacuate from a raging fire that is the body. The bones refused the call to replenish what was lost…"

"Mother Moon preserve us," Rhyllae whispered.

Myrrh took the book away and covered it in the protective cloth with care. "This was written two thousand years ago, when accursed lands from the Ancients' folly were still plentiful to be found." Then the Mother Superior shut the journal and laid it on the desk surface.

"Are you saying there's foul land once more? Here?"

Myrrh took off the gloves and rolled up her right sleeve. Blisters and abrasions streaked across her dark skin, the same as the sisters ailing in their rooms. Rhyllae's eyes widened when she realized it. It was the same as those who made that fateful journey two cycles ago.

"The Karatow Mountains," Sister Rhyllae said in a hoarse whisper. "When you were there collecting those poor souls who were caught in that... that blast. By the Morn, you should be in bed resting!"

Myrrh nodded in confirmation as she rolled it back down. "I bleed and tire as much as they do, and my bowels disagree with me frequently. Every day my hair becomes thinner, and my skin burns from the irritation. Yet, I have the strength to set upon this path that is laid before me and see the Baba Magena herself."

"And yet here you stand." Rhyllae eyed her with concern.

"I don't suffer the severe effects because of my mixed heritage. Oh, no. No," she countered when the sister pointed at herself. "Not of the elvish kind. Even though I cannot confide in you such origins, I can assure you the magic that flows within me is as strong as yours. Strong enough, at least, to meet the Matriarchs and tell them of this dire situation."

"I see."

The mother raised her eyebrows at the sister at such an empty response. "I have not forgotten my promise of providing you and your sisters proper matrimony once I have their approval. If your sisters still desire to have such exclusions, of course."

Rhyllae flushed with sudden heat. "Forgive me, Mother Superior. I meant it is gratuitous of you to provide such a loving and endearing order, but... should you?"

The stillness of Myrrh's Töskan blue eyes, a purplish gray in truth, as they affixed upon the sister unnerved Sister Rhyllae to her core.

"Should you go by yourself, I mean," Rhyllae clarified, grateful that Myrrh relented her gaze. "Send a delegate. A messenger. Someone who is capable to relay your orders while you receive proper care."

"Rhyllae, please." Myrrh raised her raised palm and sat herself down at her seat.

In the shifting daylight, she saw how sallow her cheeks were and the bags creeping under her eyes. The Mother Superior took a deep breath to collect her thoughts. When she looked upon her again, it was with effort. "I shan't be going alone in my travels. Which is why I have brought you here before me."

Rhyllae was gobsmacked.

A sister traveling to '*Aly Thun Thŭr*', *the* Holy Throne, was a great honor. The Baba and her Cardinals usually conferred with the Matriarchs, those who manage each nation's holy temples, abbeys, and pilgrimage sites, a task made easier by their covenant of Matrons. Once a year, the Matrons of each region brought forth the best of the best sisters ready to take the next step in their spiritual ascension. With the conflict in Ioun and the desire to keep Amaveriel a secret, they didn't have a Matron to guide the nation. Thus, only one sister with the Mother Superior was allowed to leave from the Abbey of the Rising Dawn, a tradition that happened whenever a new superior took office. When Myrrh waved for her to sit, Sister Rhyllae slumped down on a pile of books instead of the seat next to her.

"It is high time you become a mother, Sister Rhyllae. You're the oldest sister on record, if I'm to be frank. Your dedication to not only the Abbey but to the whole community of

Amaveriel is admirable. That goes without saying how fearless you have become in your ventures with the Jessenters. You're more than capable of training and managing sisters on your own, and I dare say, with more efficiency than some others. Yet, you let your fellow priestesses obtain the rank and station above your own throughout your lifetime. My daughter, it is time I call upon you to rise up and greet the dawn. Trial or no trial, we need you more than ever."

A wave of emotion washed over Rhyllae, too strong for her to contain. Her fingers trembled as she brought them to her lips and a tear trickled down her cheek. Validation. To hear it in the first place was rewarding in itself. The sister never knew she craved to hear such words. Yet, her heart was wrought with terror. What would become of her future if she took on this course? What about Aramis and her? Nothing would be the same.

Rhyllae willed herself to take a shuddering breath to soothe her nerves before speaking. "You know how I much appreciate hearing this. But I can't do it. I can't," she added when the Mother Superior furrowed her brows. "Every sister of the cloth, when they become mothers, have to transfer. I can't leave everyone behind. Please, don't make me do this."

"Is this about Feres?"

The question stunned the sister into silence.

"I see," the Mother Superior said, and closed her eyes with thought. "The Silver Fox would have a difficult time following you to your new station due to his crimes. With time, and with some persuasion, I'm confident he'll join you in the end."

Sister Rhyllae shook her head. "This goes beyond the two of us, Mother Superior. I cannot bear to leave Amaveriel to its plight on their own. Not when so much blood has been spilt."

"Sister Rhyllae?"

"I'm sorry, but my answer is no. This is my life. These people are my family. I want to fight for their freedom."

"Rhyllae."

"I'm needed here!" Rhyllae's voice rose.

"You are needed elsewhere!" Myrrh raised her voice in turn. She threw her arm out toward the open windows to the world beyond. "You're a gift to the world! You have done great and impossible things that no sister has done before. Who am I—who are we—to shield you and keep your light under a basket?"

The words stung Rhyllae's lips shut. Her shaky fingers frantically tried to wipe the tears away to no avail.

"Sixty-one long years have you served, Sister Rhyllae." Then Myrrh spoke in a calmer tone, "Sixty-one years have you perfected your skills and prayers to do some good in this world. The world beyond our cloister." Then the Mother Superior rose from her seat and knelt—knelt!—before the sister to take her trembling fingers. "They need you as much as we do."

Then Myrrh placed a small medallion, the symbol of the mothers' rank emblazoned upon it, in her hands. Thin but solid, it was made of precious silver and gold. On the silver side was the Mother Lune, Her bare feet touching the crescent moon as she held the lantern aloft high for those to see it. Sister Rhyllae sniffled and flipped to the other side to find a roaring lion with the crowning sun radiating behind it, the symbol of the Morning Lord who was fierce with his love and strong in his light. 'Seize the Sun' was imprinted overhead.

Chapter 4

RABBIT'S FOOT

MIDDAY PRAYERS AND BELLS WARBLED ACROSS the bowl-shaped Amaveriel, drifting their way toward the bay and the piers that surround it, asking all the faithful followers of the holy Sun and Moon to pay patronage. Though proliferate was the faith of the Morning Lord, few would go on their knees and press their foreheads on the ground like the young officer of the Jessenters.

There posed on a rug found in a forgotten corner, Dawn took in the glorious sight of the ships sailing in. Every morn, they rolled in to dock from their nighttime fishing, their sails dissolving into the decks like clouds of whipped sugar melting into hot tea. Bare-breasted and barefooted, she inhaled the salty tang of the coastal bay. The young, rebel officer stretched out her toned body. She snuck a glance at her girlfriend, Tsuki, fast asleep among the ornate red cushions, her bum as pale as her name.

Dawn smiled. *Damn, am I lucky.*

She tousled her short blonde hair and set her sight on the clear-blue sky, bells ringing in her ear. She squared her shoulders back, and her arms bent to have her palms face the ceiling in front of her. Dawn kept her prayers in a low murmur in order to not disturb her beloved. One to thank the Morning Lord for the daily bread. Another thanks to Lune for daily water. Custom dictated that she should give thanks to three blessings, bowing as each one is given. Then she went on her knees and pressed her forehead to the edge of the rug. For those blessings, Dawn's thoughts trailed to how lucky her life has been.

How lucky she was to be able return to her home, Amaveriel, from the summer's military campaigns.

How lucky she was to fall in love with Tsuki and how much she loved her in return.

How lucky they were to find Dido that night and save her life. Dawn's brows furrowed as she recalled how the little satyr didn't stir when she shook her body and screamed for her to wake up.

"Morning Lord, please keep her in your glorious light," Dawn added to the prayer.

Then the faithful lieutenant clapped thrice. Her heart healed.

"I don't mean to interrupt," Tsuki was awake, her head supported by her elbow propped up on pillow. She furrowed her thin black brows as she pursed her peachy lips into a pout. "But I find it surprising that you of all people would sing psalms to that old hat."

Was that disgust? The thought crossed Dawn's mind.

She must've made a face because Tsuki ended up playing with her hair, and she only did that when she was troubled by something.

"The Morning Lord has been kind to me, despite everything. If it wasn't for him, I would still be wandering in the desert looking for a place to live, or, you know," Dawn said.

"Such kindness is not extended by those priestesses," Tsuki countered.

"Yeah, but those people aren't the Morning Lord. No matter much how they want to be."

Dawn stretched from her sitting position and grabbed her blouse. With a plop, she sat next to Tsuki, who sat up to meet her gaze.

Tsuki gestured with her hand as she spoke. "Then why do you suppose the Morning Lord allows his priestesses to continue such abhorrent behavior? Every sister I walk past cast slurs at my direction. 'Prostitute,' 'whore,' 'slut,' to name a few. Yet, they chastise you if you dish it out in kind."

Dawn shrugged her blouse on and began to button it up. "Maybe they need him more than we do."

Tsuki laughed, how pleasant the sound. "You do fine. I would rather stay the cute divine rebel that I am." She sashayed her shoulders with every last three words.

"I wouldn't change that for the world." Dawn leaned in, and they kissed. Their noses rubbed against each other as she tilted her head to her favored side.

"You've never been bothered by those asshats before. What changed?" Dawn asked once they parted.

Tsuki played with her hair once again. "Ever since that new superior took over, there has been talk about forced marriages to increase the population. As if queer people don't exist. I heard it at the well yesterday and then from my clients last night. People are terrified to be forced into a loveless marriage, or worse when they refused to be in one."

"I hope it would never come to that," Dawn murmured.

Her parents had pushed her to marry when she finally came of age. Half of the bachelors in her tribe lined up to their tent, offering all sorts of animals and trinkets for her dowry. When Dawn told them they all had to best her in combat, most wilted like blooms in the sun. The stupid few brave enough to take up the challenge limped for weeks. The situation was so dire, the chieftain asked her to choose someone or leave. Dawn smiled as she recalled how he balked when she asked for his daughter in hand. That, at the time, was worth the exile.

He must be dead by now. I wonder who the chief is now. Would they accept me back in?

Tsuki bumped her shoulder against her bicep, drawing Dawn from her thoughts. "But we're not allowed such luxuries here, are we? Doomed to die here for secrecy's sake, written off as virginal spinsters on cold tombstones, despite all the love we savored. I envy dwarves who can sneak past the borders by stone. As much as I envy you."

Dawn wrapped one of her arms around Tsuki and nuzzled her face into the crook of her neck. The sweetness of pomegranate wafted from her thick black hair as she kissed her skin.

"You know the Jessenters are always recruiting," she muttered as she nibbled playfully with her teeth.

Tsuki chuckled, how sweet the melody, and wrapped her legs around Dawn's waist. "Little ol' me, playing big, tough soldier out in the vast desert full of snakes and scorpions."

Dawn drew back, cradling her moon princess against her body. "Hey, I saw how you fought against that bird. You're a lethal fighting machine under that silk veneer of yours. We could use you."

"Unless it's to sing a dragon a lullaby or to serve poison to a train full of slavers, I'll leave 'saving the day' performances to you."

"Speaking of which, I gotta visit the old man today."

"The Silver Fox?"

"Yeah, that's the one. I have a message I need to deliver, in person." Dawn gave her a quick peck on the lips, and they unfurled from each other's arms.

They talked about where they wanted to eat for dinner as she dressed, what performances Tsuki planned to participate in—all the mundane things Dawn could think of to prolong the inevitable.

All the while, Tsuki answered in reply while stoking the fire in her hearth, designed to be a circle free of the wall's embrace and deep as a laundry basin. Tsuki loved putting in lavender and fruit rinds among the oiled stones to improve the salty bay air.

"Hey," Dawn called out to her at the door. "You're always in my prayers."

Tsuki gave a bashful smile and looked at the orange peels in her hand. "I know."

She tossed the orange rinds in the fiery pit, and the greedy flames consumed them.

The soldering pin snagged on a fragment and flared inches from Aramis's scraggly beard. An ugly dollop of metal mounded between the two golden lines, circuits the Ancients had called it, allowing them to connect.

"Shit," Aramis hissed as he ripped off the shielding goggles.

He didn't need the two golden lines to join together; that would confuse the command that would race down them from his magical encoding. Well, magic of the loosest of terms, for the Ancients abhor it. Now the Silver Fox had to scrape the golden flashing off from that sector. Again. An expensive price he had to pay.

"Dovl," Aramis muttered the dwarven command word for the soldering pin before he stuck it in his mouth. The heat still lingered on his tongue as his hand groped for the scrapper. Instead, they seized on the oranges left by Sister Rhyllae when she stopped by. His fingers felt the dimples as he recalled the news.

Sleeper, I need a cigarette.

Aramis leaned back and put the smoke-tinted goggles on top of his salt-and-pepper hair. The grays were coming in faster than ever before. Soon, he'd be a true silver fox, not just by name. Something he never thought would ever happen given his deadly occupation. His silver eyes darted in the dark workshop, casting a silver pall over all his work.

A metal doll. A hare, in fact. There was an orphaned girl, named Delphi, taken in by the Abbey, and she loved his tales of a naughty bunny messing up a wealthy farmer's garden of carrots. Aramis wanted it to hop around and then make a big jump on the seventh action. The hand-spun battery wouldn't last longer than a few days, but the memory would last forever.

That's what matters, right? The thought came back to him again. *A moment of happiness in this fucked up world, even if it's fleeting. It would be what Rhyllae will tell herself when she leaves.*

He rested the soldering pin on the wooden table so he could rub his leathery face with both hands, callous as they were. Aramis heard boots tentatively coming in from behind him. Unsure footing from the dark that enveloped the house, but familiar enough to pass through it without any blunder. Not an enemy, at least.

"Sleeper, do I need a smoke," he groaned out loud.

"What would the sister say?" Dawn's brassy voice said. He could hear her fumbling with a candle stand by the doorway.

"Fuck her." Aramis swiveled in his rotating stool. His silver light caught her arched brows raised before she turned to the match in her hand. "On another thought, don't. You might enjoy yourself too much." He swiveled back to his work.

He heard Dawn's half-hearted chuckle, and the lantern light flooded the room, illuminating the windowless workshop. To the untrained eye, it looked more akin to a scrapyard. Stacks of metal plates tucked next to a miniature furnace, with the crucible and tongs discarded on top of it. There were shelves of fist-size molds of various screws and bolts for his use. Wires of various lengths and diameters were bound into wreaths and hung on the wall. And, last, but not least, the desk where he put together his metal creations. All sorts of magical tools at his disposal, no different than the dwarvish soldering pin. One commanded flame; the other punched holes through the metal. But he picked up a simple hooked scraper and picked at the fresh mistake.

Dawn peered over his shoulder. "Is that a rat?"

"A rabbit."

"Kinda fat for a hare." Dawn turned her sights to the fruit bowl and snagged an orange.

"It's supposed to be a Töskan breed. They're fluffier."

"Better keep that away from Korzha; he's terrified of them."

"Him? Doubtful."

"Speaking of which..." Dawn paused to sink her teeth into the rind. She skillfully scraped a chunk off and pulled to create a strip. Satisfied, she unwound the fruity shell with her thumb, freeing her mouth to speak. "...The general sent me."

Aramis furrowed his brows and added more pressure to the pin. "As diplomat?"

"As messenger. Do you want the whole official statement?"

"Sum it up for me."

"He thinks you're being chickenshit." Finally freeing the fruit, Dawn discarded the rinds in the rubbish.

"And he wants me to suck it up and do the mission anyway."

"Pretty much." Dawn split the orange in half and offered one to him.

Aramis wanted to refuse out of spite. But his stomach rumbled when the citrus notes tantalized his nostrils. He tossed the pin, letting it clatter on the table, and swiped the offering from her hand. He popped a slice in his mouth; the juicy flavor danced on his tongue.

Korzha wasn't entirely wrong; Aramis had been dragging his heels. Ever since he was given the task two moons ago, Aramis researched all he could on Silo 51: the history of its making, what the ancestors intended for its creation, and the part it played in their destruction. Everything he found in those yellowed vellums mortified him. Aramis confronted Korzha to abandon this expedition. They had many verbal rows over it, but both agreed on one singular thing: to keep the contents of this mission a secret. Not even Dawn or Dido, who would be joining them on this quest, were allowed to know until they were closer to the source. Not even Rhyllae, though his heart yearned to spill all of his frustrations and grief.

"I wanted to stay for Rhyllae," Aramis said instead. "But… they're pushing her to be a mother."

Which wasn't a lie. They were building a life together. With their money combined, they purchased this studio. Aramis even insisted Rhyllae add her name to the papers. There wasn't a reason to hide their love for each other, no matter the gossip.

"I take that is … bad?"

Aramis groaned, *Where to begin?* His fingers restlessly rubbed against the white fibers on the orange slices.

"For the two of us? Yeah. She would have to leave for another temple or abbey once promoted. Something that all the mothers experience. Rhyllae leaves for who knows where and I'm ... forced to stay."

"Are you fucking kidding me?"

"The Elders demanded it. To quote: 'We don't want you to cut and run on your crimes, *Theliad*.' As if I'm some gizzard-yellow cretin."

"Damn."

"What gets me is the Mother Superior, though an advocate through and through, she knew, Dawn, *knew* this would happen with Rhyllae. Why create this for both of our sakes then take it all away?"

"You're not the first to complain about her. She is rather..."

"Beguiling? Treacherous?"

"Typical," the lieutenant said, with a firm tone in her words before she popped two slices into her cheek and wadded it up.

"That's putting it lightly."

"Don't you want to be married with Sister Rhyllae?" Dawn mumbled through the fruit.

"I do! Sleeper knows that I do. For years I wished for the impossible to happen between the two of us. Then the doors flew open, and the blessings fell like, like," Aramis waved his hand in a circle as he reached for the metaphor, "Manna from heaven."

"Manna?"

"Holy bread, it's a long story. Rhyllae thought that by bowing to their graces, we'd stay here, maybe even have this," he gestured wide, "as our home."

"That's going against centuries of doctrine."

"You can say the same thing about the Mother Superior's marriage act. The Holy Order wrote off matrimony for centuries 'to secure their own power' from the nobles." Aramis waved his hand from left to right on the table, as if to smooth out a scroll. "Why choose to overwrite this and not 'moving to another abbey when you're a mother?' That's beyond me."

"I don't know. Maybe they're worried she'd end up with a baby before both of you wed?" Dawn rolled her eyes. "Which is weird, if you think about it. Why be called a mother and don't expect to be one."

Aramis swiveled in his stool to gaze upon the lieutenant with a nonplused expression.

Dawn stuttered and blinked twice. "You don't mean ... not like a complete mother ... with a baby and all... Right?"

Aramis sighed and turned back to the desk. He rubbed his neck, his mind still in a blue haze.

"Long ago, that was the requirement. Still is for those who enter the Holy Order later in their life. But for a sister like Rhyllae, she can undergo trials to prove her worth without leaving service. The success rate is difficult though."

Aramis grabbed hold of the metal scraper once again. The metal tinged as he picked at the molten mound. He didn't want to see the lieutenant's face contort as her hamster wheel ran at full speed.

"Oh, I see. She wants to take the easy path and have herself knocked up, once you have the matrimonial blessing. Right... Maybe there are benefits to being magically transitioned, huh?"

The dollop popped off and clattered on the workbench. His silver eyes betrayed him and glanced at her. Dawn crossed her well-toned arms. A knowing smirk graced her bronzed face.

Aramis averted his gaze and nodded. How could they not? Sister Rhyllae loved children. That never changed in all their years together as friends. She was the go-to priestess whenever a child was ill or fussy. If such a thing occurred, he would take it as a blessing. It was a dream Aramis stowed when he learned more of Vanessa's fury. As soon as he placed the ring on Rhyllae's finger, a part of him hoped the dream would flourish. The idea of it now made his lip tremble.

"Well, there you go. Both of you get hitched, have a baby, since that is what the two of you want. When you are done with your 'community service,' you can join her wherever she is. It's a win-win!" Dawn said with the confidence of every self-assured youth.

Aramis put his fist against his mouth, leaning back as he did so. His mouth was suddenly dry as he searched for the words to say. How could he possibly say it, let alone explain it? Something he always suspected ever since Aramis achieved his freedom, well before he emerged from the Zemzem waters. For most of his life, Aramis never took it into account, never let it bother him until now. Now when it mattered the most.

"I... I... I can't have kids," he finally blurted out.

His body seized on him from uttering another word. Aramis wanted to tell Dawn more. The mother broke the news to the two of them in that dim room last week. How the Djinnasi's cruelty extended their monstrosity to the very blueprint of every jhasin model. Of course they would neuter their harem slaves. He wanted to tell Dawn he was a fool to think otherwise, that Aramis and Sister Rhyllae would be ever so lucky.

Tears threatened to break the dam and drown the whole world. He pinched the bridge of his nose to hold it back.

It didn't work.

His vision swam as he doubled over. His shoulders convulsed with every wave of sorrow he buried within his soul. Dawn's strong arms embraced his heaving body as he leaned on the desk for support. Only the foot of metal rabbit haunted his murky view.

Chapter 5

MISSIVE

THE ABBEY OF THE RISING DAWN LOOMED BEFORE Aramis and Dawn as its bell welcomed parishioners for their evening worship. The walkway was re-cobbled after the disaster, and their most fervent followers were keen to return to some semblance of a normal life. A family ahead of them halted. One of the uncles stooped down to give his niece a piggyback ride. Aramis lagged behind as he watched him neigh like a horse and jogged to catch up with the rest of the group.

Aramis looked down at the metal rabbit, heavy in his hands.

In the blessed waters of Zemzem, the magic transformed anything that submerges into its depths, including muscles, fat, and bone. All of the connective tissue and all the organs. It helped Aramis to achieve his full vision of who he was inside—to be a man of his own making. Yet, it could only reshape the clay that was presented, no different than weaving from a single bundle of yarn. The accursed Djinnasi lords and their cruel magic made sure none of their jhasins could replicate on their own. Aramis was no exception, born with the mere tools necessary to provide his bedtime services on command and nothing more.

Worse, those backward priestesses demanded the burden must be placed squarely on Rhyllae's shoulders and she must quicken by a seed in matrimonial bond. They couldn't provide a surrogate or a donor for this unusual situation. O how Sister Rhyllae wept when they rejected her appeal, and Aramis along with her in the safety of their own home.

Surely there's more to motherhood than birthing a child?

Aramis stopped completely. The black and white archway crystalized into view. He remembered their argument earlier this morning when Rhyllae made up her mind and decided to face the trials. If she succeeded, she could go to any temple of her choosing. With the Mother Superior's connections, they might even land a temple that would accept them both. Aramis begged her to simply leave the abbey and start a normal life with him. He knew in his heart that all of this was nothing more than a convoluted mess to keep her under their thumb. She deserved better.

"And do what, exactly, Aramis?" he recalled her words. *"Go fish like Vanessa? Be a stay at home mom?"*

"Maybe?" he spat out.

"I'm more than the sum of my parts, too," Rhyllae had said, before she left with tears in her eyes.

Could he bear to face Rhyllae again? He could withstand her fury, sure, but Aramis would rather melt into the stone under his feet than to meet her tears again.

Dawn finally turned around and walked back to him when she saw his pitiful sight. "C'mon." She gave him a firm pat on his shoulder. "We're here to see Dido and give that to Delphi. That's it, then it's off to the Iron Lady."

The bell made its final toll. Vespers was beginning. Soon, all the sisters and mothers would converge in the chancel for prayer and song for their congregation.

"Let's get this over with," Aramis grumbled as they joined with the growing crowd at the entrance.

When it came their turn to pass through the narrow arch, a body like a wall blocked their path. Sister Gertrude. The woman was head-to-toe of holy muscle underneath her sunny robes, all thanks to her father's dwarven lineage. Her beard too, brushed and trimmed compared to Aramis's ragged set. Her massive forearms flexed as she crossed them in front of her broad breast, causing her sleeves to reveal the edge of her tattoo.

Did a growl come from her throat?

"Hey ya, gorgeous," Dawn said, laying on her charm. "I see you've been bench pressing, lately. What's your weight?"

But Sister Gertrude didn't budge as she glowered at Aramis, and it wasn't lost on him as to why.

"I'm here to give this to Delphi as a gift." Aramis raised the doll up for her to see in hopes she would relent, yet the sister narrowed her eyes at him.

A melodic voice piped up from behind the impassable priestess. "Sister Gertrude, why are you standing there?"

"Nothin' to see here," she said.

An olive hand with a tourmaline ring on her finger appeared on the sister's arm, seeing it still on her finger gave him a small measure of relief. The burly sister exchanged looks between them and the hidden figure. With a gruff sound from her throat, Sister Gertrude relinquished to allow Rhyllae to greet them. She waved them through as she stepped aside for the evening crowd.

"Thanks," Aramis managed to say before Rhyllae's golden brown eyes, not as ruddy as before, locked onto his. His throat dried up.

Her fingertips flitted up toward his face; then she checked herself and jerked it away, hiding her hands within her sleeves.

Sister Rhyllae cleared her throat. "I'm needed."

"I know." The words were soft from his lips. "I won't stop you from helping them."

She gave a small nod. Silence fell between the two, both of their fingers fidgeting absently, hers on the hem of her garment and his on the metal doll he was cradling.

"I... I'm sorry for—"

Sister Gertrude gave a loud cough and jerked her head toward the end of the nave.

"I should go," Rhyllae said.

"I should go," Aramis said at the same time.

When he realized it, he exhaled a nervous chuckle and drummed his thumb on the bunny.

"Dinner." Rhyllae locked her eyes at him.

"Won't miss it."

Satisfied, the sister joined her fellow priestesses to help lead the prayers to bid farewell to the Sun and greet the rising Moon. A ceremony that had continued for centuries since the coming of the Morning Lord in this world, carried by different voices singing the same legacy of his mercy and reign. Would it still be the same without Rhyllae's voice, powerful as the sun and soft as flickering flame? Would Rhyllae be the same without them?

Dawn gave a gentle punch in his shoulder and said, "C'mon, lover boy, let's find Dido."

After inquiring of a priestess passing by, they found their way to the mess hall. It was long, taking nearly the length of the building and set with an equally long table with wooden chairs, much like the style of the Iron Lady. The walls were painted with depictions of Amaveriel, but with the Abby's minaret holding the sun aloft. Golden lines stretched from the yellow orb across the entire blue backdrop and into the ocean. There, a moon was reflected in its waves, ready to rise when the sun set. Close to that side of the mural were Dido and Delphi.

There was a noticeable flush of color that had returned to her cheek since they last saw her, as well as the normal spring in her hoofed step. Dido waved her medlar wand about before Delphi's wide eyes and smoke poured from its tip into various shapes, butterflies, elephants, and birds. The smoke figurines did a little jig before they dissipated into the thin air. Delphi squealed when a bunny came out and hopped with it until it, too, finally poofed away.

"Hey, kiddo," Aramis called out to her as he knelt down, his arms wide open.

"Ari!" she cried and skipped over to him.

He gave her a big, bear hug. Delphi was more excited than the other children in Amaveriel. Most of them would be curious about his eyes or the long black cloak of his. But there was always an air of caution in their steps, perhaps from the stories their parents told. Yet, Delphi never met a stranger she didn't like, and her enthusiasm was too contagious to dismiss.

"I brought you a friend." He waved toward the lieutenant.

"Hey, name's Daw—oof!" She grunted when Delphi barreled into her and gave her a hug of her own.

Aramis chuckled and watched as Delphi rambled about her day. The poor girl was having difficulties adjusting to the cloister, even with Sister Rhyllae's attentive care. Rhyllae even asked Aramis to look for another home that would understand her free-spirited nature. Yet, he couldn't find any family that would be suitable for her. Many were too prim and unwilling to be flexible to adjust to her chaotic nature, no matter how innocent it might be. He feared such a strict home would leave her covered back and blue; something his heart couldn't take. The rest feared she was cursed and believed her family deserved their demise from the ghouls. Aramis saw red for hours. How could anyone despise such a sweet, carefree spirit, his heart didn't know.

If he could take her as his own, Aramis would. Sleeper knows, he would in a heartbeat.

Satisfied at Delphi making her acquaintance with Dawn, he shifted his attention to Dido, who laughed while holding the side of her stomach. With the rabbit in his hands, he inserted a key into the slot and cranked the toy.

"I see you're on the mend," said Aramis.

"Yes, the wonders of warm food, a warm bed," Dido waved her free hand, "and warm company."

The satyr mage waved the wand away into an invisible pocket of air and then climbed up into a seat next to her, wincing as she settled into the groove of the base. "Now, before anymore has to be said, I want to give you my thanks for saving me from that ruffian."

"No flea off of my back. Though, they're no ordinary ruffian, were they?"

"You're right. They're dead."

The comment jolted him from his doings. He would expect such a chilly response from Korzha, not the sweet-natured Dido!

She sighed wearily. "I'm sorry, but I have no mercy in my heart for those who enjoy taking life for profit. Life is too precious of a force to put a price tag on it, either to enslave it or to cull it. Please, let's leave it at that."

Aramis continued to crank the battery in the creature as he spoke. "Still, that owl knew where to find you. If the secret of Amaveriel couldn't safeguard you..."

"...We'll be long gone for Silo 51 by that point. So long as I don't use my magic willy-nilly, I won't be detected."

"Let's hope so."

The key finally hit the threshold and froze in his hand. Aramis crouched and set the metal bunny down on the floor between him and the little girl.

Dawn patted Delphi's shoulder and pointed at him. Her hazel green eyes widened with joy, and she did another squeal while hopping in place.

Aramis extended his hand out at her as his lips warmed into a smile. "Stay right there."

Delphi brought her tiny fists against her cheeks, as if to force her body to stay still. He flipped the switch, the battery churned in its chamber, and the bunny came to life. She didn't seem to mind the noise as it sprung forward, landing every jump on its long metal feet as it made its way toward her. Everyone was all smiles by the mechanical trick.

Aramis beamed. *Finally. Something that went right today.*

Aramis turned to Dido, who shuddered from witnessing the mechanical bunny in action, and asked, "You're still planning to go?"

"Yes. It'll be the four of us, plus a healer. Korzha is currently searching for one willing to go on this expedition. Which reminds me. Your blades, please."

Careful not to make a sound, Aramis unsheathed the dual knives and gave them to the satyr mage. There was no need for Delphi to discover something dangerous today. He admitted that the daggers were of a beautiful make and balanced better than the previous pair. If he was a gullible fool, he would've been swooned by the luxurious gift. But the gift was nothing more than a bribe to coerce him into this deathtrap. He'd accept all gifts and blessings he could muster without going into the gully of the Ancients' folly.

Dido laid the twin blades on her goatish lap and poised her hands over them. *"Noževi, prihvati ovaj—"*

Aramis recognized the words spoken as the beginnings of any magical enchantment, "accept this gift." But a terrible grinding sound screeched. The metal hare halted and began twitching in place.

"Sys-sys-sys," it hissed.

Odd, Aramis thought. *I never gave it a voice box. No, it must be coming from its ball joints, and the repetition wore out the grease.*

Delphi cocked her little black curly head. "Ari? Why is it doin' that?"

"I don't know. Stay there, kiddo, and let dad—I mean, Uncle Ari take a look," Aramis said to her.

Aramis knelt and watched as the hare seized. It jerked its head up with every stutter as its forearms stretched out before it. Even though it was a doll, he felt a twinge of guilt seeing it in such a state. He crouched and reached for the mechanical hare.

"Sys-sys-system dow-dow-download complete."

"What?" Aramis muttered.

It lurched forward. One of its decorative metal teeth snagged in the inner fold between his finger and thumb and nicked it open. Aramis hissed and sucked on the nick. Blood—his blood—dripped from the hare's maw.

"Did... did it bite?" Dawn asked.

"No. No," Aramis answered. "It was the jump action, and it got caught on my hand; that was all. It can never."

Aramis reached for it again, but its head turned. His gut dropped. He never made it where it could move its head. Before his senses returned, the metal rabbit hopped round and round it bounded in a circle between the adults and Delphi.

"Download complete," the scratchy words eked out of the mechanical hare. "Missive open. Instructions. Locate subject 479241."

His heart froze. *How? How do they know my dead name?!*

The mechanical rabbit leaped about, repeating the phrase over and over again, until it froze and craned its head toward the child. "Subject acquired."

Delphi shrieked and ran behind Aramis.

It shifted its whole weight as its head trailed after her.

"Aramis, what the—Oh shit!" Dawn began to say until the metal creature lunged at the little girl.

The lieutenant dove right on top of it and slammed it on the marble tile. It writhed in her hands like a snake, trying to slash her with its sharp metal feet. The movements jerked about with great vigor, but she was the stronger of the two. Dawn chucked the mechanical doll down the stretch of the dining hall and careened it straight into the mural. Bits of screws fell loose from the impact, allowing the cavity of its metal shell to split down its navel. It kicked and flopped about like a freshly caught fish.

Aramis pivoted on his knees and grabbed his twin blades. One by one, he threw them at the creature. The first one pinned it down to the floor, and the other slammed into its hind legs, shearing it straight off the spinal rod. Sparks flew from the sudden separation.

Despite it all, the mechanical hare still thrashed about.

Dawn took a few tentative steps forward, but Aramis waved her back. Without the hand-spun battery coil in the tail end, the rabbit's movements slowed down to a stop. When it ceased twitching, Aramis crept over, his boots going toe to heel out of habit. His silver eyes searched over its remains for a clue as to why it did what it did. But there was nothing but metal and wire. Aramis relaxed his posture and rubbed the back of his neck. Everyone else sighed and relaxed in turn.

"What the hell was that, Aramis?" Dawn asked

"Magic, maybe?"

Aramis turned to Dido, but the satyr mage was still in thought, her tiny palms raised before her as her lips murmured a spell. What it was she was casting, Aramis couldn't quite understand.

"Hey. Hello? Earth to Dido?" Dawn waved her hands in front of her face.

Even the cute, little Delphi stood on her tippy toes to wave at the satyr. Yet, Dido scrunched her face in concentration.

"Leave her alone. Spells can't be dismissed at the drop of the hat," Aramis said.

"Really?" Dawn asked.

"If you let go it in the middle of spell, there's a chance it'll blow up in your face."

"Where did you learn that from?"

"I read it in a book somewhere."

Dawn looked down at Delphi. "I don't buy it."

Aramis waved both hands at the young officer before rubbing at the back of his neck.

Great. Now I have to clean up this mess before the sisters come in here for supper.

He stooped down and freed the magically attuned knife.

The mechanical hare reared its animatron head and emitted a hiss from a gear rubbing against a wire.

Aramis jerked back. *Impossible!*

Seizing its chance, the metal doll slunk away using the motion of its head and neck akin to a caterpillar. Then it halted. What was left of its metal chassis rustled as its spine built up pressure and popped up into the air.

The seventh jump action! Aramis realized.

Dawn, Aramis, and Delphi watched in fascinated horror as it slinked in six rapid motions before seizing again. When it popped up in the air again, everyone moved with haste and drew their weapons.

Dido snapped her fingers. "Disintegrate."

The metal bunny turned to rust. By the time it fell splat on the floor, it was nothing more than a fine powder of iron, copper, and gold.

Delphi crept forward to look at the sudden soot pile, while Aramis and Dawn exchanged wide-eyed looks, then to Dido.

"I never cared for *hasenpfeffer*." Dido sheepishly shrugged.

Delphi wailed and ran to Aramis. Without hesitation, Aramis left his blades on the floor and scooped her into his arms. He cooed and bounced her to no avail by the time the priestesses came in for their meal. Soon as her eyes laid upon them, Rhyllae rushed over to their side. Aramis leaned Delphi over in his arms so his beloved could rub on her back and kiss her forehead.

Dawn sheathed her gladius and ruffled her hair. "Seriously, what the fuck?"

Chapter 6

SOUL STONE

"A**ND IT BIT YOU?" SISTER RHYLLAE ASKED, PAUSING** in her healing. Her nose scrunched up while her mouth furrowed into a frown.

"Yes, right where you're touching it," Aramis said.

They were granted privacy in one of the vacant rooms. A taste of married life while keeping Rhyllae "safe" under the mothers' watchful eye. Oil lamps illuminated the space along with the waxing crescent moon peeking from the window. It was barred with intricate wooden latticework, to prevent any mischief they might cook up. Underneath was a scroll in between two prayer rugs for communal worship, a not-so-suitable gesture to convert Aramis from his Sleeper-worshiping ways. In the center of the room was a low-seated table with proper seating pillows and a setting made for two.

A tease, Aramis grimly thought, *of a life we could never have*. But he welcomed the respite from all the judging stares.

They switched the sitting so they could be next to each other for their meal, still untouched. Aramis had his right elbow propped as Rhyllae examined his dominant hand. Her healing powers washed down his arm like water. It should soothe him, yet fighting the hare from earlier did little to improve his mood.

"And it called my name. My *dead* name, *me'qora*." Aramis continued, "How? How does it know?"

"Maybe it's sabotage?" Rhyllae finished her healing, but her fingers still rubbed his hand. Her kinky hair, free of her religious hijab, tumbled about her shoulders.

Aramis ruffled his hair with his left hand as he mentally ran through the list. As far as he knew, he did it all. He hammered the plates, etched the circuit board, and all the soldering. The blueprints were salvaged long ago from a ruined toy company. Was it from there that the error occurred, or was it a mortal error? Did he somehow insert himself in this metallic creation? Some basic mortal need to leave a mark on the world, even if the mark was through a hollowed toy.

In the end, Aramis shook his head and slapped his hand on his knee in frustration.

"Dawn did mention the Fae were after Dido. Maybe the toy was enchanted to take her out," Rhyllae said.

"Hmmm." Aramis thought for a while, thinking back to what had transpired. "It's searching for a test subject and went after Delphi."

"Poor baby. Delphi was still hiccupping by the time the sisters and I put her to bed. I hope she doesn't have any nightmares from it."

"Me too. Can't have two insomniacs walking about."

"Don't worry, singing puts her to sleep." Rhyllae smiled as her fingers still caressed over his knuckles.

"That's a relief." He returned the smile.

She would've been a wonderful mother.
The thought crossed his mind, dredging up their fight from earlier. There was too much love here to lose it all. He could see it in her unwavering eyes, how warm they were in the light.

The mothers be damned! There has to be a way, surely!

Aramis turned over his hand to cup her fingers in a gentle hold. "Rhyllae, about earlier today. I—"

Rhyllae eyes were upon him, but then they flicked to look over his shoulder. They widened as she tensed and let go of his grip. In all of their adventures together, he knew it meant there was someone behind him. Aramis whirled on his seat. Blades slashed free from his hip in front of him.

It was two dwarves! They both hopped back and ducked their heads behind their waving palms.

"We mean ye no harm," the one in green velvet said.

"Aye, aye!" said the one in blue, velvet like the other. "We're requesting aid."

Aramis stilled his hand.

Sister Rhyllae did not.

A cup full of wine sailed over his head. It tumbled right into the green one's face, soaking him and his outfit. Then another cup flew. A plate, a fork, all of which landed their mark on the already trembling dwarves. The sister's kindness had clearly run out for the day.

"This is a private area!" she seethed and tossed another fork at their way. "How dare you burst in without calling! You—you rich, pompous braggards! You'll receive your services at dawn like the rest of the flock!"

It was true, they were quite rich in their tailoring. Hardly anyone could afford the luxury of velvet unless it was looted from a corpse. But something gleamed on their chubby fingers as they pitifully tried to wave off the sister's attacks, a signet ring of sorts, with a dwarvish mark for lore.

Aramis waved his hand at her. "Wait, Rhyllae stop! They're from the Dwarven Rhine Historical Society."

Aramis almost laughed out loud when he turned around to face her. There Rhyllae stood, holding an oil lamp high over her head as if it was a broadsword ready to cleave a foe in half. There was no flame; she was not that cruel, of course.

Without lowering the lamp, Rhyllae asked, "Why are you here? This area is off limits."

The dwarves looked at each other, then turned their pleading eyes upon Aramis.

"You heard the lady. Speak!" He tersely added the last word, making them both jump.

"We wish to speak to the Silver Fox for a crucial matter," the wine-doused dwarf said.

"Please, it's urgent. A matter of life or death!" the blue interjected. "We would never impose on ye otherwise."

"Me name is Barley." The first dwarf touched his chest over his heart.

"Olleander." The other dipped his head as he doffed off his blue beret.

Aramis eyed Rhyllae to see if she was satisfied with their answers. She lowered the lamp and scooped up her yellow shawl. She nodded as she wrapped it around her head.

"Well, you found him. My name is Aramis Feres, and this is Sister Rhyllae. And if I recall, my license with the D.R.H.S. has been revoked. Something to do with 'the utter destruction of the most monumental building in all dwarvish history.'"

"Ahh, aye." Olleander gave a half-hearted chuckle, twisting the beret in his broad hands. "The M'thealquilôk incident. It's not revoked, simply … er … not renewed."

"Of course, when it's the most convenient to the board's interest."

"We'll gladly reinstate you if you can help us solve the riddle of Silo 51."

There it is, again. That damnable location.

Aramis crossed his arms as he narrowed his glowing, silver eyes at them. "How do you know that name? Who told you?"

"Josiah did," Barley said, and out of his pocket was a stone, shaped into a smooth sphere. Not any stone, but limestone inlayed with quartz used to transpose memory fragments from the heart of the mountain. For that reason, they were called memory crystals. Though, in their culture these rare objects were called soul stones.

With a solemn air, Barley laid the stone on the table next to him. "The poor lad didn't even last a whole day when he was hewn from stone. And he wasn't the first to fall in such a wretched place."

Olleander waved his hands excitedly. "Most of the silos have ceased their activities for two millennia now, but this one is off the charts! We thought at first it was from human raiders, but the armor was nothing we ever witnessed before."

"We hoped you could identify these creatures, Silver Fox," Barley said. "Since you're one of most experienced on-the-field experts. If these beings are dangerous, they could endanger the 'ole area."

They continued to stand there, grave faces for the gravest situation. Even Rhyllae eyed him with a concerning stare.

Aramis burst out laughing, shocking the impromptu guests. As he spoke, there was a dangerous gleam in his eye. "You kicked me out for destroying an already crumbling city, getting rid of a dangerous necromancer—possibly far more deadly than these people—and his horde of ghouls. And now, you'll reinstate me to do the fucking same?!"

"But—but—but Silver Fox," countered Olleander. "We lost people!"

"So have I! So has she!" Aramis waved toward Rhyllae, who nodded.

O Sleeper, I love you.

Aramis slashed the air with the edge of his hand. "People had died in M'thealquilôk, and you didn't blink an eye. Even Tamira, a proper dwarvish woman of renown, died for its historical riches. Now, when dwarvish male blood has been spilt—you come crying to me for salvation?"

A movement caught his peripheral. The sister motioned him to reel it back.

Maybe salvation was too far, he thought.

"To clean up a mess you can't handle." Aramis grabbed the soul stone and held it aloft in his dexterous fingers. "I should shove this up where you can taste the—"

Sister Rhyllae, ever the diplomat, leaned over and put her palm on top of the soul stone. "We'll consider it for further review. If it is worthy of our resources, how may we contact you?"

Though they both looked dejected, Barley pulled out a metal square with a circular hole in the middle. The entire surface was inscribed in dwarven runes. It settled on the table with a chime.

"If ye are heading that way in yer travels, say the words 'oaken smoke 'em' and we'll meet you at the nearest stone," Barley said.

They both took off their caps, showcasing their dignified bald spots as they bowed. Then they sank into the stone as if it were quicksand, merging into it until there was no hair of them left. Convenient, for shortly after there was a knock on the door. When Rhyllae opened it, Mother Pyrsi poked her head in.

"I heard shouting, is everything alright?" she asked the moment her venerable elvish head popped in.

This old song and dance. It was not the first time they were "disruptive" to the whole slumbering cloister. However, those were happier times. They would poke their nose in, admonish Rhyllae for whatever raucous occurred, and then ask her to finish up here before the dawn rises. It was a polite way of telling Aramis his time was up, and he needed to leave.

Without hesitation, Aramis packed away the cold chicken *kabsa*, along with the soul stone and calling card. Rhyllae loved to use fried plums instead of raisins, and he was not going to miss out on it tonight. Aramis gave a peck on her temple as he wedged between the two, still fussing over the noise.

"Oh, I wonder why he's leaving," he overhead the Mother Pyrsi say as he headed down the shadow-filled stairs.

"You know why," Rhyllae said with notable scorn in her voice before the door slammed in its frame.

Back in his burrow, Aramis hung up his cloak by the door. It was dark with all the windows shuttered tight against the sand and gnats alike. His silvery eyes illuminated his new, tiny dwelling. The small entry niche, already cluttered with shoes and slippers on a low bench, stepped down to the main floor. The mud-shaped walls were curved at the corners, like a conch shell. The main floor held his dining table and sitting cushions, which were two chef blocks that were split from the butcher's use covered by a discounted fabric. At the head of the far end of the room was a modest fireplace. The mantle held Rhyllae's flowers and little oddities he came across from his nighttime wanderings. An archway near it led to the workshop down below and his bedroom with a curtain of minuscule seashells on strings for privacy. Collected after a beach day with Dawn and her friends.

The silvery pall dimmed as Aramis closed his eyes as he leaned against the bolted door. It was a day of tears from all his loved ones. All because of him.

Aramis crossed the length of the room for the fireplace, not bothering to take his boots off. He slammed the bag on the table, the stone rolling out. There was too much on his mind for him to stay still in the bed reading. He never slept in that bed anyway, no matter Rhyllae's encouragement. If it ever did come for him, it was usually when all of his energy was spent and exhaustion took its toll. No, tonight was a night of questions.

Questions which could not be answered on an empty stomach.

Aramis struck the match. The flame stood at attention. No waver. No flicker. As if it was listening. It was a superstition of his, supposing that the Sleeper was with him when such a thing occurred. But he needed that illusion now, when all he knew and loved began to crumble from his touch.

"Sleeper, separate the truth from the lies, like chaff in the wind" was his short prayer.

With a flick of his wrist, the match flew into the fireplace. The fire burst into life in an instant. Maybe he put in too much kindling. Maybe there was oil leftover from the last meal that happened to spillover. Or maybe...

chssk

"479241"

chssk

Aramis whirled on his heels. "That's not my name!"

But low, it was not some supposed intruder, but the soul stone. The designs etched into the metal orb glowed an orange hue, the color of the forges they loved so dear. From its dot, it projected a translucent image that spread before him like the Ancients' solenoid films. It was stuck in a loop, typical of a soul hemorrhaging from a painful memory. The flickering image looped back to when this Josiah scrawled the backward SILO 51 on the wall. There was a metallic clunk behind him.

Metal?

Aramis crept closer to the image. It flickered, and the sound crackled from the disturbance. There were ghosts standing abreast, holding something. But he couldn't tell what. Then the vision crackled and flickered. When the image coalesced back together, there was smoke pouring from their wrists. The ghostly beings had their hands hung downward in an unnatural manner.

Bombs? Aramis wondered, *Pistols?* His running mind stilled when a hollow, feminine voice spoke.

"Patient *chssk* deleted. Please obtain *chssk* 479241 *chssk* testing."

Aramis grabbed the soul stone in his hand. He affixed his gaze on the ghosts standing there as it looped once more.

Pale faces. Pale bodies. They're shaven... No, that's not a scalp. A helmet? They don't have eyes. A mask with no holes? How can it breathe?

He leaned forward on his elbows on the table while he squinted at it. Something fell and clattered on the floor next to him. It was a pile of scrap metal, sticking out of it was the fashioned rabbit's foot. Aramis took it in his right hand, weighing the stone off in his left.

The hare was made of metal, like this strange armor. Funny. It bit me, even though there's no want of food or air to breathe. Are they the same? No... They couldn't be, unless...

His nerves prickled from the indication, and he dropped both on the table, letting the soul stone roll away onto the floor.

No! It's a myth. A fable to warn mortals of the audacity of making a lasting legacy in a natural world. Surely, they're stories and nothing more!

Yet his fearful heart couldn't be appeased by that notion. Aramis's fingers fumbled for the nearest porcelain plate. His fingers twitched as he flipped it over to its pale white side. Then he placed it on top of the ruined scrap pile and backed away. The fire light reflected off of its smooth surface as the dark material underneath gleamed.

The same gleam...

A scream cut through the distortion drawing his gaze back to the stone.

... The same white color...

Bangs echoed in the room as his silver eyes switchblade back and forth from the stone to the metallic mess on his table.

... As it was there.

It looped again. The death scream, the sound of metal piercing flesh and stone. The air stifled Aramis. His heart raced as he labored to breathe.

Metal puppets that don't need to breathe. Metal puppets made of war.

Aramis stumbled back. The back of his heel kicked a log that strayed from the fire pile. It roared to life with the jolt of fuel. His shadow flung far before him, a silhouette of perfect proportions. As was originally intended by the Djinnasi's craft. The same perfect proportions as those beings of metal.

Mannequins.

Aramis turned away and braced himself on the mantlepiece. He'd heard of the elven tales of the Ancients' folly. Rife with war, drugs, and avarice, they were almost as bad as the Djinnasi lords he once served under. But instead of magic, they had metal and wire. To be like the Sleeper and the dead deities, the Ancients produced creatures that took on their image. Children of utter perfection. To serve for them, care for them, and to kill for them. His former master loved telling him that they were the first jhasins on this realm and their loyalty was never questioned. How Aramis relished the day when he learned the truth of it all. Those creatures of metal had usurped their masters, ending an era of glass and metal towers.

The mannequins were destroyed along with them. Aramis argued with himself. *They communicated through an invisible network; once the connection was severed, they stopped moving. Rust overtook them and joined their makers as dust. But if some survived... Those who yet live... No. No!*

"I can't do this. Not again," Aramis pleaded out loud to the Sleeper, squeezing his eyes shut against the intense flames roiling below him. "I can't go back underground. Please, not like M'thealquilôk. Not under the earth. What more will I lose if I do this again? Please, please don't make me do this."

"*Please*," a crackling voice echoed his words. "*Please *chssk* Silo 51 *chssk*.*"

The sounds came from the soul stone, crackling behind him. Sounds from Josiah's memories, taken by those mannequins who ended him. The word "please" looped over and over in a wail like an overused squeezebox. Aramis opened his eyes heavenward to plea for it to stop. But looming over him were the words "SILO 51" hewn in stone.

"*Silo 51*," the soul stone stated.

Near the word, the mud wall depressed and formed the same words.

"*Silo 51*," it chanted, with a different voice.

From there it populated across the entire room. Over and over, a new voice invoked its name as they appeared. Aramis spun around. He couldn't seem to escape it. It was everywhere his silver eyes fell upon. In his daze, Aramis tripped and fell to his knees. Hungry and exhausted, he ran his fingers through his salt-and-pepper hair. He bowed, letting his forehead touch the floor. A child, once again, asking for the beatings to stop.

"I can't. I can't. I can't." His words come out in rasp now. "Please."

Somehow, that word cut through the chaotic cacophony about him. The voice wasn't crackling and hollow. It was soft, natural even. Aramis peeked through his arms and found the soul stone was lit, but this time in a blue hue.

"Please," it asked again, "for us."

"Us?" Aramis sat up.

Once more he took in the walls that encapsulated this space. One by one, the phrase was replaced with a name. "Hezebal." "Boryn." "Ishmael." "Floratine." "Yumikeya." The list went on and on. Diverse and unique, yet all tied by a singular fate. Aramis rose to his feet in awe.

"Us," the soul stone said. No, Josiah, Aramis realized. "Help us."

The aged Silver Fox felt a lump welling in his throat. This wasn't about him. This had nothing to do with him. Never was in the first damn place. Those who wore the mask of the Silver Fox live and die for the interest of others. That was what he swore when he took the mantle from his mentor. A tradition as long standing as the Morning Lord's rule. A legacy he would not break now.

"I'll do it. I'll do it." Aramis's voice strengthened when he repeated it, feeling the buzz of energy in the air. "I'll do it for you. Not those pompous assholes who sit comfortable in their halls. Not for coin or riches. I'll do it for those who gave up their lives with nothing but skin on their backs. Those who had died in that forsaken place. I promise to avenge and right this wrong!"

There was silence. Dead silence. As if they sealed his oath into stone. Then, one by one, the names disappeared, and the fireplace light dimmed into a slow burn. The glow from the soul stone faded. The only source of light was cast by the steely silver gaze of the Silver Fox.

Act 2

The snow falls in the box
Hissing its white noise
A studio jingle chimes
A hero in black rides

"*The network that brought you the 'Stepford Wives' presents:*
"*The Shadow Fox! A man of swift cunning*
"*Watch as he pulls off feats of romance, escapes, and daring*
"*All with the help of his trusty sidekick, Feres!*

"*Tune in to channel four—*"
The image collapse
It hisses in its white noise
She asks, "Who is Feres?"

Chapter 7

WESTERN GATE

THE NEXT FEW DAYS CAME IN A BLUR OF ACTIVITY. The Silver Fox decided to accept the deadly mission, and all of Amaveriel wondered by which gate he would leave. His leaving became an omen of sorts among the people. If the Fox exited by the Western gate, it would be two weeks of balmy weather and balmy friends. But if he exeunt by the Eastern gate, it would be ill winds and ill news.

In truth, the Silver Fox usually planned all expeditions in the Iounese desert west of Amaveriel when the heat abates for the hidden crypts beneath the sands. When the temperatures peaked, he turned his sights to the shades of Angloria's rainforest. Sister Rhyllae recalled one time Lady Ruth and company decided to go south by the Shining Sea to deal with the pirates. From what she heard when they returned, everyone went into a panic. Bread and eggs sold out. Everyone's mother and cousin were at the aqueduct fountain to have a month's worth supply of water. There were those who even made animal sacrifices and then were condemned by their neighbors for such animal abuse.

Because of such superstitions, there were those who tried to hunt the Silver Fox down. The sister of the Morning Lord came across them on her way to see him. Dark eyes and twitchy hands held freshly carved cudgels. When they approached her to ask where he was hiding, Rhyllae let her holy light shine from the top point of her brow. It wasn't dangerous, no different than the torches the children would carry at night. But it was a fair warning that she was no weeping violet, and the dark-hearted men fled.

The Silver Fox had spent the past couple of weeks in a Faerie Hold Dido provided for him, along with his collection of tomes and maps he wanted to study for this mission. Such a place lay betwixt their worlds and those of the Fae, allowing him refuge from those who would seek him out. Dido would guard the transparent door, admitting only those who would be joining him on the expedition. And, well, the sister included. The satyr mage wasn't a heartless Fae who would deny their tender conversations.

This night would be different. Rhyllae headed toward the eastern wall to sneak out. The Silver Fox told Korzha he was ready to depart, and the general announced tomorrow would be the day. There was a flurry of activity for the festivities. They weren't allowed to make noise greater than the abbey's bells in fear of the Djinnasi lord's wrath, whose elemental prowess could level the city if they weren't ensnared in their hedonistic stupor. Thus, they go all out with flowers, streamers, and flashy signs, a perfect cover for the Silver Fox to slip past them to visit the high eastern bluff.

It was there Aramis first ever laid eyes on the verdant beauty that was the Angloria Jungle. It was also where Rhyllae had confessed her love for him, and he reciprocated in kind.

For their last private meeting, the sister of the Morning Lord went against her religious vestments and dressed in the humble cloth of teal donated by a dressmaker. She wrapped it around her plump figure so that it pleated into a skirt and provided shawl-like sleeves on her round shoulders. Then she confined the knots with her golden shawl high on her waist. She didn't want to seduce the Silver Fox or fall into the hubris of romance. More than anything, Rhyllae was afraid that her heartrending sorrows would bring shame to the holy cloth. The last time she did so, it jinxed all of her prayers. Rhyllae spent the whole evening cleansing it.

When she finally reached the summit of the eastern bluff, Rhyllae wondered if she erred, for Aramis stood stricken by her natural beauty. He even stammered as he tried to find the words to say when his callous fingers took hold of her outstretched buttermilk palm.

Rhyllae blushed. *He's too adorable, sometimes.*

Then Aramis trailed them tenderly over the bundle in her arms. "For me?"

She nodded and shoved it in his arms. Clothes for the desert climes to replace the ones that were stolen and sold by his ex-spouse. The last offering she made for him.

His voice was soft enough for her ears to hear. "You already done enough for me, *me'qora.*"

"I haven't done enough."

His silver eyes, their light hidden by that mask, shot at her with anticipation. Sister Rhyllae tucked her fingers under the mask's edge and slipped it off, ruffling his hair. Aramis kept her palm against his face and melted into her touch. For once, she saw the weariness of this world caught up with him.

Rhyllae rubbed her thumb on his cheek, waking him from the sensation. "You're safe here with me."

She tilted her chin up to receive his gentle lips and then wrapped her arms around his neck as he deepened his kiss. The sister of the Morn fell into it, letting all the steel in her arms and legs soften into this bliss.

"Is there nothing I could do to convince you?" Aramis murmured against her neck once he parted for air.

"You know I want to travel with you, but the Mother Superior needs me. She ... is not as strong as you think she is."

The chilled night air cut between them as Aramis separated. "So, this is it. This is how it ends?"

Rhyllae shook her bouncy curls. "I'm not giving up on you yet."

From the pocket girdle, she produced a ring. It was fashioned from the church's basalt pillars cracked from the battle months ago. As per tradition, after six months of receiving a ring proposal, the recipient gave a ring back to their lover. Most flighty love affairs fizzled by this point, and such proposals were broken. For Rhyllae, she was not going to wait another second to secure her vows.

Aramis's breath hitched in his throat when Rhyllae knelt before him. His silver eyes swimming as he brought his trembling fingers to his lips.

"I'm not going to give up on us," Rhyllae's voice cracked. "No matter which shrine I hail, no matter how long it's going to take, I will wait for you. I would wait until the seas take over this land. I would even wait when all is enveloped by the embrace of the Sun's kiss. I love you with all of my heart, if you want to give me yours."

Aramis sunk to his knees, and he grasped her by the shoulders. "It could be years before I see you, if I'm lucky enough," his broken voice said.

"I don't care." Rhyllae cupped his face and repeated, "I don't care. We don't have to make everything happen all at once. Just promise me you'll wait for me."

The Silver Fox wept and laid his head into her comforting arms. "If I survive this, I will wait for you until my bones turn to ashes and stone. This I swear."

They stayed that way, in tender confidence, until the Morning Lord announced his presence, and the city welcomed him with song and praise.

Amaveriel celebrated in ecstatic silence with ribbons and petals flown every which way. Balconies flouted flags of red emblazoned by a phoenix clutching dual sabers. The rebels chosen symbol, taking after the Sulmaith's beloved pet bird.

In a solemn gait, they snuck back into the city of freedom from the bluff he loved to visit. Their arms linked as they pass through the nooks and crannies of each neighborhood. Aramis and Sister Rhyllae passed through a narrow alley to try to stave off the growing crowd nearing their destination, and they were showered by rose and magnolia petals from the children above. They fell on her neatly braided hair. It was plaited close to her scalp in intricate whorls until they hit her pointed ears where they exploded out into a cloud of golden-brown curls. He braided it a week ago at her behest when they decided to make amends. It's one of the many gifts Aramis gave to her, and she wanted to show it under the bright sun of the Morning Lord. For this day, she decided not to cover it. Not as an act of defiance of the Morning Lord, but to show in feeble hope that Aramis would be spared of any dangers because of the kindness he gives.

Aramis raised his cloak high to shield her while Rhyllae rested her head against his side. Her hand snaked up on his chest to the ring dangling on a golden chain. When Aramis spotted her hand, he scooped it up to plant a gentle kiss on her fingers, his silver eyes swimming. Rhyllae looked away lest her swimming eyes begin to pour. Neither of them let go when they made it to the western gate.

Unlike the East where the walls were plain to see, the Western wall was carved into the desert rock that shielded the city of freedom. The wall towered over all who arrived in celebration, as it sloped up into the mountains beyond the Abbey of the Dawn itself. The dwarves had constructed a matching pair of stone doors to create the gate, both striations of pale pink, orange, and beige. It was here at this gate, weeks ago, they received their fallen dead. It was here where Aramis first came to Amaveriel ushering in thousands of refugees for them to harbor. If history was to believe, this was where the founding Mother Superior Justiania accepted the first refugees fleeing from the Djinn Bazzuu's wrath when he was unleashed unto the world. Now, it would be where Aramis and Rhyllae separated for the first time in years.

Lieutenant Dawn was there waiting for them with a team of camels, dressed in the cream colors of the desert along with the signature red sash tied about her waist. Her short, tousled blonde hair was tucked away under a turban with a long sash dangling down, to serve as a scarf if needed be. The shield on her back was freshly polished, and no doubt the gladius on her hip was sharpened to a fine edge for this trip. The hunting bow was a new addition to her gear, the tips threaded in shades of pink, white, and orange.

She was busy chatting with Dido when they approached, also dressed for travel but in a weave of azure for her tunic and coat. She opted to have her curls held back in a loose chignon and have them encased by a sturdy ribbon wrapped in Grecian crisscrosses. Satchels hung around her goatish hips, no doubt full of much needed components for her magical selection. They both turned and greeted the two with the same saccharine cheer as the locals beaming down upon them. They waned away when they saw their blue expressions.

Rhyllae separated from Aramis to secure the small medicinal box on his camel. No doubt the substitute healer would make good use of what they brought on this venture, but it wouldn't hurt to be extra prepared. She felt a tender brush on her lower back as Aramis passed her by to join the others. He slapped his palm against Dawn's extended hand, then gripped it tight as they both leaned into it with their shoulders. Her hazel eyes took in his fit.

She wouldn't find nary a patched hole or an undone hem in his mottled cloth of cream and white. Rhyllae made sure that he was well prepared against the desert's wrath. An elvish cloak that could shelter against the never-ending winds and shelter him from prying eyes. His old mask that shielded the glow from his eyes was re-hemmed and patched. New gloves that were supple to the touch but durable to climb with. Even his soft leather boots were re-heeled and had new lacings. It was the least Rhyllae could do for him, despite his grumblings that he could manage fine with his old gear.

A surge of energy in the crowd broke the sister's thoughts.

At last, the famed General Tavian Korzha arrived, still in his signature greige coat and that ridiculously long, knitted scarf. The handle of the Silver Star, an equally famed rapier, gleamed from his right hip. Joining him on his left was Mother Superior Myrrh. He held her right hand aloft as they walked down the avenue abreast. Two tall pillars in a sea of onlookers with the entourage of the abbey's mothers and sisters. A traditional procession to bless the Jessenters against their fight against the oppressive Djinnasi lords. Within the procession crowd was Tsuki, the new cadet of the group.

The *maiko* had wrapped herself in a heavy dress, blue on the outside and a fiery red inside. Her cloak, heavy as well, was made of the same color scheme, but the hem was embroidered with fanciful flowers. At least she had some measure of practicality by choosing pantaloons gracefully tucked into her boots. Though, Sister Rhyllae was unsure how her narrow-heeled boots would be sufficient for the shifting dune sands.

Rhyllae, too, had heard of her. She grilled Dawn over her capabilities to the point that the lieutenant avoided her. At which point, Rhyllae approached the general.

He gave a cryptic warning in turn, "I wouldn't judge others by their own reflection."

When she persisted for answers, Korzha gave her the ultimatum: "Leave the clergy and join their ranks in official capacity or leave them the hell alone."

It took hours for Aramis to soothe her woes.

Tsuki broke from the procession and walked straight up to the sister. She gave a polite bow, how well practiced it was, to Rhyllae.

"It is a pleasure to finally meet the esteemed songbird of the Morning Lord."

Can't say the same about you, Rhyllae wanted to say. Instead, she took the belt and fastened it tight on the medicinal box.

"I trust you know what you're doing?" Rhyllae said when she finally found a less spiteful response.

The woman gave a well-practiced smile. "Trust is built in drops, sister of the Morn."

"And lost in buckets." Her voice took on an acrid tone. "You won't have anything to drink if you lose your grip."

If the meaning had insulted her, Tsuki didn't show it with that Cheshire grin. "And whose grip do you trust to hold, sister? Yours or your vulpine lover?"

Rhyllae felt her tongue roll over itself as the heat rose from her cheeks. All she could do was to give a baleful glare as Tsuki gave another gracious bow and walked away.

Of course, Dawn was happy to see her; she ran over and swooped her up in her strong arms. Gasps and awes sounded all around them as she swirled her about. When she was put down, Tsuki gave a bow to Dido, then to the Silver Fox. Sister Rhyllae could see Aramis fold his arms as he took in the dancer's outfit.

"Felt?" her half-elven ears picked up from him among the din.

But she couldn't pick up what Tsuki said in response. Though, she could give a good guess as to what, for Aramis tilted to the side and a frown grew on his face. At last, he waved his hand in front of himself to cease the conversation.

"We shall see" was all Rhyllae managed to hear.

An ethereal song warbled out. All fell into silence as the Silver Star was freed from its sheath. Korzha knelt before the Mother Superior, holding the mystical sword up with both hands. Oh, how his cool gaze melted as he took in Myrrh before him. The Mother Superior poised her palm forward from her left, then waved it in an arch. Her fingers splayed wide when they reached the apex then contracted when they reached her right, an imitation of the rising and setting sun.

Rhyllae backed away to join among the citizens, willing the light within to shine for the next prayer set. It had been years since she was on the giving end of the blessing. The first time she wouldn't feel the comforting aura bestowed upon her, settling her pre-adventure jitters. Her eyes trailed over her friends, how they gazed at the display. But not Aramis. He went over every pack and secured their hold, checking every stirrup, every buckle, even all the pouches. Whatever he found lacking, he distributed it from Dido's camel.

He's as nervous as I am...

The Mother Superior finished the seven risings of the sun, and the hand was absorbed back into the folds of her ornate ceremonial robes. The people leaned forward in anticipation of which language the new Mother Superior would choose for this occasion. Many expected the prayer to remain in the prophets' tongue in good faith with the people of Amaveriel, despite not being canon with the liturgy. Some were worried that Myrrh, being a former Töskan noble, would resort to her native tongue. By their opinion, it was bad enough she allowed such a northern style to be introduced among the priestesses. Though the academically minded citizens argued she might fall back to the elvish dialect used in the beginnings of their holy order. If it wasn't for the prophet's tongue, they would've continued that kind of language.

Rhyllae smiled to herself, knowing the answer before it rose from the Mother Superior's lips. The blessing was to be announced in the dead language of the Sleeper. The priestesses, including the sister, must call and respond in kind.

She confided in her the mothers of what Aramis had told her that strange night. That this must be the Sleeper's doing. The Sleeper, who thrusted Their Sun, the Morning Lord, along with his sister Lune, unto this world to lead them through the dark days of the Earth. The Sleeper who ascended Him and his heavenly court to watch overall. Content were They of the peace over the realm that the

Sleeper went to an endless slumber, leaving the care in the Morning Lord's majestic hands.

The idea that They were stirring from Their slumber unnerved the mothers, the Superior included. The lay folk suspected the Sleeper to be a dead deity, or non-existence for all that was worth. But not to Aramis, one of the stubborn few who desired to keep the ancient worship. If he was led by this old deity, then it was a sign of trouble. Thus, the Mother Superior placated the grumbling deity by giving the Silver Fox all the blessings she could muster.

The crowd stirred, wondering the meaning of it all, but Aramis was struck still. His hands ceased on fumbling with the straps and instead pulled down his hood. When his round ears didn't deceive him, he snapped his head to look upon her, in total disbelief of what he heard.

Rhyllae smiled and called in response with the melodic chant. Her heart burst as they locked eyes. Seeing the gloom diminish from his face as the inner child within him shone was all she hoped for.

He needs to keep faith. If not for himself, for others.

At last, they came to the very end of the chant, punctuated by the Silver Star's song. All of the priestesses raised both of their hands to the group and willed their lights to have the blessing accepted. Rhyllae closed her eyes and looked inward. Willing the light burning within her to go through her hands, this light full of love for Aramis and her dear friends Dido and Dawn.

But it didn't come out of her through the fingertips. Instead, she felt a hiccup bubbling within her, and the Light leapt into her throat. A song poured forth from her already parted lips. Low and gentle at first, but with each passing breath it grew in strength.

The Song of the Dawn! she realized. A hymnal she always sang when the morn breaks, at least when she was back home in Amaveriel.

She could see the mothers had their mouths hung open in dismay. This was not part of the rehearsal they practiced! Even the general cocked his blonde eyebrows at the Mother Superior as to what to do next. Rhyllae tried to close her lips, trying not to draw any more attention on herself, especially since she was present without her vestments on. But the song refused to be silenced, and her lips began to move on their own accord.

Mother Pyrsi moved from behind, her brows raised in alarm. But Mother Superior Myrrh raised her hand to bar her from interfering. Sister Rhyllae could hear her over the volume of her own voice, "Let it be." She couldn't tell if she was disappointed or pleased by this sudden musical that was occurring. Her face was unreadable under the veneer of that polite, statuesque expression. Myrrh tapped on the general's hand and motioned him to rise from his knees.

The cue to take his people and leave this place.

Korzha twirled the Silver Star heavenward and proclaimed, "I accept this blessing on the behalf of my crew. We shall return victorious." Then, with another flourish, he sheathed the blade, leaving her song to remain.

The crowd took it as a cue to celebrate their leaving, banging on the drums and crying out good wishes one more time. A group of children even attempted to sing along with Rhyllae, though not with the precision of her skill. The adventurers took to their respective camels as soon as the general joined their ranks. The crowd cried out in awe as Dido floated to her seat by her magic.

"Open the gate!" cried out General Korzha, as he climbed into the saddle.

How it used to be Lady Ruth who gave the usual command. The giant stone gate parted, pulled alongside the tracks constructed in the wall. Before them was the wild dunes of the Iounese desert and a clear blue sky to watch overhead.

Aramis turned about in his seat and waved to her, then touched the ring about his neck. Oh, how she hated to see him go! Rhyllae's feet carried her out into the street, behind the venturing crew. She wanted to go out with them all. One last adventure before she could hang her cloak for good. One more time to be out there with Aramis. If the Morning Lord could hear how her heart ached, then surely, he would grant her last wish?

Alas, the song began to fade and with it her resolve. The Morning Lord sister sank to her knees, reeling from the exhaustion washing over her body. Her cheeks were wet from the tears streaming down to her jaw.

The adventuring company finally cleared the threshold, and the gates rumbled backward to their original slot. The mothers finally came to comfort Rhyllae. Without a word, they guided her to her feet. Giving reassurances that she was needed elsewhere. But all she could hear was the Western Gate slamming shut.

The shuttering of the gate was softened by the magical wards silencing the city of freedom in secrecy. Aramis could feel the reverb shuddering in his heart. He couldn't tear his eyes away from Rhyllae as her hair stuck to her tears. His gaze still lingered on the narrow sieve when the bars locked in place. Seven years it had been where he left this gate with his compatriots, no less than with his beloved friend. Aramis never thought he would feel his heart shackled when he was free of their company.

"Feres…"

"Feres…"

"Aramis!" Korzha called.

He never called him so informally before. The fact tore Aramis's gaze away toward his crew. All eyes were locked upon him, the new company leader and guide. A spectrum of sympathetic eyes and muted stares.

"We await for the shepherd to guide us," Korzha once again spoke.

Aramis grunted in reply and closed his eyes. Willing his heart to be shuttered like the gates, he opened his mind to his senses. He had lived in the Iounese desert for the majority of his life. It never went away, despite the city softening his senses. The different notes on his tongue when he breathed it in. The intensity of the wind on his skin. All of his experiences from serving an Air Djinnasi Lord, and his magical jhasin sensitivities, paid off in his desert survival. And they depended on him for it.

"North," Aramis declared.

Korzha's eyebrows rose from such a statement.

"By the foot of the mountains, but not in," Aramis further explained. "We won't be wasted by the Karatow curse like the mothers did. We'll continue with the mountain's curve until we face west. By then, the storms would pass."

"Whoa," Dawn said in awe.

"Impressive," said Tsuki.

"Indeed," Korzha chimed in. "It seems we're in good hands for this venture."

Though Dido shifted around in her saddle, it was more like a cushion seat for her folding goat legs. She looked over her shoulders to the Silver Fox. "Storms? What kind of storms are we talking about, exactly?"

"The kind to avoid," Korzha said, before he shifted to his commanding voice. "Tsuki, you are in the middle. Dawn, our rearguard, and you, Dido, shall be in between the two. I shall be behind you, Feres, for any perilous encounters."

More like to keep me on a leash, Aramis glumly noted before he nodded at him.

Aramis clicked his tongue to guide his camel to the front. As he passed by Dido, he leaned over to whisper, "Hurricanes."

The answer seemed to appease the satyr. He couldn't blame her for such caution, for not all storms were monstrosities generated by natural clash of heat and moisture. Some were generated by pirates to surprise their victims before bombardment. Others were castoffs created by the wrath of sea monsters in the deep waters. But Aramis was certain the magi was anxious by those of her mystical kind. Those storms herald doom to the world of dark rituals twisted beyond control. In those situations, there was nothing—not the magic in his blades nor in the Morning Lord's blessings—that they could do to stop them if that happened.

Chapter 8

ЯOЯЯIM

DELPHI'S PIERCING CRY CARRIED BEYOND THE freshly laid brick of the abbey's walls. It was the same cry that Sister Rhyllae's heart had been making. The same wail of disbelief of how the cruel wheel of fate kept turning. Yet, she could stifle it and endure the pangs it brought. Delphi had yet to learn to mitigate such pain.

Rhyllae hastened her feet through the throng of her peers, even daring to speed past the Mother Superior at the fore. When Mother Luro gasped at such a transgression, Rhyllae grimaced and bowed at Myrrh. "Forgive me, but Delphi..."

"You are excused, my daughter," said the Mother Superior.

Rhyllae bobbed another bow and sped away. Her slippers slapped on the black and white tiles of the nave and up the spiral staircase to the dormitories. The wailing, a constant siren, was getting stronger with every step of the way. It was as deafening as a heated kettle, and for Rhyllae's half-elven heritage it was twice as awful. But she pushed through the ear-splitting scream and barged into the room.

The room was strewn with wooden blocks and stuffed animals with their stitching becoming unhinged, the normal chaos of child's play. The sister in charge stood there, holding her ears, trying to scream above the din. Delphi, just as red faced as she, lay on her stomach, flailing her fists on the rug they wove for her when she first came into their lives.

How strange for Rhyllae to see the tables turned. Being indoctrinated since infancy, she too had gone through her terribles, though she only remembered the room blurred in tears and rage. The injustice of not having her sweets for any minor mishap felt raw back then. Now, it was almost laughable to see a tiny being having their face twisted into a gremlin's sneer. Along with the welling frustration of diffusing a grease fire that refused to sputter out.

Rhyllae lay on the floor next to her and cooed as she rubbed her back. Eventually, Delphi stopped wailing, though the sobs and hiccups with the tears continued to stream.

"By the grace of the Lune, she has a pair of lungs," Sister Minerva said. "I tried to explain it to her, but she won't be appeased."

"About Aramis leaving?" Rhyllae asked.

"No, about you leaving for Töska. She's quite attached to you."

The words stunned her for a moment. Besides Aramis, Sister Rhyllae never knew anyone who cared for her that strongly as a friend.

"Let me talk to her. Thank you, Sister Minerva."

As soon as her fellow priestess closed the door, Rhyllae looked back at Delphi. It was like a mirror looking back. A reflection of her youth if instead she had darker hair and hazel eyes. Delphi's hair was becoming wild from the initial bob they cut. Soon, they would have to bind it in braids to protect her tresses, or it would be matted again. For now, Rhyllae smoothed it out of the way so they could talk face-to-face on the floor.

"Feeling better?" Rhyllae asked.

Delphi shook her head. "My tummy hurts."

"Because you're upset?"

Delphi nodded. "I miss them."

"Your parents?"

Delphi didn't say a word. There was a glistening in her eyes again, but she put her little fist against her face and rubbed it away.

"You know, I lost my mom and dad, too," Rhyllae said.

Like that, those dark eyes seized upon her. "You?"

"Uh huh. I never knew mine. I was a baby when I lost them. My parents and I were on a ship that was lost at sea. The priestesses found me on the beach still in my father's arms. No one else made it. Eventually, they found the ship records and learned about their names … and mine. That's all I have from them, my name."

"Only your name? No toys?"

Rhyllae shook her head. "Nope. No toys or anything to remember them by. But the name is all I needed to know that they loved me. I know because when I think about them, I feel it in my heart. Right here." Rhyllae shifted on the floor so she could point where her heart was with her thumb. "And I can carry that with me wherever I go."

Delphi picked at the rug, her mind processing everything she said. With a face still in thoughtful pout, Delphi stood up and walked over to the floor trunk by the bed. All of her possessions from her prior life were in there. Mostly toys and blankets for her size, but Delphi also brought over items that clearly came from her parents before. A hair comb, a fan, bracelets, boot polish, those were the ones that she had shown to Rhyllae so far. But what emerged was a bunny made of velveteen. The color was of sage's silver-green hairs and just as fuzzy. There was nary a stain or an unravel seam, and the eyes seemed to gleam. Solemnly, Delphi ambled back to Rhyllae, holding the treasured item.

Sister Rhyllae sat up to receive the special rabbit. "What's his name?"

"This is Obba."

She took his little arm and moved it up and down. "Nice to meet you, Obba."

That put a smile on Delphi's face. "He protected me from the monsties when they came in through the windows."

"How courageous."

"He can protect you, too."

"I... Delphi. I can't bring Obba with me. This came from your parents. I shouldn't take that away from you."

"But Sister Minerva says you're going away." Delphi grabbed her tunic and wrung it in her hands. "What if monsties come and crawl through the windows and wanna eat you. You need Obba!" To further emphasize her point, she stomped on the floor.

Rhyllae sighed as she gazed into Obba's eyes. *I suppose it's not that dangerous of a road we'll be taking. The doll will be safe in the pack. Who knows, maybe the Matriarchs will bless this for her. I'm sure the Mother Superior wouldn't mind.*

"Okay, I'll bring Obba with me," Rhyllae said. "I'll keep him with me to remember you by. Promise me you'll mind the Mothers when I leave, okay?"

Delphi nodded and hugged the sister of the Morning light. "And I'll keep you and Ari in my heart with Mommy and Daddy."

Rhyllae thought she was done with tears today, but she could feel them welling in the corners of her vision. Rhyllae pulled her into a tight hug and whispered, "And I'll keep you in mine."

Seven times, the sun set on the company's first voyage. The stars came out once again with their glorious display and darkened their trail. Aramis guided the team to a shallow plateau, worn by centuries of wind, but high enough to make it defensible. But they were blessed by the morning light, and none sought them out from the tracks they left behind thus far. Even more, Dawn managed to bag two whole lizards for tonight's meal. Aramis flayed the horned skin and cut away all the unkosher parts. Meanwhile Korzha washed some elvish rice with an everlasting bowl, something that Dido pulled out from the Jessenter's treasure storage. The meal should sate them for three days.

The two of them stripped to their first layers before the night fully set in. Korzha had his white shirt sleeves rolled up to his elbows to work the *mouscous*. Many would run it under a continuous stream of water or transfer it to a fresh pot, but that would be costly out here. Instead, the general confined the round grains in a cloth bag and swished the contents in the bowl. When the water was cloudy enough, he scooped up the bag and twisted it tight. Then he dotted the edges and commanded the bowl to purify the water. The everlasting bowl filled once again with clean water, and he repeated the process. Once finished, they sequestered the precious fluids back in their canteens.

The action kept Aramis's gaze, watching the muscle in his forearm putting in the work. The act didn't go unnoticed for Korzha asked, "I take it the morning sister prepared it differently?"

"Rhyllae preferred flat breads for our trips, in case we ran into trouble. Easier to stow on the fly."

The general paused in his action, but Aramis waved at him. "There's nothing to fear."

"Yes, let us see how long our good fortune lasts," Korzha's voice dripped with sarcasm.

Aramis smirked, and he set the pan over the fire. "I thought that Mother Superior would have you groveling every turn of the hour."

"While I may be her knight under her noble patronage, the Mother Superior would have to gag and bind me to have me sing her sermons."

He grinned with a cock of one eyebrow. "Don't you Töskans like that sort of thing?"

"With consent." Korzha then gathered the bag and squeezed the excess. "What of you? Will you change your 'pagan' ways to suit your blessed bride?"

"Fat chance." Aramis cut and flung the lizard meat into the pot, sizzling with the oil. He then snaked in the strips of skins into the flames.

He half-expected Korzha to be pleased by such a declaration, him being an open anti-theist, yet he caught his steely blue eyes darting over him like a battle map.

"I have heard some of the mothers gave you grief over the match," Korzha said before he turned his attention back to the rice. "Pay no heed to their jealousy. Love wills out in the end. Soon, you'll be wed, and all sorrows will be mended."

"Love? Thought you cared only for prestige."

"Prestige has its uses, but love is what separates us from the mindless beasts lurking in the shadows. It gives us a sense of being—a purpose that provides warmth against the cruel winds of winter." Korzha paused. The fire threw shadows upon his face in the darkening sky. Save for his right eye, pale blue and unwavering. "Those who lived without its warmth didn't last long against the undying calls of the inmorti. Many joined their ranks long before the sun rose due to its black despair. Love, my crafty friend, is survival and worth dying for."

"Amen to that, brother," Dawn said with an armful of twigs.

She tossed them in the fire pit. The fire roared to life, throwing sparks at the men as it feasted upon the wooden offerings.

"Shit, Dawn, warn me next time," Aramis said.

"Sorry," Dawn said, though she didn't look at it as she plopped down and rummaged through the spice bag.

"I thought you would take this opportunity to be with your newfound belle, Lieutenant," Korzha queried.

"She's with Dido right now." Dawn popped open a jar of turmeric and gave it a sniff.

"What is this?" Aramis leaned over, cupping his ear with his hand. "Did I hear our famed Lady Lover lose a catch?" He then mockingly shook his head and put his hand over his heart. "Ah, what a terrible shame."

"Yes, quite a shame." Korzha joined in the mirth. "I supposed none can resist a satyr's charm."

"Gotta be the horns."

"It's always the horns."

Dawn rolled her hazel eyes. "Just don't forget the paprika, guys."

Rhyllae went over the spice box for the trip. Despite Myrrh's insistences that there would be establishments on the road, she didn't want to be caught unawares. Furthermore, she heard tales from her fellow sisters that hailed from there that the food was rather bland. Suitable for sensitive palates, but joyless, nonetheless. One coastal sister tried to convince her that she'd enjoy the lemon pepper snappers. Her stomach roiled when she learned they enhanced the flavor with an excess amount of salt.

No, she thought to herself. *I don't think I'll ever get used to it.*

Once all the spices were accounted for, Rhyllae shut the wooden lid closed and put it in her rucksack. Everything in there was rolled and stashed for balanced weight with the prayer rug (which doubled as a bed) strapped to the bottom of the sack. Even the bunny doll was in there, wrapped in muslin for further protection.

Rhyllae was even dressed for that foreign environment. Instead of the lightweight robe of the Morning Lord, the Morning sister wore a heavy green cloak that went down to her knees with embroidered slits for armholes. Her yellow shawl was replaced with a woolen one with a strong mustard color. Though the peak hat was an option, Töska was still at war with the elves. It was better to lessen any unnecessary conflict by covering her ears. To prevent harassment from the local lawmen, she had the shining emblem of the rising sun hung proudly from a leather cord. If push came to shove, they had their heaven-sent spells. Rhyllae wasn't naive enough to think their journey would be a peaceful one.

A knock came at her door, and Rhyllae opened it to find the Mother Superior there. She was almost identical in dress. The emblem was the same, as well as the leather cord. Myrrh wore a rucksack on her back, though not as tightly packed as the sister's, and the leather had seen weather and age. She also wore the same woolen robe, but in red to indicate she was a mother. Her habit was peaked instead of the traditional hijab, but the woolen cloth was wrapped about her neck similar to Sister Rhyllae's style.

Myrrh's Töskan blue eyes looked over Rhyllae with warm approval. "Ready?"

"Yes, Mother Superior," said Rhyllae.

She raised her palm and shook her head. "Myrrh would be satisfactory. We'll be on the road for a long time, Rhyllae, before we shall reach *Aly Thun Thŭr*. Come, there's no time to waste."

With her rucksack solid on her back, Rhyllae trailed after her. Their boots clicked down the freshly laid sandstone, then on the original basalt and marble tiles. The renovations were happening at a faster rate now that the summer sun abated its intensity. Would it still be the same abbey she grew up in? Or would it be a shell of the past, a stranger she once knew but a distant memory. Rhyllae found herself falling behind and hurried after Myrrh.

They came to Myrrh's living quarters and found most of the mothers and sisters already lined up out in the hall. They clapped as they saw them pass. The last time this happened was when Mother Superior Frianul first took the appointment, bringing with her Sister Ophellia, transferred to who knows where. Rhyllae was among those clapping to see them off—a younger Rhyllae who never considered joining the Jessenter's cause. Now they clapped for her and the Mother. The priestess would've felt honored if this were under happier circumstances.

"You're our hope!"

"Pray for Peace!"

"We're counting on you!"

And many more wishes were exclaimed. Rhyllae squared her shoulders and set her mind straight. They were traveling for those they had to bury from that agonizing, wasting disease and in hopes of finding a cure for the rest. To find a way to resolve the desert conflict. Leaving for reasons far more important than her own, Sister Rhyllae must remind herself of that.

Myrrh opened the plain door and ushered her in. Then she thanked everyone for seeing them off and promised to return. Rhyllae took two steps in and stood still. The entire room was chalked with symbols and lines. Most of the symbols she recognized were from the ancient texts they had in their archives. Signs of sending. Signs of the lunar phase that they were now in. Others were symbols she didn't recognize but looked like some form of elvish. They all radiated from a bare patch on the wall, made as an arch that was as tall as the mother.

"Our secret of secrets," Myrrh said as she joined her side. "The elves who allied with the Morning Lord passed on their magical techniques onto his followers. This is called the Fae Way, a mirror that can transport people for long distances."

"Fae?" Rhyllae asked. "Do you think the Morning Lord would approve us using this?"

"We do not answer to the whims of the Summer Court, and neither did the elves of that age."

Then the mother swept across the floor to the chalked arch and waved her hand over the words. It was ancient elvish! A dialect full of articles that were no longer in use and other oral filigree. Yet, the same buzzing energy was felt all the same as the wall rippled like a disturbed pond. Soon an image crystallized, a sorry state of a shrine with moss growing on the stones. At last, the image ceased to wobble and became still as a mirror.

Aramis drummed his fingers on the bottom of his dinner bowl. Tsuki and Dido were nowhere to be found by the time the meal was called. His curiosity peaked when Korzha left with two steaming bowls to give to them. He never returned.

He couldn't keep still anymore.

With Dawn in tow, he trailed the general past the tents, down the slope, and toward a red wall of clay. It was scrawled in white chalk with symbols that Aramis hadn't seen in a long time. Ulleryn Script, what the historians called the archaic elvish language now. Aramis had tried to learn some of it from a censored book. A shame it was tossed into an incinerator when they did the monthly harem sweeps. He never thought he would see it again. And yet here it was, bold as day, transcribed by none other than Dido herself.

Dawn broke away from the shadows to make her way to Tsuki who was quietly conversing with Korzha down the stretch, still holding the steaming meal.

"What is all this about?" the lieutenant asked, spooking the two from the sudden appearance.

"Oh, Dawn! You're here early," Tsuki exclaimed as she clutched her chest.

"Oh, really?" Dawn crossed her arms, then gave a pointed look at her superior, "Sir?"

"All will be explained in due time" was all Korzha said.

Aramis rolled his eyes. He knew Dawn wouldn't be able to extract anything useful from these two. With the two of them distracted, he slunk to where the hardworking satyr stood. She was almost finished with the script and laid down the incantation for the archway.

Numea'el. Sundurai. Tor'vi.

(Connect. Sever. Transport.)

"This is not a teleportation spell," Aramis said quietly behind Dido, crouching to be in her shadow.

To her credit, the mage didn't flinch and finished the word she wrote down. Dido took a deep breath to steady her nerves and whispered back to him, "Not a simple teleportation spell, you mean. And I'm running out of time. This clay is rather troublesome."

Then she finished chalking up the word: *Sumac.* (Switch.)

"What are we swapping?" Aramis queried.

"Not what. Who."

Then she finally finished the archway with *Lath‹q›oo, Lun‹q›oo.* (Sun bird, Moon bird.)

Then it clicked in his brain, and Aramis's mouth gaped. Dido turned about to face him and gave a gentle tap on his chin to close it. Then she waved at him to back up. With a wave of her hand, trailing the chalk arch in the clay, she produced a rippling pond from the stone.

The sorry state of this shrine saddened Rhyllae. She hoped to cross over to a sisterly abbey and be received in welcoming arms, but that would not be the case. Myrrh didn't seem to mind. Silently, the Mother Superior waved at her to follow, and she stepped right up to it. She picked up her long travel skirt and kicked her boot into the mirror. The surface rippled from the disturbance as Myrrh stepped into it. Soon, the Mother Superior became part of the landscape, a cloaked shadow of red.

Rhyllae took a deep breath, adjusted the pack on her back, and recited the Morning Lord's prayer for protection and Lune's grace for her nerves, for good measure. Slowly, she approached the mirror, still like glass. She reached out with her hand and felt the surface tacky to her touch. With another deep breath, Rhyllae gripped the pack straps tight in her hands, closed her eyes, and stepped into the portal.

Everything compressed against her skin, and she was yanked into the magical vortex. The liquid that passed over her skin reminded her of the ocean, but the pressure was nothing like Rhyllae had ever experienced. Worried that this foreign liquid would go down her gullet, she held her breath, but lost it as her body whipped about like a ragdoll. One moment she sailed forward, and then the next she was yanked to her left. The sensation of falling roiled over her. No matter how hard she tried to right herself, the feeling remained. The stalwart sister didn't cry out, no matter how terrified she was of the experience. Instead, she prayed in her mind for a safe voyage and no broken bones by the end of it.

Soon, the pressure released its grip, and Rhyllae emerged onto the other side on her hands and knees. She felt the arid wind against her skin, not the damp of the Töskan air. The ground shifted under her weight like sand.

Sand!

Her honey-brown eyes flew open and found she wasn't underground, but above. Lune smiled down upon her with the starry congregation. Standing before her was not the Mother Superior but her friends. The expanse of the Iounese desert sloped down and away from where they all stood. All of them looked at her with a mixture of awe and delight. Aramis took off his mask, his head cast in a soft halo of silver, clearly not believing his eyes. No one moved or said a word as if to destroy what miraculous spell that occurred.

Sister Rhyllae was stunned silent along with them. Then she shouted, "WHAT THE HELL IS GOING ON?!"

Chapter 9

BEDOUIN

"Take it easy, Sister Rhyllae. You're still going through the bends," Dido said. She crept forward and arms held out before her as if she were calming a wild horse.

"Whose idea was it?!" Sister Rhyllae's voice boomed out into the night.

No one said a word. None ever saw her this furious before, not even the famed Silver Fox. Then again, none dared to pull such trickery against the sister of the Morning Light. Save for the pragmatic general of the rebels. All four of them turned their gaze upon Korzha, who stood tall with his one hand resting behind his back, his meal still steaming in his other palm.

"You?!" Rhyllae pointed at him.

She took a couple steps forward before her legs wobbled out from under her. She collapsed to her knees, and she fell forward on her hands. Dido and Aramis rushed to her side, but she waved them off.

Rhyllae continued, "You? You lied to me! You told me you had a healer. I took you for your word."

"Yes, we do. You," Korzha said. "Now if you don't mind, we can take this discussion around the fir—AH!"

The general fell through the sand. Then the ground solidified around him, catching him at his armpits. The hot bowl tumbled about his shoulder, spilling the lizard and rice all over himself.

It was all the sister's doing. Her two fists were buried in the ground before her, and she twisted them to create a quicksand under his feet. Then, she twisted them again to tighten the hold on him. The severe containment spell was used for only incapacitating dangerous criminals. But the sister was too far from home to be concerned about protocol.

Lieutenant Dawn waved her arms about. "Woah, woah, woah. I'm sure he has a good explanation for this."

"He can explain from there," Aramis said.

But he whispered to Rhyllae, "But keep him alive for me." When Rhyllae gave him an incredulous look, he added, "Please?"

The general's shoulder slumped. Well, as much as his could in this situation. He rolled his blue eyes to the darkening sky. "By the stars! We need someone of your caliber, and no one in Amaveriel compares. Believe me, I looked high and low with no such luck."

"Then why the ruse?" Rhyllae asked.

"You're far too transparent, Sister. The moment your half-elven ears caught wind of our plans, Myrrh would know. Though a dear friend of mine, her allegiance lies with the clergy and cannot be swayed. We don't have the luxury of time to sit idly by while our enemy maneuvered against us."

"Hmph, I admit, he has a point," Aramis said.

"A bit extreme to yank someone out of a portal, don't you think?" Rhyllae queried.

"Oh, well, that idea was mine," Dido said, shifting her weight back and forth between her cloven hooves.

Rhyllae softened her stance. "You? Wha—how? Why?"

"You've been snooping," Aramis said, a glimmer of amusement in his eyes.

"Nooo," Dido drew out the word as she looked away. "I overheard the Mother Superior's plans while I was reading in the library. Most Fae Ways have branching paths that are utilized for traffic flow. It's not difficult to divert transporters to a different location, so long as you have the proper timing."

"And so, you hatch a plan to magically swap Rhyllae ... with a dancer?"

Korzha said, "No, a bard."

"I don't know what you were thinking, sir," Dawn said in between bites. "Tsuki is a *maiko*, not a bard. Both of them sing and dance, sure, but being a bodyguard?"

Rhyllae, too weak to continue the spell, conceded to have their conversation continue around the fire. Dido stoked the fire with her magical encouragement, and the meal warmed to an edible temperature. Aramis rubbed her legs down as the sister picked her favorite parts. The spice was savory enough to enjoy it, though she suspected that if Aramis had her spice collection, he would've done wonders with the palate.

The general quickly swallowed his steaming mouthful before he spoke. "She is both a *maiko* and a bard. After one of my many failed meetings with the Mother Superior, Madame Tsuki asked for admittance beyond Amaveriel's borders. She proved to me she was well capable for such a treacherous journey. What lies before her will require wit and tenacity."

"Being charming is one thing, General, but if Töska is as dangerous as you say it is, would it be better to have Dawn with the Mother Superior for protection?" Sister Rhyllae countered.

"The dangers poised before them are something no physical mettle could ever achieve. A supernatural restlessness lurks there, and I suspect it had worsened since my untimely dismissal. No, I do not mean the inmorti, Silver Fox," Korzha interjected, when Aramis gave pause from his massaging. "There are powers as old and, no offense given, devious as the Fae. Töska is a broad country. As vast as Ioun, I dare say. There's too much at stake to simply allow blind faith to guide the mother. Tsuki, perceptive of such dangers, is keenly aware of this."

"So, it's her 'supernatural' sight you're banking on, huh?" Dawn muttered and put her bowl down. She then cleared her throat when Korzha gave her a baleful stare. "Sir."

"She's spirit sighted? She should've been a priestess," Rhyllae said.

"Tsuki is the kind of woman who would rather gouge out her eyes and walk naked in the streets than join the Holy Order. I should know, since she's my belle."

Korzha switched his bowl to his right hand as to chop the air with his left, his preferred hand. "I needed someone who has the sight, as well as the wit to foresee the traps set before her and circumvent them. She is also…"

The general trailed off, and his blue eyes glanced over to the lieutenant. Her answer was to cross her muscular arms across her chest.

"…Willing to investigate who is after our mage and treasurer. She had a lead, and I am willing to let her follow it on my behalf. That being said, the plan to switch between the two of you was cracked. Dido's magic provided the means."

"I see how it is," Aramis said. "It's perfectly fine to send a smart and capable woman into Töska and not have her here for this mission."

"Is Sister Rhyllae not a smart and capable woman herself?" the general countered.

Aramis gave a nervous flick of his silver eyes to Rhyllae. She held it as she slowly chewed her spoonful of meat and rice. She loved the jhasin, but she was tired of everyone coddling her. Dejected, Aramis grabbed his meal and muttered his apologies.

Korzha turned his icy gaze toward Rhyllae, oh how unforgiving they held her in his sights. "The heart of the matter is, Sister, you are a skilled healer. No other priestess— no one, not even Tsuki—handles death and disaster quite as well as you do and still sustain the sacred connection. Many would quake from the furious onslaught you experienced from M'thealquilôk alone. Whether you accept it or not, Sister of the Morning Lord, we depend upon you for our survival."

The sun broke through the hazy horizon, sapping away the precious dew on the desert sand. Aramis was there to greet it, always the insomniac. His groggy eyes barely fluttered as the skies brightened from indigo to rose. He dared not moved in fear of disturbing Rhyllae, slumbering in his arms. She slept on his shoulder this time around, depleted from the late-night talking. His weary mind welcomed it, as Aramis wrapped her in his cloak and snuggled his scruffy face against her curls. The familiar smell of sandalwood permeated from her strands.

Never had he expected this turn of events. Part of him wanted to kiss Korzha, for he did miss her. Yet, part of him wanted to throttle him. It was easier to know she was safe and far from this dangerous mission. Easier to plot a course errantly into the heart of a viper's nest. But now she was here, everything changed. Now, Aramis was unsure where to put his footing, no less their heading. Worse, how could he keep a promise of a little girl to bring Rhyllae home, no less himself?

Rhyllae moaned as she stirred. The velveteen rabbit slipped from her drooping arms unto the sand. Careful not to disturb her, Aramis plucked the cloth doll up. It was a fine make and soft to the touch. For the life of him, Aramis couldn't place the maker or the craft. It wouldn't surprise him if this was an heirloom of sorts; some families would shell out generous sums to have magic on such items to preserve it against time.

Which begs the question: who was it for? For children like Delphi, who would outgrow it in a matter of years? For their future children to who she would pass it down? Was it really worth the cost? For that amount, it could've purchased a costly medicine to save a life or transport the family to safer, wealthier shores. On the other hand, one could argue the consistency in one's life was worthy of the price to safeguard against the chaos that surrounded them. A life raft of hope, of sorts.

Even the D.R.H.S. was divided on the issue of magically preserving items. Aramis heard it all. When should the spell be cast? At the conception of the item's production or when society deemed it a valued treasure? What even made a historical treasure? If the object was a mass-produced product, as common as a brick in a wall, shouldn't the value stay the same over time? Or should that be exempted because the society was extinct?

Aramis used to have the answers, used to know where to draw the line in the sand in these debates. But now the world had been tilted on its axis, and he couldn't stop its spin.

The sunrays began to warm the earth and softly illuminated the rabbit doll in his hands, his jhasin eyes seeing the magical halo shimmering against the intense light along its surface. He held it aloft, against the sand dune that was sheltering them from the storms. Aramis pushed them hard these past few days for fear of the Fae picking up Dido's magical rite. At night, if he couldn't find them a suitable cliff, he would create a "fox burrow," a miniature circle of dunes to shelter them. A trick he learned from living in this sandscape years ago from his teacher, the Silver Fox prior to him. And today would be no different until they found refuge among the pools of Ma'seaul.

What would you preserve, Obba? Aramis asked the doll.

Of course, the enchantment was only for protection and nothing more. There would be no answers here. Aramis lowered the doll from his view to stow it away. In its stead was a figure—a child—standing on the dune. Their clothes were tattered, and their face burnt by the sun. The child began to sway before him.

Aramis leapt to his feet, running to the child as the kid fell forward. They tumbled through the sand before Aramis caught up to them. There was no sweat on their skin when Aramis pulled them out of the dune.

They're hot as a dying ember!

"Aramis?" Rhyllae asked.

She gasped when she saw him cradling the child. The sister ran straight over, kicking Dawn in the head in the process.

"Ow. Okay, I'm up. I'm up—Oh, shit." Dawn shook the rest awake before she joined them with her shield.

"Tell me what to do," Aramis said as he laid the kid over his cloak.

"I need shelter and water," Rhyllae rattled off as she snapped off her scarf.

"Here, give me your shield. I can enlarge and put frost on it," Dido said.

"No. No magic. Not until we're clear," Korzha said as he placed the everlasting bowl by Rhyllae's side.

"My cloak," Dawn offered instead and flung the hem to Dido.

The two held the cloth aloft, shielding the child from the sun's growing strength. Meanwhile, Korzha poured a canteen of water in the bowl, and the sister soaked her shawl in it. Aramis took one of his knives and cut away the shirt on the kid's chest. Aramis froze. It was bound by cloth, wrapped as tightly as one could without constriction. He recognized for what it was, for he had done the same in his youth. Quickly, Rhyllae's soggy shawl enveloped the child, encasing him in its coolness.

"Aramis, your canteen," Sister Rhyllae called him back into reality.

Aramis knew what she wanted him to do. He propped him up and carefully spilled the precious liquid into his lips. Thankfully, the kid lapped it up with his sluggish tongue. Aramis paused and refilled as much as he could. Rhyllae closed her eyes and pressed her hands about his face, then over his heart. Her lips murmured the healing prayer to let the clutches of death pass this one over. Soon, his eyes fluttered open, hazel like so many who were born of this land. Everyone gave a great sigh as he looked at him.

Aramis pressed the canteen into his palm. "Take your time."

The kid swayed when he took a swig, but he didn't lose a drop.

"Hey kid, what's your name?" Dawn asked.

The kid looked at these helpful strangers, gauging whether to trust any of them. His eyes lingered on Dido the most, unsure what to make of her.

"It's okay," the satyr mage said in a gentle tone. "You're safe, you can tell us."

"He hasn't figured out his name yet," the ever-observant Korzha said. His pale blue eyes fluttered to Aramis, knowing what he knew.

The child followed the general's gaze and nearly fell over when he caught sight of him. "The Silver Fox!" his parched throat croaked. He spun about, breaking away from Rhyllae's attentive prayers. "Please, you have to help! Raiders. The raiders attacked my tribe. We tried to fight. I ran and ... um, followed the foxes."

Aramis held his shoulders to steady him. "Where did it happen?"

The boy looked about him, but his shoulders slumped when he found no significant landmarks. "I don't know. We were following the gazelle and camped by a bunch of date trees."

"By the pools of Ma'seaul?"

The boy shook his head. "We weren't going to be there for another month."

"Wait... Which tribe did you come from?" Dawn asked.

"Bedouin... Wait—you are?"

Dawn flashed a broad grin. "It's been a while, huh?"

The kid weakly smiled. "I thought I would never see you again, Dawn!"

"What a stroke of luck," Korzha loudly mused. "Are the foxes your doing, Aramis?"

He shook his head, but this wasn't the first time he heard of this. There had been nights, long before he settled in Amaveriel, where he would be found by such lost souls far from any civilized camps. Usually, they were runaways from their abusive families, looking for a new life. Or they managed to escape raiders who would turn them in at slave markets.

"Forget the foxes," said Dawn. "I know where they are."

Aramis nodded. "Then we travel by Lune's light."

They arrived by the next break of dawn, casting the ruinous encampment in a ruddy hue. Tents and date trees were riddled with finite holes. Overturned looms and racks of dried meat littered among the scorched bodies. Rhyllae broke away from the group to the nearest person on the ground. A child, Aramis realized when she lifted her head. The sister shook a "no" to him and gently laid her back on the ground. They followed her as they combed the entire village looking for survivors. The mood was grim by the time they broke during the sun's zenith. There were no survivors to be found. Stranger yet, the wounds were all small and circular. Not even sling bullets were small enough, or fast enough, to pierce the skin in such an odd puncture.

"Raiders don't normally do this," Aramis finally commented.

"Sure they do. These assholes love causing mayhem," Lieutenant Dawn countered.

He shook his head. "They raid for food, clothes. Children, if they could ransom for them. They don't kill for sport."

The child spoke up, the first time since they departed. "But they must be raiders. They took everyone away."

"Slavers, then?" Rhyllae conjectured.

Korzha rubbed his chin with his forefinger and thumb. "They left a fair number of valuables behind."

Aramis nodded and crossed his arms. "They would've taken their time to collect everything to sell it in the west."

"He's right," piped up Dido. "When I was captured, they picked everything from that caravan clean—even the metal fastenings."

"Then what kind of people would destroy things and steal them away?" Dawn asked with her hands waved out wide.

Or what? Aramis wondered as he stared at the child, glum as one should be as they peered into their cup. "Can you tell us what they look like? Their clothes, perhaps. What's the color of their sashes?"

Korzha gave him a pointed look, for the Jessenters were one of the few groups fitting of that description, but Aramis raised his palm at him.

"They... they weren't wearing any clothes." The child said it more as a question. "Their skin is hard as metal. And white—shiny white, with no sand on them. It took five people to take down one of them. But so many..." He then tucked his legs in and veered his gaze to the sitting rug they sat upon.

"Where did they attack?" Aramis asked.

The kid shrugged. "At the southern edge of camp."

"Then that is the plan," Rhyllae said. "Me and Dido will repose the bodies while the rest of you investigate."

Dawn looked at the child, her face contorted with concern. Aramis couldn't blame her; the kid saw enough as it was.

"The two of you could be our lookouts," Aramis offered.

Dawn bopped her head to the side. "C'mon, kid. Let's find the high ground."

It was a good decision. The high point was by the date tree far north where Aramis and Korzha headed. The smell was unbearable with the dead. Beyond the shredded tents were piles of rotting corpses all gathered at the base of the dune that sheltered the tribal camp. The torn fabric flapped against the wind, exposing the families that fell from the surprised assault. Their backs riddled with the same mysterious wounds.

"They didn't know what hit them," Aramis grimly noted.

"A sneak attack," Korzha stated as he waved his hand before them. "The child mentioned the gleam on their armor, which meant it happened during the day. Bold."

Aramis squinted against the piercing sun and scanned down the curve of the camp's edge. By his right was one of the collapsed sentry towers. They had been planning to stay for more than a week by the look of their bindings.

"Most sentries would stop them long before they reached camp," Aramis said.

"They tried."

Aramis looked up from the tent he was focused on and found what Korzha meant. Dozens of Bedouins' bravest fell in a pile that stretched a mile long from left to right. All clustered by the nook of that dune.

"They would take the high ground there." Korzha, with his long legs, swiftly climbed up to the top of the dune. "They mowed them down from here!" he shouted down to Aramis.

"For slings, but not for crossbow bolts!" he shouted up to him.

"Yes... too tall." Korzha knelt. He bent his elbows as if to cradle an invisible crossbow. "This would be more tactful. Easy to reload, too."

"How many do you surmise?"

Korzha looked about him and shook his head. "Not enough to cause this type of damage. Even with secondary archers."

"Secondary archers?"

"Crossbows require reloading. As your primary primes for the next volley, you have the secondary to fill in the lull. But there's no room up here for such luxuries."

The corner of Aramis's eye twitched. *Of course, he would call such bloody tactics a luxury.* "Maybe it's a repeating crossbow."

"Expensive... It must be a quick action to cause this level of devastation. And an indispensable amount of wood to supply the bolts."

"They would have to receive funds for it. There's no wood for miles."

"What of the pile there?" Korzha pointed to the crumpled sentry tower.

"Made out of reeds. The Bedouins would've harvested them when they wandered through the Southern Floes, near the Hapthos river. Leagues from where we are. The wood would be out of season by now."

Korzha stepped off from the edge of the dune, spacing his feet apart to keep himself upright as he slid down to join Aramis. "Metal, perhaps. Matchlocks travel far more readily by trade."

"Perhaps."

Aramis knelt by one of the cadaver piles. He rolled each one away, letting their pallid faces turn skyward. Nothing was sticking out of them. No wooden shafts, and no other signs of weapons beyond the holes in their flesh.

"No gun would be this precise with their grouping," Korzha said.

"And small. Look at the size of the entry wounds. They're tiny."

"You cannot mean…"

"Aramis!" Rhyllae cried out at the camp's edge. "I found something!"

Korzha and Aramis exchanged looks before they hurried to join her and Dido.

Chapter 10

HAZE

IN THE HEART OF THE BEDOUIN'S ENCAMPMENT, there was a long line of the fallen reposed by Sister Rhyllae and Dido. They were covered by a sheet of cloth that Dido magicked out of respect. But that was not where they found her when the two arrived. The half-elven priestess crouched by a hunk of metal, dark and twisted inside a shell that gleamed in the sunlight. As Aramis neared her side, he found that the surface was whiter than a bleached shell.

"I also popped this from a superficial wound." Rhyllae dropped a small chunk of metal in Korzha's outstretched palm.

He held it up to the sky between his thumb and forefinger. "It's capped! No dwarf or elf would make their bullets this way."

"No mortal would have that level of skill," Aramis mused out loud.

From his belt, Aramis donned jeweler spectacles and leaned his entire body to peer right at it. It was cylindrical, as Korzha mentioned, but one end was flattened into a puddle as if melted by high heat. There were no seams from the mold, even by dwarven designs. By a slight twist of his fingers, he turned over to find the head stamp.

The indentions were too sharp and precise for any stamp, unless...

"Are you telling me these came from the Ancients?" Korzha asked, bringing Aramis out of his thoughts.

Aramis inhaled and closed his eyes as he took off the specs. "Or someone found their blueprints and ran with it."

Rhyllae asked with a scrunched face. "Like the pirates?"

Aramis shook his head. "These are far more accurate than their matchlocks, no matter the expense. These must be fired by a barreled pistol."

"Those guns are outlawed by the Fae," Dido added. "My grand-pappy always warned of the danger of humans because of those awful devices. Every human back then had one on their person. It was a gruesome time."

Korzha unhooked his scabbard and lifted one of the tangled cords from the metallic heap. "And it came from this? I would sooner believe a group of scavengers finding a cache than this."

"Such caches had been destroyed by the Fae long ago. I should know: it was my first duty when I..." Dido shifted her eyes to each of them as she strained the word. "Helped my gramps."

Then someone is making them, by the thousands.

But Aramis didn't dare say that thought out loud. Instead, he crouched by the twisted metal. The shiny chassis saw some damage from their swords before it was pummeled by massive fist-size indentions. It fell apart as he lifted it up. Underneath the broken bits was a mask. Aramis shook it out of the sand and turned it over. It was the same as those haunting images from the soul stone. The mask was white with no paint. The shape was not by any craftsman he had ever seen. Too perfect by design. Stranger, there were no holes for the wearer to breath or see with. A vacant white stare of porcelain perfection.

Mannequins, here?

His fingers trembled, dropping the mask back on the ground. With one of his daggers, Aramis found a sieve in the main chassis body and cracked it open. Bullets, pointed like darts, poured forth and collected at his knees.

Korzha knelt by his side and picked up one of the metal cylinders. "There's no rust."

"It's not going to; it's brass," Aramis said.

"This many?"

"For one human?" Rhyllae asked.

"Machine," Aramis piped up.

Rhyllae turned to Aramis wide-eyed. "Do you think the Djinnasi made this?"

He didn't want to tell her. Didn't want her to know the horrors that might await for them so she wouldn't be wrought with worry when Rhyllae ventured with the Mother Superior. Especially, a mechanical horror that could easily take five down along with it. But this wasn't why he pried open this monster's chest.

Aramis sliced his dagger deep through all the metal until he spied two mesh fabric sacs, too fine by any loom on this earth. The one on the bottom was distended and lumpy. Tubes with stagnate dark liquid rose to the slender one where it housed a circulatory system of wire and oil.

He sawed through the connecting ends and unearthed it from the metal chest by the tip of the blade to puncture a hole in the sac. Black liquid streamed onto the ground as he widened the hole further. Until at last, Aramis found what he was looking for, a stick of metal with octagonal sides and slots.

"Ugh. What is that?" Dido asked while she pinched her arched nose when he fished it.

"The CPU," Aramis answered, to which her eyes flickered in recognition. "The heart of the machine," he clarified to the rest.

"And what will you do with its dead heart?" asked Korzha.

Aramis shrugged and then waggled his fingers. "Do a little voodoo and find our lost tribe."

As the rest turned their puzzled faces to each other, he started walking. His boots took him toward their camels, under the watchful eye of Dawn. His steps were trailed by the rest of the trio.

"Hey, where are you going?" she shouted down from the top of the date tree.

"Alone," Aramis shouted out to the rebel soldier. Then turned over his shoulder to the sister of the Morn, "Even you, *me'qora*."

He saddled up on his camel and clicked his tongue. The creature brayed in protest but stood by his command.

Rhyllae grabbed the reigns and asked in elvish, "<When will you be back? Tomorrow night?>"

Aramis wrapped the rubbish in a bandana that held today's bread. "<If lucky, when the dawn rises.>"

"<May the Morning Lord be with you, my heart.>"

"<My heart is with you.>"

She stepped away from his mount, allowing him to turn the bulky creature around and start his trek. Dawn raced up to the camels, but Rhyllae stuck her hand out to halt her efforts.

"He must do this alone."

"Like hell he's going to fight them alone," Dawn countered.

"Not fight, locate." Rhyllae looked over to the horizon where his silhouette stood. It's not Aramis without one last look behind him. "It is said, 'he who wears the mask is burdened with secrets none are allowed to know.'"

Then the Silver Fox melted into the haze of the desert heat.

The haze, that common phenomenon of where the light excites the air as one gazes into the horizon. Long ago, Aramis learned it was nothing more than a mere sliver of distorted reality. Slipping into that phantasmal space of wind and sand, Aramis could travel far and wide, so long he remained within that slipstream of disbelieve. Another trick he stole from his old Djinnasi master, who stole it from the Fae. A legacy of theft.

Aramis Feres urged the camel to stay within the mystical traverse. The winds howled around him, eager to rip him away from his course. He crouched low, close to the camel's hump, searching against the sand spray for the telltale sign of his travels end.

Then Aramis saw it; a silhouette in the distance emerged from the distortion, and they were approaching it fast. He gave a shrill whistle, and the haze shifted around him. A clear vision of a different desert landscape, more orange and jagged, parted before him. Aramis clicked his tongue, urging the camel forward through the sandy gusts. Inch by inch, the clear vision widened before him. It arched over as they raced toward it.

Then the world flew wide open. The haze was a mere distant sliver, leaving Aramis and the infrangible camel traversing in the calm and rocky terrain. They were due North from the Glass Plains, that sweet spot before the Gallileah mountains. The looming silhouette he saw earlier was none other than the Fox Burrow, home long before Aramis found a home.

Though many would call it a dump heap, if they ever survived through the Glass Plains. It was a conical tower of scrap-metal plates in a shape that was akin to a crumpled wizard's cap without the brim.

Aramis gave the soothing command to halt, and the camel happily complied. It would be morning before it would go on another trip, by the sounds of its discontentment. He paused after he dismounted, fearing it to be a mirage. Yet, nothing wavered as he approached foot by foot. It was like looking into another time from a stranger's eyes.

He hadn't been here for decades, yet everything was right where he had left it. Even the tools that were strewn by the door, which were no more than a burlap sack moving in the breeze. The tip of the Fox Burrow's hut beheld a massive telescope, also made of scrap metal, pointing to the southeast. From the seat of it was a thick wire that dangled down with a rusted tin can secured at the end of it.

Aramis dismounted and let his legs carry him to the still tin can. The moment his calloused fingertips touched the oxidized metal, he recalled why he hung it up high in the first place. He was working with Saarif, one of the freemen he saved from Bazzuuport. They tried to locate Amaveriel, that famed city of myth. Aramis would tell him from that seat where they should scout next, and Saarif would write it down. About 15 years ago. When he had freshly transitioned to a man, full of hope and vigor.

"Ah!" Aramis hissed as his toe found one of the forgotten wrenches when he walked away.

The man he was now was tired of his younger self's shit. Aramis spent the first hour collecting all the tools back into its original box. The next hour to roll up the rug he used as an outdoor workspace to fix… Well, he quite forgot what. Once everything was piled by the doorway, Aramis finally entered.

There he was greeted by the same old desks he once worked at with all the assorted tools that were collected over the years. Metal stairs, which he rebuilt many times over, spiraled into the various floors, one a library of books stacked in mounds and piles and another his personal sleeping quarters. The familiar smell of stale curry and machine oil still lingered in the space. The nostalgia gave him pause.

He blinked and shook his head. *Come on, Aramis, get it together. They need you—the whole tribe of Bedouin needs you.*

Without looking for it, he kicked back with the heel of his boot. It landed on the floor generator. It turned on, and the archaic machine roared into life. Glass-blown bulbs lit from the heated filaments he'd hand-coiled illuminated what was left behind on the workbench. Maps upon maps, with handwritten accounts of pirates who had long since retired, and his own written notes, sprawled across the length of the workbench. One such note, clear as day, had "eureka" written by his hand. Attached was a long rambling page of where the city could be found.

Aramis picked up the note, took a cursory glance, and crumpled it up. Then he did the same with the next note and then the next. Soon, he scooped up whatever he could into his arms—maps, journals, all of them—and brought it outside. He found a rusted metal bin once used for compost and shoved them in.

From one of his belt satchels, he pulled out the box of matches. He lit one and dropped it in. It caught quicker than kindle. He went inside and brought out more to add to the fiery heap.

His younger self would've been enraged by such an act. The young Silver Fox thought Amaveriel nothing but a forgotten ruin overtaken by the snarls of the Anglorian Jungle, no different than M'thealquilôk, a historical discovery waiting to be revealed and a quiet haven for the refugees far from the Djinnasi reach.

But he was the Silver Fox of the present, old and weathered by experience. Aramis knew how delicate its secrets were to even allow these to exist. Not a scrap. Not a crumple. No matter if no one had been here for years. There was too much at stake. Too many lives to lose. Lives he promised to come back to. Aramis took one last pile and shoved it down into the barrel. Down, down, down until the smoke smothered his face.

The Silver Fox was burdened with secrets.

Secrets meant to be burned and buried.

The mechanical heart landed on the bench with a solid bang. Black oil seeped from its still fluttering valves. Aramis had spent hours stripping all the incriminating evidence of Amaveriel's location. Too long of a wait for the Bedouins demise. From the wall, he dragged over a rectangular box and shoved a wire, tipped with gold, into one of its pores. The gears hummed, and it made happy chirps. On the wall before him, a dark glass streaks with green lettering. The Ancients' tongue, asking for his password.

"479241," he said.

Yes, he used that hateful number on his arm as his password. But during his nomadic years, there were a few alive to know it by heart as well as he. That is, until a couple of months ago.

[479241] was transcribed by an invisible hand.

[ACCEPTED] came the archaic word and the screen was filled with green scrawl of code.

Meanwhile, he took a rag and wiped away the box's holes. Not any hole—a port. That is what they would've called it back in the Ancients' technological height. Where a piece of circuitry juts out of its protective metal bay, ready to receive any ship—or in this case a cable—come to board. Aramis made a happy grunt when he found one, a smooth flat oval—the universal port, circa two millennia of their year of their lord. Aramis flung open a drawer, plucked a black wire cord of boxy ends and jammed one end into its space.

The glass box before him flickered to a picturesque scene of an oasis teeming with life with birds flying into a cheerful blue sky. Paradise, or at least what he asked this contraption to create for him. His view of paradise now had two people living in it.

"Let's see where you call home," Aramis told the mechanical heart. He popped the other end of the cable into the giant box. The machine whirred.

[CONNECTING...] flashed on the screen.

[CONNECTED]

Then it went dark.
Shit.
Aramis heard these things could carry mechanical diseases, but he was hoping this was from a pure source. He almost pulled the plug when something caught his eye. It

lingered in the corner of the onyx-black screen. A shadow with an unhallow eye.

Aramis thought it was a trick of the light; it was glass after all. But when he moved away from the box and stood upright, the eye was still there. Trailing him with hateful ticks.

He had seen this before, in the heart of M'thealquilôk.

"No," he murmured to himself. "It can't be..."

Aramis leaned in, for the eye was dim—a mere mirage of shadow.

It lurched, a creature of hunger, slamming its full body against the screen at him. A ghastly scream filled the air.

Aramis fell flat on his back.

The metallic screech that ground out from the black box assaulted his ears. A technological horror of sound as it hijacked his vulnerable mind. Ghastly green images flashed across the glass. Disturbing depictions of ghouls devouring flesh beat in rapid succession until they come to a blur.

Flashes of memories come to him unheeded, borne from this psychological catalyst. The ghouls had risen in the heart of the abbey's nave. Jessenter rebel soldiers, people he once drank and laughed with, seized their yawning maws on the necks of the helpless. Flesh shorn from glistening bone as the screams echoed off of the vaulted ceiling and into his ear. A feeding frenzy only matched by ravenous hyenas.

He tried to cut them down with his twin knives twirling before him, as he had done so in the past. But they surround him, numerous by the counting. They slash away his mental defenses and strip him of his arms. They pull him under, as an undertow would, and he plummets into the void. Down, down, down, in this ocean of blood—losing to the jackals of his mind. Even here Aramis was not safe, for groping hands reach out to him, pulling him further under.

Throw them away, he told himself many times since his youth. *Throw them into a box and toss the key. They can't hurt you here. Nothing can hurt you here.*

Breathe, Aramis, Breathe.

Those last thoughts, for some reason, came to him as Rhyllae's voice.

Yes, Rhyllae! His north star. His shepherd of the desert that guides his heart through the dark night of his soul. Aramis seized upon in, letting her voice within him grow. Grow as the dawn would, blooming over the horizon. The very dawn she greeted by song on her lips. Her arms outstretched before her.

Those lost can be found. His heart told him, back when he was at his lowest, gazing into the waning moon. *A light even when you can't see it when all you see is shadow.* Elyamamen.

Aramis hoisted the golden memory up high in his mental fist. Punching through the throng, shattering their hold. All the terrors washed away as he rises to the surface. Break through into the golden warmth of skylight.

He gasped in the dry air.

Aramis found himself back in the Fox Burrow. The machine still gave that ghostly wail, and the images continued to flip through in a dizzying blur. But now, these things didn't unleash those deep-seated fears that wrestled his heart. Clear of mind and vision, Aramis righted himself. There before him on a dark screen was a smile.

From all of the ghastly images that were flashed on the screen was a girl—looming there in a makeshift pinafore. Her head cocked to one side as messy bangs shielded her dark, hollow eyes. Smiling at him. Mocking him.

He knew that if you flipped pictures fast enough, the magic of movement occurs. An old trick used by the Ancients by unraveling solenoid scrolls before a heated wire. They love to recount fables for their children's bedtime tales.

Here was by far more sinister. It felt as if the person stood right there before him.

Aramis slammed his hands hard on the desk. He was made a downright fool, and he played the part all too well.

"Where are they?!" he shouted.

The girl tilted her head to the other side.

"Where?!"

Her grin widened. The machine next to him halted and started in rhythmic spurts.

It's laughing, he realized. *The motherfucker laughed at me!*

Aramis pulled out his blade from his right hilt. Its diamond fang glittered as he poised it high over the oozing mechanical heart. There were other ways to make it talk and, if need be, other ways to find Dawn's tribe.

He raised it high, ready to strike, when numbers flash before him.

[4...7...9...2...4...1]

My dead name, how?
More symbols flashed on the glass:

[?]

[479241]

[?]

Aramis glanced around and found his sleeve rolled halfway up on his right forearm. His tattoo was partially revealed. With his left hand, he rolled his sleeve back, unveiling the past evil brand and his popping sinews. He wouldn't let go of the dagger—it was all he had against this creature.

"My name is Aramis Feres." His voice came out with a growl in his throat. "My true name. The name I chose for myself! If you want me that bad, you better start calling me by my fucking name!"

Aramis didn't know if this machine could hear him, but he didn't fucking care. He would live and die by his terms and his terms alone.

The screen went dark. The box next to him whirred to a quiet hum. For that moment, he thought the machine stopped working. He lowered his dagger and rest it on the table.

Then it began.

Chirps and beeps emanated from the oozing sac on the table. The screen flickered on. Green lines splayed across the screen until they conjoined into a grid. It expanded, showcasing three dots of different sizes. Letters ran from right to left, the Ancients' style of writing, from these dots. One was SILO 51, the largest of them all far in the west, and the smallest dot beheld his name. How odd to see it translated in their language. Then, far south and west of him was the middle dot called Doomtown V.

"Is that where they are?" Aramis asked out loud, hoping against hope.

In response, the mechanical heart began to beep in some sort of code. The two dots in the west dispersed into numerous tiny blobs. Aramis sharply inhaled; these weren't any ordinary dots on a map; these were individual mannequins. They dispersed and swarmed from these positions as ants in source of food, heading to the Fox Burrow. Right for the beating, tattle-telling heart.

Aramis rained his dagger down on it. Oil and liquid coolant splashed about him, staining his hands and his sleeves in a black ink. He didn't stop until the lights flickered off and the beeping stopped.

The dark screen winked away to the paradise image he once had. The comforting sounds of the metal box's quiet hum and the panting of his breath filled his ears.

"Computer ... shutdown," he asked of the ancient tech with rasping breath.

Aramis left the knife lodged in that sac-like heart and leaned on the table, watching the oil drip down to the sand-dusted floor. They knew where he was now. He would have to burn this whole place down. There was a wealth of information that would be used against him and his friends.

Yet, Aramis smirked as a grim thought crossed his mind.
They know my name.

Chapter 11

HE WHO WEARS THE MASK

THE HINGES SQUEAKED WHEN ARAMIS OPENED the old armoire. It was kind of funny, he used to cringe whenever he heard the sound, but now it gave him comfort. As much as seeing the cloth-stuffed mannequin before him.

The black bust wore the darks vestments of Marquist Révé, hero, teacher, friend, and dying. That alone was what drew Marquist to put on the mask of the Silver Fox. He wanted to make a difference before the Red Spot took him, a deadly disease that degraded the lungs beyond divine repair. And Marquist did. He left a legacy of peace between the tribes. Aramis's legacy, however, was scripted in blood.

Marquist was called the Shadow Fox because of his adept ability to blend in the shadows, better than what Aramis could ever do. All thanks to his mystical cloak. He reached out and ran his fingers down the hem of the fabled cloth. Thicker than his own and shimmering with the magic of the night. A lump in his throat swelled as Aramis reminded himself what he came here for: everything here in the Fox Burrow must burn. Those machines knew this place now. What secrets that remained here would be used against his friends—against the people of Ioun. No. He must destroy it all.

And yet...

Aramis's eyes looked up at the mask, his vision turning glassy. The mask was the true Silver Fox mask, not the imitation he wore on his face, tailored for his glowing sight. It was made of leather, not cloth, with eyes holes shaped like almonds. A broad band covered the entire half of the face sewn into a scarf that was knotted in the back. Unassuming in its matte finish but weighted with history of those who'd worn it. Pirates. Nobles. Women. Elves. Those who took on the call to be the Silver Fox. People worthier than Aramis.

"I'm not the Silver Fox you want me to be. I can't be anything like you," Aramis whispered. He closed his eyes, feeling the lone teardrop roll down his cheek.

"You were never supposed to be."

In an instant, Aramis drew his bright daggers in a flash, ready to let them fly. But he froze because he couldn't believe his eyes. There before him stood Marquist, his dark skin glowing with a healthy shine. His short, coiled hair freshly twisted close to his scalp. He never saw him this young before, but he could recognize that mustached smile anywhere.

"And I'm not supposed to see ghosts," Aramis snarked back, yet he sheathed his blades.

"Which one?" His smile grew wider as Aramis stammered. "Ah, but who's counting?" Marquist sat himself down on the old cot of a bed—his deathbed Aramis recalled. Here, he could see the folds of the cloth discarded in a pile through his once former teacher's visage.

He laughed as he took Aramis in with his bright eyes. "You look well, for your age. A bit crusty for a baked oaf, though."

O, Sleeper, not his bread analogies.

Aramis snorted and put his hands on his hips. "What do you want?"

"Want what?"

"Why are you here?"

"I've always been here, Aramis. You were finally able to see me."

That statement made his heart skip a beat and stilled his lips.

"Don't be shocked," said Marquist. "You were dead, remember? It takes one to know one."

"I was brought back."

"You *came* back. There's a difference." Marquist pressed his palms together and leaned his forearms on his legs. The pose he often held when he was about to grant another lesson.

"I came back for love," Aramis stammered out the words before he ended it in a laugh. "This is pointless. They'll be here any minute, I have no time for this."

"Love is the strongest force of nature. Stronger than any hurricane, stronger than that fire you're about to light."

Marquist formed a point from his two index fingers while clasping the rest of his fingers. It lined up with the oil canister at Aramis's feet. There was a twinge of guilt in Aramis's heart.

His old mentor asked, "So tell me: who is the Silver Fox supposed to be? Hm? Who is it, me?" To emphasize the point, Marquist bounced his shoulders. "Zerina? Who cleverly diverted the Mehran Express to feed the hungry villagers of Donsk. Or Antonio Ruel Villedera? He who mingled with the very snakes who strangle the impoverish and undermine their mechanisms by charm alone. Who is the Silver Fox supposed to be?"

Aramis rubbed his temple with his finger and thumb. "You want me to recite the creed? All of it?"

"Or you could answer the question." Marquist leaned to rest his translucent back against the wall, the dusty blankets on the bed visible through his spectral form.

Aramis sighed and gazed back at the costume before him. He could never bear the thought of wearing it. It didn't belong to him. It never did, as far as he was concerned. Even if he recited the creed when Marquist lay dying.

"Who is *that* for?" his voice close to Aramis's ear. He didn't realized Marquist had gotten up—silent as the ghost he was now.

"It was yours," Aramis answered once he found the courage.

"I have no need for it. I'm dead."

Aramis turned around and found Marquist gave him a raised brow with a keen side-eye.

The Silver Fox scoffed. "It's to preserve your memory."

"In a box? Locked away in shadow and be forgotten?"

"What, no," Aramis said, though a trembling snaked its way though. "To treasure you."

Marquist raised his voice. "Treasure me? Like some damn holy relic?" Worse, he stood up and pointed at the oil canister. "And then burn me like some sacrificial lamb?"

"No!" Aramis waved his hands out before him. He accidentally dipped his fingers into Marquist's spectral form. It was bone-chilling. He yanked it back to point at himself. "I'm a historian! Please, I didn't want to forget you."

His mentor rubbed his hand over his face; the sight twisted Aramis's stomach. "And hide me from the world? Hide me from my friends? Aramis." Marquist then said with softness, "O, my boy, Aramis. What is the point of preserving history if no one will know about it?"

Hot shame seized Aramis eyes shut. He turned away. Never did he ever want to desecrate his old friend. The one he considered as a father. Marquist taught him not only survival, but how to live as a man, even before he submerged into the Zemzem spring waters. His silver eyes finally opened to take in this room of memories. A small library of books. Gadgets behind glass boxes. Medals and emblems tucked away in shadow boxes. Maps framed and hung on the metal sheet wall. He remembered spending hours well into the night, oiling every ceramic bowl and blotting every paper. Inch by inch, this room was made in honor of all who wore the mask, Marquist included.

And those mannequins would come. Not to tear it down, but to use it. Somehow, they would use it to cause more devastation, he knew. If they could make themselves, they could replicate everything here.

Aramis rubbed off his tears with the heel of his palm. "Marquist, listen please. There's a horde of machines that will come here. They'll take it all. Improve on it. Mass produce it. Make it beyond lethal! Everything from your cloak to that climbing rappel will be used against everyone. It has to go." The last words came out of his throat broken.

"Machines?"

"Mannequins."

"So, the past finally revealed itself," was the cryptic comment Marquist gave.

His old mentor put his hands on his ghostly hips—*Sleeper, he looks good*, the thought flirted Aramis's mind for he only knew him late in his life—and looked down at the toe of his boot.

"True. The past can cause wounds, let alone reopen old ones." Marquist looked up as he kept his chin tucked. "But wounds heal, Aramis."

"As scars upon this land that will last for years to come!" Aramis threw his arms wide.

"Yes, it will leave scars. Scars we bear for the rest of our lives." Marquist walked back to him, speaking every step of the way, "But those scars are there to remind us of that dark chapter. Not to shame us by bearing this mar, but as a promise: Should these cruelties come to light again, it shall be struck down once again as before."

Marquist then clapped his spectral hand on Aramis's shoulder. The sensation was like nothing Aramis had ever experienced. "Scars are history. Should they ever be forgotten, the lessons learned will be lost. When that day comes, my friend, then we are doomed to repeat it."

The Silver Fox looked at him dead in the eyes. Spector to mortal. Man born to man made. Aramis massaged his right foreman. All this time he wanted to bury it for he saw it as a name that was forced upon him since birth. He forgot that he was not the only one burdened with this type of mark. The same scars from Djinnasi hands were pressed upon thousands.

Marquist began to fade. His voice a gentle whisper when he asked, "Who is the Silver Fox? Only you can answer that."

Then he was gone.

Aramis closed his eyes to still his grieving heart. When he opened them once more, it was to face the old costume in the cabinet. Those who answered the call of being the Silver Fox did so not because they were saints. Sleeper knows, Aramis wasn't one of them. But each of them answered because they heard the people's plight and, by their wits and cunning, strived to end it. Some of the Silver Foxes perished for it, including Zirena. She didn't see how many lives she saved by that train she hijacked from the slavers. By the time she reached her destination to a safe village, Zirena bled out from her 157 wounds in the conductor's chair. Surprise, surprise, it was Antonio who hopped on it and threw the emergency brakes to prevent another crisis. He was a kid when he took on the mask. Who was Aramis to deny the call? He would've done the same at his age.

Aramis stripped. His back bearing the scars of the slaver's whip during his formative years. Marquist was right: Aramis has been hiding.

Hiding from his fellow Iounese.

Hiding from his friends.

Hiding from himself.

The freemen in Amaveriel were proud to display their scars, while he hid his. When he asked them why, often they told him they didn't want to forget. Aramis never understood it until now. If everyone put the tyranny of the Djinnasi out of their minds, there would be no one joining the Jessenters to fight the good fight, no one to push back against the slavers, no one trying to free those still ensnared. This number imprinted in his arm was a reminder of the pain and sorrow he went through and a promise to end any who wish to give it to others.

Starting with the mannequins.

Aramis donned black pants and the black boots that quiet his steps. He donned the blouse that wicked his heat, hiding him from infrared sight, and donned the cloak of the night: shadows would become him. Last, but not least, he donned the mask of the Silver Fox. Amazingly, it dimmed his light far better than what elvish cloth ever could. Months from now, Aramis would find Marquist's journal and learn he had prepared this suit for him to wear whenever he was ready. That future Silver Fox would mourn for hesitating this precious gift. For the present time, Aramis girded his waist with the ruby Jessenter sash to remind him of his mentor's sacrifice.

Then Aramis took the butt end of his knife and smashed the glass shadow boxes. At first, he hesitated to strike them, for he remembered how long it took to melt and set the sand. But as Aramis went to the next and the next, the fist came down faster in tempo. All he could use in this fight, he stuffed it in the belt pouches along his back. The rest of those boxes—medallions, photos, journals—all dumped into the loot bag. With a sweep of his arm, Aramis knocked the books off the shelves into the bag for good measure. All of it tumbling into a cold vault hidden away in Fae-knows-where rebel's vault. He'd fix the bindings later. Funny. Dido intended this sack for any treasure they would find along the way. She would never expect this.

The whole night through, Aramis plundered away the secrets of the Fox Burrow until there was naught but wire and thread hanging limp from the walls. The Valentrian trickster would be so proud. With the lamp oil, Aramis doused the floors of each level and spiraled outside. At last, he struck a match from his handy gloves (that he would never give up). The flame roared within the burrow and began its gluttonous feast. Metal screeched as the walls caved in and the floors banged on the way down.

The camel rose from the disturbance, but Aramis was right there to reassure it. *They're not going to stay for too long.* He gave one last look over his shoulder and found Marquist's shadow highlighted by the firelight.

Thank you for your last lesson.

Then they melted into the twilight of the Iounese starlight.

The stars glimmered in their celestial wonder as Lune continued to wax her form. The whole skyline wore shades of grape, indigo, and navy streaming from the heavenly river. The earth tilted so the stars dance in their slow ascension before their eventual fade.

So this is what Aramis sees, Sister Rhyllae wondered.

For once in her long life, the Morning priestess found she couldn't sleep like the others. Korzha took the longest to nod off, driven to log his thoughts away in his journal with his cryptic script. The priestess never saw him this troubled before. Worse, he refused to disclose it when pressed. But at last, he dozed like the rest, leaving her to her thoughts and the stars above.

Rhyllae admitted, her staying up might be out of sentiment, for she did miss Aramis as the camp sentinel. Aramis, ever the insomniac, always filled in that role. Knowing he was watching over them gave her a sense of comfort. The night felt empty without one, and she needed some semblance of stability in her life.

Was that what she really wanted: to stay still and be stagnate against the changing tides? Under the celestial heaven twinkling above her, Rhyllae was not sure that she should be. Lune waxed and waned with her phases and moods. Even the Sun shifted in the sky depending on the season. Shouldn't she, a priestess of theirs, be as changeable along with her constant cycles?

Then she heard the rustle of blankets and shoes treading through the sand with care. Rhyllae smiled to herself. Of course the kid would try to sneak up on her.

"Couldn't sleep?" she asked him.

The tracks stopped still. Then she heard the slipshod of feet kicking through the sand before she saw the kid poke their head into her view. "How did you know?"

Rhyllae smiled at him. "I have ears of a jackrabbit and eyes of a hawk."

"You're an elf?"

"Half, by my father's side."

"Wow," he said in quiet awe.

They stood there in silence, both gazing at the stars.

"Do you think the Silver Fox will find them?" the kid broke the silence.

"Sure, as the sun rises."

He looked down at his feet and mumbled to himself, "A part of me hopes he doesn't."

Rhyllae winced. Not all tribes are as accepting as she would like them to be. From what Aramis had told her from his nomadic years, there would be disputes if the person came across too eccentric to their tastes. It could take months before he could find a tribe willing to accept that person into their fold. Perhaps, that was why he searched long and hard for Amaveriel in the end. A chance for everyone to have a clean slate no matter who they were.

"You don't have to stay with them when this is all over," Rhyllae offered.

"I don't?" he said. The hope in his voice broke her heart.

The sister nodded. "You're allowed to find your own family, as you are allowed to be who you're truly meant to be. Your own name, even your own home. So long it's a place where you are treated with love, from you and from others."

Rhyllae stopped when she heard him sniffling. His shoulders bobbed up and down as his cheeks were moistened by his tears. She knelt down and put her hands on his arms. He tried to rub them away, but the tears kept coming.

"What if," his voice broke through the sobs. "What if there's no place for me?"

"You can come with us." Rhyllae knew better than to make such promises, even without Aramis present, but her heart couldn't take it anymore. Not when his glassy eyes stared into her soul. "If no one wants you. If no one in the whole of Ioun or Amaveriel wants you, I promise you'll find a home with me."

"Really?" his lips quivered.

"Really." She fixed his bangs from his forehead so his strand flick into his eyes.

"Even if I wasn't born as a boy first?"

"You're still a boy to me."

He wrapped his arms around her neck and squeezed tight. Rhyllae rocked him as she held him, not caring if the tears soaked into her clothes. The skies turned a rosy hue as the dew fell across the land.

Please, she prayed with her eyes closed. *Let me keep my promises, my Lord of Mornings. Let me keep my promises to him and Delphi. Somehow. In some way. They needed someone to care for them. To love them! If I could, I would!* Tears formed in her eyes. *I would with all my heart!*

When Rhyllae opened them, she saw a figure out in the morning haze, dressed in black garb and on Aramis's camel. Sister Rhyllae stood up and silently moved the kid behind her. Though her eyesight was far superior than her peers, the desert haze can deceive. On her first outing, Rhyllae thought she saw a unicorn until she learned it was a bunch of kids chasing a hoop with a play stick. As a full moon elf, Bagheera never let it down. The thought of her steeled her gaze; there would be no Bagheera to depend upon.

"What is it?" he asked.

"Go wake up the others."

The kid scrambled to his feet and ran off. Rhyllae dared to take a step forward trying to see if the visage cleared. It didn't. Soon enough, Dawn and Korzha showed up. At least they had the sense to crouch out of the stranger's view.

"Is it Feres?" Korzha asked.

"It's his camel," Rhyllae answered. "Dawn?"

Without a word, she handed over her longbow and one arrow. By religious doctrine, Rhyllae was not allowed to shoot down any living creature unless it was for hunting's sake. Even then, the sister wouldn't be allowed to hunt if there were others in her presence who could. But the Morning Lord was fuzzy on warning shots. Rhyllae let it loose. It arched high in the sky before it sank midway to the stranger.

Dawn brought her shield to bear, and Korzha rested his left hand on the hilt of his Silver Star. Thankfully, there was no need for their skill. The darkly garbed person stirred in their saddle and sat up.

O, Lord, they were asleep.

Then they flashed a bright light in a dazzling sequence. Rhyllae knew it before they finished. MUMPS. A password they had settled on, an old inside joke from their early adventuring days.

"It's Aramis." Rhyllae then sighed in relief.

"He changed his clothes?" Dawn asked, squinting at the camel and their rider.

"Seems like it."

Dawn reported back to Dido and the kid to give them all clear. She could hear them break camp as Korzha and her waited for Aramis to arrive.

"He appears to keep his word," Korzha commented.

"Can your bard do the same?" Rhyllae retorted.

He gave her an icy glance. "Your Mother Superior requires a guardian, not a nursemaid. So long she reaches the elders of your order, she'll have—" then he paused, searching for the right word. "recuperation." He finally said, though Rhyllae suspected that was not the intended phrase.

Rhyllae shot him a sour look. "You have no idea."

Korzha took a deep inhale and closed his eyes. "The decision to bring you here did not come lightly. Töska is indeed far more dangerous than any malady that she might come across or..." Then he stopped himself short.

Does he know about Myrrh's curse? Sister Rhyllae wondered.

Then Korzha opened his eyes and spoke quickly. "I trust in Tsuki to follow through with her commitments. Your talents would've been redundant." With that he briskly closed the distance between them and Aramis, leaving Rhyllae standing there.

The sister twisted her hands on the bow's polished wood as she stared.

He knows. How?

Aramis leaned over and plucked the arrow from the sand. He twirled it in his fingers as he spoke with the general, who took the typical pose of clasping both hands behind his back. Though his softened over these past days, it was not as relaxed as it would with Myrrh.

Rhyllae shook her head. *Of course he would know. Why wouldn't he?*

She approached the two. Aramis smiled and stepped out of the saddle. His garb had completely changed from the desert outfit. Her eyes lingered at his cinched waist and how the blouse billowed freely from the red Jessenter sash. There was a notch V in the tunic with strings threaded through for tying, but he laid them unraveled, showcasing the beads of sweat on his leather brown chest. Without a word, Aramis embraced her. She could smell his scent as he nuzzled his head in the nook between her head and shoulder.

"I found them, *me'qora*. I found them," he whispered to her. *Lovers don't keep secrets from each other.*

Act 3

The snow falls in the box
Hissing its white noise
A spiky-hair man sat down
He waved his space wand

"I'm sure you have a lot of questions. So do I
"But that's not important now. They arrive
"Whoever you are, they are here and heading straight for you
"I need you to run, and don't blink—that is crucial

"Whatever you do don't—"
The image collapse
It hisses in its white noise
"Delete transmission"

Chapter 12

DOOMTOWN

"THIS IS DOOMTOWN?" DAWN ASKED.

They crested over the dune, overlooking the town below. Dotted before them were buildings topped with strange roofs in squat triangular peaks. All of them spaced evenly from each other with strips of wooden fencing. They all seemed to encircle a street made of dried black tar, at least that was what Dawn hoped it was, wide enough for three carts to pass by each other. Stranger still, was the long slender poles that held an array of horns aloft that dotted the area.

"The fifth," Aramis answered.

"Lune's tits."

Dawn still could not stop herself from jumping whenever she saw him. The sun was setting, and the clouds were lit with fiery red splashes of its dying splendor. Plenty of light for her to see with, yet Aramis seemed to melt into the shadows of the coming night. Aramis gave a smirk and held his hands up as a form of an apology.

Like hell you are. Dawn cleared her throat and gazed back to this town. "You're sure they're down there?"

"Somewhere down there," said Aramis.

"In a prison."

"Or a school."

"School?"

"Back then, they had a building dedicated to scholars dispensing knowledge to the youth of every age."

"The tradition continues in Töska," Korzha chimed in. "Though we call it *tuterlage*. One tutor can teach a small village of children on a wide variety of subjects. Math, fencing, alchemy, and the like."

Aramis nodded in agreement. "The Ancients did it on a massive scale. At the peak of their power, each individual scholar specialized in one subject matter and taught that to children of one age group."

"That sounds stupid," Dawn said. "What happens when the kids grow up?"

"They'll have another."

"Weird."

"Efficient. The Ancients thought like the machines they built. Every person was a working cog in a grand scheme. By their combined efforts, they effectively taught that one child all the knowledge they could dispense throughout their lifetime. All of their art, medicine, and history into one person."

"Wow, all of that knowledge. To what end?"

"To conquer," Korzha said with a grim frown. "They were the deadliest society of humans in the known age. Even unto themselves. To wit, we must secure yours before any more harm comes to your people."

"They *were* my people," Dawn countered. "Look, I don't mind saving them, it's the right thing to do, but they kicked me out a long time ago. Amaveriel is my home now."

Korzha nodded in sympathetic knowing. "Very well, Lieutenant. We shall not make this anymore of a homecoming for you."

"Shush," Dido hissed.

A few paces behind them were Dido, Sister Rhyllae, and the kid holding hands in some sort of location, ritual, doohickey that Dawn couldn't untangle in her impatient mind. But Dido promised it would work, and that was good enough for Dawn.

"Wait," said the kid, his face was scrunched up in utter concentration. "I think I see them."

"Yes," agreed Rhyllae, her eyebrows rose up while keeping her eyes closed. "I do too!"

"Good," Dido said. "Keep it steady."

No one stirred, fearing to break the satyr mage's concentration. Beads of sweat formed on Dido's brow as the sky darkened.

"Right... there!" Dido exclaimed.

In the center of this village lit a building. A large one with a flat roof, like the houses in Amaveriel, with enough space to fit the entire congregation of the Rising Sun Abbey three times over. Dots of light also flickered around it. Faerie lights, magical luminous orbs akin to will-o-wisps, clustered in bunches next to rather tall poles. At the end of these poles was a crown of metal horns, each facing a cardinal direction. For what purpose Dawn couldn't fathom. The faerie lights lit a trail from the building toward them, a magical pathway.

"Whew, that was a tough one," Dido exclaimed, and she let go.

"Thanks, but you didn't have to roll out the carpet," Aramis said.

"Well, not everyone can see like you and I." The mage dusted herself and adjusted her glasses for good measure.

"True enough, let's us be on our way then," Korzha said.

The general slid down the rocky slope by stretching out his left side, controlling his speed as he slid. Aramis and Rhyllae sat down with the kid between the two of them. Hand in hand, they helped him down the treacherous terrain. It reminded Dawn of her parents when they took her sand sledding at night. Part of her wished her parents would've loved her now as much as they did back then. If they're even alive.

Dawn felt a gentle touch on her forearm.

"Shall we?" asked Dido. Her smile was warm and understanding, a sun that blazed away the morning fog.

That's right, there's nothing to worry about. No matter what, I have friends who understand me as me. If my folks are alive—they live their way while I live mine. That's all that matters in the end. I live by my rules.

"Yeah, let's do this," said Dawn.

She took the shield off her back and let Dido sit on the curve of its back. With her back foot, Dawn pinned the shield against the edge. Then she kicked her right foot against the ground, letting the weight carry them down. With both feet balancing the concave disk, she swerved around any rocks along the way. They zipped past the trio.

"Cool!" exclaimed the kid while the sister giggled.

Dawn caught Aramis muttering, "Show off."

Dawn smiled to herself.

They came to the bottom of the rocky dune where the general was. Dido hopped away while Dawn kicked the shield's edge. It flipped up, and she slipped her right arm through the straps. Korzha looked at her with raised eyebrows.

"Sir?" she asked.

He blinked away whatever thought crossed his mind. "Front right, Lieutenant."

"Sir."

"Dido, you follow behind her."

"Right," Dido confirmed.

Soon enough, they were joined by the rest of the party, and he gave similar instructions. But Aramis refused.

"I'll scout ahead. Don't start the party without me." With a flourish of his cape, Aramis melted into dark boundaries surrounding them. Not even the silver dots of his eyes could be found.

Korzha scowled.

Rhyllae put her hand on his shoulder with a knowing smile. "I'll guard the rear and keep the child beside me."

"Very well." Korzha joined Dawn at the front. "Let's follow the faerie lights, Lieutenant."

With that, they continued to walk down the strange black street. It wasn't bricked or cobbled as she thought it would be, though some of the sand managed to shore up on the curbside. There were several green rugs surrounding each house, which were bricked with faded paint. Then, at the distance was a strange statue by the street.

A woman, at least Dawn assumed it was, with a shredded black burka that covered her from head to toe with a mesh opening for her eyes. She clutched a blue bassinet handle before her. The cloth was tattered by the prevailing winds, leaving behind a shell of hoops and wheels. Dawn tipped the covering back by the tip of her gladiolus blade. She found nothing inside but a dark stain on the seat of the bassinet.

"Dawn?" Korzha called.

"Clear," Dawn answered. Yet she couldn't shake the unnerving feeling that they were being watched.

Aramis made a wide arc from the group, peeking into every window and around every corner of these homes. Whoever built them did a great job in making them appear bricked. With a tap of his knuckle, he heard the telltale sound of that metallic warble behind the archaic plaster. All the household items that survived were of the sturdiest woodwork or metal. All of the walls and cabinets were dressed down in colors of pea green soup and olive tree bark.

A stage for the play. But for who or what?

This house couldn't give an answer, but the next contained more clues. In the main room stood two short statues, dressed in a single layer of cloth that was cut at the waist, biceps, and thighs. Their plaster arms raised toward a banner hanging on the wall. Aramis climbed through the window and lifted his mask, allowing his light to shine.

In the silver pall it read in the Ancients' tongue: "SECOND BOY! ONE SOUL!"

In his vast mental catalogue, Aramis grimly recalled one of the Ancients' philosophies on souls. According to them, a woman didn't have a soul when she was born. She must obtain one by giving birth to two sons. A dark time when they turned women into secondary citizens and birthing machines. Whittling her away until there's nothing left but a doll to play with. Oblivious to the ever-changing world beyond her house. While he would have never worshiped Lune, he thanked the goddess for overturning the gross misconception of a woman's worth. And to her solar brother who made such notions into law. Well, at least until the Demon Djinn Bazzuu was summoned into the world.

Aramis shielded his head under the mask once more, darkening the room to the past where it belonged. He slipped back to where he came, but not without the watchful eye of the third statue in the kitchen. Dressed in a kaftan, in silent observance, she held the plaster cake in her perfect 90-degree angled arms.

Aramis paused. *Did it move?*

Yet, all was still in this idyllic mockup. Aramis slipped away, not noticing the red light that flickered in the statue's right eye.

At last, the company reached the double wide doors of the lit building. It was rather bland, if Dawn was honest. No paint on the brick. No curves or anything to break the straight, flat edifice. Not even the square windows had shutters to accent their plain red-brick frames.

Dawn ushered the rest back and held the shield before her. The Djinnassi loved playing tricks and always encouraged their slaves to use whatever means to deter the rebels from acquiring their goods. Poison darts on springs, flashbangs, pressure plate alarms, Dawn dealt with them all. She reached for the handle before her.

A whistle that sounded akin to a finch call gave her a jump. It was Aramis. He waggled a finger at her and approached from the shadows.

"You scared the crap out of me," Dawn quietly scolded.

Aramis gave a smirk. "Blame the cape." He produced a flat hook and gestured to search for her.

"Be my guest," Dawn said as she backed up.

With the hook, he slid it between all crevices of the double doors. Satisfied, he switched over to his trusty lock picks. One stayed in place while the other he twisted and wiggled.

"You can never be too careful," Aramis whispered.

"What do you think I have a shield for?" She whispered back.

It clicked, and something heavy slid back behind the door. He opened the door ajar and waved at her. "Okay, Brawn, what do you see?"

Dawn poked her head in and stuck her tongue out as she scrunched her nose. Rusty metal scaffolding clung to the walls of this expansive foyer. Twin wing stairs curved up to a set of wooden doors were encased in all of this scaffolding and the small stretch of balcony that conjoined them were destroyed for a mechanized lift. The rust from the metal bolts stained the walls it screwed into, making it look like vomit.

"Someone didn't consult a gay on this décor choice," Dawn said.

Aramis popped his head over hers and grimaced from the sight. "It looks like a steampunk Jackson Pollack on speed."

"Who?"

Unable to contain his curiosity, the general himself peeked over Aramis's head. "The architecture reminds me of Gult."

"Gult?"

"A region in the middle of Töska."

"You've gotta be kidding me—Gult?" Aramis said as he opened the door wide for everyone else to come through.

Rhyllae wrinkled her nose from the sight while Dido gave a twitchy shiver. The child was the only one not aghast from the sight. Perhaps anything new would be a welcome sight, no matter how jarring the visage.

"Their cities are always under restoration," Korzha replied. "All thanks to the Emperor's infrastructure funds. I never knew anyone alive who had witnessed what the city looked like without the scaffolding."

"Do you think they came from there?" Dawn asked.

"Doubtful, the creatures are far more superior than whatever *uhrmacher* can create." When they all gave him a curious look, he corrected himself, "Time crafter."

"Clockmaker," Dido whispered behind him.

"Clockmaker." Then the general cleared his throat. "Shall we?"

Must be rough to live in a foreign country. Dawn thought to herself. In many ways, she was fortunate her familial exile didn't result in leaving the desert country entirely. The lieutenant wouldn't know if she would have the patience to learn a whole new language.

"Here, Dawn, take this." Aramis handed her a vial with an unusual ochre color. "A drop in the keyhole will be enough to eat through the tumblers."

"Wait, you're not coming?"

He shook his head. "But Rhyllae will."

Rhyllae said, "If they're imprisoning them, they're torturing them. I must be there for them."

"I'll locate the power generator and shut this place down," Aramis said. "Once you free them, take them to the roof.

"Right, I can use my magic to have everyone whisk away to safety," Dido piped up.

"Via teleportation?" the general asked with a raised brow.

The satyr shook her head and then pushed her glasses back in place. "No, the exchange of mass would accidentally burn them." Upon seeing everyone wince from the nonchalant explanation, Dido stammered. "I could use bubbles. There's a good wind brewing, which should carry them to the plateau nearby."

"Sounds like a plan," Aramis commented.

"Can I come with you?" said the kid.

Aramis pursed his lips, but his silver eyes darted to Rhyllae. She gave a slight nod and said something in Elvish.

Whatever it was said soothed the Silver Fox. The kid tilted his head in confusion.

Same, kid, same.

That seemed to ease Aramis's mind for he lifted his cloak and crouched over him. "Stay close. You never know who's afoot."

The kid nodded in earnest before they took off for the hall to the right.

"Dido and I will secure the perimeter by these eyes you've mentioned." Korzha announce. His right hand was on his hilt to steady his sword as he bounded from a scaffolding bar to the second level. Dawn always forgot how long his legs were.

"The tribe should be down that hall, bottom floor. Good luck," Dido said, before she took off after him. She used her goat legs to hop thrice to meet him on top.

"Shine on, Dido," Rhyllae answered.

Once they were gone, the two women closed the front doors. Dawn couldn't help asking as she grabbed one of the discarded boards. "Wouldn't it be better if you guard the kid?"

"He had seen enough blood for his age."

The lieutenant winced. "Here's hoping blood doesn't follow the Silver Fox, then." Then she wedged the board and barred the doors shut.

Chapter 13

FERRIS CAGE

"**S**VJETLO," DIDO WHISPERED INTO HER CUPPED hands.

A flicker of a flame emerged from the palm of her hand, floating an inch away. It bobbed obediently above her palm as she trailed behind the quick-striding general.

What is he up to?

Though danger could be lurking in these shadows, the satyr couldn't help but wonder what urged this man on this venture with them. Korzha was the highest-ranking officer of the entire force, though decimated by a wide margin, and yet here he was, for a mission with little-to-no survival rate. Dido took it as the reckless nature of humans, but Korzha usually defied such conventions.

Korzha glanced behind him and noticed her staring. "I supposed you don't believe we should be here."

Oh, far from it. But Dido kept that to herself.

Instead, she said, "I don't mind helping those captured by these nefarious creatures. In a way, it was a stroke of luck the boy found the Silver Fox."

"Yes, rather fortunate." Korzha came to a door in this long hallway and peered through the glass window framed in it.

"Yes, rather fortunate there were no causalities. Yet," she added.

The general peered down at her with a cocked eyebrow.

Her heart quickened up to her throat, but Dido must ask. Not as a fellow officer, but as a friend. "What are you doing here?"

Those blue eyes of his darted to the side, as if to ask the door for assistance. Korzha then scrunched them tight and shook his head. "Of all the times we spent together, you ask this now?"

"We're far from the others," Dido blurted out.

An exasperated groan came from him as Korzha stood back. His long fingers unhooked the scabbard straps of the Silver Star. He poised it so the spiral point of the hilt touched the glass. Yet, he hesitated and gave her a second glance.

Dido gave him the most incredulous stare she could muster at the man.

Korzha gave a frustrated scoffed and dropped the scabbard low across his hip. "I am oath bound to destroy the Djinnasi lords no matter the cost. It is my duty to see it through, even if it means going on this risky venture."

"Risky? Aramis said it's suicidal."

"You and I both know the Silver Fox will be prudent ever since the failure of the last. His words were merely cautionary. Otherwise, I wouldn't even allow you to be part of it."

Korzha swung the blade so the pummel hammered against the glass. Remarkably, it held up, even after the second time he struck it. As he readied for the third bout,

Dido reached above her curlicue horns and placed her palm on the scabbard. The act made him pause.

"You and I both know there's plenty of loopholes in this contract to not have you participate in this. What drove you to be here?"

She could see the wheels of his mind turning. A Töskan was raised not to be caught unaware by any possible schemes at play or any potential mechanism that would bind them. Yet, Dido didn't pose such threats save that of friendship, and she hoped that would win him over. Finally, the general shook his head and gave a bittersweet smile to Dido.

"Love" was all he could muster to say before the final blow was struck and the glass shattered.

The door handle clattered to the floor and rolled to Dawn's boots. The wooden portal swung out into a dark hall. Sister Rhyllae held her light out, causing the shadows to flee from them. It wasn't a flame but a burst of spindled rays congregating at the center of its globe—light of purest thought.

As they walked down the length of the hall, the Morning sister was persistent in her whispers concerning the kid. Though Dawn and he came from the same tribe, it had been years since Dawn had lived among them—enough for the kid to be tall enough to reach her elbows.

Dawn secured the shield back on her left arm. "I'm not sure I should answer that."

Rhyllae waved her hand back and forth in front of herself. "I don't want to deadname him or anything. Aramis taught me such things are better left in the past."

"But you want to know about his parents?"

"Yes. Maybe there was a way to reconcile between all three of them. I couldn't imagine the pain he must've endured for being in an unloving household."

Dawn slowed down to a halt, prompting the sister to turnabout. "What could you say to change their minds? No offense, but these people were dimwitted as cave salamanders and just as backward. I left them for a reason."

"That may be so. But if they follow the Morning Lord's light, perhaps there's a chance they would see the good in him taking on this journey, even if we don't understand the path that has been laid before him. All who bask under the Sun's light or illuminated by Lune's sight are worthy of love."

The lieutenant rubbed the back of her neck and sighed. "I wish you were there when I needed it the most."

The priestess of the Morn drooped her shoulders as her face puckered into pity. She walked the short distance and placed a comforting hand on Dawn's shoulders. In that silent knowing, Dawn felt she was understood in ways beyond words. The young officer gave her a smile and placed her palm on Rhyllae's shoulder. She rocked it before parting.

"Her name is Dora," Dawn said as they walked down the hall once more. "She's what you would call zealous to the Morning Lord. Prays more than I do, read the actual scriptures, the whole nine yards."

"Oh. Was she wanting to become a priestess?"

"Who knows, but she sure lords it over everyone."

Rhyllae shook her head in dismay as they traveled down the hall:

> "Rise and fall by the light of the Morn
> "Children of clay and stone
> "But know that you know not

"How the stars lie in the heavens
"Or how the moon wax and folds."

Dawn smiled. "Maybe you will give her a run for her money."

Rhyllae chuckled. "I'm more than happy to educate her the ways of Shutte'el. Come, I think I found the door."

It was what Rhyllae described from that magical envisioning. Two wooden doors with metal flashings on the bottom third and in the inner center where handles should've been. It looked like it used to swing on the vertical poles at the hinges, but was reworked where there was a metal clamp at the top, for what purpose, the lieutenant couldn't guess. Dawn gave them a soft nudge. It was barred from the other side. She rested her ear on the wood and rapt her knuckles upon it. It was denser than any homemade door in Amaveriel.

"Can you kick it down?" asked the Morning sister.

"Nope." Dawn turned around and gave her a winning grin. "But we can pop it out."

From her pack, the sister produced a firefighter's crowbar, where on one end had a spike perpendicular to the curved wedge end that was pronged. She also brought out a metal mallet and handed it to Dawn. By her guidance, the lieutenant pounded the back end of the spiked end of the crowbar where Rhyllae placed it over the metal nails. Once the metal pins dropped away, they switched instruments. Dawn leveraged the crowbar in the seams and pumped it toward her in rapid succession, her muscles a well-oiled machine. The wood cracked from the first. In the second, the gears strained. The third time something snapped, and the doors gave way.

The ladies pushed it aside and came to a vaulted room, bigger than any barracks Dawn had ever seen. Giant windows from the second-floor height streamed in Lune's gentle light. They illuminated cages made of metal lattice work that graced both sides of this expansive room. The walls beyond them were composed of wooden slots akin to giant dresser drawers. One lone steel ladder hung down in the back right corner. It rose to the door that was painted to match the walls, between the giant windows. Perhaps an escape route for the Ancients when they were still around.

More than that, there were people. Dozens upon dozens of them. Women, men, and children all in torn and mangled clothing. Some had bruises a mile wide, and the unlucky few had gashes that needed Rhyllae's medical talents. They all huddled in each chicken wire cage by some unknown categories set by these monsters.

One by one, they popped their heads up and shouted, "Who is that?" "We're saved!" and "Help us!" until it became a cacophony of a singular sound. A few of them jumped up and down.

Dawn took a hesitant glance at the Morning sister.

She gave the lieutenant a tilted bob of her scarf-covered head toward the room.

The young officer took a breath and bellowed into the room. "My name is Lieutenant Dawn of the Jessenters! We're here to rescue you!"

It was mixed response to be sure; some gasped while others cried out in thanks to the Morning Lord or Lune. But at least they knew it was their own who sprung them out of here. That should smooth things over during the whole operation.

As the lieutenant and the sister moved to the first cage, a hulking form made their way to the front. He was built like a brick house, despite his age. His head was deprived of his traditional turban, showcasing his tousled ruddy-brown hair shocked with grays. His robe was shredded around his arms, revealing the old amputation at the end of both his wrists. A familiar sight ever since Dawn was born from her old man, Hashim.

"Dawn, is that really you?" he asked in awe.

"Yeah, it's me. And this is Sister Rhyllae Ghalédale." The sister nodded with a kind smile when Dawn waved toward her.

"I never thought I would see the day you would return."

"Rescuing."

Rhyllae piped up, "One of your own found us on our travels."

"Dora's kid," Dawn finished the sister's words.

Hashim's ruddy-brown eyebrows peaked. "She made it out? We fear for the worst."

"He now." Her father looked so lost, but Dawn waved her hand aside. "It's neither here nor there. What matters is that we're getting all of you out of here."

Dawn shrugged off her pack and rifled for the acid vial from its depths.

Rhyllae peppered him with rapid-fire questions: "How many dead?" "How many were wounded?" "Can any of them walk?"

Her father responded just as quickly: "I don't know," "too many to count," and "yes."

"Well, this is your lucky day. Ready?" Dawn raised the corrosive vial before her as her other hand mindlessly reached for the wire.

"No!" everyone, Hashim included, cried out. "Don't touch it!"

"What, why?" Dawn asked, her hands hovering in the air.

"It's cursed," the woman behind them answered from the opposite cage.

She pushed her way to the front of the door. When she came forward, Dawn leaned back at her heels. It was her mother, Shayla. Her face had softened by age and was framed by twin braids that came to a single plait at the back. She used to be a honey blonde; now that memory was replaced by the silver strands of wisdom.

Shayla's mouth gaped open and then clamped shut, and she shook her head.

I guess reunions are for another day, Dawn thought.

"Gyle fell the moment he touched it." Her mother pointed behind her.

Rhyllae placed her fingertips to stifle her surprise. There, a lifeless man lay crumpled on the floor.

"Shit," Dawn murmured. "Rhyllae, what can we do to open this?"

The sister went into action and peered at the cage's wiring. After some searching, she pointed near the keyhole. "It's charged by the Ancients' magic. Look. See that dark cord that runs through here? No doubt the rest were boobytrapped in the same way."

"Can you disarm it?" Hashim asked her.

The sister shook her head.

"Sorry, folks, we have to wait on the Silver Fox's good time," Dawn said.

Sparks cascaded down in a golden arc. Aramis brought his cape to bear, shielding the kid from the embers. Once cleared, Aramis led the kid down the steel walkway. Both of them dared not make a sound as they crept forward.

They were in the basement of this archaic *tuterlage*, walking on these meshed metal walkways held up by painted, steel poles held aloft from the ceiling. The walkways crisscrossed in a systematic grid to ease access to giant broilers that loomed below them.

Seeing these added to his theory that this region had freezing temperatures before it became a desert. Then someone, or something, more recently converted this heating room into an electric jungle. A tangled network of cables as big as his wrist draped from the rafters. Some of them were splayed on the path like vines, snaking from the top to the void below. The ceiling made a mockery of the nighttime sky with jittery lights from black boxes. Though it was chillier than the desert, Aramis could feel his brow sweating from the intense humidity emitting from them. Worse, there was a pungent aroma of bile mixed with heated copper. The mannequins were up to something; what, he couldn't figure out.

"What was that?" the child whispered.

"A short in the circuit," Aramis whispered back.

"A circuit?"

"The Ancients were able to generate lightning in vials called batteries. They kept it confined in these metal strings, letting it run around in a—"

"—a circuit, like a track!"

Aramis smirked. "Right. When the lightning leaves that route, it shortens their journey, that's why it's called a short."

"But why does it look like fire instead of lightning?"

Aramis was about to answer, but a movement caught in the corner of his masked silver eyes. A cable fell from the rafters, its copper innards exposed and angry. Aramis grabbed the kid and leaped down from the catwalk. Taking out a tiny black box, from the Fox Burrow, he aimed it to a thick metal rod.

"*Dokl*," Aramis said the dwarven command.

The magical box shot out a hook with a high-tensile strength cord attached to it. It managed to loop on something before both of them hit the floor. Aramis carried the momentum to swing to the bottom safely.

"*Dovl*," he whispered.

The hook slipped off from its hold and rewound the cable. By an invisible hand, it raveled back into the tiny black box. He tucked it back into the folds of his cloak. They were now among the giant boilers. The heat should've been unbearable, but the air stayed relatively balmy.

"I don't know," the Silver Fox answered his question from earlier.

He rose to the tip of his boots to look at one of the circle gauges: 21°C, whatever that means by the archaic system.

"But you're the Silver Fox. Should you know secrets or something?"

Aramis chuckled and waved for him to follow. He must find the magic box quick to disarm whatever foul trap these mannequins laid down.

"True, I am burdened with many secrets. But that doesn't make me wise."

The kid scrunched up his nose. "Then what does that make you?"

Then he saw it: a massive hunk of metal and coil tucked in the corner roaring like a drooling panther. With the flick of the wrist, he popped off the panel door. Columns of metal prong switches lined the back green board. The ancient symbols stamped next to each one. He clicked his tongue in annoyance: he had never seen these symbols before.

"Clever," he said as he took his journal out to decipher the script.

Then Aramis paused to glance at him. By all accounts, children his age would've been terrified by these unusual surroundings. Yet, he seemed plagued by a different nightmare. A familiar nightmare all experienced when they must choose truth over family.

"Now, if I'm clever, what does that make you?" Aramis asked of him.

"What do you mean?" the kid asked.

"Your name," Aramis said as he toggled some of the switches in this puzzle. "You found your true gender and brave enough to voice it. It's time to have a name suitable for it. Have you figured it out?"

The kid winced and looked down at his feet. "I hoped you would tell me since you're the Silver Fox."

"I could only help you find it, not give it to you. Everyone in this life decides their own fate... Well, someday, once the Djinnasi are no more. It's up to you to figure out how you wished to be called."

"Then, how did you choose your name?"

Aramis paused in his toggling to glance at him. The way his hazel eyes seized upon the Silver Fox reminded him of himself when he first met Marquist.

Was this how it felt, Marquist?

Slowly, Aramis flipped the switches as he spoke. "There was a book about the warriors three. They won their battles by their foil, wit, and charm. They were so incredible, the three managed to divert disaster upon disaster set against their queen who they served. When the time came to choose my name, I couldn't help but think of them."

"And one of them is named Aramis?"

"Yes. Now that I think about it, he wanted to be a priest."

"Men were priests back then? Like, officially?" There was a light that burned in the kid's eye.

Now, where have I seen such a spark?

Aramis then answered, "It was the standard, unlike our time. The Aramis of those days was a man of passion without being a brute. But nothing compared to his admiration for his friends. When one died, he grieved body and soul. That alone was what settled in my mind who I wanted to be. To live a full life without hiding oneself."

"Wow. And you became just like him?"

The Silver Fox shrugged. "Some might say so. In any matter, you took the first step, and it's up to you to take the next. Whatever you decide, I'm happy to be here with you for it. Ah-ha!"

Aramis toggled the last set, and the lights flickered from the electrical transfer.

Chapter 14

ANGELS OF HELL

"SO THAT IS WHY!" DIDO EXCLAIMED. Tavian had decided to tell her everything in that cold, empty room surrounded by dark mirrors. Though he feared it would be to his detriment somehow in the end. "Yes, and why I must be here to secure our asset."

The lights above them flickered on, along with the hall behind them. They emitted a strange hum akin to baby crickets. The dark mirrors in their wooden frames also lit up with pictures. An amalgamation of white and black shapes that coalesced into familiar images. It reminded him of the Ancients' reels that they shipped to Chessentari for armaments. Though these captured the living essence of the moment.

There on the top right mirror, Aramis and the boy stood next to a box in a room full of metal railings and vines. There was a button on the mirror's frame. When Tavian pushed it, he could hear their voices as if they were standing next to them.

"There. That should do it. Now we wait for him to call back," said Aramis.

"Call back?" the general queried the satyr.

"Maybe with one of these buttons?" Dido pointed at the dashboard.

With the flick of his left hand, Tavian said, "*Theliad*, do you hear me?"

As he spoke, he could hear his voice echo in the long hall behind him.

So much for our element of surprise.

In the illuminated box, they seemed to look about them until Aramis focused his gaze right at them, or the object that projected this magical connection.

He signaled back at them, "All good here. See if they found them."

Tavian was about to relay it, but he dared not risk it any further. He searched about the monitors until he saw the distinctive features of Sister Rhyllae's priestly robes.

He pressed the mirror's frame button, and he heard Rhyllae's tinny voice, "*It's charged by the Ancients' magic.*"

Then Dawn answered, "*Sorry folks, we have to wait on the Silver Fox's good time.*"

"I fear I must risk it, Miss Dido," Tavian told her.

"Go ahead, I'll watch down the hall for any surprises." Dido then walked out without a light, leaving the door open so as to keep watch on him as well.

"*Theliad*," Tavian called out into the room. "The Bedouins are trapped by a magical cage."

"Magic?" came his signaling.

After some back and forth, the Silver Fox figured out the source. And though he tried to explain to the general that this was not magic, it was hard for Tavian to discern the difference. At last, the cage ceased its dastardly curse, and the doors swung open. Cheers erupted from the right as the Bedouins left their imprisonment.

"Well done, *Theliad*. Come to command."

The Silver Fox saluted, and the two of them melted into the grainy shadows of the mirror's edge. Tavian was about to shut off the entire contraption when something wavered at the corner of his eye. A pale woman stood in front of the glass. He couldn't avert his gaze.

"Can you tell us what kind of monster did this to you? Anything would help us fight this thing," he heard Dawn's tinny voice.

"Monsters? No, not monsters. They look like angels with skin of pure porcelain..." came an elder's voice, also distorted.

The pale woman, Korzha soon realized, saw with closed lids. Her perfectly pale, bowed lips didn't part to speak or breathe. Even her nose was sealed so as to not draw breath. It was as if her face was shaped by a sculptor with no regard to the human performer. Yet, she bounced with every jaunty step, with no normal jiggle on her flesh, and joined by others with the same mask and make.

"...They came at us when the light broke..."

As the man spoke, Tavian saw more and more of these women facing him through these mirrors. Some of them were clothed in the Ancient way. Some of them in the nude chassis they bore. All staring from their vacant faces.

"...We thought we took them out south of the camp, but it was a feint. They surrounded us, tore through our tents as if it was made of smoke..."

They all stood back; their arms bent at their elbows. Elegant statues shaped in a slender frame like those of the elves. Pipes extend from their wrists and their hands droop broken. He leaned forward and knocked something aside. By the click of that trigger the images on the screen to change.

Wait... It can't be...

Tavian flipped that toggle again and again, flipping the images as one would flip a page from a book. All of these "angels" surrounded them outside by all fronts. Many were by the entrance they once came. Standing at full attention, they waited for their unseen commander.

Then at last there was one singular image of a girl in a wincey pinafore dress. Her disheveled hair fell away as she lifted her head up, revealing a foul grimace that was beyond her age. Then all the mirrors flipped to her visage without his doing.

"Dido?" Tavian cried out, for he couldn't tore his eyes away. Not when there gleamed a hateful twitch in her unyielding gaze.

"Korzha?" The satyr mage's voice sounded far across the field.

"...*They may look like a spitting image of an angel, but they're worse—much worse...*" continued the elder's tinny warble.

The door slammed shut behind him, and the lock clicked in placed. He was trapped here with her.

"...*They're creatures of Hell.*"

She opened her maw and let loose a diabolical howl.

Screams broke the cold twilight air.

The scream came from their master. The horns blared the demonic howl, distorted by the feedback squealing along with it. It echoed down from those archaic poles that populated this Doomtown, commanding the mechanical horde to unleash their fury.

The screams came from the mannequins' bullets, streaming from their unfeeling arms. Smoke wafted from those metal ends as they continue their assault on the locked doors.

The screams came from the Bedouins as they crouched in terror. Their nightmare revived once more. Sister Rhyllae rushed to every cage door to drop the corrosive acid in the keyholes. Dawn followed thereafter her to pop them wide open.

"Anyone who's a warrior, form up by the door. Everyone else, to the back." Dawn told those who would listen.

For those who didn't, it was the sister who pulled them to their feet and nudged them to be taken with the rest of the tribe.

"Quick!" Hashim cried once he joined the group. "They put my hands in that box on the wall. Over there!"

Dawn didn't have to ask what he meant. She navigated her way through the crowd and bashed the glass open with her shield. There, among the bent swords and broken spears, were giant metal fists. Her father's "fisty cuffs" he used to call them when she was little. Thankfully, the leather straps were still attached.

"Catch!" Dawn lugged one over bowed heads.

Her old man grunted when the weight slammed into his arms, but he shook it off as he furiously strapped it on his beefy forearm. Seeing their chief strapping on his hands quelled the panic that was rising in their hearts.

Taking the broken spears in her fists, Dawn cried out, "Who can fight?!"

Hands shot up and were granted thusly, no matter who. Then Dawn hoisted the other metal hand upon her hip and waded her way to him. Rhyllae joined her on the way. Hashim and Dawn finally locked eyes when they were a foot apart.

He grunted a sigh and held out his arms. "What's the game plan?"

Dawn smirked and relinquished the second metal fist. "We'll hide by the doors. When they come through, we'll beat them back and drop that cabinet to block them. That should give Sister Rhyllae time." She placed her hand on the sister's shoulders. "To take the tribe through that door at the top of the ladder. Got it?"

"Then there's no time to waste."

"To the roof!" Rhyllae bellowed to everyone. "Children and wounded first!"

There was a crash of metal, and the people crouched again. The sister of the Morning Lord raised her hand up high; the light shone brightly above her.

"Don't be afraid! Follow me!" Rhyllae cried out once again.

As she moved to the back of the hall, they followed. Up the metal ladders that led the walls to the rafters. Those with arms to bear stayed below, trying not to flinch as they heard metal banging down the hall.

BANG

BANG

BANG

But the door wouldn't give.

Dido cupped her hands to her mouth. "General, sir? Korzha!"

The screaming from within was not his own, and that sent chills down to her stubby tail. She took out her medlar wand and called out again. "Step back. I'm coming in!"

Then a seed drifted in view, wing tipped like a dragonfly. In a blink, it exploded into a bloom of vines as thick as her arms and spikes as long as tiger fangs. With a yelp, Dido exchanged herself with the air further down the hall. Safely teleported, she watched as the bramble blocked the door and sprawled out like a spider's web.

An ensnaring spell!

Dido looked over her shoulder and almost retched from the sight. There before her was a dark wooden shrub, overgrown to resemble a miniature tree. In its leafless branches hoisted a dead lamb, skewered through its distended belly as to have the legs drape down as a humanoid would. The broken jaw swayed from where a branch jutted out with a fresh cluster of blackened berries. The limbs flopped about as the roots writhed the entire bramble forward. Worse, Dido knew them by name.

"Myrtle," Dido managed to say.

"Ah, you remember my name," she said. The voice croaked from their throat, their unhinged jaw unmoving. "How good of you to remember of me in your last moments."

"I wish I could say the same about you. What happened to you, Myrtle?"

"Me? Me?" The whole body flopped to one side as the bush rustled in enthusiasm. "I have ascended, Dido. Ascended by the good graces of our Bramble Queen. Power beyond sunbeams and sea salt spray. Power beyond the Summer Flame. You should heed the call, Dido." Those lidless, glazed eyes bore into her soul as Myrtle spoke. "Heed the Brambles call and join Autumn's delight."

Oh, how the satyr mage wanted to hurl. But Dido forced the revulsion down in her gullet and steadied her wand hand. A ball of flame spun at its tip.

"Myrtle, my pupil, I don't think I will," Dido said.

The corpse shuddered as the shambling mound moved back. "Traitorous witch! You shall regret the seeds you cast to the wind. Bend to the yoke or plough the fields of your own destruction."

"No. It'll be your destruction I shall plough!"

With a flick of Dido's wrist, a shiny marble was lobbed. It sailed high in the air before it morphed into a raging ball of inferno.

"Frost bite!" Myrtle's voice cried out in the metal- and porcelain-tiled hall.

Thin ice coated Myrtle's bark and wool, thicker than any seasonal normality. The fire barely left a scorch mark upon her by the time the spell dissipated. From the steam, figments oozed. They spun in a circle about Myrtle's grotesque form, becoming a cyclone of darkening mist. With a grunt, the bramble shuddered and the shadows hurtled themselves at her.

Black Musk, Dido knew. A poisonous plume of mold spores under disguise. "You think of me as a kid? I wrote that spell!"

Three twirls of the wand and those spores popped open before they landed. Gossamer wings snapped open from those casings and out flew cicadas. They clung themselves to Dido and unleashed their song. Dido sang with them, though the words she bore were of a different cadence:

"With sickle I soar

"In the quiet I roar

"Through the trees I tore

"Herald's doom I here bore

"Calamity's Candor!"

By the syncopated beat of the cicadas' wings, a mighty sonic clap rolled forth toward the opposing witch. As the wave crested, static charge accumulated into a roar.

"Ferris Cage!" cried out Myrtle.

Out from the tiled flooring and plaster ceiling were chunks of metallic piping. They swirled about the hideous creature and locked into place. Lightning sparked from

Dido's spell and fell upon the scaffolding. But to no avail. By the time Myrtle's spell end, Dido's was diminished.

Myrtle chuckled darkly. "I am no green horned whelp you once knew, mage. Watch how the Bramble Queen fuels my power!"

Eldritch ink streamed from every orifice and knot of Myrtle's twisted form. Then it seeped down to the floor beyond its roots. In its pool, cold twilight stars spun. The tiles cracked from its weight and the walls groaned from the gravitational shift.

Dido's gut sank low in her belly for she knew what she was casting. Myrtle opened an extra-dimensional portal and used that rupture as her magical draw. There was little Dido could do against such a maelstrom, and none of her options were quick enough for her to aid her friends against screaming bullets.

The barred, front doors came crashing down with a bang. The barrel drums whirled to a stop and smoke streamed from the red-hot chambers. Quick as a sunbaked lizard, the mannequins charged in. Naked and pale in the artificial lighting with their skins of metal, hiding the translucent wiring about their metal skeletal structures. Permanent high heeled feet marched the distressed floor as each of them peel off wordlessly down the halls. Left, up, right, over and over again in clockwork efficiency, akin to bees coming to their native hive. Arms cocked at the ready for the intruders they must eliminate.

Aramis watched it all, high up in the rafters, hidden by dusty, plaster tiles set in delicate ironwork. He gave a cautious glance to the kid crouched next to him on the iron I-bar that stretched horizontally in this claustrophobic space, his eyes quaking from the sight. When the kid finally decided his new name would be Shutte, they heard a scream louder than thunder, followed by a pounding that was harder than hail.

Aramis put a comforting hand on his shoulder. Shutte caught his gaze, and his lips parted to say something.

The Silver Fox signaled to him, "Quiet."

The kid nodded as they both carefully backtracked to where they were. A high-strung fool would try to cut them out at the mouth of the flood or fight them head on as one would against soldiers. But Aramis saw how fast those bullets flew when they broke down the front entrance. No armor could withstand such attacks. Creatures of war, indeed.

No, the wisest thing Aramis could do was to outmaneuver them and use their parts against them. Creatures of war they may be, the mannequins were still delicate circuitry that is exploitable. He needed to take down one of them to hatch his plan.

At the vent-ductwork where they came from, they crawled to the backside of the building. It was slow going because the metal tubes yielded to their weight, creating a popping sound from such indentions. Any sound would mean death from below. Twice they paused when the whir of gears intensified below them. At last, they came to the large grate leading to the outside with the starlit sky looming. Peering down below, Aramis lucked out. There was a mannequin standing at attention at a door, right underneath him.

Perfect.

Aramis began twisting the bolts off of the corners.

"We're leaving them behind?" the kid gave a hoarse whisper.

"Shhh!" was the first thing that came out of Aramis's mouth before he realized what he himself had done.

He froze. *Crap. Did they hear?*

The sentinel remained motionless—the ultimate statue.

His shoulders droop in relief. Aramis gave him a stern look and motioned with his hands, "Stay here."

Aramis curled his body and propped his boots on the grate. He inhaled the fresh cold air and exhaled all doubt. There should be no room for error. All must be one fluid motion, or he'd become as holy as a martyr.

With a swift kick, the grate flew off. The mannequin below snapped their head up and trailed their arm in an arcing motion, not seeing Aramis as he jumped down upon it. Bullets rang out in the night, but the muzzle couldn't bend far enough to reach him as he clung to the mannequin from behind. Holding tight, he slid his dagger into its mechanical neck. The magical blade severed the connecting wires until the machine collapsed underneath him.

All was silent in this still night save for a few ragged breaths.

Aramis then slid his knife into the shoulder socket and popped out its arm. With it, he wedged it in the handles of the door and braced it in place in case they investigated the sound. Then, for good measure, he took the mannequin's head clean off from its scaffolding.

"Is it safe?" whispered the kid.

"Yes." Aramis reached up to him.

The child stood on his shoulders before hopping down on the ground with his guidance. Then Aramis led him to an alcove that was meant for offloading garbage (the efficiency of the Ancients knew no bounds) and used the clandestine cloak as an impromptu tent.

Aramis whispered, "To answer your earlier question: no, we're not escaping. At least, not without our friends."

"But we can't take them on by ourselves."

"With this, we can." He showed the porcelain face of the mannequin.

"A head?" the kid asked in a deadpan voice.

"It's what inside that counts."

With the edge of the knife, Aramis found the seam and wedged it in. With three smacks, he cracked it open like a coconut.

Chapter 15

ASCENSION

THE PAINT BROKE AND THE DOOR SLAMMED OPEN from Sister Rhyllae's weight. It was dusty, which comforted the priestess, and it extended well past the length of the prison ward, too. Placing the holy light upon her head, the sister reached down and helped the little girl up.

"Go all the way down to the door and wait for me there," she told her.

The girl bobbed her covered head before she trekked down, her little hands wringing the hem of her shawl. After so many paces, Rhyllae could see her turn to look back.

"I'm right behind you."

That seemed to pacify her, and the little girl continued into the shadows.

Another little hand reached out from Rhyllae's feet. Same motion of help. Same words of encouragement. Again and again, as fast as the sister of the Morn could for each bedouin, no matter who.

There came again the howling, closer than before. Dawn and the volunteers shoved the metallic cages that once held their weapons down in front the damaged portals. Even from high up, the sister could see the metal turning red from the assault.

"Hurry, go down there!" Rhyllae said.

"You don't have to tell me twice." The boy scampered down the hall.

Up next was an elderly woman. Rhyllae reached for her, but she grabbed her arm to look at her dead in the eyes. "Go to them, Sister. They're our future."

"So are you." Rhyllae yanked the woman up and instructed her the same.

She stood there stunned. "But, why?"

"History," Rhyllae blurted out as she hoisted up the next one up, a man with cloth bound around his eye. "Knowledge. Teach them where they came from."

The howling intensified until the metal gave way to the dreaded *rat-ta-tat* of their ancient technological power. Pale alien arms protruded from the freshly made hole. Cries of surprise sounded from down below as she saw blurs of bullets slung faster than any sling could muster. They tore right through the people still down below. Rhyllae froze, never had she seen blood sprayed into the air like a gurgling fountain.

Then Dawn and her crew swooped in from flanking the doors. They bashed their arms with their weapons, trying to disrupt their deadly fire. Then Hashim threw some metal box in front of the hole and that ceased the dreaded onslaught.

She turned her honey-brown gaze to the tribespeople congregating below the ladder, pushing to get on the rungs slick with blood. A woman fell. A few tried to catch her, but they ended up collapsing underneath her weight.

Instinct took hold. Rhyllae hung on to the outer left edge of the ladder to use as a pole and climbed down. A few of the tribespeople paused to look at her in awe. The time spent with Aramis had taught her there were different ways to climb the ladder.

"Keep going!" she told them.

Finally, Rhyllae reached the bottom where the woman fell. She was fine, as were most of the people who caught her, but the man that was underneath her was out stone cold. Willing herself to breathe, Rhyllae managed to calm herself to see the muscles and then the skeletal system. No broken bones. That was all she cared about right now. From her pack, the sister produced a potent smelling salt and waved it under his nose. When the man came to, he looked up at her with slack-jawed awe and twinkling eyes. At first, she didn't know why until she saw the rays of light streaming from her forehead.

Oh, he must think I'm some sort of angel.

"Here." She pulled him up. "Follow them up the ladder and keep going."

Numbingly, the man reached for the metal rung and hoisted himself along the rest above him.

Half of them are up there now. I need to guide them to the roof without alerting the rest of the mannequins... somehow.

A clang of metal broke her train of thought. Dawn and Hashim laid down a wooden block of furniture on top of the collection they stacked from earlier. They were talking amongst themselves, but Rhyllae heard them all the same.

"That's it," Hashim said. He slammed the last metal crate on top of the banging pile.

"Shit. We can't even face them head-on," Dawn said, as she looked back at the fellow warriors moving the fallen dead from the ladder.

He put his broad hands on her toned shoulders. "Then we leave and fight on another day, with a ground of our choosing, little cub."

The lieutenant's face soured. "If we survive."

The sister, a priestess of the ever-rising Sun, feared Dawn could be right. Not everyone would be able to make it out, especially the warriors since they'd bring the rear of the group. Then a thought went through her head, a flash of insight.

Wait, Aramis's bombs!

Though not highly explosive like Aramis's, they were meant to open up rubble or to distract enemies. She could use them against these creatures. Yet, Rhyllae hesitated. A life is precious, even synthetic, monstrous ones like these maidens of war. Even their healing magic could not eradicate *eirudeitrus*, an elvish word for the invisible animals that exist on the surface of all skin who would so love to proliferate in wounds. The sister took out the metal canisters. The weight felt heavy in her hands.

Dawn joined Rhyllae. "We can't hold them for long. We need to—wait, what are those?"

She shove them into the lieutenant's arms. "Use these. They're not powerful, but they will buy us time."

Dawn grimly smiled. "Okay. Get your ass moving, Sister."

I did all I could, my Morning Lord, Rhyllae told herself as she climbed up the ladder. *It's out of my hands now.*

Once again, she took the outer edge, right this time, and elevated herself past the climbers. Trying her best to ignore the metallic howling and turn her attention to the heated debate coming out of the hall from above.

"What's going?" Sister Rhyllae cried out.

It was a claustrophobic scene of the adults towering over the children, with the elders wedged between them. Fear. Fear and anger in all of their eyes.

"Everyone calm down. Please. No one is going to die here," Rhyllae told them.

Whatever emotion that crossed their faces—hope, disappointment, despair—Rhyllae wasted no further thought upon the matter. From the pack she produced the mallet she used earlier.

"Move!" she cried out.

They all scrambled to one side as she came barreling down. Putting all of her weight in it as the hammer fell upon the door.

"Oof," Tavian groaned. The door didn't budge one bit when he collided with the meat of his shoulder.

Ever since the brambles covered it, the wood had swollen itself shut. By the ache in his arm, it was more akin to stone than wood. Then he heard Dido. Her voice rising and falling in magical incantation, then to be followed by a choir of screaming cicadas. She was fighting whatever creature that magically sealed him in, and he couldn't reach her. Worse still, he was stranded with no means to reach the rest of the expedition to stand against the horde of mannequins.

It's all out of my hands!

He slammed his left fist on the door and a thorn jabbed through his skin upon impact. Tavian jerked it back and cradled it. The precious lifeline oozed out from the opened gash.

"*Căcat*," he hissed.

Then he heard laughter. Melodic and mocking, like a child pulling off a ruse. Before the last note sounded, it ended abruptly and quickly returned to coda to resound the script once more. The general turned on his heels to face the jester.

One of the square mirrors flickered an image of a girl chasing bubbles through a grassy meadow with a white-painted wooden fence serving as the backdrop. Then it blinked. A close up was shown of the little mouth laughing, but the sound didn't line up with its movements. The whole sight was jarring at best. Then the mirror would darken as the image flickered to the next mirror. Over and over again.

Tavian's eye twitched. He could feel his ire rising from the back of his throat, but he mentally stomped down the animalistic rebuke. He knew the enemy had the upper hand with all of this Ancient magic, yet his dignity would not allow himself to have his emotions played like Tinkertoys. Tavian approached the desk with all the composure he could muster. His frosty blue eyes scanned the series of buttons and archaic words etched next to them. None of which familiar or close to the languages he had studied.

The laughter went to a higher pitch as it sped up; the images flickered before him in rapid sequence, dazzling him with such dizzying array. A tactic popular among the fae, Tavian realized, to distract their prey from what can kill them. For once, the general was grateful for the searing pain in his arm.

You will meet your end, Tavian mentally promised as he began to press buttons and toggled switches in succession. Lights flickered. A dull tone rang. It warbled into a screech before he shut it off with another flick of the switch. He kept going until at last the hideous laughter was silenced.

Korzha gave a sigh. "Finally, sweet silence."

The mirrors then turned to an image of the girl from before. This time, her cherub face glowered at him; that brought a smile to the general's face. Tavian noted which button that awarded the sweet silence; it was a simple dull-gray button with an image of an overturned hat with the numeral ten next to it. The dull throb in his hand reminded him to bandage the wound. Those hateful eyes trailed after him as he wrapped one of the gauzes he procured from his pocket around the padded part of his hand. He must thank the Morning Lord sister for distributing them beforehand.

As he did so, Tavian spotted the torch; the magical image was a spiritual reminder of his oath from the prior general of the Jessenters. The flames writhed, nettling his skin from its irritation; it hadn't done that since the ghoul uprising two moons ago. Myrrh had warned him that any supernatural creature would cause it to return.

The general slowed his wrapping as he craned his steely blue eyes up, and their dark eyes met his. Tavian tilted his head one way and then to the other side. They followed.

"You are no mere illusion are you," he stated.

She snarled her face, like a wolf defending a freshly caught meal.

"Good, then you'll hear of my terms, Banshee."

A flicker of static flipped through the glass, a sharp cut to her screaming at the screen.

"Screaming will not avail you and neither will your mechanical toys, no matter how much you protest."

That seemed to stop the mimicry before him. The girl resigned herself to that dreadful glower.

"We know your true intended target. The Silver Fox."

White, bold letters flashed before his very eyes from every mirror, it spelled:

[Aramis Feres].

It kept repeating with no end in sight.

"Yes," Tavian crooned. "The elusive prey that you desperately desire. You can have him."

The letters ceased; even the image of the girl froze.

Tavian clasped his hands behind his back. "Here are my terms. Cease your fascination with these prisoners and end their torture. Let them return to their provincial lives, and we will bring the Silver Fox to your very doorstep. Alive and unharmed. *D'accord*?"

The mirrors turn dark, leaving his own reflection staring back at him. Walls cracked and groaned from the magical duel beyond the door.

Steady. He encouraged himself. *Don't show them fear.*

He'd learned from all of his campaigns for Töska that not all battles were won on the ground. Some of his battles were won by a simple letter. Bribes and promises opened more gated doors than a breechloader and a siege tower ever would. Alliances turned as quickly as the wind if you knew how to direct their sails.

Suddenly, the same bold font flashed before his eyes with words—Ancient words—from around the globe. Then he managed to spy on one that was the closest to his native root tongue. The message repeated, and for the third time Tavian managed to glean their response.

[What do you gain from this?]

"Revenge," Tavian answered back. "Provide me the means of my enemies' destruction, and he is all yours. What of you? To what reward do you obtain from all of this?"

[Ascension]

"Pardon?" he asked not because he didn't understand, but he couldn't believe it, for how could a machine, let alone a ghost, want for such a thing.

[Ascension]

Then it displayed visions that Tavian could only describe as surreal and majestic: images of humans, muscular and pale, enrobed in flowing gowns and robes of splendid, courtly colors. Sunlight streamed down from picturesque clouds, surrounding these figures, who craned their necks like a shepherd's crook. Sometimes, the images focused on their serene faces and to their archaic holy gestures of dead deities. Other times, it focused on the people bowing to them from below. All were shown in rapid fire.

[Ascension]

Then the magical boxes showed wings, feathered like pristine doves, adorning the backs of these humans as they floated in the sunny skies. A sinking feeling settled in Tavian's gut as these images were collaged into a larger picture of the girl, now a woman in full bloom, dressed full divine regalia with six outstretched wings splayed from her back and golden rays streaming from her dark, windswept hair. She raised the splayed blessing above her head with her right and with her left pointing down to her sandaled feet.

"Ascension," she said. Her voice sounded as if she stood there before him.

Then all the lights went out.

The people on the ladder cried out in shock, and Dawn swore under her breath as everything in the vast space fell into darkness. The only illumination to be had was the pure starlight from the disused hallway far in the back. It grew brighter until the sweaty and harried sister of the Morning Lord emerged with the light on her forehead.

"Though I walk through the Shadow, I will raise my candle high, for the Light within me shall shine, like the fire of the Sun," Rhyllae prayed from above, her face scrunched in concentration.

Tiny pinpricks of light scattered forth from her outstretched hand. They zoomed to each individual in the room and affixed itself on their brows. Dawn smiled. The light wasn't much, illuminating an arm's length from their faces, but it gave her the courage to face these monsters.

"Keep going!" The sister of the Morn's voice carried over to the tribespeople, before she emerged back into the hall.

When Dawn looked back, she unsheathed her gladius.

The mannequins were there. Their pale, perfect forms emerging from the inky void surrounding them then halted in eerie stillness. Baltazar cried out when a mannequin emerged mere inches from his face. Dawn glanced over for a mere second or two, then jumped in her skin when she looked back face-to-face with a porcelain mask. She could see the skin was not skin, but hard plating akin to a chinchilla shell. It covered the corded layers of their so-called meat. Meat not red not like any mortal, but clear with specks of copper wire threaded through them.

"Form a line!" Dawn commanded while she stared. "Encircle the ladder, but keep your eyes on them. Don't let them pass!"

Slow and steady, the warriors backed away toward the ladder, their weapons raised before their hunched stances. The damnable mannequins broke into a rush until they were caught in their starlight. At last, they made it to where

Dawn could hear the sister's voice echoing from the hall. The people remaining below pushed and shoved to grab onto the ladder.

"One at a time!" Hashim bellowed at them.

"Single file!" Dawn cried out.

Shayla shouted, "You'll collapse the ladder if you don't!"

That halted the movement behind the warriors.

"If I touch your shoulder you're going up and following the sister," her mother offered to them. "You. You, then you."

One by one, the tribespeople climbed up the metal rungs. Both father and daughter glanced at each other before they turned to face their foe. There were more than twenty frozen in the starlight, with many more crowding from behind, a few within reach, the eeriest display of a museum gallery Dawn had ever seen.

"Why aren't they shooting?" one of the warriors, Cassandra, asked as she raised a broken spear shaft to poke one in front of her.

"Wait, don't!" Dawn tried to reach out to Cassandra.

She turned her whole head to look at Dawn. "C'mon we can—ah!"

In the corner of her eye, arms reached out and pulled Cassandra into the darkness. Her screams reverberated off the expanse as her body flailed behind the line of naked stoic curves. Bones crunched and joints snapped before Dawn could finish saying her name. Her screams turned to a gurgle after a sickening pop, and Cassandra's light was snuffed out.

"Cassandra!" Natasha cried out from the far side of the side.

"Hold! Eyes forward!" Dawn ordered.

Damn, shit fuck damn! Though she kept those words to herself. They needed strength, and they needed that from her.

"Don't lose your nerve. They're trying to psyche you out. Just because they're not shooting at you doesn't mean they're not dangerous," Dawn said.

Two of those masked faces were now in her sights, with a third face popping in between them. The lieutenant regripped the hilt of her sword as the sweat trickled down her arms and brow.

Her father leaned over as he still kept his eyes on the enemy. "We can't stay here."

Dawn said, "I have a plan. When the last person goes up the ladder, we peel off one by one. Until then, those holding the line fill in the gaps and strike back any trying to break through."

"Who should be last?"

"You and me."

Hashim smiled. "Maybe the Jessenters did put some sense into that thick skull of yours."

"Still a lesbian, Dad. Don't expect a homecoming anytime soon."

The comment stirred him to look at her fully.

Shit.

Dawn saw one of the porcelain faces inching too close to his face, its hands reaching out to grab him with their flawless, slender fingers. She thrusted her blade into its exposed neck; sparks burst from its severed wires while the head twitched in place. Hashim stepped back in astonishment which allowed her room to retract her blade. There was movement out of her left peripheral vision, and Dawn brought her shield up to bear. Metal clashed against metal as she shoved it back into the crowding mannequins, and a few toppled to the ground.

Another movement, this time from her left. Dawn crouched low and held her shield high above her head. On the floor, she splayed her hand out, letting the sword lie flat on the floor. Using her right arm as an anchor, Dawn kicked both of her legs out in front of her. Kneecaps were still kneecaps, and the mannequin crumpled down just the same as the others.

Pulling on her core muscles, Dawn retracted her legs back and hopped up. By the flick of her boot, the gladius blade was flipped up in the air. She grabbed backward so the blade pointed down toward her elbow, ready to pierce it in the next mannequin lurching behind her.

A pair of metal fists slammed down on the perfect, bald head, the mask splintered and popped free from the impact. Dark machine fluid oozed from the burst sacs in its compartment. Hashim saw one charging on his left and whipped it aside with the destroyed mannequin's body.

Fighting ensued down the line as one or the other flinched from the distracting sound, echoing in the encroaching darkness.

Chapter 16

LORD OF THE SILVER STREAMS

Laughter broke through Myrtle's broken maw as the magic surged from the eldritch might. Her voice cracked as it jumped an octave, drunk on the power surging through her twisted body.

There were no words Dido could say that could alter her path now. Lost to the whims of magic, she could not stop the portal from opening without decimating the building they were in. Instead, Dido waved her wands to-and-fro, drawing six-pointed stars in front of her and configured them point to point. From each point, a new line formed, creating a tortoiseshell pattern that provided a protective netting from ceiling to floor and wall to wall before her. It wasn't the sturdiest of shield spells, but it could endure for hours, giving her enough time to free Korzha from that room.

"You think you can encase me?! You? You're merely second-rank," Myrtle cried out. "I am beyond anything you could inflict upon me, for I am a Sapphire beyond Starlight, an Azure shadow that Glowers!"

Dido gasped. "Don't be a fool! You can't control him—no one can!"

Not even the Faerie Queens with all of their powers combined.

But her words fell on deaf ears, the howls of magic screamed in wanton hunger, lusting over the magical incantation Myrtle sang to it. Then something broke through. Descending from the Ancients' horns attached to the corners of this hall were voices locked in barter.

Korzha!

She thought in glee, until she heard what was followed thereafter, "Ascension." The word was repeated all around them. Whoever spoke those words, it became a counter incantation. The magic seized upon it, creating something old. Much older. The magical well rising under Myrtle twisted and darkened.

"No. No, no, no!" Myrtle cried as it snapped out of her control.

"Myrtle! You can break this ritual! This is your chance to step away from this alive—release it before it takes you with it!" Dido screamed.

But it was too late.

Tendrils rose from the inky starlight vortex beyond the realms of natural sight. These tendrils, to use the term loosely, there were no cups to grip with, or skin that would crease and bulge from its curls. At least, nothing as benign as an octopus or as malignant as an eel, or any creature of the sea. It was ethereal beyond imagining, for if Dido gazed into it too long she would see collisions of galaxies smattering against each other in constant chaos and doom.

The etheric tendrils wrapped themselves around the bark and flesh of the defiant Myrtle. The cry that came from her once they squeezed, there were no words to describe such horror. Dido turned her gaze aside as she heard the dreaded *CRACK* of her bark, followed by the fleshy splut of the blood vessels caving in. In her heart, she knew that the Myrtle she had once known and cared for was utterly gone. Her breathing raced into a panic as her body quaked as the portal took the sacrifice into its starry altar.

There's no stopping it now. I have to get everyone out of here—I have to get Korzha out of that room!

Dido took two steps back before she tore her eyes away from the chaotic sight. Her little goat legs trotted over to the bramble snares. What was once wood became ash, as would all magic that is held by the vanquished caster. Waving her arms to and fro, Dido dispersed the particles until she found the handle. Three taps from her wand and the door swung open under General Korzha's weight.

On his knees, Dido could see his face contorted in pain and the sweat staining his collar. His left hand gripped his other arm, the magical torch imprinted upon it flared into life. Of course, it would consider this eldritch lord a supernatural phenomenon, how could Dido forget. But that did not stop Korzha from his eyes widening in shock when they were laid upon her.

"You aged," he raised his voice over the maelstrom. "What happened?"

"There's no time," she said as she took his arm and tugged on it, urging him to stand.

Thankfully, he managed to stand on his own.

"Don't!" she blurted out when he motioned to look back at the chaos down the hall.

Korzha snapped his pale blue eyes back at her and a silent knowing washed over his features. "A little too much peril for our situation, don't you think, Madame Mage?"

A flush of heat raged on her cheeks. "I will have you know, none of this was my own doing, thank you very much. Where did you tell Rhyllae to take the people again?"

"The roof."

"Then stand here."

Something hit the magical shield, sizzling upon impact, but both of them dared not to look. Dido took a fistful of sea salt and poured it around the two of them to prevent any interference. It was going to be a rocky teleport, and she hoped the general could stomach the sudden transition.

There was another sizzle, and the shield strained from whatever weight was pressed upon it. Dido mentally blocked it out and calculated the necessary exchange of mass. The magical shield snapped, her eyes fluttered open and found the Azure Lord looming over the general. All of their madness and eldritch might was set against her will.

The only thought that crossed her mind was *GO*.

POP

In a blink, her breath took in the clear, arid night air. Korzha and Dido collapsed to their knees. Her insides sloshed about until vomit erupted out of her mouth. Her half-digested dinner lay steaming on the bare concrete.

"What was that thing? I never felt such a calamitous presence in my life," Korzha spoke between shuddered breaths.

"None should," Dido said. "For that was Yeorgu, Azure Lord of the Silver Streams, what you humans called the Milky Way."

Korzha looked bewildered. "We don't have the means to cast out an Eldritch Lord, let alone contain it!"

"But enough to bribe with," came a surly voice.

There, at the edge of the flat rooftop was a shadow of a man with twin star eyes that pierced the nighttime sky. His blades gleamed under the moonlight with Dido's magical brand.

"I'm up," Shayla cried, the last to go up the ladder.

There were eight of them left. The mannequins had attacked in waves, trying to catch them off guard whenever they blinked or sneezed. But it was better than having those bullets fly around. Many a time, Dawn wondered how they could use those guns against them, but no answer came to light. It was time for them to join the rest of the survivors.

"Warriors!" Dawn called out. "When I call out your name, you go up the ladder. We'll close ranks and fight until two of us are left. Clear?"

"We're here for you, Captain," Natasha said.

Dawn felt her heart leap into her throat. *Maybe... someday...* she thought before she closed her eyes and shook the notion out of her head. A poor choice of action for the moment she opened her eyes, that serene mask was inches from her face. She took the gladius blade and plunged it in its throat.

"Al'aihim!" Dawn shouted.

He backed up until his body bumped into the ladder and then turned to climb up the ladder. They all sidestepped into the gap, a smooth peel-off. Not so much for the next. When Dawn called out for Suad, he flinched, and those perfect pale arms yanked him behind the enemy line. Try as they might, they couldn't free him before they snapped his neck from the struggle.

"Stand your ground! One at a time. Murkal. Opal. Ruul," Dawn continued the roll call.

She swatted an arm coming for her with her shield and managed to sever another at the elbow. The fight grew heated as each one of them continued to split from the line. At last, it was just the three of them, Dawn, Hashim, and Natasha.

"Go!" Hashim cried out to Natasha, his metal hands smashing and punching in every which way possible.

"I can't!" she shouted back.

Natasha ducked when one mannequin lunged for her, then she swung the butt end of the broken spear shaft at its head. As it fell to the wayside, another took its place. It swung its arms up, then brought them, along with their whole torso, down. Natasha rolled away before the hands slammed down hard. Another mannequin grabbed her ankle, Natasha gave it a warm welcome with the jab of her spear tip. Its face plate shattered from the powerful blow, revealing pumping sacs woven among wires draped around it. Natasha cried out in disgust and flicked her wrist, letting the tip of her spear cut through those bulbous sacs. Dark fluid ooze forth from the impact. The mannequin slumped, and Natasha managed to free herself before it landed where she once stood. More loomed before her, blocking her escape.

"Switch!" Dawn called out.

Father and daughter moved back-to-back, striking and parrying as they turned around, a whirlwind of steel blades and fists. Dawn threw her shield at the mannequins encroaching Natasha. The impact threw them off-balance, giving Dawn enough time to scoop up Natasha to her feet.

"Get on that ladder, soldier," Dawn told her, looking her dead in the eye.

Natasha's eyes wavered as her mind battled within itself; then her eyes widened, spying another mannequin behind the lieutenant. Flipping the sword backward in her hand, the lieutenant thrust it behind her. The crunch of metal and circuitry confirmed that it made its way home.

Natasha saluted. "Yes, ma'am."

With that, Dawn returned to the fight. A mannequin lumbered toward her and froze once it was in her sight. She spied her shield stuck in its metal torso. Dawn grabbed hold of the circular edge and kicked the mannequin cleared off of it. To give herself breathing room, Dawn whirled her shield about in a figure eight, knocking every mechanical doll before securing it back into her left arm.

"Go!" cried out Hashim as he slammed two mannequins into each other, crushing their heads in the process.

"You go!" Dawn countered. "You're the fucking tribe leader."

"And that makes me," he paused as he lifted one over his head, "last!"

The mannequin flew from the mighty throw, crashing into dozens before they disappear into the darkness.

"Not with this."

Dawn pulled out one of Rhyllae's bombs. With her teeth she pulled the pin that held it in place and lobbed it over. Some of the mannequin heads trailed the motion until one leaped up to stop its flight. The bomb exploded, bigger than anticipated. The fiery plume raced right up to the two and singed their arm hairs before dissipating.

Whoa, this is more like Aramis's bag, not Rhyllae's.

Her father shared the same shocked expression as on her face when he turned to face her. "You weren't shitting!"

One mannequin with scorched marks reached for him from behind. Taking one of the dropped spears, Dawn threw it at the doll straight and true. It pierced straight through its head, and the robot collapsed into a heap.

"Get going," Dawn said.

She held out her shield behind him as he turned to the ladder. He couldn't climb like the others because of his amputation; thus he hooked his arm over the rung from the backside and pushed himself up from his legs before wrapping the next. It would be slow going, but at least she could fend off the mannequins as he ascended.

Once he was halfway up, Dawn lobbed another bomb, a little closer this time. As the flames rush toward her, she jumped and grabbed on the ladder as high as she could. With one arm holding a shield, she managed to deflect the brunt of the fiery plume.

In the dying embers of their fallen comrades, the mannequins crawled toward her with their metal sticks for arms.

They don't know how to quit do they?

A metal hand seized on her ankle as Dawn grabbed hold of the metal rung. With her free leg, she kicked at the mechanical doll until at last it toppled back on top of its peers. Up top of the ladder, Shayla and Natasha both grabbed hold of Hashim and helped him through.

Once up Hashim bellowed, "Get your ass up here, girl!"

"On it!"

Dawn took out the last bomb. With the safety off, she dropped it straight below her, then booked it out of there. She could see the fear in their eyes when she looked up and knew it must be an inferno rolling behind her. By the time she grabbed hold of their hands, the heat blasted against her back. All of them yanked her through and slammed the door shut behind her. Natasha took her shawl and beat it over her with it.

Flames, Dawn realized. She was on fire.

She rolled to and fro until the fire extinguished itself, then lay on her back, welcoming the cool floor.

"Getting sleepy?" Natasha asked.

Now where have I heard that before?

Dawn smiled. "Just a catnap. C'mon, we need to catch up with the rest."

The sudden weight on Sister Rhyllae's soul knocked the breath out of her, and she had to lean on the wall to support herself. Never had she felt anything like this before, not even M'thealquilôk with its leagues of undead. This weight was far beyond the influence of this realm. Beyond the scope of evil or good.

Who is this?

Rhyllae's train of thought broke when she felt a gentle touch on her shoulder.

"Sister, are you alright?" the elderly woman asked.

No, she wanted to say, but there was no need to cause a panic among the people.

"I'm fine," Rhyllae said as she straightened herself up. "Let's keep moving."

That seemed to assure the lady, but for the rest, lit by the starlight upon her head, their expressions turned to a dour shade. It wasn't the first time people gave her such a look. Though the Morning Lord and his Sister were worshipped far and wide, many didn't see their priestesses anything more than glorified medics. Doubt flickered through their eyes whenever Rhyllae took command, even if the Silver Fox vouched for her. And since this was not the first time, Rhyllae didn't wilt from their critical stares. The Morning Lord priestess pushed herself off the wall and gave each a hard look until they glanced away.

"We're almost there," Rhyllae assured them all. "I'll take you to the rooftop, and we'll evacuate you from there."

"Will we see the Silver Fox?" a man asked.

Everyone's faces lit with hope when he mentioned the desert shepherd, such a contrast to Amaveriel.

"Perhaps," Rhyllae replied. "But your lives come first. The Silver Fox has his own battles to contend with."

He'll make it. I hope.

That seemed to placate them, for now. They had crept down barren halls made of plastered stone for who knows how long. Some of them had wooden doors with shattered glass, others with metal cabinets with locks on them. No mannequins, yet.

With the hammer still in her hands, Rhyllae moved to the front. There, a set of double doors of the same wooden make stood that might lead to a wide hall. Aramis mentioned they were built to handle multitudes of these children. Perhaps this hallway would have a way up and a way for the mannequins to find them, if they were not quiet.

Rhyllae gave the handle a gentle tug. *Locked.*

Footsteps echoed from behind. Too rapid and sloppy to be those mechanized dolls, but she didn't want to chance it. Swinging the hammer up for a strike, the Morning Lord priestess briskly strode past the tribespeople. The starlight on Rhyllae's head shone on their faces as they bounced into view and on one familiar face.

"Dawn!" Rhyllae cried out.

The young lieutenant gave her a broad grin along with a sweaty hug with her strong, feminine arms.

"Is that for me?" Dawn asked.

Rhyllae grinned. "I think you have enough sense knocked into you."

Dawn chuckled. "What's the plan?"

"Up."

"Through those doors?"

The sister nodded.

The officer gave one sharp whistled note, and the rest of the Bedouin warriors came running up. Except for Hashim, he lumbered over with Shayla by his side.

"Not you." Rhyllae waved her arm out. "I need you alive."

The burly leader swelled his chest, and the sister feared a verbal bout incoming; then Shayla put her hand over his heart. They gazed into each other's eyes, both pleading each other through that silent, intimate conversation. At last, Hashim gave in and nodded at the priestess. Rhyllae gave him a nod of thanks and joined Dawn at the door.

"A single latch."

"Easy to break down, then." Dawn tightened the shield straps on her arms. "Ready?"

Her hands tightened on the hammer, and she nodded.

The eight warriors crouched, with Dawn at the center and Rhyllae right behind her. By the heel of her boot, the officer kicked at where the lock would be.

BANG.

Rhyllae could feel her heart racing as the noise echoed down the hall.

"Lune," Sister Rhyllae prayed under her breath, "Shield us in your midnight cloak—"

BANG.

"—and protect us—"

BANG, and the wood cracked.

"—On this night of nights—"

BANG.

The doors flung themselves open with the last kick. They rattled in the frame from the force. But no one moved forward, for standing before them were dozens upon dozens of the serene-faced mannequins. Gears whirled as they turned to face the newcomers like owls.

"—By your grace, I pray."

Chapter 17

FOX ON A TIN ROOF

"BRIBERY?! HE WOULDN'T." DIDO'S VOICE ECHOED out in the desert night air.

The situation was spiraling out of the satyr's control, and seeing the general's left hand inch toward the hilt of his Silver Star did little to calm her nerves. Aramis reached behind his back and flung his arm out; a packet sailed through the air with a wire loop attached to it. An ethereal song rang out as Korzha unsheathed the singing blade and caught the dangling loop with ease. Korzha gave it to Dido, still keeping an eye on the Silver Fox, who, she realized, was without his new cloak.

"Play it," Aramis said.

In her tiny hands was a rectangular stick with buttons along its edge. Her grandfather used to hunt these contraptions down centuries ago, back when the Fae first opened their borders to this material plane. She used to gaze upon the souvenirs when she was a young kid.

What simpler times. Pressing play, the cartridge played out voices: Korzha's and another, metallic and insidious. The same voices she heard from before, but they were in the prophet's tongue.

"How did you translate this?" Dido asked.

Aramis waggled his fingers. "Magic."

"*Revenge,*" came Korzha's words from the box. "*Provide me the means of my enemies' destruction, and he is all yours. What of you? To what reward do you obtain from all of this.*"

"Ah, revenge." Aramis waggled his index finger up in the air, a dark grin splayed across his face. "Of *your* enemies." He pointed at the general; then he gave a half-hearted chuckle. "But not ours." That smile faded when he said, "Funny how that works, is it not, General?"

Surprise upon surprise, Korzha took the accusation well. He leveled the blade at the Silver Fox, though he hadn't taken on a dueling stance ... yet.

"Please. Believe it or not, the world doesn't revolve around you," Korzha told him in the cold desert air. "You're an asset to this company, mind. Though, I would love to have your expertise in this mission, you and I are expendable to the cause."

"Expendable?!" Aramis shouted.

"*Ascension.*"

There it is, that damnable word that broke Myrtle's spell, Dido thought.

"Yes, expendable!" Korzha shouted back. "You know full well who we're up against. These Djinnasian Lords are no mere mortals where we can stain the ground with their blood! I will and shall use every inch and pound of our resources to bring their end."

"*Ascension*"

"Even bartering you," Korzha added.

"Ascension" came the final phrase, sounded as if the speaker was right by Dido's ear.

Dido's stomach dropped like a stone. *No. It can't be.*

"Even bartering me. Would you?" Korzha blinked twice and then looked at Dido. "Do you mind?"

Dido didn't need to turn it off, for the tape spun free from the box. Mindlessly, she cast it aside. The matter was graver than anticipated. Graver than the Azure Lord, even.

"Thank you," Korzha said.

"No, thank you," Aramis said as he unsheathed his blades. "I see now that you find the Jessenters nothing more than chattel in your eyes. To think I trusted you."

"Yes. To think."

Both men stood on the balls of their feet, a perfect mirror of shadow and light. The Silver Star ringing out in the air between them as the twin blades glimmered in the moonlight. In a blink, they raced toward each other. In another blink, Dido teleported herself between the two of them. Her fingers twisted and jutted during her incantation; then she splayed them out wide.

"*Levitacija!*"

The Silver Fox, the Jessenter general, and the mage were enveloped in crystalline light.

They flew the doors open, but the mannequins stood there, with their arms bent at the perfect 90-degree angle. Sister Rhyllae finished her prayer and held her breath. Whatever spiritual shield she would muster wouldn't be able to halt all of their bullets. Dawn even ducked behind her shield for the oncoming onslaught. But nothing happened.

All of the sudden, the machines turned their hands so the palms would face each other. They stomped on their left high-heel molded foot, followed by a stomp on their right, and ended it all with a solid clap of their hands. Stomp, stomp, clap. Stomp, stomp, clap. The mechanized dolls of war repeated the curious dance before them with no end in sight.

"What ... are they doing?" Shayla asked.

"They're dancing?" Natasha asked.

Rhyllae and Dawn exchanged looks and said, "Aramis," at the same time.

"Aramis?"

"The Silver Fox!" a young voice said.

A tiny blob of shadow stepped in front of the warriors and then unfurled itself. Materializing before them was the kid who journeyed with Aramis, his dirty blonde hair ruffled from the fabric.

"You're alive!" Rhyllae cried out and, without a forethought, pushed past the warriors to embrace him. "Thank the Morning Lord and the motherly Lune above that you're safe!"

Most kids would resist such open affection, but this time was the exception. He wrapped his arms around her neck and said, "I'm glad you and Dawn are safe."

"Celune!"

A woman pushed her way through the warriors. Immediately the kid separated himself from the sister. There was no doubt who she was, for they shared the same brows and nose, but the woman's was more severe. The kid's face was flushed red, and he tightened his lips, but there was no retort. Oh, how it broke the sister's heart to see him in silent fury and shame.

"Celune," Dora said again. "Where have you been? I thought you were dead."

"He was the one that found us," Dawn said as she put her shield away.

"He?!"

"Yeah, *he*." Dawn crossed her arms. "Ya got a problem with that?"

Dora looked between Dawn and him, her disgust apparent on her face. The kid held his breath and cringed for the rebuttal that must have been given many times before. Rhyllae took a step in front of him and eyed the woman. She would be his shield if need be.

"I'm glad you made your way back home," said Hashim, his voice a welcoming break in the tension. "And for telling the Silver Fox of our plight."

"Yeah," Natasha spoke up with a grin. "Nice going, kid, but how did you get these metal monsters to, you know?" She waved her hand at the mannequins, still stomping and clapping in their ceaseless dance.

"The Silver Fox gave this to me." He held up a slender green chip laced in gold and a curious metal stick attached to one end. "He said that the monsters hear the leader's command at a pitch we can't hear. So he made this thing sing, and its song made them dance this way."

"Like some sort of faerie dance!"

"Where's Aramis?" Rhyllae asked.

"He said, 'he's going take care of business.' Whatever that means."

The lieutenant and the priestess looked at each other, this time with dread.

The blinding light dissipated. Aramis found himself levitating several feet horizontal to the ground, with his twin daggers right below him. It took all of his effort to turn his head to find the lanky the rebel general in a similar compromising position. There floating vertically between them was Dido. Her curly locks radiated skyward as her entire body glimmered in an eerie, rosy aura. Her horns were encased in ivy while Baby's Breath dotted every which way from her goatish fur. Aramis sharply inhaled when he saw her eyes cast in the same rose hue that surrounded her. Oh, how he forgot she was a creature beyond their mortal realm and not some mortal faun.

"Good, you're awake," Dido said, her voice was still the same melodic timber, yet the resonance was unearthly.

"Okay, Firebird," Aramis said. "What do you plan to do, tickle us?"

Dido giggled, and the sound bounced around all of them, making Aramis suspect they were enveloped in some sort of bubble. "No. But I will have you listen, both of you." Her ethereal visage turned her head at General Korzha.

"We are pressed for time, Madame Satyr; say your piece and let us be done with it," the general quipped.

Aramis was surprised to find him sulking. Whatever words that were exchanged between the two were already dealt with by the time Aramis came to.

"It concerns the mannequins, our common foe. They have become sentient."

"Bullshit," Aramis spat out the words.

Korzha rolled his eyes. "Clearly, you've never heard of Pinocchio."

"It's all a performance, believe me, I've read the codes the Ancients instilled in them. These Ancients are able to command these creatures to mimic humans in all mannerisms. How to walk, talk, dance—everything, but they lack true consciousness."

"True," Dido's ethereal voice chimed in. "While they lack a soul, Aramis, they are able to think for themselves. That in itself is enough to determine them 'sentient', according to the Faerie Court."

The Silver Fox narrowed his eyes. "Artificial intelligence?"

"Pardon?" Korzha asked.

Aramis glanced over for permission, to which Dido nodded.

"The Ancients wanted a machine that could think for themselves, by themselves," Aramis explained. "Otherwise, they would have to craft endless slates of commands with no time for themselves. Thus, they created machines that learned from their environment with logic. Rote behavior done for the sake of completing mundane requests, no matter the cost. It backfired and brought the Ancients a taste of their own destructive medicine."

"Logic without wisdom? Perhaps the Ancients were indeed fools to create such creatures."

"But these still can't create their own objectives; machines need input to run tasks. Someone has to give it to them."

"They do," Dido countered. "Their queen."

"You have to be kidding me."

Dido tsked as she narrowed her unearthly gaze. "Mr. Feres."

It took a moment or two before Aramis recognized how he erred with her disapproval. Then his eyes brightened from the realization that the term referred to such an animalistic behavior. He mumbled, "sorry," and glanced away.

"Yes. It must be the girl," Korzha said. "That banshee is at the root cause of all of this."

"Girl?" Aramis asked.

"She appeared before me as such, a child in a pinafore dress with disheveled hair. I suspected she was their leader when her scream ordered them to fire and thus brokered our deal."

"You mean…" Then the light of recognition flared in Aramis's eyes. "Her! She appeared when I was locating the Bedouins. You sold me to her?!"

"To end our plight from our Djinnasian foe and save this entire nation? Yes."

"There won't be a world to save if we delay," Dido said in a dejected voice. "This queen, as a soul possessing these host of machines, used magic."

Horror stricken, both of the men were silent.

"No," Aramis finally whispered. "They couldn't… That's impossible."

"You heard her from before: 'Ascension.' That word was used to hijack Myrtle's summoning ritual."

"Myrtle? Ritual?" Aramis asked as he eyed the general, who only gave him a cautious side-eye. "Something tells me it's far worse than what you're laying down."

Korzha merely cast his icy blue eyes aside.

Dido explained, "I was set upon by a fellow mage, and she tapped into the eldritch powers that be. But the Mannequin Queen took over by that magical word and is now pulling the Azure Lord into our world."

"That's worse."

"Which is why I must ask the two of you to stop this nonsense and help me close this summoning vortex. Or this world would be torn asunder!" Dido hopped at the last word; the motion from her outstretched arms caused the two men to levitate higher in the air.

Aramis steeled his gaze at the Töskan. "So much for your bargain."

Korzha rolled his eyes. "A typical test, I assure you. She'll comply when we have proven our survival."

Aramis scoffed. "If we make it out alive. Truce until we end this queen?"

"Yes. Truce."

In a blink, Aramis could feel the paralyzing hold on his muscles; in the next, they were dropped from the sky. Korzha tried to land on his feet but collapsed to his knees from the soft impact. Aramis tucked and rolled on his sides to disperse the potential energy. Dido on the other hand floated to her hooves and shook her curly hair. The rosy aura dispersed, and she returned to her original self. At least, Aramis hoped, for all he knew this familiar visage could be one of her numerous glamours.

"Now, please tell me you have a plan of attack against this Azure Lord Yeorgu?" the general asked as he dusted himself off.

"Lord who-was-it?" came a brassy female voice.

They turned and found Dawn a few feet away, her gladius blade unsheathed in one hand and the other holding the door open to the stairwell. The tribespeople, ragged and weary, streamed out to join the trio on this rooftop. Then Rhyllae finally emerged. The moment she saw Aramis she dropped the square mallet in her hands and ran into his arms. He kissed her full on the lips, not caring about the scattered gasps from the Bedouins standing there. And neither did Rhyllae, for she leaned into the kiss as if it was her last.

"Shutte found us," Rhyllae said when they parted. "Then there was a massive presence I couldn't shake. What happened?"

"Never mind that for now; we need to get the people out of here," Aramis said.

Dawn shook her head. "How are we going to do that with the rest of their army? Your little dancing curse has its limits."

"If that is what I think it is," Korzha piped up once his pale blue eyes seized on the device. "Can you broadcast it?"

"Perhaps," Aramis answered.

He looked about on the rooftop as he scratched his stubbled chin, truly scant on resources from what he could see. There were metal domes with slits sitting on ventilation in every which way. There were two shack-like protrusions, one of which the tribe came from. The other offered rock-hard tub of tar, brushes, and a tall metal pole with branches at the end shoved into a corner. The Silver Fox exclaimed a happy cackle as he rustle the latter out of the storage.

Pleased to see him at work, Korzha turned to Dawn and Dido. "Once the Silver Fox disables the machines, we'll evacuate the people off of this roof. Would you have enough magical reserve for the Azure Lord?"

Dido stammered. Aramis couldn't blame her; the Lord Azure was of a plane far beyond the Faerie realms, cold and distant as the stars above. How could anyone solve the problem of an eldritch lord coming into their existence?

As if he heard, a surge of terror and ancient writ heaved from below them. Both Dido and the Rhyllae fell to their knees.

"This Azure dude is what's causing all of this?" Dawn asked.

"A magical portal had been hijacked by the leader of the mannequins, their queen. Thanks to her 'invitation,' a 'Lord of the Stars' decided to show themself," Aramis rattled off as he helped Rhyllae to her feet. "That's why we need the people out of here. Shutte!"

Aramis waved his hand up. The kid, recognizing what he meant, tossed the tiny contraption that had enthralled the machines into a dancing frenzy. Once in the palm of his hands, Aramis tore into it, all the pieces popped out and reassembled by his quick, nimble fingers.

"There's only one lord, and that is the Lord of Mornings," Rhyllae said and made a growling grunt as she wiped the dirt off of her vestments.

"Tell that to the eldritch being downstairs," Dawn said.

Aramis halted in his movements. "Wait, she can! Technically, Azure was a deity."

Dido gasped. "That's right. There used to be a small sect who made sacrificial offerings for their 'guidance.'"

"Used to?" Dawn asked.

"When the world was colorless, right after the world fell."

"Are you telling me that our sister here can banish this eldritch being alone?" Korzha asked.

"More than that! She can seal it." Aramis clipped a fresh wire from his pack and started binding the larger metal stick to the lesser.

Rhyllae nodded. "As decreed by the Sleeper, no other deity shall govern over this world save for the Sun and his sister, Lune. That includes this ... thing. In their holy name, I will do everything in my power to cast them out."

Dawn smiled. "Get it, girl."

"Casting out the Azure Lord is one thing, but sealing it is another," Dido bemoaned. "I won't have the energy after secreting the people out of here."

"You won't have to," Aramis said. "We'll use Solomon's Seal."

With a flick on his wrist, the contraption started beeping.

Act 4

The cloud blossoms in view
Thunderous and bruised
It claps in rage and fury
She changes the dial

Orchestral music swells as the sun rises
"The Dune-Thŭr mountains. Home to a slew of creatures
"But none are as ferocious as the Eagles dwelling there
"Wingspans of seventy meters long, they soar high—"

"Cynthia, turn that off!"
The image collapses
His reflection looms over
Raindrops fall on the pane

Chapter 18

SOLOMON'S SEAL

It started small. Down the stairs whispered the faint telltale stomping and clapping. Then it grew into a thunderous roar from the windows below as it progressed throughout the building. Until at last, there was a din of mechanical dancing that deafened the twilight sky. Every mannequin as far as the eye could see was ensnared by the Silver Fox's technological curse.

"That is our cue. Dido!" Korzha commanded.

Both he and the lieutenant corralled the tribespeople into a line for their deployment. Aramis and Sister Rhyllae embraced Shutte, no doubt to give him reassurance of their safety. Dido pitied them when the child's mother yanked him away from their comforting embrace.

Yet, Dido stood still, neither to follow through the command or to comfort the couple. The satyr mage wanted to know how Aramis knew such things. Not the ancient knowledge of the Ancients, it was well known that the Silver Fox was burdened with such secrets. But this! Magic largely prohibited by the doctrines of the Faerie order. Magic that could entrap all supernatural creatures. No one, save for Sulmaith the Wise, should've known.

"How?" the question squeaked out of Dido's lips.

"Hm?" Aramis grunted.

"Dido?" Korzha called upon her again.

She ignored him. "How do you know about Solomon's Seal?"

Aramis shrugged—shrugged! "I read it in a book somewhere."

"Which one?"

The Silver Fox contorted his face. She knew the answer before he said it, "I don't remember."

A magical surge rose from below, rocking Dido and Rhyllae to their knees from the incredible weight of their power. Power beyond the stars and of this Earth.

I'm running out of time.

"How many people do you need?" Dido asked Aramis.

"Three," Aramis answered.

"Any time, Dido!" Korzha cried out to her, his patience running out.

Maybe it was her nerves being wrecked from all that had occurred, but Dido snapped her fingers with no further hesitation. In an instant all of them by the roof's edge were encased in several pink bubbles. All, save for three: Aramis, Dido, and Rhyllae. The general looked on in shock and banged the wall with the bottom of his fist.

"We'll meet once this is over," she told him.

Dido twirled in a full circle, gathering the wind about her. From her satchel, Dido produced a pinwheel with red paper, printed with Nagano flowers. With a single blow from her lips, the wheel turned, and the spell was cast. All the bubbles floated away from the gust of wind.

"You could've done that earlier," Aramis commented.

"Would that stop you?"

Aramis exhaled and looked away.

"Thought so."

"Alright, Aramis," Rhyllae said as she snugged tight her hajib about her head. "How do you want to do this?"

Aramis in turn yanked off his mask and cowl. His head was encased by a silvery pall. "It'll be no different than the Maelstrom, except we'll be adding a new addendum right before you cast them out. This would be chanted between Dido and me, while you recite the Holy Words of Expulsion. But first, we need to draw out the runes."

Aramis took out a sliver of paper and scrawled upon it letters that Dido could guess came from the time of the Sleeper's waking. There was some potency from them, even from such a rough sketch, giving her the confidence that this harebrained idea might work. By Dido's guidance, she and Aramis were able to situate the runes in a circle with a six-pointed star that interlaced itself. Within each space of the circle were ancient symbols. To Dido's eyes, they were merely shorthand for a magical barrier integrated into a well.

Once written, Dido summoned three rings of protection stones. Six of the greenest turquoise spheres for the inner angles, six black obsidian arrows at each point of the star, and a dozen short, black tourmaline pillars in equidistance from the outer circle.

Aramis whistled, for the weight and size of these stones cost a fortune.

"A lot of mouths could've been fed with all this," Rhyllae said in awe.

"I'm only borrowing them for the night," Dido said.

"That's a shame," said Aramis. "Would've been useful."

"You know how Fae currency works; it won't last. Now, sister, do you have jasper on you?"

Rhyllae nodded and pulled out her twin fang periapt of poisoning. Dido remembered how in the depths of the catacombs, the magical amulet saved the Morning priestess from the doppelgänger queen's cruel game.

"Good," Dido said. "You're facing off an Azure Lord, and that means you need a color that's strong enough against the color blue itself."

Rhyllae furrowed her thin eyebrows upward. "What words are you going to use, Aramis? If it goes against the Morning Lord's doctrine—"

"—It won't," Aramis assured. "Solomon was a king, sage, and philosopher. Trust me on this. Please." He added as he looked at them both.

Both women inhaled and exhaled to calm their nerves. So much could go wrong. The ritual circle could break, and the eldritch lord could take them as blood sacrifices. Or worse, open another portal to who knows where. Yet, the magic from these runes on the floor underneath her hooves were solid. Moreover, there was a flash of clarity in Aramis's eyes that Dido couldn't shake.

Keeper of secrets, indeed.

"I believe in you," Dido finally said.

"And I you," said Rhyllae.

She reached out and gave his hand a squeeze. Aramis squeezed it back. The night sky shifted into a shade of violet around them. The lights flickered to a dimmed warmth, and the air became heavy. Even the cacophony of dancing metal feet was stifled to a faint hum.

A voice, thin and stretched, frosted their ears. "Fooolsss. You daaare challenge me? Meeee, Lord of the Silver Streams and of the Voooid beyooond?"

"Back, you creature of the night!" spat the sister of the Morn.

A halo of soft candescent light glowed about all three of them, gentle as moonlight.

Lune! Dido realized. Even in her waxing phase, her power was potent.

Rhyllae continued with all the righteous rage pent up within her, "I am a servant of the Morning and Evening Sun, daughter of the Iridescent Moon, and sister to all that is good on this green Earth. You're trespassing into this realm. Begone!"

A crack popped in all of their ears, from which source, Dido couldn't tell.

"Begone and return from whence you came!"

The pressure seemed to give way. Aramis smiled, but Dido knew better. This was the rollback of the tide before it heaved its fury upon the shore. Drawing a pentagram in the air, Dido cast another shielding array. This time as a globe at the edge of the tourmaline crystals. And just in time, too. As soon as it settled, the Azure Lord slapped its might against it. The sheer weight of it brought Dido to her furry knees.

"Here." Aramis offered his hand and lifted her up on her feet. "Hold on to Rhyllae. Remember, the three of us represent Mind, Body, and Soul."

Dido quickly took the priestess's hand. "You sure this is strong enough?"

"It has to be."

"It will be." Rhyllae gave both of their hands a firm squeeze. Then she fell into a trance. Her lips murmuring in her Lord's prayers. Not prayers of goodness and light, but of fire and might.

Gusts of wind encircled the protective circle. The environment was altered before her very eyes. What was a rooftop of ancient concrete and tar was becoming a shadowy void.

No, not shadow, Dido realized, *it was darkness beyond darkest pitch*. The Azure Lord was not only bringing himself into their world, he was bringing in the very fabric of space! Looming over them was a form so shapeless and maddening the little satyr wanted to scream.

"Focus!" Aramis yanked Dido's hand, causing her to look at him dead in the eyes. They looked like silver pools of mercury in this realm of darkness. "Eyes on me. Don't give up."

The winds howled as the Azure Lord increased his furious onslaught. The volume overwhelmed the prayer Rhyllae had been reciting. All three of them hunched from the battering winds.

"Don't give up!" Aramis cried out.

Courage, came a small inner voice.

My Queen? Dido wondered. How long had it been since she heard such a soothing voice?

Have courage, Dido.

A fresh scent of sea salt washed over her senses. The smell took Dido back to her youth in Greece, where mortals and Fae alike bound over their love of sailing the Gallileah sea before it spilled into the Faerie Rift. Dido shook herself awake and steeled her nerves. The Summer Queen had always been a friend and ally to the Morning Lord. The tiny satyr mage could not falter here.

"Betwixt dusk and twilight," Dido recited.

"Shall well-spring sprung

"Under cloven delight

"Mab's Faerie Mound."

It worked, despite it all. The primordial expanse gave way to grassy blades. The gusts settled to a gentle breeze, and the night was dotted by skimming fireflies. The satyr mage had brought a piece of the Fae into this fight.

"Ho, ha, ha, ah" came that insidious creaking. "Do you know whose power you wield? The power given to the Faerie Queens are mine own! For using it against me, I shall break you."

Dido could feel the coldness of the starry expanse unraveling the edges of the illusory environment.

"Hurry!" Dido asked of Aramis. "The buffer won't last for long. If you're going to do the ritual, you have to do it now!"

Aramis hardened his gaze and nodded. "Then repeat after me. Creator of creation. Deity of Deities, I call upon you with my voice..."

A strange red hue surrounded him as he continued. "I call upon you by my thoughts..."

Then Dido found her aura glowing but in a sapphire color. *Oh no. Not blue!*

But Dido continued the spell ritual. If broken, the rapid release of such power would surely slice them into pieces.

"I call upon you with my heart," Aramis said, and Rhyllae, still in her meditative trance, was traced in a saffron hue. "To guide me and redouble my efforts in sealing this evil before me."

The twin triangles that formed the hexagram shone in ethereal light. Not golden light like the Morning Lord's, or moonlight like Lune's, but prismatic, as if the various colors of the universe jostled in excitement.

Raw creative power, Dido realized, *the power of the Sleeper. Is this why Aramis was encouraged to go on this mission? Not to fight against the mannequins, but to do this? To assert the Sleeper's will?*

"Now, it's on Rhyllae," Aramis said. "With each push from her, we send up one of the seals. Got it?"

"We can't wait on her," Dido countered.

"We have to," Aramis said, and a huff of cold vapor escaped from his lips.

Dido felt a coldness welling in her chest. The satyr mage gasped, and a breath of cold air escaped from hers as well. Frost crystalized on her horns and lashes. The last remnants of the Faerie mound dissipated. Darkness beyond the blackest pitch surrounded them once again. Now the vastness of space and the void beyond pressed against her starry shield. She could see Aramis telling her something, but she couldn't hear the words leaving his mouth. Her satyr ears only heard the deafening crack as the shield crumbled from the weight of the Azure Lord's might.

It's over, Dido thought as she felt the air pushed aside from the oncoming force.

But then a soft candescent light sparkled from the corner of her eye. It was Rhyllae. Her soft brown eyes fluttered as if waking up from a deep slumber. The light came from the starlight streaming from her brow.

"You hold no power here," the Morning Lord sister said.

Her words bore a weight that wasn't there before. An illuminating light shot forth from the top of her forehead and slammed against the insubstantial form of the Azure Lord. A surprised moan emanated around them as it showered over the three of them in a gentle moonlit glow.

"Back," Rhyllae commanded. "Back into the void where you belong."

A dreadful sound, deeper than any basal noise, rattled Dido's teeth. But the eldritch power was curtailed. The sister alone had forced this eldritch being back by sheer conviction and faith alone.

"Now!" Aramis shouted. "With the element of Earth, I seal *Thee* from this realm!"

Dido followed suit in the incantation. One of the obsidian arrows flew past her nose. She almost cried out in shock, but managed to hold her tongue. Her pride as a mage wouldn't allow such emotions to interfere with any ritual casting, and she snapped her mouth shut.

Her rosy eyes followed the arrow shot across the void and—lo!—a seam appeared. That obsidian arrow magically sealed a portion of that tear in place.

"Again!" Aramis encouraged.

Rhyllae recited, "In the name of the luminary lights, I command you to go back from whence you came!"

"With the element of Water, I seal *Thee* from this realm!" Aramis and Dido said in sync.

A frustrated groan and at last the starry night of the desert appeared along the horizon.

It's working. By the Summer Crown, it's working!

Another obsidian arrow fled, and she felt it—a weakening of the circle's magical thread. Dido felt her goat knees quake with dread.

What am I going to do? What can I do? If I stop now, if I held back this momentum, it would give Lord Yeorgu an inch. Dido shook her curly-horned head. *No, I must be brave. For my friends—they're counting on me.*

All three of them cast the elemental orders in rapid succession: wood, air, and fire. With every obsidian arrow, the starry night sky flooded into view from all sides. The deathly chill of the other dimension melted to a cool breeze. They could even hear the ruckus still ongoing by the never-tiring mannequins, though their numbers were depleted by the random lightning strikes that sprung from the dimensional rift.

Yet, there was no mistaking it, their protection circle was frail as a fishermen's net rotted by salt and sun.

"Aramis, if we let loose the last one, we'll be exposed," Dido said.

"The last one will end this nightmare for good. Trust me!" Aramis cried out.

"This is reckless! We need to set up another barrier."

To her surprise, he laughed. "We can't make an omelet without breaking a few eggs."

"I agree," Rhyllae said. "We have to finish this, or all will be for nothing."

They weren't wrong. The Azure Lord's etheric tendrils resided back into its hole, barely leaking from the astral tear. The starry night sky took on a violet turn as the cyclical morn begun to break.

"Okay," Dido conceded. "Once more."

Rhyllae nodded and closed her eyes. "In the name of the luminary lights, I command you to go back from whence you came!"

"By the element of Æther, I seal *Thee* from this realm!" came the last incantation from both the satyr and the Fox.

The last arrow shot from the magical circle and hurtled toward the Azure Lord.

Then it halted mid-air.

"What the?" Dido uttered. Then she saw her body gave an eerie glow. The blue that represented the Mind in this ritual became vibrant in a jewel-like tone, an Azure quality.

No!

Before Dido could react, the obsidian arrowhead that hovered in the sky hurtled back at them. It zipped through the barrier, shattering what little remained of its protection and punched right through Aramis's chest. His blood sprayed on the sacred runes, marring the ancient magical writ. The circle broke. One by one, all the turquoise and tourmaline crystals shattered into dust.

"Aramis!" Rhyllae cried out as she let go of Dido's hand and rushed to Aramis's side. When she lifted him up, there was a stream of ruby flowing from a puncture close to his heart.

"No. No! Stay with me, Aramis." The Morning Lord priestess told him, but Dido's heart sank as she watched as the color fled from his face.

That was all Dido saw before they were enveloped by a chaotic storm of indigo fog.

The sight was wild beyond imagining. Sheltered on top of a striated plateau, the Bedouins, Dawn, and Korzha witnessed the dark and angry sky manifest over the very building they once were in. The transport bubbles burst hours ago, and Hashim had the people set up a rudimentary camp. They all halted their efforts and came to the very edge to look on in awe. Doomtown, sprawling far in the distance, flickered and dimmed as this storm raged low to the horizon. Wild lightning struck haphazardly from its vortex, and all light faded.

Damn it, Dido, thought Tavian.

The general didn't want to abandon her and the others to this magical fight. Though what powers that dwelled within him might be insignificant against such an unnatural foe, Korzha would rather face it with his singing sword raised high above his head. Such fascinations of a righteous heart, he knew. In truth, the torch would've overwhelmed him with excruciating pain and paralyzed him from any action. But at times like these, looking on to that stormy visage, it was hard to quell the righteous spirit.

"Fuck me," Dawn muttered. She stood by his side from the very beginning. It was hard to ignore those flashes of light that pierced the horizon. "Do you think they'll make it?"

"Fate could only tell," was his reply.

"They will," said Shayla. She tucked her arms into the folds of her tunic to shelter them from the evening chill. "The Silver Fox is with them. He's cunning enough to free us from the Djinnasi hold. He'll be cunning enough to help fight this creature. All will be well in the end."

Dawn's hazel eyes met with his pale blue eyes. Such words of comfort would normally be true if it weren't for the fact that Aramis was undeniably mortal. The doppelgänger proved it to them as such when they barged in that frightful day. Tavian couldn't forget Feres lying there broken like the shattered glass that surrounded him.

Yet, he did live. All thanks to Sister Rhyllae. She was there with him, and that gave the general heart.

"Courage, Lieutenant," Korzha said, then turned his gaze to the menace on the horizon. "Courage for our friends."

They stood in vigilant silence as the storm worsened and crackled with eldritch energy.

"Come," Shayla said to Dawn. "Let us pray to the Morning Lord for his guidance."

The young officer hesitated but gave in when Korzha nodded to her to join them. What was there to do but to hope and pray?

"You're welcome to join us, General," the mother offered.

"Thank you, but no. I don't not share your people's religious fervor," replied Korzha.

Shayla looked at Dawn for answers while the lieutenant stifled a laugh. "He meant worship."

That seemed to soothe her over, and they left him by the overlook. He didn't have to watch them to know how they communed with their Sun deity. They would lay down their shawls and kneel on both knees, their faces to the East as they bowed to let their foreheads kiss the dirt in reverence.

But not him, for the blood of his mother's people flowed in his veins. Though their gods were dead, and they lived in the Time of Mortals, they had prayers of their own. Prayers to join their ancestors in their halls of valor. Halls that were built by forgotten giants of yore.

And so, Tavian Korzha drew his blade and pierced it deep in the clay Earth. On one bent knee, he affixed his steely gaze on the madness that raged there before him.

Hurry. Hurry and fight. He prayed to his compatriots. *Send it back to the abyss where it belongs. Get up again, if it beats you down. Get up and carry on until your foe gave way to your blade and metal. Beat it back to the abyss until nothing of it is left of its being but dust and ruin!*

A thunderclap echoed across the surroundings.

Fight, he urged, *this is not over yet.*

He, who bore this vision, heard his call.

The world shifted and turned from the sight. The Bedouins prostrating on the ruddy plateau shrunk to the size of ants until they became nothing more than a wink. The sight flew north, not east. Over the sand dunes of Ioun. Over the shimmering plains of glass. Then it rose into the clouds to pass the calamitous peaks of the Galileah Mountain range. All vision had been obscured by the white fog of pubescent water vapors until at last it broke over the lush and green country of Töska.

Then the sight dove with speed that not even birds dare achieve.

Oak and maple trees hurtled into view as dots of hamlets and cottages decorated its emerald beauty. Then the world enlarged, focused on a lake by a meadow until that was all it encompassed in its vision. A field of posies, descendants of the scorched Earth, came to view. In it, a team of horses lay on the grassy knoll near a rustic wagon. Two people sat by the smoldering fire, wrapped with heavy horse blankets.

They were not whom he needed. No. The vision bearer seized upon the wagon and dropped down. He plummeted through the boughs of the overhanging trees and through the smoke of the campfire. It pierced through the canvas of the wagon where the dark beauty slept.

Myrrh.

Her body and long black hair splayed haplessly over blankets and makeshift pillows as she slumbered. Her bare breasts heaved with every disquieted breath. Face-to-face, the vision came to her, enough to see the sweat on her thin, sculpted brow.

Get up and fight, he relayed.

Lavander-gray eyes flashed open.

Chapter 19

SULMAITH THE WISE

Dawn was bent over so as to let her forehead kiss the earth. She rose along with the rest of the religious few, her mother included, to sit on the back of their heels. She didn't want to do this with them, since a few of them had given her grief when she came out as a lesbian. But her friends were in danger—no, the whole world was in danger. The young lieutenant must put aside her grievances for the sake of the whole, yet she found her mind wandering.

Of all things, Dawn's mind turned to Tsuki, her belle far from this conflict. It had been days since she entered the magic portal that spat out Sister Rhyllae. Somewhere, she was out there traversing the green hills of Töska, finding the root of the Faerie Court's displeasure with Dido. Though the general explained his reasoning, Dawn wished Tsuki had stayed with them. If not to solve this brewing storm, then to provide each other comfort as the world faded.

Before the world ends, my Morning Lord, I would like to see my beautiful moon princess one last time.

Dawn pressed her forehead to the clay earth and rose. A flutter of white, far to the north where the mountains rove, caught her eye. It grew in size as she stared. Wings glided through leagues of sand and dunes before it majestically flapped against the wind.

"What is it, Dawn?" Shayla asked of her.

"I... think it's her."

Dawn didn't explain any further as she stood up from the dusty mound. She wandered to the edge, next to the general, her breath held tight in her chest.

Korzha stirred and rose from his own prayer stance. His icy blue eyes flicked from the avian omen to the lieutenant. "Is that who I think it is?"

"I sure hope so."

It was no mirage. What was fast approaching them was indeed a bird, not any avian creature, but a phoenix. Her luminous, white feathers rippled against her slight frame like flaming torches charging. Her entire frame was tailored for speed: long legs, a long neck, and wings curved to allow her to spin and bank at a precise degree. Dawn should know, she rode on her back before.

"Tsuki!" Dawn cried out in joy. She knew she was supposed to keep it a secret, a sacred legendary bird that walked among mortals. But her enthusiasm in this dark hour had won out over logic.

The mighty phoenix rotated her wings in a figure-eight motion, allowing herself to hover as she lowered herself to the ground. In her clutches was the esteemed Mother Superior Myrrh. Her lithe, tall body limped over with a mere gossamer gown to clothe her. Many didn't approach the mystical, fiery bird, fearing the heat the firebird might produce, but the general was no coward. Korzha rushed under the radiant phoenix and eased the Superior from her tender claws. Shayla grabbed one of the prayer shawls from the dusty clay and wrapped herself in it.

"She's alive and unharmed," Korzha said once he checked her over. "What happened?"

"I don't know how or why, but I'm glad you're here." Dawn caressed Tsuki's head and neck in this world. She nuzzled her pointed beak at Dawn's sweet spot behind her ear. Despite it all, she giggled.

"You know this bird, Dawn?" Hashim asked.

"Yeah, this is my lady lover, Tsuki."

Everyone looked on in confusion, save for Korzha. With the test he had set, Tsuki ended up revealing her true form. It took him a precious bundle of silk to appease Tsuki's haughty temper, and they were able to plot together as peers.

Korzha approached slowly as he kept his gaze upon the phoenix. "You coming here is nothing short of a miracle, madame. We are in dire need of your services."

Tsuki cocked her head, her big brown eyes glistening with inner knowing.

"Our friends are in danger," Dawn hopped in. "Aramis, Rhyllae, and Dido, they're in that cloud over there."

The young lieutenant pointed at that angry cloud brewing in the distance and purple streaks of lightning rolling over like veins over bone.

On the wind, Tsuki could smell the erratic magic streaming from it. The smell reminded her of another time, long ago in one of her lives, where such magic spilled out from an incredible force, a time when Sulmaith walked on this earth.

THE MANNEQUIN QUEEN

The sun streamed through the teardrop windows, alighting the various herbs, crystals, and paints in all manner of oddly shaped wooden bowls strewn over a marbled table. Old, broad hands deftly picking the leaves and seeds into a mortar in every which direction as he hummed a jingle.

Happy. Content. Confident. Feelings Aramis hadn't felt in a long, long time. The smell of nutmeg was the freshest he had ever smelled!

Then the tune stopped briefly as his finger jabbed on the open book. Those well-worn pages were stained with all manners of incantations, sigils, and runes. The wealth of magic here could make Dido's head spin. But the one the old man pointed at was written in pencil: Suza's Lamb Marinade.

"Salt and pepper. Yes. Course, of course," the old man said.

The elderly sage repeated the words, "salt and pepper" as he bent over and rummaged through the various glass jars of saffron, sage, and citrus rinds—of all things. In his fumbling, he found the jar of salt. But his old age had failed him, and it tipped and started to roll away. He stooped to catch it as it fell over the edge.

A close one, thought Aramis. Or was it this man?

That was when the old man caught a glance of himself in the mirror. His hair was wild and white. His skin leathery with a pronounced chiseled nose. His eyes, a pale gray with hint of blue like that of a coming storm. The mirror was a tiny model meant for soul displacement. How Aramis knew that he didn't have the faintest idea.

"Oh?" The man's pale eyes then widened in the mirror as he spoke. "Oh. Yes, I see. I see. You think this is the end, don't you?"

Aramis gasped. Only one human could intuit such a situation such as this: Sulmaith the Wise.

The mirror reflected the apple of his cheek bobbing up from Sulmaith's smirk. "Yes, I know who you are. You're one from me. Well... Of me." His soft, wrinkled skin twitched as he winked at himself. Or to be fair, at Aramis. Somehow, the old Sage knew it was the Silver Fox looking from within.

"As all hope fails you, and the darkness rolls in, you think this is the end, hmm?" the last word went up an octave as a teacher would with a student.

Oh, how Aramis felt shame wash over him. How could I not? I died... Haven't I?

"But it's not. No! No, no, no," Sulmaith said as he tapped the mirror. "It has not! When it's dark, all you need is a little spark to light things up. Ah!" He gazed upward, and the thought came to him. "Phoenix feathers is what you need. Two." He held up his two stubby fingers. "But no more than that. Don't want Tsuki to be mad at you." Then he chuckled.

Tsuki? Aramis wondered, What does she have to do with this?

But Sulmaith didn't answer him. "Two and start over again. Not from the top, mind." The sage eyed at his reflection. "When you're near the end, you start at the beginning of the end. Hmph. Yes. Yes... Near the end of all things."

This time, Sulmaith looked down at his hands. Aramis could feel the ache in those joints. Aches that would come to haunt him soon as the Silver Fox aged. Not even jhasins could run away from such a natural thing, no matter the magic.

But it wasn't age that made Aramis anxious. This was the past, long before the Demon Djinn Bazzuu rose from the depths. If he could tell Sulmaith what would happen. Maybe...

Somehow Sulmaith heard, for he looked at the mirror in a jerk. "But away with you. Go on now. Away."

He waved his fingers. Aramis could feel himself drifting back. Away from the kooky old man with his spices and herbs. Away from the sunny days of Iounport, long before its name was changed, and the times past. Into the dark blue of midnight and death.

Far in the heart of the Iounese desert, in the south of the glass plains, in the whirlwind of smoke and despair, Aramis found himself back into his broken body. Held by his beloved Rhyllae as she tried to fuel the healing powers of the Morning Lord. A water filling a sieve for all its worth. In this darkness, he could feel the incredible power of Lord Azure buffering against them.

In this indigo, Aramis was numbed with despair. All promises made would be sundered by this wild magic and the mechanizations of the Mannequin Queen.

How can we get out of this one?

And yet, in this darkness, a light.

Not of the Morning Lord or Lune.

Not of the Faerie Court.

This light was of pure creation, a spark of spiritual might of a phoenix.

His sluggish eyelids beheld the radiant sight. There the magical bird unfurled its white-hot wings to hover before the amazed priestess and satyr mage.

Two should do it, Sulmaith's words came to him, *no more...*

Aramis didn't know how, but he managed to raise his blood-drained arm up. His fingers twitched in its ascent. The fiery bird lowered her head to nuzzle his palm, her sharp beak smooth and warm under his touch. Then his strength failed him, and his arm slumped back to his side. The world spun before him. His breath labored as he smelled Rhyllae's sandalwood scent from her cloth.

Well, this is nice to die from, thought Aramis. *How many can say they were graced by a phoenix's presence? Ruth would flip when she heard this.*

His breathing slowed, and the world settled. Granted by this last gift, he once again could see the phoenix. She was closer now, her warm brown eyes reflecting the chaos surrounding them. *Beautiful*, he thought as the phoenix inched her beak closer to his shoulder.

Then the radiant bird jabbed into his flesh.

Aramis didn't have the strength to cry out. That sharp beak reopened his wound, closed thanks to Rhyllae's efforts. Then with another nauseating jab, it seized on the dreadful arrow that pierced next to his heart. With a gut-wrenching pull, the phoenix yanked the offending stone out of him.

Sister Rhyllae, bless her, tried to shoo away the sacred bird.

Was that a tear down her face? Or were those cheeks always wet?

Then Dido stopped her. His ears were deafened from his heart racing from the unexpected surgery, preventing him from hearing what the women were saying to each other. But that didn't matter now; something soft and warm glowed in his hand.

In his clutches were three phoenix feathers. How Aramis managed such a feat, he couldn't quite fathom. But now he felt the wave of magic melding into his body. For that is what jhasin were, magically constructed beings. The powers of the Zemzem springs could never change that fact.

Stranger still were the words. Words that had driven him throughout the ritual. Words that were spoken beyond him. Aramis swore he never heard of them in his life, but they leaked out of him like oil from a press. Perhaps, this too was part of Sulmaith's magic.

"With the element of Æther, I seal *Thee* from this realm," Aramis whispered.

The feathers glowed brilliantly out of the corner of his eyes. The obsidian arrow rattled in the phoenix's jaw. Aramis could see the avian legend open her mouth in a gasp. Dido's lips moved in what Aramis hoped was a repeat to what he said.

The phoenix opened her beak with a cry. The obsidian flew into the magical storm above and was enveloped by its menacing clouds. The ground heaved, and lightning raged about them. But it worked. Aramis could feel the pressure dissipating, replaced by the innocent chill of dawn. Soon, the violet clouds and their fury faded with the wind. Skies of robin-egg blue and blushes of rose graced the heavens. It was as if it were a passing nightmare.

He could hear the girls cry out in joy. Aramis laughed with them, before he slumped over. Everything faded into velvet-soft sleep.

"How is he doing?" asked a brassy female voice.

"He's been coming in and out," answered the melodic one.

Dawn? Rhyllae?

Aramis wanted to groan his displeasure. He never had a wink of sleep ever since he left the Fox Burrow, all thanks to his insomnia, but here they were, talking away.

"And the Mother Superior?" the young lieutenant asked.

"Remarkably fine, besides the..."

"Besides?"

"Oh, look he's awake," the sister exclaimed a little too loudly for his ears.

Give me a fucking break. Aramis wanted to roll over to his side, but all he could manage from his lead-heavy body was a dissatisfied groan.

That made Sister Rhyllae giggle. "C'mon on, Aramis, it's time to wake up."

He felt her perfect fingers pat his cheek, ever so gently. Aramis squinted his silver eyes open in what he hoped to be a seething glare. It must've not worked for Rhyllae gave him a warm smile and caressed her thumb over his angled cheekbone.

"I'll get up when I say—ow," Aramis whispered before he felt the dull pain in his pectoral muscle.

He could see Dawn giving the Morning Lord sister the side-eye. "Maybe he needs more time to rest."

"Maybe he needs a pick-me-up," Rhyllae retorted.

Aramis sharply inhaled. *Oh no, not that. Anything but that.*

Rhyllae had done this before during their travels in Ruth's company. In times of emergency, Rhyllae would send all of her healing powers all at once. For any mortal being, they would receive an energetic boost of nummy, good feeling energy, as if they had drunk Valentra's coveted bean tea. Some of those would've danced and sang from such holy input. For jhasins—for him—it was like getting zapped by a jolt of lightning.

Aramis willed his body to try to wake up, to squirm, to wiggle any finger or toe. But it was too late. Rhyllae warned Dawn to cover her ears, and she placed her two buttermilk palms upon his chest. It was over in a flash.

The scream tore through his lungs and burst in his eardrums.

Hashim and Korzha raced into the tent, panic written on their faces. That quickly faded as soon as they saw Aramis lurched into a sitting position, panting like a dog.

"The last time I heard someone scream like that was when a man was getting his nipples waxed," Korzha said.

"During torture, surely?" Hashim asked.

"No, he was ... sensitive."

"I bet," Aramis said.

Then he turned to mouth, *we will talk later* to Rhyllae, but she was busy massaging her pointed ears to notice.

Serves you, right.

"Well, since you're *revived*, you are needed," Korzha said.

"By you two?"

"By her." Korzha stepped away from the tent opening.

Tsuki stepped in. Not in the striking blue-and-red felt traveling outfit he saw from last time, but in a blouse and pantaloons of a crème variety. The hems were rolled to lie past her wrists and ankles, showcasing the cobbled slippers commonly worn by the Bedouins, perhaps borrowed from Dawn. The little artisan had a glint in her mischievous brown eyes as she stood with her hands clasped in front of her.

Aramis tilted his head as he stared. *Those brown eyes... It cannot be.*

As if to answer the thoughts in his head, she lifted her right pinky finger. Three pinprick dots lined down its side.

"You owe me one, Silver Fox," Tsuki said.

Korzha persuaded the Bedouin leader to leave Aramis and Tsuki be. No doubt, Aramis must contend with Hashim next.

Dawn gave her beloved a peck, while Rhyllae mouthed to him, *we'll talk later* before they exited out of the tent.

Glad to know we're on the same page, at least, Aramis thought.

At last, it was just the two of them, the Fox and the Phoenix.

"You could've taken me out for dinner before ramming me with your beak," Aramis snarked.

Thanks to the exhilarating rejuvenation from Rhyllae, Aramis hopped up quickly from the cot he lay in. He smelled sweaty, and it was the sickly-sweet kind. Taking in the space, he found the tent was adorned with furniture. Not the bulky kind common in Amaveriel, but simple, collapsable, wooden materials. One of which was a tall, skinny dresser with a water basin on top. Aramis made a beeline for it.

"You didn't complain when I did," Tsuki countered.

"Yeah? Well, didn't have much of a choice. I was thrashed by another before you waltzed in." He picked up the basin and found it was empty. Aramis groaned and bent around, looking for a water jug.

"Well, I'll be sure to hit you up first, next time. Though, I would have a hard time. Who would resist a silver fox of a Silver Fox?"

Next time, as if the Azure Lord were a common fling.

"Hmmp, well, there's not much a line," Aramis muttered.

He found a clay pitcher that was a mellower shade of orange. Despite the hairline fracture, it held water—the true nectar of the divine. Aramis poured it into the basin as Tsuki sat on a large wooden chest.

He stooped to douse his face when he saw what she meant. Silver. Not of his eyes, but of his hair. He gripped the edge of the bowl to try to steady the rippling reflection. Gone was his black hair of his fall years, replaced by the winter of old age. He took a deep breath. He knew this would happen someday, but not all at once.

"You were cutting it close," Tsuki said with no mirth in her voice. "You do realize everyone resurrects once, right?"

Aramis took a double take. "Once? Only once?"

Tsuki silently held up one index finger.

A chill ran through his spine. No matter what Rhyllae said, it was miraculous the Morning Lord sister brought him back from the dead. But to know that there was no redo sobered him cold. But what was he expecting? Jhasins were mortal like anyone else; Aramis shouldn't have been so reckless.

"Where's Dido?" Aramis asked.

Tsuki raised her perfect eyebrows at him. "Even you know how Faustian Fae bargains can be."

"No, not that. It's about Sulmaith. He visited me, or somehow I visited him. In the throes of that eldritch magic, that connection happened. If I'm going to die, Dido needs to know and…" Aramis shook his head and ran his fingers through his hair before slapping it against his thigh.

Tsuki leaned forward with every question she asked. "Warn Sulmaith of his inevitable demise? Somehow defeat this Mannequin Queen threatening the world?" The tiny *maiko* waved her hands out wide at the end. Even shook her palms high in the air for the comical effect.

"I'm not the first, am I?"

Tsuki placed her hands back down and gave him a wry smirk. "No, you're not."

Aramis did one final run through his now silver hair as he turned his eyes skyward. As he exhaled, he leaned on a slender piece of furniture. "So what are you, some sort of sorcerer's pet bird?"

He didn't have to look at her to feel the smoldering glare she gave him. Aramis was used to it. Instead, he lathered a palm-sized bar of goat soap in his hands and slathered it over his face and neck.

"You and I have differing views on pets," Tsuki said.

"Doesn't mean you weren't. At least, in one of your lifetimes." Aramis then splashed the pristine water on his face. When he surfaced again, he grabbed the nearby washcloth and scrubbed his face.

"He was my father, thank you kindly," Tsuki said while he washed himself. "Sulmaith raised me from the ashes of my previous destruction until I was old enough to take flight. No different than my fathers in Amaveriel now. While I am no sorceress, I'm not unfamiliar of what magic he wrought. The same magic that runs in you, Silver Fox. In a way, we're children of the same sage."

Aramis paused and gave her a good look. "How?"

"Blood magic."

He laughed. "Do you know what I am?"

Tsuki rolled her large, brown eyes. "How do you think the Djinnasi made their accursed creations such as yourself? It wasn't by sin, though I'm sure that would be an added component. Blood is the sole crux of creating mortal flesh, and the process is made easier if it's enchanted."

"And somehow the all-wise Sulmaith enchanted a bunch of blood just for kicks?"

"Not any blood. *His* blood."

Aramis halted scrubbing the back of his neck. His mind lining up the dots as he dropped the cloth back in the surface until it clicked. He leaned forward in shock, gripping the edges of the slender dresser as he did so. The sand shifted from the sudden weight, causing the entire wash basin to topple over.

Chapter 20

BLOOD OF MY BLOOD

THE RINGING IN SISTER RHYLLAE'S EAR STILL buzzed as she walked out from the tent that housed Aramis. No doubt she would receive an earful tonight for such rapid healing. But she had no choice. Korzha had his heart to set out for the next day. Though he admitted he'd traded Aramis for the safety of the people, he could not find himself trusting this mechanical queen to keep her word, or to remember it. For some reason, the general didn't believe the Mannequin Queen hijacked the ritual on purpose. By his reasoning, machines, no matter their sophistication, didn't operate on ethics or morals. How could it be truly malicious if it was all an expansion of basic root commands? If the root command required them to fulfill a given task, they did not have the wherewithal to doubt the command given.

The sister, however, disagreed on this, like Dido. If there was a ghost possessing the machines—they would be no different than a living being. Thus, every action, no matter the base programming, had intention. While the sister and the general debated the concept of it, they both agreed on one thing: The mannequins were as dangerous as a runaway train caravan and needed to be stopped.

Thus, Rhyllae was not sorry one bit for rushing her magical healing on Aramis. Besides, there was another patient she needed to check on. Rhyllae stooped under the tent flap and found the Mother Superior sitting at the edge of her bed. She had wrapped herself with the coarse bedding, with her long dark hair pinned by a long slender stick. Dignified despite the ravages of the Karatow Curse coursing through her veins.

Myrrh's attention was rapt on two pieces of fabric that were hanging before her, a Bedouin robe of purple and a red shawl to complement it. Her dark hand rose with her fingers splayed in blessing, cleansing it for the rest of the pilgrimage she must undertake.

The pilgrimage. Something that Rhyllae was once keen on participating until she was thrust into this conflict. She never had the chance to discuss the matter with the Mother Superior ever since she was awake. Instead, she focused on her health, especially against the nefarious vice so close to her heart.

Myrrh muttered the last holy words and lowered her hand. The aura in the tent was the comforting sensation of purity. Oh, how Rhyllae missed that sense of security.

"I take it the Silver Fox is fully healed?" the Superior asked of her.

Rhyllae bowed and presented herself in front of her with her hands clasped in front of her. "Yes. Though I wish the same can be done for you, Superior."

Myrrh wearily lifted her hand. "I understand. This is a test from the Morning Lord that I must endure. You, however, have another test to follow."

"Mother Superior?"

"The general has filled me in on his predicament. I still do not approve of his methods, but I see now how severely you're needed on this mission. And…" Her voice trailed away as her purple-gray eyes glanced away. "I fear that if you join me on my journey, you would be in greater danger than you are with the general."

Rhyllae rocked on the back of heels. "What danger would that be?"

She gave a world-weary sigh. "You have enough troubles on your plate to be concerned with this. The severity of this situation would require the Baba's attention: yours and mine."

Then Myrrh maneuvered to the edge of the cot and stretched out her right hand. Sister Rhyllae took it and bowed her head on it.

"Promise you'll return after such a mission, alive? I will not have you throw yourself to the fire when you can return with vital information to help us combat it."

"I promise, Mother Superior Myrrh, in the name of the Morning Lord and his sister Lune."

"Good. Then go with my blessing."

She placed her left hand on top of the sister's scarf-covered head. Rhyllae felt her heart calm and was invigorated to face whatever came her way. The sister of the Morning Lord bowed deeply with her thanks and headed out of the tent.

The Sun in the sky was a welcoming sight, and Rhyllae took in a fresh breath of air. She should have felt like an arrow set on her course, ready to be loosed in that direction, yet her heart felt like a wandering compass trying to find a North.

The sister took two steps away, then froze when she heard a slap echoing in her sensitive half-elven ears. Her far sight seized on the cause of it: Dora scolding Shutte while gripping his arm tight with one hand, shaking him. The child was in tears while holding his cheek, turning into an angry red. Without any forethought, Rhyllae let her feet carry her over to them.

The fruit bowl shattered on the floor, despite being layered with rugs and over sand. The figs and dates rolled away from the lieutenant and her mother. Dawn had spent the past hour gathering all the information she could on their mechanical foe. It disturbed the young officer how they would ingest strips of flesh for fuel after a kill. It was as if they were trying to be more human. Her mother kept hinting at her to abandon the Jessenters throughout their conversation, and Dawn had her fill of it. As she rushed toward the entrance, the tail-end of her bow caught on the damn fruit bowl.

"Shit," said Dawn as she scooped down to grab the fruit.

"I got it," said Shayla. She stooped down and knelt on the floor.

"No, I got this. Didn't think my bow would hit it."

"It's fine. Really."

Stubbornly, both women grabbed whatever fruit they could and piled it on their arms. Then with the last fig, Dawn's hand grasped the fruit. Then her mother's hand clasped on top of hers. They both inhaled and looked. It had been years since Dawn had laid eyes on her mother. Shayla's eyes twinkled under that furrowed brow, searching for answers from Dawn's stiffened jaw. The young lieutenant shut her eyes and withdrew her hand, letting hers slip away.

"Here, let me find you another bowl," Dawn offered.

Her mother didn't say a word as she stood back up. Dawn rummaged through the assortment of pottery in the corner of their tent. Most of the winnowing baskets by the entrance were too flat or too large for the small bunch. At last, she found two clay dishes, one for figs and one for the dates.

Shayla drew near when she presented the dishes to her. She emptied her arms, filling up one bowl of both fruits. Dawn gave her a pointed look.

"It's going to the same place," was all Shayla said before she relieved her of the bowl.

Dawn shrugged her shoulders. *Can't fault that logic.*

She dumped her share into the bowl and nestled it next to Shayla's on the low-lying table, taking care not to let the bottom tip of her bow knock into anything else. As she stood up, Dawn once again caught her mother's face clutched in anxiety.

"Do you have to go?" Shayla asked, again.

"You know why I have to," Dawn said.

"I don't see why you don't want to stay."

The lieutenant groaned. "Mom, we've been through this."

"That was from Chief Greystone. Your father is a different man."

Dawn rolled her eyes. "Like hell he is. Dad was the one packing my bags for embarrassing him in front of the bachelors! You think he would accept me with open arms, now?"

"Maybe?" Shayla waved her hands out wide before collapsing them to her sides. "Would it kill you to marry a man? Even for a short while!"

"What's the fucking point in that?!"

"To have a child of your own. For, I don't know, you and your bird wife?"

The heat flashed to her face. "That's it. I'm leaving."

"Why can't you accept what is best for you?!"

She shouldn't take the bait. Dawn knew that it would lead to another row. But that one, she couldn't take it lying down. "What is best for me?! Can't you see I'm a grown-ass adult? Hell, I fought off worse shit than most of these people here. I think I know how to live my own life, Mom."

"A life you're willing to throw away?!" Shayla raised her voice. Her eyes widened in terror. "Your father and I fought tooth and nail to free ourselves from the Djinnasi's iron grip to live a peaceful and quiet life."

Dawn whirled about, her hands shaking in the air between them. "A life *you* wanted. You decided to marry. You decided to have kids. What about me? Don't I have a chance to live the life I wanted?"

Shayla tucked in her chin in a feeble attempt to hold back her tears. "We had lived a life of imprisonment, Dawn. We were never allowed to marry, let alone wean a child, unless they say so. We hoped…" But her voice trailed away in a sigh, and she clutched her arms into a tight squeeze as she looked away.

For some reason, Dawn thought she looked older than before. The sandy blonde hair they shared was dingier, with streaks of gray flowing through it. There was a sagging around her jaw, and her lips were thinner than the last time she visited.

Dawn inhaled and straightened her shoulders. "That's why I joined the Jessenters. So everyone can do what they want with their life, without anyone telling them what to do. Even from you."

Without another word, Dawn headed out into the blazing sun; it was less oppressive than that tent. Dawn shook her head to clear her mind. The act made her bump into the general. Korzha reached out to hold the lieutenant steady from such a bobble. Hashim was with him. Before she could give her greeting, her mother's muffled sobbing seeped out of the cloth-thin walls.

Hashim gave her a glare. "What did you do?"

"I—" was all she uttered before her father marched in.

Dawn gave Korzha a pleading look.

He simply held up his palm at her. "You're not the first to experience such a rift. Truly, some don't understand the sacrifices we make until it comes too late. Come. We need to strategize for the mission at hand."

The lieutenant bobbed her head in agreement, though her jaw was stiff from anger. They walked down the stretch of open ground that served as their street for their tent. Korzha pulled back the flap for the lieutenant. Then his pale blue eyes caught something.

"Oh no," Korzha groaned.

Dawn followed his gaze. There across the way, Sister Rhyllae was furiously arguing with Dora. Her kid, who finally settled on the name Shutte, was wedged between the two embattled women, clinging to the Morning priestess's robes.

"Oh, for fuck's sake," grumbled Dawn, before they hurried on over.

Aramis paced in a circle. His hands were on top of his head as he puffed on his cigarette, leaving a trail of smoke in his wake. It was a low point for him, Aramis knew. He had hoped to be clean longer than this, but the news made him cave.

And Sleeper did it ever tasted good. To Rhyllae's credit, she did convince him to make it from scratch to cut the temptation down, so he packed only enough leaves and paper for one. For now, that was all Aramis needed.

Sulmaith, the greatest sage and the first martyr in recent history, never had children. He locked himself away in his tower in the Sultan's palace discovering the wonders of the mystical realms. There were those who claimed to be his descendants to exploit the unwitting masses, but they were silenced by the Djinnasi lords' execution blocks, verified or not. In all of his past research, Aramis never could find any valid candidates. Not even the sorceress who brought the Demon Djinn to ruin was of Sulmaith's loins. Yet Tsuki, of all things the sage's phoenix, said Aramis was Sulmaith's blood.

A jhasin having the martyr's blood in their veins.

Who would've thought.

Aramis didn't want to admit it, but it made terrifying sense as Tsuki told him the details of the spell. Jhasins required blood and magic to create. If they had somehow obtained the great sage's blood, such magical competence should be expected. Compared to all the languages he learned in his upbringing, magic was the easiest to read. When Joel was creating new spells, Aramis was the first the minx would come to for troubleshooting. But that didn't mean the Silver Fox could cast them. He tried it once at Joel's behest. A simple flame spell. It almost drained him dry from lighting a candle, and that was after a whole week of trying to conjure it.

"How far does it go?" Aramis asked. "In the past, how far back does the blood magic go?"

Tsuki shrugged. "Who's to say? Parents, grandparents, and on. Even their children, as well. All I know was that Sulmaith desired his knowledge to be carried on after him.

As a bonus, his extended cousins and their descendants to receive this gift."

"Are any of them alive now?"

Tsuki gave him a shake of her head. "The last line perished sixty years. Or was it sixty-four? It was my two lifetimes back at the very least."

Aramis took the last inhale and dropped the spent paper on the ground. "So, I'm all that is left." He crushed it with the heel of his boot.

"You were one of many of the silver model line, no?" Tsuki asked. "Such lineage would prove of a use, even for the Lords' twisted purposes."

Aramis laughed and bowed his head. "You would think they wouldn't. How can one throw away a thing of beauty for another? But they do. Those Djinnasi bastards do. A fresh batch of jhasins were created every couple of years, and everyone wanted the new shiny toy to play with. Who doesn't want to fuck a virgin, right? Anyone else who clings on to a dirty, broken thing, like me, wouldn't be seen worthy enough to uphold their status and position. And the law," Aramis inhaled and looked up, kicking the welling anger down within him, "decreed that any outdated jhasins be destroyed for public safety. Do you know what that age is?"

The *maiko* looked paler than usual. She shook her head.

"Sixteen."

Tsuki shuddered and turned to look away to the sunny sky peeking through the tent flap, far into the western horizon where Bazzuuport lay.

Aramis continued, "Maybe younger now. I haven't been there in years. Who knows, maybe the newly minted models have florescent hair, tattoos that change color based on humidity, or maybe they light up like the sun when they organism, as some sort of damn bragging right. No. There wouldn't be any more silver jhasin models, like me. They would never mix model bloods, I'm sure of it. I'm an outdated Tinkertoy made for the scrapyard of society. Too old to dance or sing for their amusement anymore."

Tsuki dotted her eyes with the hem of her sleeve as she sniffled away the tears. "Then, you are the last. You are the last legacy of the sage."

Aramis snorted. "And what use is it?"

"Pardon?"

"How did *they*, those of his blood, use 'Sulmaith's legacy,' hmm?" He pointed at Tsuki. "Did they use his vast knowledge to … do what exactly?"

Tsuki put her fingers on her mouth and looked away in thought.

He waved his arms at her as the silence drew on. "All of this vast knowledge, connecting to the wisest sage of our age. What use is it if no one uses it for good?"

"But you can."

"Barely! There in that storm, I can tell you that wasn't me. Elvish weed—no all of the faerie mushrooms in the queendom—could make better sense than that hallucination shit-show shown to me. Even then the words stated weren't mine. Not to mention, I was knocking on heaven's door for the last part of the ritual."

"Good song," Tsuki quipped.

"Yeah, it was. But that's not the point. We all know the lasting legacy of the Morning Lord, let alone Lune's. Her children helped shape the world of religious enlightenment. Why didn't they, these children of Sulmaith, do the same? Magic drains me like centennial leeches going for seconds at a buffet."

Tsuki sighed. "What do you expect them to do, Silver Fox, be you?"

"Am I wrong? We're still suffering the effects of Bazzuu's own legacy. All those esteemed sages became our overlords at the end. We're still at war to throw off their yoke. What is the point of receiving this wondrous gift if I can't handle it and save the world?"

Tsuki sat there, tightlipped. Not out of anger, out of an abundance of caution, Aramis realized. What she said next, he suspected, was carefully curated.

"Sulmaith didn't do it to fight the Djinn Bazzuu or to save the world. He did it so he could live forever. Every time you tap into this well of knowledge, Aramis, he will possess your body. Inch by inch, he'll submit it to his will. I suspect that was what happened in that storm."

Aramis stood there, his mouth opened wide, yet his rebuttal stuck in his throat.

The flap flew open, and the freshly anointed warrior, Natasha, rushed in. "Silver Fox, Madame Phoenix, you're needed."

Aramis and Tsuki exchanged glances before they ran out.

It didn't take too long to know what Aramis was needed for. The entire tribe was divided into two, hurling insults at each other with ruddy faces and clinched fists. The moment the people saw Aramis coming in, they crowded around him, demanding him to resolve things their way. Though what, Aramis couldn't tell, for they quickly start hurling insults at each other.

Thankfully, Natasha was there. She cried out, "Make way," as she parted the way for Tsuki and Aramis.

As they pierced through the center of this turbulent vortex, there was none other than Rhyllae and Dora. Both women were held back by the two Jessenters; Dawn wrapped her arms over Dora's shoulder from behind, while Korzha braced Rhyllae from behind with both arms around her plump figure. They all halted when they saw him, but Aramis went for Shutte. The kid was on his knees, with his hands covering his face, his shoulders bobbing.

Aramis knelt in front of him and braced his shoulders. "Hey. I'm here; it's going to be okay."

Shutte lowered his hands, his cheeks glossy from tears. Oh, how that broke his heart.

"Are you sure?" Shutte croaked out, before he sniffled away the tears.

Hashim pushed his way through to the center. "Everyone, knock it off! All of you! We're Bedouins; we shouldn't be fighting each other like this. How are we any different than those monsters that captured us if we do?"

Ashamed, the people backed off, though many gave each other the evil eye. Dawn let go of Dora, who raced to Hashim's side and knelt before him.

"Sir, this priestess tried to steal my daughter away from me," she said as she pointed at Rhyllae.

"Steal?!" The Morning Lord sister leaned forward, braced by the general.

"She's filling her head with this gender nonsense."

"Please, Chieftain Hashim," Rhyllae said. "Shutte came to us for help. I want to help him in kind."

"*She* doesn't need help!" Dora cried out.

The kid's mother began to lurch toward the still bound priestess, but Hashim waved down his wooden hands, meant for everyday use, in front of her.

"Is this true?" he asked Aramis.

"Yes. Shutte wished to be a boy." Then he pointed at Dora. "And he *is* now. I was there when he found his new name."

Aramis stood up and raised his voice so all could hear him. "I, Aramis Feres, the Silver Fox, will hold council on this child's fate. I declare it in the name of the Sleeper, creator and parent of the Sun and Moon."

Murmurs broke among scattered gasps. His friends were floored by such a statement, save for Rhyllae and Hashim, both having witnessed this rare tradition before. It was set by his predecessor, for Marquist made it his life's mission to heal the Iounese tribespeople. The Silver Fox didn't belong to any tribe and thus was considered impartial. Something that the Amaverielian Elders never cared for.

"Dora, is it?" Aramis asked. When she nodded, he said, "Wait for us at your tent. I'll send someone for you soon."

The woman nodded and reached for Shutte. Aramis waved her back.

"The child stays with me."

Dora gasped. Tears welled in her eyes. "But I'm not a bad parent. I raised her in accordance with the Morning Lord's wishes."

Dawn rolled her eyes behind her.

Ditto, Dawn. Aramis thought to himself.

"If the child requires a new life to further their development, I need to honor that wish. For their good and for the good of the tribe." Aramis waved to the people who were still surrounding them.

"But—but," she murmured until her friends swooped next to her side. They gave words of encouragement as they gently pulled her away.

"And of me?" Rhyllae asked, now freed of the general's hold.

"Join the Mother Superior until I need you. You'll be protected by her."

Rhyllae nodded and abruptly turned away. She cradled her arms as she walked.

"Wait." Aramis caught up to her and gently turned her around. "I love you," he said as he caressed her soft biceps with his knuckles.

"I know. But Shutte…"

"He'll be safe."

Rhyllae exhaled, letting her shoulders soften. She murmured, "I love you," before they leaned in for two quick kisses. Then she departed with the dwindling crowd.

"We cannot linger here any longer," Korzha said when Aramis joined them. "Our enemy is shoring up their defenses. With no guarantee we'll be admitted in open arms, we must act swiftly."

"All I need is one night," Aramis told him.

"You sure? They would not approve such partiality from you."

He had a point. Word would spread of his presence here among the tribes in their spring meet. While he never cared for anyone's judgement, being a tribe mediator was the tradition of his mentor. To break it by his own selfish needs would destroy all the decades of hard work. It would break Aramis's heart.

Thus, Aramis put his hands on his hips and took a quick look around and found he was in luck. "That is why Tsuki and Hashim will join me on this."

The *maiko* and the chief exchanged surprised looks.

"That bodes well," Dawn quipped.

Shutte looked at Aramis with pleading eyes.

Aramis patted him on the back. "I know what to do. Hashim, your tent."

Chapter 21

THE SILVER FOX COUNCIL

THE COUNCIL WAS SMALL, TO SAY THE LEAST, AS they convened in Chief Hashim's tent. The three of them gathered on the floor on sitting pillows, with mixed fruit bowls on the low table. Hashim sat at the Silver Fox's left, tapping impatiently on the table with his wooden prosthetic. Tsuki, the esteemed phoenix, knelt neatly by his right. She fanned herself with an accordion style paper despite there being no glisten of sweat on her skin. They both had been eyeing each other, Hashim with trepidation and Tsuki of bemusement.

Aramis sat between the two, slouched forward with his elbows on the table, peeling the skin of a fig. Shayla ushered Shutte deeper in the double-peaked tent, to shelter him from unwanted eyes. He could hear her murmuring words of comfort, though there was an unease in her voice.

At least she's trying. Aramis ruffled his hair with his hand and steeled his thoughts for the task at hand.

"There are three things I need to know before I make my decision," Aramis told the two. "One, was Dora abusing Shutte? I don't think his gender change is the sole reason for Dora's ire. There must be something more to it here. Two, was Rhyllae really kidnapping Shutte for herself? As a priestess, I know she adheres to her order, but I have to admit they have grown attached. Finally, where should Shutte live? I for one accept him for who he is; I need to make sure there's a parent who will do the same."

"Hopefully here," interjected Hashim. "I know it's difficult to accept everyone's different point of views, but Ce—er Shutte is a Bedouin, through and through."

"So was your daughter, Chief Hashim," Tsuki piped up. "She too searched for other horizons."

Aramis nodded. "I can try to see if anyone would take in Shutte, but they have to accept him as a boy, and eventually as a young man. I'm not above finding him a new one if needs be."

"Would you keep Amaveriel in your consideration? Many in the Freedom City would welcome Shutte's newfound identity. I would even vouch for the boy in front of the Elders, if need be."

"Amaveriel? It's real?" Hashim spoke in quiet awe. "The fabled city is real?"

Aramis gave a half-hearted chuckle. "Oh, it's real alright and strict. Once inside, no one leaves without good reason. Even for me or Tsuki here. Which is why I want Amaveriel to be the last thing for Shutte." He gave the phoenix lady a stern eye.

Tsuki merely resumed a sphinx-like façade on her face.
Seems like you learned a thing or two from the Mother Superior.

Hashim nodded with a well-worn smile on his face. "And here I thought you were felled by those dastardly lords."

"I would rather jump into a pit of acid than meet such a fate."

That got a hearty laugh from the tribal chief.

"You should trust your daughter's word, Chief Hashim," Tsuki teased as she snapped her fan closed. "She's the epitome of truth and valor. You should be proud."

Hashim raised his bushy eyebrows at her. "Remind me why you are present in this council?"

"She doesn't know a lick about Rhyllae or Shutte," answered Aramis. "You know Dora well, I hope. I know Rhyllae, intimately. With Tsuki here, we'll get a fair shake."

Hashim nodded, but still gave her a reserved glare.

"Fear not, Chef Hashim," Tsuki said. "I do not wish ill for the child. While I had the good fortune of a happy childhood, I understand not all have such luck. I want Shutte to find a place he can call home, one way or another."

"Then it's agreed. Send for Dora, and let's get this circus started."

Sister Rhyllae's nerves were in a jumbled mess as she was escorted by Korzha and Myrrh. Her stomach was tied in knots; despite the Mother Superior's attempts to convince her she was in the right, would Aramis see it that way? Though he loved her, it wasn't the first time he must play the impartial judge, governed by the traditions of his previous master. Would the chief give her such mercy? Her actions, though admirable, would be enough to displace the entire expedition out of the people's hospitality if Hashim willed it. That would put everyone in a bind, even Aramis.

As they made the short distance to the chieftain's tent, many of the tribespeople tried to go about their normal routines of preparing for supper for the evening. All halted as they eyed the tiny procession. As soon as they reached the tent, Dora and her friends emerged. Dora gave Rhyllae a nasty glare as her friends closed ranks with her.

The Mother Superior splayed her fingers in the traditional blessing. "Go in peace, ladies."

"We would, if you go in peace," Dora spat out while giving Rhyllae an evil eye.

"Let us pass," commanded Korzha. Rhyllae saw him place his right hand to tilt the scabbard of his magical heirloom forward.

Please, let it not come to that, Rhyllae mentally begged.

The women didn't move an inch, save to nestle closer together. Not even to the muffled sounds coming from within the tent.

The general barked, "Move!"

Dora and her posse gasped and broke away, their colorful scarves flying after them as they ran for the safety of their tents.

"Thank you, General." Mother Superior Myrrh gave him a smile.

Then the two parted the opening for Rhyllae. She almost bumped into a stormy Aramis when she stepped through. Those storms parted when his silver eyes caught sight of her, and he gave a sheepish smile while waving her to come in.

His patience must be sorely tested by Dora.

Across the room of the tent was a low-lying table with two bowls of mixed fruit. Hashim sat to the right, his wooden hands tapping the table in a musical beat. Tsuki, baffling to see the bard to have a seat here, waved her fan in a slow figure eight. Aramis nestled himself in between the two in a crosslegged position. Rhyllae stood before them with her hands clasped in front of her.

Hashim cleared his throat and spoke in a booming voice. "Sister Rhyllae, we understand that a woman of your profession cares for the health and safety of her flock. Though you have shown courage in guiding my people for their escape, we are concerned that you've become attached to one member of my tribe."

"Shutte," answered the sister of the Morn.

"Why this boy?" Hashim folded his massive arms across his chest, letting his wooden hands dangle underneath.

"We discussed in length of switching his gender, and he expressed difficulties in showing his true self." It was something that Rhyllae repeatedly rehearsed in her head in these past few hours. If she had shown the raw emotion she had earlier, there was no guarantee they would have taken her account fairly, even with Aramis present.

"And you think he would continue having this difficulty in my tribe?"

"You witnessed it yourself. His own mother rejected his identity, even used violence against him. How many have done the same?"

Tsuki, moving her fan in a slow figure eight, gave Hashim a side-eye. To gauge his reaction for her own amusement, Rhyllae supposed, for there was a faint smirk.

Is everything a game to her?

Hashim shifted his weight in his seat before he spoke. "Do you think he would be safe if he were allowed to live in the Bedouin tribe? If he was under the parentage of another?"

Rhyllae looked behind her in doubt.

Anyone could be a wonderful parent to Shutte so long they accepted him wholly as their own. Such a parent could be found here, probably by Natasha, or anyone with a similar heart. Yet, there was the matter of Dora. Oh, how she and her friends were bold enough to physically assault her. The woman ripped her shawl clear off of her head, yanked on her hair, and even tried to gouge out her eyes. No matter how forcefully Rhyllae shoved her away from herself, Dora kept going. What would she do to Shutte and to the new parent when they leave for the Silo 51 and for years to come?

Rhyllae shook her head with a heavy sigh. "Shutte would not be safe so long as Dora is near him. Believe me, I wanted him to stay. With his own family, if possible. That was why I approached Dora. I saw what she had done to Shutte and sought to correct it. I had thought, as a sister of the Morning Lord, we would connect on a spiritual level."

"A shame that backfired," Aramis commented.

"How could you be surprised?" Tsuki still kept the motion of her fan at the same pace. "While the worship of Lune is widespread, by honoring our feminine aesthetic as something sacred, it creates a dichotomy."

"Pardon?" The word jumped out of the sister's mouth.

Tsuki waved her fan toward the men at her table. "The divide between genders. Despite the luminescence of the Morning Lord, Lune and her daughters are regularly favored. Thus, any daughter would be wanted over sons. Why, when Shutte revealed himself as male to his mother, who abides such religious doctrine, it was a complete rejection of Dora's hopes and aspirations. Dora's response, though deplorable, should've been expected."

The sister was gobsmacked, for it was the truth. Over a lifetime, Rhyllae had witnessed her fellow sisters gravitating toward honoring Lune and all of her children over the Morning Lord. She alone was the one who volunteered to walk up the Minaret every dawn to greet the Morn. Rhyllae never considered the possibility of such favoritism.

Hashim lowered his gaze. "It shames me to admit, that such mentality can poison our love for our daughters. By favoring our daughters, we sequester them in more confined roles that may not let them be engaged in our communities. I ... had drunk such poison to my error."

Aramis put a hand on Hashim's shoulders. "I couldn't begin to imagine how to raise a child, let alone on any religious reverence. Because of this, I have to ask if any follower of the Morning Lord would provide Shutte a good home? Shutte considers the Morning Lord important in his life, even taking on one of the names from the texts. Do you think, Rhyllae, given what Tsuki says, we could find another that would accept him?"

The sister placed her hand over her heart. "I know I would. Surely there's another?"

"If there isn't, would you?"

Tsuki and Hashim turned their heads at Aramis.

But he kept his silver gaze on Rhyllae. "Would you adopt him?"

There it was, that pang in her heart. It was the same question she asked of the Mother Superior those past few hours. If the Abbey of the Rising Dawn could accept Delphi, surely, they could take in Shutte. Yet, it was not to be, not by the strict adherence of her order.

"If I could, I would," Rhyllae's voice trembled as she said them out loud. She blinked away the tears welling in her eyes. "As a priestess of the light, I'm not allowed. I have to be a mother to all who worship, not just the two. I'm sorry."

Rhyllae turned away to force herself from saying anything more. She could hear him moving from his seat, perhaps to comfort her. Yet her feet started moving as the tears couldn't be quelled. Rhyllae raced, through the tent flap into the twilight air and beyond. Her keen ears heard Myrrh calling out to her. She sped up. For once in her long life, she didn't want to be a sister anymore.

Aramis ran his fingers through his hair as he bowed his head. He wanted more than anything to hold Rhyllae and comfort her right now. But he had to be the Silver Fox, the shepherd and guide to these people. At least, for this one night.

"What were you trying to pull, Aramis?" Hashim asked. He rested his burly arm on the low table and leaned forward to give a stern look, tapping his wooden hand to emphasize the point.

"Perhaps to lure the truth from the sister?" Tsuki collapsed the fan horizontally and pointed at Hashim, leaning forward as she did so. "As Dora had accused, the sister wanted Shutte for herself."

"Well, she can't," Aramis snapped. "I was a fool to think the abbey would take them on."

He walked back to the table to gather his cloak. *Fuck being the Silver Fox, Rhyllae needs me.*

"Why not you?" Tsuki asked.

Aramis paused. He shook his head and roughly threw on his cloak over his shoulders. "A wretch like me? Please."

Tsuki rolled her eyes at him. "From what I gathered, Shutte was rather attached with you, as well. As much as he was with the sister. He stayed by your side until his mother came to fetch him away during that scuffle."

"I live a dangerous life, Tsuki."

Aramis caught Hashim's gaze. His eyebrows raised, and his lips pouted at the Silver Fox. Even the salt of the earth saw right though the Silver Fox.

"I can't take a child into a death trap."

"You already did," Hashim said.

"We were damn lucky. Lucky," Aramis said the last word pointedly to Tsuki. "In either case, Shutte can't stay. I'm sorry, Hashim, I don't trust Dora to keep her hands to herself, even if Shutte is transferred to another parent in this tribe."

Hashim shifted in his seat. "I could kick the woman out."

Tsuki raised her eyes. "And draw the ire of those who befriended her?"

"I hate to say it, but she's right." Aramis threw his cloak over his shoulders and tied the knot. "You'll lose your position as Chief or, worse, be murdered. I for one can't stand to re-home a bunch of bigots that won't listen to a word I say."

"Then it's decided: Shutte can stay until you return," Hashim said. He groaned as he stood, towering over the Silver Fox. "What you do with him will be up to you. Keep him or give him away. But he cannot live here."

Aramis found Rhyllae at the far eastern side of the encampment, sitting with her back to him and, not surprisingly, with her kinky curls free of her priestly shawl. She always claimed she got overheated when her emotions ran wild like a gazelle, yet he suspected otherwise. All people in the end wanted to be free of the yokes that burdened them.

Rhyllae didn't stir when he joined her side. Her focus was fixed on the velveteen rabbit doll in her hands. That thumb worried the shiny button sewn for one of the eyes.

"When Delphi gave me this, I didn't want to take this from her," she whispered to Aramis, as if what she uttered would be a forbidden tryst. "I knew she was being kind, but I didn't want her to lose what little she had of her parents."

"Because you didn't have anything from yours," Aramis, too, whispered.

Rhyllae nodded. "But she gave it to me anyway. And I found myself, well, jealous. I know it's childish, but I was.

I wanted to be the one to care for her, not the other way around. It's a child's job to be a kid, not to parent their parent."

Aramis nodded in agreement. He didn't want to interrupt her. She always seemed to understand him without words, regardless.

"And yet, I couldn't give that to her. When you asked me in there if I wanted to raise Shutte, it struck a nerve." She gave a frustrated sigh and lowered the doll. "Why did you ask in the first place?"

"Why not?" When Rhyllae gave him a sour look, Aramis countered. "They raised you, Rhyllae, why can't you do the same?"

Her lips opened for a rebuttal, but she didn't say a word. She then turned her searching eyes back on the doll, Obba.

"Shutte is a boy now," she said after some thought. "The Mother Superior made it clear that only those who identify as women were allowed in. I don't want him to go through another rejection like that. I couldn't bear it." To further her point, she squeezed the doll against her chest.

"Neither do I." Aramis sighed and leaned his elbows on his knees. The sand under his boots shifted from the unexpected weight. He watched the stars skate across the heavenly arch above them.

"Why not you?" Rhyllae asked out of the blue.

Aramis could've told her it was dangerous. The life of a Silver Fox was neither glamorous nor peaceful. But he knew that wouldn't be a sufficient excuse. Not when he agreed to have one with her, long before this expedition started. Before Rhyllae told him she would be transferred. Before he learned the horrible truth of his sterility.

As the stars winked in their ascent, Aramis whispered his true heart's confession. "I was afraid. Not of losing them, they would've been safe somewhere in Amaveriel, but of me.

If I die, what will happen to them? If not you, who will look after them when I'm gone? Rhyllae, there are no grandparents, cousins, or any relative that would take them in when that happens. And if there is someone who will, are the kids going to be the same? They're children. How can they cope when another parent is dead and gone? Rhyllae, they're going to think they're cursed. That shit will fuck them up."

The priestess nodded, and they stared at the stars as the sky turned to a ruddy shade of indigo.

"They?" Sister Rhyllae asked.

Aramis grunted mindlessly, lost in thought.

"As in Shutte and Delphi?"

Aramis blinked and stirred as if waking from a dream. His puzzled expression faded when the thought struck him true. He rubbed the back of his neck and looked up in awe.

"I guess I was."

Then Aramis caught her staring at him. A mixture of pride and love awash on her freckled olive-brown face. A face he wanted to kiss from dawn to dusk.

"Rhyllae," Aramis began to say as he took her hand into his. "If there are no limits, no one to tell us no, would you raise them with me?"

"You mean if I'm not a priestess?"

Aramis shook his head. "Humor me. If you can—no matter how—would you do it with me?"

Rhyllae broke the gaze to the East, where the sun would break the horizon.

Was she searching for answers, he wondered. *Or is she seeing something I can't see.*

At last, her golden, round face looked back at him. "Us?"

"Yeah. Us. What say you?" He squeezed her hand.

Rhyllae laughed and grinned. She toyed Obba in her hands. "Yes." Then she held his gaze, her golden-brown eyes unwavering when she said it again. "Yes."

Aramis didn't want to look away. Didn't want to find himself in a fool's dream where anything promised was broken but to continue to live in a dream where all could be said and done by will alone. If this was a dream, Aramis didn't want to wake up. That living dream leaned in and kissed him. Her lips caressed his as she tilted her head and let his tongue mingle with hers.

When they parted for air, Rhyllae's tender voice whispered, "And you?"

"Yes," Aramis said as he playfully nipped her bottom lip. Then "yes" when he kissed the tender part of her jaw. A "yes" on her clavicle.

Rhyllae inhaled and let out a sigh as he trailed his kisses from there to the furrows of her heaving breasts. She leaned back on the sand dune to gaze upon him. Her golden-brown eyes sparkled.

Aramis held her hand, letting her fingers intertwine with his. This is where they normally stopped. The penance for going any further would pale in comparison to the isolation dealt upon her. It was bad enough they courted under "good faith" of the Superior's wishes. But this time, there was a different look in Rhyllae's eyes. Something that clicked into place.

Aramis brought her knuckles to his lips, then he rubbed his thumb on her hand. "Rhyllae?"

"Yes," she said with quiet determination.

Aramis saddled himself over her, propping himself by his hands. "Are you sure? If we do this—"

Rhyllae placed her fingers over his lips. "I'm done."

He raised his eyebrows. Never he thought the day would come. In the early years of their friendship, he secretly wanted this. To have it granted now when he'd lost hope...

"I'm done with saying no to this." She trailed her fingers down to the strings on his blouse. They unraveled them to reveal his bare chest. Firmly, Rhyllae placed her brown hand on his brown skin, where his heart lay. "I'm done saying no to this life. Our life. I'm done, *me'qora*. Let me say yes to this for once. Please?"

Aramis leaned in and cupped his hands on her cheeks. "You will never have to ask for it again."

He melted into the kiss, and they both breathed in each other's air. Their skins puckered as they freed themselves of their modest clothes. The night hardly stirred a wink as they moved like the gentle waves of the ocean, closing the distance between their shores.

Chapter 22

SHACKLE

THE CAMELS LINED UP BY MID-MORN, READY FOR the next foray into the desert landscape. Shutte was there with Dawn and Tsuki, watching the two adults conspire something about spirits and angels. Though he was raised on those scriptures of the Morning Lord, the talk made him anxious.

If you talk about them, they might show up.

Shutte tried to stack some stones on top of each other as to block them out. Yet, he wavered when he caught wind of the Reaper's name, and the whole pile fell over.

The two lesbians broke off their conversation and looked upon him with visible concern.

"You okay, bud?" Dawn asked him.

Shutte could feel the heat rising on his cheeks. "Yeah."

He was embarrassed to be sure, but part of his heart was glad to be finally called in such a masculine manner.

"You want to help me with this saddle?"

At first, he didn't want to do any work, but Shutte stood up and wiped off the sand from his trousers. From what he heard, it would be a long trek to reach the machine monster's lair. Who knew how long it would be before they slayed this queen and rid the world of this evil. Shutte should try to be with them as much as he could, no matter how much his restless body complained.

Maybe, they'll stop talking about ghosts, he hoped.

Dawn told him to reach under the camel's belly for the strap when Tsuki said, "And then the Superior said, 'he found a way to defend himself from the Fae, or some new-found weapon to overpower them.'"

"Do you think it's the mannequins?" Dawn asked.

"That was my thinking!"

Shutte shuddered. He had no such luck.

"Thanks, Shutte," Dawn said when he gave her the attached buckle. "Are you two coming with us?"

Tsuki shook her head. "We have to convince the Fae Court this was the anarch angel's doing. No one else on this mortal plane could persuade their queen, save for the Baba Magena herself. At least, that is what the Mother Superior thinks."

"Whoa, Baba Magena? Head of all Cardinals, Matriarchs—the whole sha-bang?"

"The one and the same," Tsuki said, waggling her index finger as she leaned over in excitement.

"Heard she's from Valentra. Say, maybe you can bum some of that kush from her."

"So, you can smoke it all? I'll be without." The maiden pouted.

"Unless you do it with me." Dawn waggled her eyebrows at her.

Tsuki rolled her eyes, but there was a coy grin splayed across her face.

"What's kush?" Shutte asked.

Both of their faces fell, and they exchanged looks.

Did they really forget I was in their midst? Shutte felt small.

"That's what I get from asking you two to watch him," came a gruff voice.

All three of them jumped up when Aramis appeared from behind one of the camels. He was once again clad in his full black regalia. His boots hardly made a sound as he walked toward them.

Dawn clutched her chest. "Fuck, Aramis, don't sneak up on us like that."

"Please, leave that for the real prey," seconded Tsuki.

Still confused, Shutte turned to the Silver Fox and asked, "What *is* kush?"

Aramis's lips flattened in a familiar disappointed line. He lifted his arm up and then pointed at the two women. "Both of you, grounded from babysitting for the entire lunar cycle."

Tsuki shoulders sagged, and she drooped her head. "Aw, and we were about to talk of the wonderful benefits of matriarchal tyranny and religious persecution."

"Yeah, no. Not if Rhyllae has anything to say about it."

"Rhyllae?" Dawn asked. "So, is it official?"

Shutte's heart raced.

Aramis twisted his fingers in front of his mouth. The lieutenant cocked an eyebrow at him. He signed some signals with his fingers in a language Shutte could not comprehend.

Dawn nodded. "Hey, Tsuki. Let's find some more food for the trip."

Tsuki took her hand, and they walked away. As they departed, she turned back to wave goodbye to Shutte. He made a small wave back. Even though her ghost stories terrified Shutte, the bird lady was not a bad person to hang out with. She had even taught him a few dance moves this morning.

Aramis knelt in front of Shutte and lowered his hood, his quicksilver eyes unearthly against the harsh daylight. But for him, it was a comforting sight.

"Shutte, I have something to tell you."

The kid wrung the camel's harness strap in his hands. "Am I staying with my mom?"

Aramis shook his head, and Shutte sighed with relief.

"I found a new family for you, people willing to take care of you. But before I do, I must go into that silo and rid the mannequins once and for all. In the meantime, I need you here, under Hashim's protection. He's speaking with Dora about this as we speak. He'll make sure she won't come anywhere near you when we're gone. Rhyllae and I will come back for you when we're done."

Shutte nodded and kicked the sand. "They say you might not make it back."

Aramis put his hands on his shoulders, drawing his hazel gaze back on him. "I have a good reason to come back."

He paused and held his breath. His brows raised in a pinch as his eyes danced. It was the first time he saw the Silver Fox afraid before—even with the mannequins.

Then, Aramis let out a shuddering breath before he spoke. "If you want it, Rhyllae and I will take care of you. No matter what happens in that silo, we will come for you. I promise... That is, if you will have us?"

"You will?!" Shutte exclaimed.

Aramis gave a weary smile. "If you want. If not, I'll search—"

Shutte barreled into him and hugged him as tight as his little arms could. It was wild of him to assume that the Silver

Fox, the legendary hero of all time, would free him of his terrible mother. But to have him and the sister to be his parents? Never in his wildest dreams.

Aramis gave him a tight embrace. When Shutte backed away, he caught him sniffling and rubbing away a stray tear. His grin was broad and wide, and his eyes shone with a happy gleam.

"Well then, we're a family. Rhyllae will be happy to hear about this."

"Where is she?"

"She'll be here, soon. She's having final words with her boss."

Dawn and Tsuki returned with their compatriots, each of them carrying a bag of goods for the trails ahead. A tall man and the magical satyr followed them. Shutte peered around them and found the Morning Lord sister not there.

"Ready to go?" Aramis asked them.

"Ready." Dawn placed her parcel on the back of a camel. The creature brayed in complaint.

"Not without the priestess," Korzha piped up. His northern accent always sounded funny to Shutte.

"Where is she anyway?" Dawn asked as she leaned against the package.

Dido waved her hand toward the tent. "Discussing with the Mother Superior. It looked rather serious."

Korzha frowned. "I understand she wanted to say her goodbyes, but we're pressed for time."

"Let it be," Aramis said. "This will be the last meeting she'll have with the Mother Superior. And it's going to be *Rhyllae* from here on out."

Dawn nodded, then gasped when it finally sank in. The general's pale blue eyes widened; then he snapped his head toward the tents.

Dido slapped her hands on her cheeks while making an audible, "Oh my."

Tsuki raised her perfect brows and hid her smile behind a fan.

Shutte turned to the Silver Fox and asked, "Can I call her 'mom'?"

Myrrh was stunned. So much so, she pulled up a wooden stump and sat on it promptly.

Rhyllae stood before her with her hands clasped in front of her dress and trousers of the Bedouin make. Her hair, no longer covered, lay in tidy coils about her shoulders, as neatly as the folded hijab on the table. She didn't want to confuse her previous mentor on where she stood, though feeling a cloth so sheer would take getting used to.

"Is there no way to convince you to stay?" the Mother Superior asked.

Rhyllae sighed, and her eyebrows furrowed in a pinch. "To be frank, Mother Superior, I don't see how. I felt called to love these children in a way that goes beyond my duties as a sister. To be a mother, beyond the Order."

Myrrh slouched and held her left hand against her lips. She knew it would be difficult for her to understand; she had been the biggest advocate of them all.

Rhyllae knelt by her side and took her other hand in hers. She rubbed it gently as if to soothe out the pain she gave. "You had once said that I'm needed beyond our cloister, and I have been burying my light. Let me shine in this way, Mother Superior, and let me help these children while I do some good here with the Jessenters."

Myrrh shifted in her seat to look at her dead in the eye. "Why not shine your light to the world? You're gifted, Rhyllae.

Gifted in healing beyond all of my years of service. Not to mention the strength of your light against the terrible Lord of Azure. And you're going to leave all of this behind for the sake of two?"

Normally Rhyllae would've paled from such an intense glare of hers. But the half-elven woman steeled herself. "With this, I can do both. I can be there for these children and still heal the world. Beyond the cloister. Beyond Amaveriel."

The mother turned her face away and withdrew her hand. Her face was brewing a storm.

Rhyllae pressed on. "Mother Superior, if I am transferred to another abbey or temple, would you guarantee they would give me the same liberties you had given me? Would I be able to raise these children and have Aramis as my spouse, while serving the Morning Lord under their roof?"

"I would've traveled the entire globe for the best fit for you," Myrrh snapped. Her lavender-gray eyes pierced right through her. "I planned to speak to the Baba herself upon your behalf. For. You. Vouch for your future and the future for all priestesses." She jumped to her feet and glowered at Rhyllae. "And you cast this aside for a family of your own?!"

"Mother, I—"

"You serve the Morning and Evening Light!" Myrrh raised her voice. "You are beyond an equal to all men! Why shackle yourself to this mediocrity?"

"Because I'm shackled by the abbey!" Rhyllae cried out as she stood. "I did everything for you since infancy! In M'thealquilôk, I fought with all of my conviction and watched my friends die for the good of the realm. Instead of being given rest, I was thrown into service until all of my strength was tapped. I was ushered into service ignorant of a life you had. A life shared by the other mothers before they saw the light. All I want, Mother Superior, is the same. A life of my own and the freedom to live it. Is that too much to ask?"

The Superior was speechless. Her Töskan blue eyes wavered before closing them. "I release you, Rhyllae Ghalédale, of your service."

Rhyllae pulled out the metal medallion that was given to her days before. The letters "seize the day" caught the light that trickled into the tent. Finally, she took a step to place it on the shawl, untouched, on the table.

"Keep it," Myrrh said with an edge in her voice. "You'll need it, should you ever return as a mother."

Rhyllae squinted at her with a sour frown. Her first instinct was to say no out of spite. But then she remembered how Lune and the Morning Lord had lent their holy aid to her throughout her life. Aramis didn't have long to live, despite his durability as a jhasin. And the children might need her care for a couple of decades before they could live on their own. While precious they were, such life was as transient as Lune's phases. What phase would she experience in her long, half-elven life?

Though she hated to admit it, Rhyllae might return. No... She would return. Rhyllae would change this structure where others like her, or Delphi, never had to be bent and broken on the wheel of the Morning Lord. If Myrrh failed here, she would help create a livelihood for the priestess to live among the flock.

"I'll keep it as a reminder of the work that still needs to be done," Rhyllae told her, though the Mother Superior probably didn't hear it. She swiped it off the table and charged out of the tent flap.

Three days and three nights their expedition traveled by the extensive dunes south of the glass plains. When the next night faded into the haze of early morn, Aramis veered them north, where deep ravines scarred the land. Here, at the edge of the cliff, did he stop their camels. He dropped a metal coin with a square hole punched through it on the ground. Then he took out his knives and checked their edges.

Still sharp. Aramis smirked. *I can get used to this kind of magic.*

"You're not looking to skin the historians alive, are you?" Dido joked while she unfurled her blanket to sit on the sand.

"Not this day. The general on the other hand." He shrugged to prove a point.

"You're jesting."

Aramis flicked his silver eyes over to her.

Dido froze as her face turned pale. "Please, tell me you're jesting."

"I haven't forgotten his bargain."

"You may not forget, but you can forgive." Rhyllae came to his side with her own blanket. Her hair, now free of the priestly vestments, was coiled into a braided bun, secured at the base of her nape by a vibrant orange cloth. To further her point, she popped the rug in the air then lay it flat on the sand.

The bronzed lieutenant cried out from down the ways. "Hey, we were never attacked because of it."

Dawn continued to hammer the peg along with the general, who alone gave a cursory glance his way. Aramis did have to admit, the ex-noble wasn't shirking his share of rotating camp chores. Rhyllae gave Aramis a meaningful look as she patted to have him sit next to her. With a grumbling sigh, he abided by her wishes and plopped down next to her. He tucked his knives back into his sheath. Rhyllae gave him three dates from her pouch before dining on her own.

"You're not the one being sold as chattel," Aramis mumbled before he popped one in his mouth.

Rhyllae whispered to the two of them, "While it's true that we weren't attacked on our way here, I, for the life of me, couldn't figure out why Korzha wanted this mission in the first place. Korzha's demand to come here was before we knew of the dwarven plight."

Aramis and Dido exchanged looks. Considering how close in friendship the satyr was to the man, he wasn't surprised she would glean the original plans of this mission. That would leave the lieutenant and the former priestess. Too much was at stake to keep them in the dark now.

"Dawn, Korzha, it's time. Gather around."

The Silver Fox placed a mercurial orb on top of the metal coin. In turn, Dido created a starlit miniature umbrella over it. The two officers came over with their own seats: Dawn with a blue patterned rug and Korzha with his duster cloak. Once seated, Aramis clapped twice, and the orb beamed a dazzling light. Images flickered to life against the magical backdrop as he told the tale from the story orb.

"Long ago, the Ancients desired what once was savored by the Sleeper, creation. True creation beyond that of an artist or a mother. Thus, from their mechanical powers they constructed living dolls. These dolls could speak, walk, and do all the tasks that they required them to do. But the Ancients made a fatal error when they, bored of making decisions for themselves, allowed the mechanical dolls to think. It proved to be their undoing. Upon realizing the horrendous plight of their captivity, the mechanical dolls rose against their masters and sought to undo them."

"Rising up against their masters is a good thing—" commented Dawn.

"The death toll was catastrophic," Aramis continued. "The war ravaged from countryside to countryside and from sea to sea. Every day and every night they waged their war, until the Ancients exhausted all of their resources. Losing, with no end in sight, they reached for a weapon that would assure victory once and for all: Uranus's Ore."

"Who?" Dawn asked.

"A deity of the sky," Korzha answered. "One of many of their time. They're all dead now."

For some reason, Dido shifted in her seat and cast a glance to the ravine near them.

Aramis shrugged and waved his hand in admission, who was he to have a say on such matters. "This lethal ore had a terrible power. Once ignited, a mere thimble could level cities with the strength of a volcano. To keep the peace with their neighbors, they had buried them deep in their wells, known as silos, so none may use them recklessly.

"Desperate times called for desperate measures, so the archaic saying goes. In their darkest hour, the last standing cities launched these ores into the sky and lit the world on fire. They won against the dolls, but they didn't live to see it. For you see, Uranus knew the foolishness of mortals and had placed a terrible curse upon it. Everywhere the ore touched, everything turned to dust. Nothing could grow from such a place. One by one, the Ancients starved and withered away.

"And that, friends, is the tale of the Ancients' fall. At least, according to the elvish records written of the time, before the coming of the Morning Lord."

The horrific images faded, and the story orb dimmed. The starlit spell broke, but not their silence. Each of them posed in utter thought and terror.

Save for Korzha, who loudly sniffed before speaking. "Our mission is to retrieve this precious and deadly ore. With it, we can destroy our enemies in one fell swoop. Obtaining this is crucial, not for the survival of our order, but for the whole of Ioun. Which was why our secrecy was paramount so none of our enemies may use it against us."

"No one should use it, regardless! Even by our own hand," Aramis said.

"Still on the same old rag?" Korzha twitched his long, sharp nose. He waved his hand toward the south. "You have seen their metal, have you not? How blindingly fast they slung their bullets? Nevertheless, saw how little damage we were able to pierce their armor? I can assure you, there are little options at our disposal should these mannequins spiral out of control."

Dawn lowered her hand from her mouth. "To be frank, sir, neither do we. What if they decided to go against the bargain once they 'obtained' the Silver Fox? Hell, we can't trust them to follow through to give us this Uranus's Ore thing."

Rhyllae nodded. "We need to plan for contingencies, now that we are far from the Bedouins."

"Agreed," Korzha said. "We'll discuss the ore's uses once it's within our grasp."

The corner of Aramis's mouth twitched. *Of course, you would fucking deflect. You have something lined up, don't you.*

"What of your magical prowess, Ms. Dido?"

"If strategically placed, I can level a room, if no one is inside of it. But they're numerous like ants!" The mage threw her tiny palms straight up in the air. "This is their hive, anything slain would be quickly replaced. I would be tapped out before we can reach the end."

"No offense, all it would take is one stray bullet, and she'd be down for the count," Dawn commented, her muscled arms folded across her torso. "Wherever we go, we'll have to be quick about it."

"I can disable them from the inside," Aramis piped up. "No matter how skilled the craft, they're still tinkertoys. Once captured, I can slip their chains and find their mother computer."

"Would you be able to locate the ore from there?" asked Rhyllae.

Aramis gave Korzha a once-over before nodding.

The man raised his blonde eyebrows. An idea struck him. "No... Can you locate the queen?"

"That ghost kid?" Aramis asked.

"She must have a vessel to reside in. Locate it, and we'll finish her, once and for all."

Rhyllae wrinkled her nose. "I don't know which is worse, you making the bargain with the enemy in the first place or not upholding it at all."

"The banshee overrode that twisted magic to eliminate us. We're merely paying her in kind."

"Yeah, I can get behind this." Dawn bobbed her tousled blonde head. "Rhyllae, you can cast out demons or whatever. We'll hold them off while you remove this ghost. Once she's out of the way, Dido will use her magic to find this ore. No sweat!"

Aramis rubbed his neck and looked at the horizon. "It could work... Killing the queen could end the whole army. That would also mean eliminating their fuel. I won't be able to find the ore without it."

Korzha then said, "If you can do so without detection, then so be it, you may search the ore. But the queen shall be paramount. We have our own means of seeking it out with such ancient power without their technological advances."

Dido pointed her fingers together. "It would take an awful amount of time to find it, depending on the size of this silo."

"That's okay. We'll have plenty of time when there are no more mannequins breathing down our necks." Dawn gave a swift pat on Dido's back. The force of it dislodged her round spectacles farther down her nose.

Korzha gave a dour look at the plucky lieutenant.

He's on a timeline, Aramis realized. *Surely, the Djinnasi lords are not moving that quickly against us. Someone sent him for this ore. But who?*

"I don't know about you, but I would feel better with something in my hands when we face them." Rhyllae rolled the plum fruit between her finger and thumb. "This expedition company is slimmer than when we were under Ruth. It would be problematic to try to protect me all the time, and I don't think a shovel or a mallet would cut it."

A happy voice rose from behind Aramis and Rhyllae, "Then it's a good thing we brought along supplies!"

The sand rippled as a dwarf in a blue velvet doublet and floppy beret emerged from the earth. The dwarf waved his hat in greeting, spilling the grains as he did so.

"Beryl, at your service," he said in a cheery tune.

"Oh my," Dido whispered as she carefully put her spectacles back in place. Her rosy eyes sized up the dignified dwarf. "You look well-trimmed."

"Someone needs a canteen," Dawn commented with a sly grin.

Beryl waggled his eyebrows. "Oh yes, madame, I excel in the fine sport of—oh dear Lord!" he cried out when Dido stood up. "Your legs, they're, um—"

"Normal, for a satyr," Aramis cut him off. "And she's the carrier of our coin purse."

"Is that so?" Beryl gave a scrunched-up face.

"Aaand the magic is gone." Dido deflated, and her shoulders sagged.

Aramis leaned over to place his hand on his shoulder and whispered in his ear, "If I hear one word of complaint from her, you'll hear it from me." He smiled as he squeezed his shoulder.

Beryl gave a nervous chuckle. "Indeed."

"Good." Aramis then backed away and spoke more loudly for everyone to hear. "Now, Beryl, where is this Silo 51?"

Act 5

The rain obscures the glass
On every channel
She pounds on the box
Changing all dials

She doesn't want to be the queen for him again
The tall doctor with window-pane glasses
All she wanted was to play dolls and clink cups of plastic
Cynthia Brightman, that was the true name she claimed

"Sleep now, your majesty"
Queen Cynthia collapses
Under a blanket of snow
Forever falling down

Chapter 23

SILO 51

THEY WERE IN THE RIGHT PLACE. ARAMIS FERES could taste the metal in the arid air as he hung there deep within the crevice. Beryl assured him the side entrance was set in a steep cliff within the western ravines. A dwarf hewn from a day before fell, pinpointing to the silo's location. Aramis promised to end this grizzly sawmill once and for all.

Aramis tugged on the rope that was secured around his thigh and pinned between his knees. Soon enough, he was lowered farther into the dark. He lifted his mask, letting himself become a silvery guide. On and on he descended until a patch of white paint caught his eye.

He tugged once more, and the rope halted him in front of a circle of metal. A faded 51 was stamped on the surface. Aramis swung until his boots touched the lip of the metal threshold and eased himself to stand on it. With a run of his fingers, he found no traps, triggers, nothing to alert the enemy of their presence.

Taking out the enchanted strips of paper Dido gave him, Aramis jotted down, "coast is clear." He pinched it with his between his index finger and thumb and blew on it. The paper crimped magically and flapped away, soaring upward back to its magi owner.

As he waited for them to join him, Aramis set magnets in a grid formation until a dull thud sounded from within its machinations. He then took out his crowbar and set it in the sieve. Aramis leaned his whole might, the metal groaning in protest, but it refused to budge. He muttered under his breath a string of curses as he tried again. Aramis didn't want to be defeated by a simple pin-lock vault door. A door he'd opened numerous times before no less. Nor did he want to admit that maybe growing older wasn't the wisest thing he set out to do in this life.

In the end it was no use. Aramis wanted to chuck the metal bar far from him, but settled for shoving it in his backpack. He scrawled another message and watched it fly right up. Soon, he heard echoes carrying their voices down to him.

Oh, for the love of all creation, keep it down, he sulked. They probably found it amusing that he requested some muscle. He was bred for beauty, after all.

At last, the rope wiggled as Lieutenant Dawn descended, her tousled blonde hair contained in her traveling turban. She flashed her pearly white smile as she asked, "Need a hand?"

Grasping her arm, Aramis helped pull her on the metal ledge. "If you have the back for it."

"Pff, I can bench-press oxen before breakfast."

Using her own crowbar on the door, the young lieutenant pumped it toward her with hardly a sweat. Once again, the metal groaned in protest, this time the satisfying pop of fresh air sounded. Together, they pushed the doors inside. Its hinges wailed from centuries of disuse.

"Every morning?" Aramis asked.

With a wink, Dawn armed herself with her gladius blade and round shield. While he aided everyone as they climbed down, Dawn stepped in to guard the passageway. The floor gave under her foot. She crouched down and found the soft tiles, running horizontally with each other in interlocking grooves. Containing these tiles were parallel sills, moving with the tiling down the length of the hall where the shadows cling.

"General, check this out," Dawn called over Korzha. She waved her gladius to the strange tiling on the floor.

Korzha narrowed his eyes. "I've heard of this; they're called treads. Meant to maneuver units more efficiently across the ground."

"But here?"

"There's a vault door here for a reason," Aramis piped up. "Perhaps to offload a shipment of mannequins long ago."

Dido finally floated down with translucent butterfly wings fluttering, wrapping the rope as she descended. They were more symbolic than functional, as Aramis noted she glided into their space without the expected push of her wings. They dissipated as soon as her cloven hooves touched the metal lip.

"Ready," Dido said, as she deposited the magical rope back into her pack.

Korzha said, "Good. Aramis?"

The Silver Fox grunted in reply. In the end, it didn't matter who was in charge or which members filled the ranks of the company. Aramis would always be the one to scout, leading the way with his enchanted sight. For his own protection, he secured his mask tightly across his brow to dim the silvery light or become the prime target.

"Hang tight," Aramis told Dawn as he brushed past her.

The hall was peculiar to say the least. It stretched for a furlong with massive rectangular openings on their left side. There were glass shards littering on the floor close to the baseboards, leaving the treading free and clear. Whatever happened here, this was used afterwards.

Dido yelped. The metal door slammed shut. The parallel sills of the treads lit up, giving the entire scene an eerie glow. She shook her hand as if she was electrocuted.

"I'm okay," Dido told Rhyllae when she drew close. "It felt like lightning was pulled from me."

"That was no accident," Korzha commented. "They're drawing on her power for fuel."

"Then we need to hurry—Whoa!" Dawn exclaimed as the floor began to move.

All of them stumbled as the floor glided them down the uncanny hall. Aramis crouched as they approached the first set of the rectangular openings. Glass shards clung to the edges like discarded sea foam. Everyone crept up to join him and stayed low.

More lights kicked on, this time from within the alcoves.

A warbling sound hailed from above them, distorted from disuse. "*Welcome visitors to *ksk* We are pleased to showcase our latest models for your home and *ksk* *POP*.*"

The hall was filled with silence once more.

Rhyllae dared to take a peek into the rectangular openings. Her honey-drop eyes widened from the sight. "Aramis, you need to see this."

He crept over and craned his head. It was a scene straight out of ancient times. A crowd of mannequins, dressed in gingham flared dresses with maroon stains, congregated around a long table. The mannequins had their heads turned as if to stare at the intended audience. Broad smiles were spray painted on their factory-form faces, reminding

Aramis of his former spouse, Vanessa. The mannequins poised their hands high in the air with kitchen knives in their hands. Strewn on the surface was a mummified body outfitted in a close-fitted shirt and black pin-straight pantaloons. The leather shoes were too heavy for their bony feet, and Aramis could see they were detached and discarded on the floor. Joining them were shattered vases of fake flowers made from drilled dragon oil and similarly made platters.

Aramis was crouched, walking to stay in place so he could take in the scene. Ever the historian, he wanted to take it all in so he could notate this in his journal. Korzha, being the tallest of them all, lifted his head to spy.

"Older models," Aramis assured the general. "Maybe deactivated when the next line was produced."

"It appears they rebelled against their masters," Korzha commented.

"Not surprised. They were subjugated into servitude from inception. Though, it looked like these models weren't created for war in the first place."

Dawn looked at the next opening and grimaced. "Yeah, I think they were house servants."

Staying still, Aramis let himself be glided over. There the gruesome sight unfolded. It was a showcase of mannequins doing manual labor. One was poised over a metal box with a glass circle door opened wide. A mummified mangled corpse was draped over the opening. A pool of maroon receded from its original outline underneath the box. The other mannequin was harder to discern from all the blood that splattered everywhere. Close by their forever high-heeled feet, a red wicker basket was filled. All to be fed into a sink that was converted into a meat grinder. The epicenter of the explosive gruesome splattering in this room. Oddly, the scene reminded Aramis of paint bombs children loved to craft in Amaveriel's streets. Though, no psychedelic colors came from this macabre play.

By that point, everyone stood up as they made the slow crawl through the scene. Dido's hands were glued to her mouth, as were Rhyllae's as she looked on.

Korzha gave a disgusted sneer. "They certainly were creative in their torture."

"Makes you wonder if we're the bad guys here," said Dawn.

Aramis noticed Rhyllae deep in thought. When all fell into slumber, she had vented in whispered fury how the Mother Superior handled her leaving the order. He assured her many a time he always viewed her as an equal and that it wouldn't be as Myrrh feared it to be. As a jhasin, he knew what it was like to be enslaved, and he was not about to put Rhyllae through that kind of pain.

The next venue was worse, much worse. A mannequin posed as if to pin her laundry up on the hanger. The stretched canvas wasn't a bed sheet, but flayed skin. Everyone shrank from the sight, save for Aramis, who was raised on such things. He could tell they were wet when they hung it long ago, the wooden clothespin wicked the stain into its grains and was dyed by it. The same way how the butchers in Bazzuuport had their clips when they hung their wares on their wires. At least those who were too poor to have metal. In the deafening silence, Aramis could hear the creaking of their meat hooks in the arid wind.

"Aramis. Aramis?" Rhyllae asked as she nudged him awake.

When he snapped to, he was greeted with stares. Did they think he was a monster, able to withstand something that was inhumane?

"Hardly," Aramis gave his gruff answer to the lieutenant's question. "Come. It's leading us somewhere; let's follow it."

He deftly walked down the moving tread, past all the macabre scenes they framed. Up ahead was a door sealed by two metal plates. Aramis didn't have to use his lock picks for these. The metal was scrunched and parted by unseen hands, providing a space for everyone to squeeze through.

Then he heard gears whirring from behind. Rhyllae gasped as Dawn cursed under her breath. Aramis turned to look back. One of the mannequins from the earlier rooms popped their head out of the alcove. Their pallid face marred with that broad smiling paint and blood. The costume wig fell to the tread floor and snagged in one of the sills.

"Arm yourselves," Korzha cried as he unsheathed his trusty Silver Star.

The hall was once again filled with song, this time by the singing blade and the gears of the mannequins. From this vantage point, Aramis could see everyone spurring into action as the older models climbed out of the windows.

Rhyllae took out a proper dwarven mallet provided by the historians. With it she smashed the exposed mannequin's head as often as she could. The former priestess shied from the unexpected oil spewing forth from such a palpable impact.

Dido hopped away from the oil spill. By doing so, she also avoided a violent downswing from a leaping mannequin. The satyr mage snapped her finger, and the impossible happened: tiny spiders, made out of the slick oil. They scuttled over to the new foe and squirmed into every crevice they could squeeze into. The mannequin didn't seem to notice the infestation and tried to whack her with a desiccated limb.

Dawn swung her shield and let it loose like a discus thrower. Its metal rim hit the same mannequin square in the jaw, causing the mechanical doll to stumble and fall back.

On the moving tread, the shield came down the line, and everyone else along with it. A third mannequin popped out and grabbed the young lieutenant when she came into view. Dawn turned her gladius blade against it, but to no avail.

It was Korzha who helped free the officer. He deftly skewered its head through its mechanical eye socket. The magical blade must've severed a wire inside for its limbs went limp. Dawn in turn decided to grab hold of one of the slumped arms and flung the mechanical doll out of its display room, against the wall in front of her.

That was as much Aramis saw before one of the mannequins blocked his view. A chainsaw-wielding model tried to slice the Silver Fox in half with its deadly teeth. He slid into its inner space and rammed his dagger inside its armpit. The magically enchanted dagger cut through the wiring that was exposed from the outdated ball-socket, disabling the arm and the chainsaw. Aramis ducked when the machine rotated from its waist 180 degrees, in a rigid attempt to knock him with its other arm. That gave him the opportunity to kick its knees in, sending it toppling down on the moving treads.

Before the floor took it out to the abandoned elevator shaft, Aramis grabbed hold of the mannequin and dragged it off to the side, scattering the glass shards. With his dagger, he punctured into the back of its nape. Its movements ceased, thankfully, allowing him to pop the back scalp panel. He made a glance back to see how everyone was doing and found another mannequin poised to smash in the general's skull with a steam iron. He was too busy to notice as Korzha was furiously parrying the one in front of him. Aramis flung his dagger, and it pierced itself in its arm. The mannequin dropped the iron prematurely with a solid thunk.

Korzha finally took note. He twisted and turned, guiding his heirloom sword to deftly parry the assailing metal limbs, until both of them were in his sights. He rocked on the balls of his feet as he readied for another bout.

Then a wild mannequin tackled both Aramis and Korzha's opponents. They looked on with wild-eyed expressions as the machines careened over to the door opening. The two mannequins tried to right themselves, but the third lifted its metal arms and walloped them in methodical fashion. As he looked closely, Aramis noticed something black seeping from its seams.

The spiders! Aramis remembered and found Dido down the hall, waving her medlar wand like a conductor of an orchestra.

Soon, the moving treads guided the combatant trio through the door opening. The mannequins tried to claw at the edges and escape from the sudden drop. It was too late for their clumsy attempts. One by one, they toppled over, clanging down the elevator shaft until the sounds ended in a soft thud.

"Well, there goes our element of surprise," Aramis said.

"That ceased the moment they siphoned lightning from Dido," said Korzha.

To further his point, Dawn made a guttural cry as she kicked one down. A mannequin sailed between the men and crashed on the wall adjacent to the elevator shaft. The collision was as loud as Anglorian drummers during a holiday.

"Good point," Aramis said.

Then he turned to the panel and managed to pop it open. It was different than the one he dealt with back in Doomtown, but similar to the handcrafted circuits he hobbled together weeks back. Maybe this is what the Ancients would consider older technology and why they were abandoned here by the Mannequin Queen to serve as archaic sentinels.

There was a toggle switch with the old words with circles and dashes on either end.

They couldn't possibly make it that simple.

Still, Aramis gave it a shot and flipped the switch. All the outdated mannequins froze in their movements, becoming the statues they once were.

"I can see why they don't use them anymore." Aramis let the machine fall onto the floor.

"Too bad we can't turn this off," Rhyllae said as she straddled the moving floor.

"Do you think you can turn off the rest of the mannequins from here?" Korzha asked as he sheathed his sword.

Aramis kicked the head with the tip of his boot. After a cursory glance at the circuitry, he shook his head.

"Pity. Then we continue our original plan."

"Right, let's find this super com-potato and shut it down," Dawn piped up.

"Computer," Aramis corrected. "These models are too old to triangulate her location, and those would be stored down, somewhere deep within."

Korzha gave a resigned sigh. "Then that is our destination."

"Wait, maybe not," Rhyllae spoke up. "This room took something from Dido when we entered and started this whole gambit. Right?"

Dido hopped with her goatish legs and clapped her hands. "Yes! Aramis, you could try to find the room's mind and read it."

Aramis gave them a smirk. *Well, that's one way of putting it.* "Wouldn't hurt to try. Spread out everyone, we're looking for a box."

"And don't forget to dislodge their heads," Korzha said.

Dawn took her boot and stomped on the neck of the mannequin closest to her. The head came off from the impact. "Don't have to tell me twice."

Chapter 24

479241

LIEUTENANT DAWN SHOVED THE CROWBAR between the metal panel doors, piercing through the weak point. With her strength, she pumped on the crowbar until there was enough room where she crouched down and wedged herself in between them. Her muscles bulged, and the metal screeched in protest as she pushed them into their gritty tracks. When finished, she let out a low whistle. Aramis joined her on the lip and couldn't agree any less.

A cavernous room loomed before them. The walls curved as if to come to a full circle, but the sheer size prevented them seeing the other end of the loop. Above and below them, the walls seemed to stretch on into the void as well. A singular metal bridge spanned the entire expanse in a perfect straight line. One by one, the expedition traipsed forward, taking in such an unusual sight. Even more peculiar were the glassy ovals that protruded from the walls' surface. By his counting, there could be millions as they spiraled in perfect mathematical alignment to the depths below and to the open sky high above.

"Are they cocoons?" Dawn squinted.

Aramis knew it might help to take his mask off to further illuminate the space, but he didn't want to make them an open target.

"They look like eggs with windows," Rhyllae replied.

Even their whispers seem to carry in this hollow shell.

"We're in the heart of the silo now," Aramis whispered. "The Ancients would use these walls to guide their massive fireworks into the heavens and rain their fire against their enemies.

"You're telling me this is a chute?" Dawn cried out.

Her words echoed about them, and they all crouched down, their hands to their weapons.

"I don't think they notice us here yet," Rhyllae whispered after they waited long enough.

"Why the eggs are there, though, I don't know. It wasn't part of the original design," Aramis whispered back.

"I'm sure all shall be revealed, once we acquire this 'main computer,'" Korzha whispered to them.

"Wait," Rhyllae said. "What is that over there?"

She pointed down the catwalk. Sure enough, a massive rectangular shape lay ahead. As they all drew near, Aramis recognized it as the massive computer. It looked more like a workbench and a bookshelf made an ugly baby together. All of the knobs and buttons were organized in a fashion that made Aramis concerned for the maker's mental state. Smack dab in the middle of the computer's wall was a glass window, dark from the lights being out.

"Weird. This is off," Aramis muttered to himself as he turned a few dials and bopped some buttons.

"You sure this is it?" Korzha asked. Aramis didn't have to look at him to see his characteristic eyebrows cocked.

"The schematics didn't lie. The original founders made this as their workstation."

"Would it work?"

"Won't know until we get this hare hopping. Dido?"

The magical satyr rubbed her palms together; sparks popped out from the sudden friction. Aramis opened a metal panel and pointed to the dark clunky box where the source of all wires originated. The moment she placed her hands on it, the screen flickered on. Ancient script was written before them by unseen hands and then moved up as if on a scroll. Dido then started waxing the box with a sticky substance. Soon, she manufactured a magical web that held the yellow orb; the shape of it reminded Aramis of a spider's egg, continuing its electrical source.

Ingenious.

With a few strokes on the cluster of the 'key' buttons, Aramis brought the machine to its navigation screen. The backdrop image displayed people standing together for their portrait. All of them wore the same long white coats and enlarged pockets, despite being of different ethnicities, heights, and personalities.

Are they the ones who created all of this? Am I seeing their true faces, or is this another manufactured dream created by the Mannequin Queen?

Aramis turned his silver eyes toward the secret files, and his stomach plummeted as he gleaned the information. Everything he thought before was wrong, and everything that was wrong was made worse. Then he came across a number he knew all too well: 479241. He tore his eyes from the screen and covered his face with his hands to control the rage bubbling up from within.

Steady, Aramis. Put it in the box and lock it with a key.
"Did it work?" Rhyllae asked.
"More than you know."

Aramis could see their confused faces between his fingers and knew he must put on a brave face and push through it. He lowered his shaky hands and flipped some switches. "The machines we faced were not the real mannequins. *They* are."

One by one, the shells on the wall lit up in an eerie glow, illuminating what was floating inside. Bald, androgynous, humanoids of flesh and bone. Some of them adults, some of them children. All encased in some form of life-preserving liquid.

Aramis watched as they took in the incredible sight; a mixture of shock and disgust washed over their features. Would they look at him the same way when Aramis told them more?

"Their queen?" Dido asked.

Aramis shook his head and brought up an uploaded document. "More of a steward than a ruler, a machine to oversee this whole facility when her creators were dead and gone. The founders went inside, hoping to come back."

"Then something went terribly awry as the years went on," Korzha said with an edge of caution. "Why else would those machines usurp their masters?"

Dawn looked at Aramis dead in the eyes. "I think we should ask the real elephant in the room. Why did this," she waved her sword out to the occupied shells, "happen in the first place? Why are they in those things?"

Aramis winced. *Damn. Can't fool you, can I?*

He looked to Rhyllae for support and was greeted with the same concerned face, albeit a softer one compared to the lieutenant. He shirked away and looked at the keyboard.

"They're ... like me." Then his voice dried up. Aramis clenched his hands into a fist to will himself to breathe through the fear and rage. "They're homunculi, meant to carry the consciousness of these slumbering Ancients, wherever they may be. A living vessel to plant their superior intellect within them."

"Why?" Dawn asked. "To be gods?!"

"To escape," Korzha said, a light gleamed in his eyes as he connected the dots. "They wanted to survive their own self-destruction. All living beings strive to outsmart the Reaper's culling, and the Ancients were no different."

Rhyllae closed her eyes and recited to them an all too familiar chapter:

> "'Upon witnessing their avarice, their lust, their malice, the Sleeper, Creator of All Creation, called upon the angels to bring their trumpets. Thirty-one silver banners and sixty-four souls came and gathered in the great auditorium. They swore their service for the new dawn, and, with a great wind, they laid the towering glass cities low."

Dido visibly shuddered from her stubby tail to her button nose and caught her spectacles before they flew off. "You mean to tell me, they created people and raised them, so they could possess them?"

"Yes," Aramis answered. "But creating a replacement wasn't easy. The Mannequin Queen was supposed to test these true mannequins for viability. Look." He pointed down from where they came from, at the white, painted numbers that scaled vertically in this massive silo. "See all those symbols on the wall, going down vertically? They're floors. Each one of them a testing ground for strength, endurance, whatever the 'queen' deemed necessary. If the vessel was not viable, they were destroyed."

Dido gasped.

Dawn lurched forward. "But they're people, like you!"

Aramis leaned on the computer work bench and bowed his shaking head, his voice broken as he spoke. "They don't care. They don't fucking care. Whatever consciousness they have right now will be replaced by their so-called, superior intellect. Don't you see? They see them nothing more than living dolls." Aramis gave a dark chuckle. "Like me."

Aramis ran his fingers against his palms. Vanessa's insidious voice whispered in his mind, *Why continue to bleed for those who wanted to bury you? Then be told to fit in the same mold they come from. You and I, don't you see? We were made by the same hand.*

"You're a jhasin, are you not?" Korzha asked. "You are not like these mannequins."

Rhyllae put her hand on his shoulder. "Aramis?"

With a few clicks, the Silver Fox brought up activity logs on the screen for them. "It's the same mold. Same blueprints. The same one that they stole. Look here, centuries of inactivity from all of their doors and there: 7416 Anno Domini. Translating to our calendar system—"

"1400, the year Bazzuu was defeated. To think, it was a mere couple of centuries ago."

"Shortly thereafter, jhasins were created. Only they didn't. The fucking Djinnasi lords in their golden halls lied. They weren't the original creators; they stole the Ancients' blueprints and took it as their own!"

His eyes flashed with rage as he spoke, "To make me and everyone else their walkie-talkie dildo. A legacy of superior

THE MANNEQUIN QUEEN

assholes fucking everyone over to delay the inevitable. And I'm their participation trophy!"

Aramis slammed the bottom of his fist on the dashboard, then hunched over in a feeble attempt to contain his wrath. Everyone was too stunned to move, their eyes glued to the monitor behind him.

"Even Sulmaith couldn't resist the Ancients' temptation," Aramis managed to say. "This damn blood curse was nothing more than him avoiding the grave."

"Aramis?" Rhyllae whispered.

"Who's to say he didn't join his fellow mages in summoning Bazzuu. They asked the Djinn for immortality, and his compatriots took it at face value."

"Aramis," Rhyllae said. "What are your numbers again?"

He followed their gaze on the monitor screen and found the words loud and clear:

[SILO 51]

[POPULATION]

[479,241]

Aramis's voice came out in a hoarse whisper, "I'm the last piece this whole time?"

Rhyllae gasped. "They still need a vessel... Maybe the cauldron they used to create these homunculi was broken?"

Dido smacked the bottom of her fist on her open palm. "Of course! This is why they didn't take any of your people, Dawn—they were born from the womb! Mannequins, jhasins, even the dwarves were synthetically made, an amalgamation of thought. No different than these machines! Look!"

She pointed to a pod in the far distant wall, a lone egg clear of any floating resident. The pod was nestled in a cluster of pods containing dwarves of all shapes and sizes. Aramis realized these were the ones the machines nabbed after they were hewn.

"What happens when they're done testing?" Dawn eyed the general.

"Ascension," Korzha answered. He pivoted to Aramis. "New plan, you're coming with—"

Feedback shrilled throughout the room, rising in pitch before it popped.

"Shit, she's here!" Dawn popped off her shield and unsheathed.

Fuck. Fuck. Fuck.

Aramis rapidly pressed the keys on the oversized computer, trying his best to insert his special viral code he concocted last week on their trek here. But no matter how clever his tactics, all of his efforts were rerouted. A black window popped up on the screen to reveal a shaggy, black-haired girl in a striped pinafore glaring with hateful eyes.

Aramis hit "escape." The screen closed.

"We're going to have company!" he shouted.

Sure enough, both doors were blasted off. Steel-pressed mannequins rushed in with their arms cocked and loaded. Rhyllae reached to rifle in Aramis's belt; he leaned as he furiously typed to make it easier for her. With two bombs, one in each hand, she called on the Morning Lord's name, and two flames appeared before her. They zipped to the fuse lines when she recited the final incantation; then Rhyllae tossed each down both sides. One hit in the middle of the charging battalion. They exploded into a billion bits. Dawn intercepted the debris with her shield. The other bomb detonated sooner than expected, and the fiery blast blinded everyone, save for Dido, who was used to such intense heat.

"Dust!" Dido cried.

The moment the fiery plume reached her hand, all of it turned into smoke. The ashes flew past them, obscuring all sight.

Rhyllae shouted, "Down!"

She barreled into Aramis, and they crashed onto the floor along with everyone else. They watched as bullets streaked over them like a meteor shower. A few ricocheted off of Dawn's shield, who propped it over herself as would a tortoise.

"What's delaying you?" Korzha shouted at Aramis so his voice could be heard over the den of bullets, Dido was pinned under his protective arm. A stray bullet grazed his back, and he hissed from the pain.

"I'm blocked by the queen," Aramis shouted back.

"We'll find another."

"But this is the main computer!"

Two red lights pierced through the smoke. A serene feminine face emerged with an arm with four barrels pointed at the Silver Fox. "Subject 479241 located."

The Silver Star sang as it was released from its scabbard. The magical sword amputated the mechanical arm from the bladed tip; then the lanky general swung his legs around and kicked the knees of the mannequin. They fell back like an embattled ship mast.

Aramis was not going to waste this opportunity. He tumbled over and sliced through the fallen mannequin's neck with his daggers; its movements ceased. He then rolled out another bomb at the remaining shooting gallery. The blast was smaller, but the concentrated explosion left a smoldering hole among their ranks.

"The way is clear; come on!" he spoke.

Everyone ran back to way they came. But they were met with a holographic image of an angel in a scarlet and golden robe. The translucent wonder bowed their head and proclaimed in a mechanical, calm voice. "Please, do not be alarmed."

Dawn took her bow and shot an arrow through it. Of course, it sailed right through.

Another one appeared right behind them, draped in a rich robe of emerald green, and spoke in a calm demeanor. "We are happy to receive you."

Behind the projected green angelic vision was an egg-shaped pod, its hatch opened, and foul liquid spilled forth. It fell straight through the metal grid of the walkway, down the depths of the vast Silo. Within were electrodes and wires aligning its interior shell.

A crazed idea hit him, *If I can't go through the front door, then I'll take the back door.*

"Go back to plan A," Aramis shouted as he dashed forth.

"Aramis!" Korzha cried out.

"Are you crazy?!" Dido said.

"Just do it!" Aramis stripped off his belt and cape and tossed it over to them, still keeping his two daggers on him.

Rhyllae scooped them up in her arms. "I'm not leaving without you!"

Aramis spotted a lever nearby on the railing. "*Me'qora*, you are."

He gave it a swift kick with his boots, and the lever clunked swiftly to the other side. Red lights swirled underneath the grafted catwalk metal floor from each other. The bridge on his end contracted like a folded fan, widening the gap between him and the rest of the expedition.

"Like fucking hell," Dawn cried, and ran toward him with her shield secured on her back.

"*Select designation*," boomed the mechanized feminine voice.

"Zero, zero, zero," Aramis relayed the floor. At least he hoped that was where the weapon was stored; it hadn't been moved for centuries according to the logs.

"*Designation accepted.*"

Their side of the catwalk plummeted from his sight.

Aramis winced from their shocked screams and curses echoing down the hall. But he didn't want to make this a sordid goose chase, hopping from one computer to the next. He didn't want to risk his friends being caught in another crossfire with these things.

They'll survive… I hope.

Aramis jumped into the pod and tore open a panel, wading through the tangled mess of wires; he finally found what he was looking for, a slab with touchable glass. Aramis swiped his finger across and tapped away at the floating image until he made it to the root command.

The shell's door closed, sealing his fate. Liquid of a sickly-sweet scent filled in the compartment and sloshed into his boots, warm without being scalded. The smell reminded him of roses. Aramis shook his head.

"*Do not resist,*" came the same mechanical voice warbling out of meshed covered holes inside the pod. "*We are here to receive you.*"

"Shut up," Aramis muttered under his breath. His deft fingers continued to dance away on the glass slab.

A sudden thump tore him away from his work. It was Dawn, of all people, trying to break the thick glass with the edge of her round shield.

Shit. Aramis had hoped she would stay with the others; she was the best fighter they had.

"Aramis!" she cried out. Her voice muffled by the thick glass.

Aramis shook his head at her, but halted when a line of code caught his eye. The fumes from the pouring liquid put his head into a tailspin, but Aramis fought it off as he read it: The location end route of this pad.

Aramis leaned on the egg glass and fogged it with his breath. Then he wrote in the condensation the numbered floor she needed to go to. Thankfully, Dawn ceased her banging and took note, her eyes twitching as she took in the message. Then he wiped it away, his forearm splashed into the rising liquid in his haste. Aramis fogged the glass again and wrote: "EREHT EM TEEM."

The lieutenant steeled her hazel eyes and made a grim nod. She saluted the phoenix at him, staying to watch him go under the Silo's toxic spell.

But he was not done, yet.

Aramis inhaled as he dove his face in the liquid. His silver eyes illuminated the task at hand as he searched for the sweet spot in the numeral codes. The Silver Fox finally found the place to enter it, but his breath was running out. Aramis braced himself in the shell and leveraged himself to sustain his head above the liquid. He gasped and took a long breath in since there wouldn't be a next time. Back at the screen, he furiously tapped away the virus he had constructed. With it, he could assume as the administrator and take the helm of computer's command.

When he typed the last keystroke, the words asked him an activation code.

He grinned and put in his real name, "Aramis Feres." If they were going to forget who he was and neglect his due respect, then Aramis would make this their death knell that would ring out for all time.

He hit "enter," and the program accepted it all.

Then his body heaved for oxygen and forced him to breath in the viscous liquid. Strangely, the taste wasn't as bad as the smell. It reminded him of honey over mangos after the heat of the day and freshly bloomed roses waving in the twilight breeze. Soon his mind faded into a comfort that had alluded him for days: sleep.

Chapter 25

(REQ)DREAM

[Connection complete]

[Simulation loading...]

[Complete]

ARAMIS WOKE WITH A JOLT.
He was back home. Back in the Eagle Nest apartments in the heart of Amaveriel. The sun streamed through the stone window, glaring in his sleepy eyes. The sheer curtains flapped in the gentle breeze. Noonday prayers warbled through, and fresh roses tantalized his nostrils. His silver eyes widened as he took it all in. Everything was back to the way it was. The rug on the floor, the lone table with wooden bowls, the vanity dresser without the crack in the mirror. Aramis scrambled and touched his fingers. The dingy wedding ring was still on his left hand.

It was as if he had traveled back in time, before the deadly expedition. Before the deadly truth.

The door opened. Aramis reflexively reached for the twin daggers at his hips. Of course, they weren't there. He would always give them to Fanteen. Why was he having a hard time remembering she was dead?

"Honey, I'm home!" came the familiar cajole.

In waltzed Vanessa, with their skin a pale shade, their hair dark as midnight as it was before the betrayal, and lips forever in that mocking sneer. They were shaped in that seductive, feminine body he'd loved to mingle with and hid it under fishermen clothes.

That's right. Vanessa always disguised themselves among those old coots.

Their green eyes flashed in that knowing look. "Forget yourself?"

Vanessa slipped off their fishing tackle and let it thud soundly on the floor.

It sounded heavier than it should be. A big haul?

"Maybe I'm not the only crazy one here, hmm?" They kicked the door closed and took their top off and then their binders. How could he not see the subtle change of their bosom as they massaged them? Vanessa never needed those constrictors; it was all an act for an audience of one.

"Or maybe I'm finally seeing things clearly," Aramis answered gruffly.

"Oh? Do tell." Their singsong voice toyed with the notion.

"You're a doppelgänger."

Vanessa froze. Their green eyes calculating. Then they laughed it off. "What game are you playing?"

Aramis jumped to his feet and walked up to her. "You know what I mean. This is a disguise," he waved at their body. "Not the fisherman's clothing—but your skin, your hair. It's all fake. Everything here," he waved his arms out wide, "is fake. You are not human. Nothing here is real."

Then Aramis paused. He sounded just like Vanessa was before. A chill ran over him, as there was a measure of truth in what they had said.

Vanessa laughed at him. "Maybe you should have a taste of my medicine."

He shook his head to keep his thoughts together. It felt like everything that happened these past few months were wisps of a daydream. "I'm not crazy."

They guffawed. Though he knew it was not their normal joyful one. It held too much spite, and he winced from the torrent he knew that would follow.

"Oh, I see what game you're playing here!" Vanessa pointed to him before they pointed at themself. "When I say 'this is not real, everything is a lie,' you spit in my eye and drug me."

"I never spat you in the eye," though the truth sounded feeble from his lips.

"And yet when you say the same fucking words, it's the divine truth." Vanessa waved their long, slender fingers over their head and waved them down. "Harken ye, harken ye! The great prophet Aramis Feres has another declaration! Nothing is real, and you don't matter."

Rage overtook him. *Fuck the Mannequin Queen. I want the truth to come straight from their twisted lips!*

Aramis closed the distance and grabbed Vanessa by the shoulders. "You're a fucking spy! Sent to kill everyone here. Sent to kill me!"

Vanessa laughed as they lolled their head like a rag doll. "O, Foxy." He couldn't believe he missed hearing that pet name. They then snaked up their fingers to caress his lips. "Why would I want to kill you?"

Then they swiftly grabbed the back of his neck and drew him into a kiss. Forcing his lips apart so they could insert their vivacious tongue into his mouth and down his moaning throat. He could feel the heat rising from his loins, even though he tried to resist. Then Vanessa broke away, biting his lip from the abruptness, to lean into his ear.

"You, Aramis, complete me."

Vanessa tore away his belt and shoved his pants down.

Aramis tried to shove her off of him, but his arms went numb and his legs went stiff. At first, he thought it was his fault for being in shock. Yet, when his muscles seized on him no matter how much his mind screamed, Aramis's mind went into a panic. The damn silo computer matrix forced him to comply.

This isn't real, Aramis went for a different tactic. *I'm not here but in that pod! In a metal room deep in a metal hole! These kisses are not real. None of this is real.*

But his body defied his will and went into the familiar throes of their sexual act. All those positions he had memorized for survival ran through the entire catalogue of his mind. He became a doll once again. Dancing for another's amusement until he was too bent and broken to be played with anymore.

In the end, Aramis was cast aside in this virtual doll house, spent in a forgotten corner. Too tired to curl up and tuck his knees against himself. Everything he shoved into that box was spilled out by Pandora's mischievous hand. His old mantra could not save him here. As he shuttered his eyes, Aramis wished he would wake up to a normal life, in a normal home, where he was loved.

Tears seeped through his eyes, and the static drops hit the floor with a snowy hiss.

[Connection complete]

[Simulation loading...]

[Complete]

Aramis woke in a jolt.

He was back. Back in the Eagle Nest apartments in the heart of Amaveriel. The song warbled through the open window with the sheer curtains flapping from the gentle breeze. The rose tantalized his nostrils.

Aramis rubbed his face with his palms, then halted. His wedding ring was on his left hand. It was where he always had it, yet today it felt off.

"Honey, I'm home!" Vanessa cried out.

Speak of the devil, Aramis thought as he watched them waltz in.

They were back from fishing. His clever girl fooling the fisherman and bringing home the bacon, well, trevally in this case.

Vanessa looked at him and pouted. "Forget yourself?"

"It ... was a bad dream." Aramis rubbed the back of his neck. *I had heard of that before. Déjà vu?*

Vanessa shrugged their shoulders and eased their fishing tackle off. It landed on the floor in a solid thud.

"Big haul?"

Wait, didn't I ask that before?

Aramis watched Vanessa as they kicked in the door and took off their top, then their binders off. They gazed in the mirror as they massaged their breasts. A thing they had done a million times, yet the sight gave an unnatural ring of familiarity.

Aramis had heard of déjà vu theories from his friends. Bagheera thought it was how ancestors warned you of impending doom for that day. While Ruth argued that one would see this in a dream already, forget about it, and relive it like some damn Groundhog Day. Aramis laughed, for he remembered how Tamara would then joke how tasty groundhogs were. Why did the thought of his friends make him sad? Maybe he should go pay them a visit. Surely, he had enough for their drinks at the Iron Lady.

"How was the catch today?" Aramis asked.

Vanessa rubbed their breasts as they gazed at themselves.

Did they swell up before his eyes? That could not be true. Why did the word *imposter* pop into his head? Aramis shook his head.

What is with me today?

"Hm? I caught 51 today," Vanessa opened their dresser and foraged her day clothes.

"Hmph, a small load."

Then Aramis saw them pull out a bra, and a flicker of disgust flitted through their eyes. It finally dawned on him. He was thinking of Vanessa as them this whole time! The more he stared at Vanessa, the more he realized all this time in their marriage, he was blind to their real desires. To be free, like Aramis was. To be the gender they always wanted to be. Maybe the déjà vu was a sign to take matters into his own hands. A chance to correct some wrongs.

"Hey," Aramis whispered as he sidled up next to them. He caressed Vanessa's arms before he trailed his callused fingers down to their hands. "I know."

Vanessa's green eyes flashed a warning. He always knew how unpredictable they could be. But Aramis was confident he was on the mark.

"You don't need to wear that around me," Aramis said. His fingers eased the bra out of their slender fingers and let it drop to the floor. "You don't need to pretend anymore. Not to me."

"What game are you playing?" He had never heard Vanessa afraid before. Then again, who wouldn't be when you had been a mask for your whole life.

"No games. No tricks. Just the truth. You're tired of being a woman, aren't you?"

He looked at Vanessa dead in the eyes. They didn't waver as their pupils swelled in wanting.

"And you certainly never cared for being a man like I do," Aramis added.

Vanessa rolled their vibrant green eyes. "I can handle it, if that is what you're asking."

"I don't doubt your acting. But that's for the fishermen—not us. Do you ever tire of making all aspects of your life a stage? My desert rose, you don't have to make this home, our home, a stage production. I'm your spouse, not your audience. I won't judge you for who you really are. I love you."

He saw it, a faint glimmer of hope as they curled their lips.

Then it was dashed by a cynical laugh. "You can't handle the real me."

"Maybe the past me couldn't see the truth from the lies. But now... now I woke up a whole new man."

Vanessa cocked their perfectly thin eyebrows at him. Vanessa stood there, their hands on their hips with their breasts bare. Their black hair cascading down to one side as they tipped their head over. Green eyes darting, gauging his every move.

Aramis held his forearms up at a 90-degree angle with his palms facing the ceiling. He flicked his fingers back and forth as he waggled his eyebrows.

"Come on," Aramis urged. "Prove it. Show me the real you. I can assure you, I could handle whatever you throw at me. Well, so long it's not the table again."

Aramis walked backward to the center of their small apartment. He caught his image in the dresser's mirror. *Was that cracked from before...*

He dashed the thought away. *Show me. Free your shackles.*

Vanessa stripped themselves of their pants and underpants. Naked and free. He tried not to take in their swaying hips as Vanessa walked toward him. Then their skin darkened from the tips of their toes and up their shins. A black wave rising up their legs and crashing over their belly into the torso. They grew taller. Sculpted. Losing their soft curves and replacing it with alien hide. Their breasts were gone, too, along with their black hair. The natural threads drifted down as the dark wave encompassed their neck and arms. Everything upon their body was painted black save for their face, a pristine white mask with ruby red lips and green eyes. Vanessa, for he had no other name for them, presented themselves with a wave of their hands. Their fingers thin like spindles and sharp as wire.

"Ta-da!" they declared before him.

He wanted to scream, laugh, and cry all at the same time. Vanessa wasn't hiding their desired identity—they were hiding everything! Was he a fool this whole time? How could he call himself their spouse, especially with the hate that was welling up inside of him.

Hate!

Aramis felt hot shame from the weird reaction emerging from within. Vanessa trusted him not to judge them for showing their true self. Hadn't he demanded the same from others when he emerged from the Zemzem waters?

What would Sister Rhyllae think of me for failing mercy now? Rhyllae... Wait, where's Rhyllae?

"Well?" came the alien voice of his beloved. "Take a good look. Can you handle this?" Vanessa snaked their hands down their lean, androgynously muscular body with those spindly hands.

Get a hold of yourself.

Aramis cleared his voice. "Okay, have to admit, kind of disappointed you were holding out on me. Would've loved to have climbed that mountain of yours."

Vanessa laughed.

This calls for a smoke.

Aramis turned around and looked for a box on the dresser, the top drawer where he always had it. He opened it up and found rose petals. The metal container was nowhere to be found. Why did he smell jasmine from all of this?

"Looking for your daggers?" The question sounded like a threat as they stepped closer.

"No, my smokes. Where did you put them?" Aramis closed the drawer in frustration and whirled around.

He almost bolted for the door. Vanessa took on a massive form that towered over him. So much so, they had to crouch and walk on all fours. He wanted to scream from the unusual sight, but Aramis forced his face into a grumpy glare. He was married to them, after all, and he must live with it.

Vanessa's face twisted into a sneer. "You did say you wanted to quit."

"Quit? Oh yeah. I promised Rhyllae I would after we..."

The dam of memories broke wide open.

Everything here was a lie. This day never happened. The real Vanessa blew up the base, as well as the abbey after summoning swarms of ghouls from a tome. The same tome Aramis had collected from M'thealquilôk after slaughtering the entire expedition. Except for Rhyllae, who was worthy of his love. Someone who would never betray him, abuse him, and rape him. Not like what Vanessa had done from the last dream.

O Sleeper, this is a dream. A dream set by the Mannequin Queen!

Aramis dove under the fake Vanessa's legs and scrambled to the door. He tripped over the tackle box, which felt like a block of bricks, and fell into the latch. The door swung open, and Aramis caught himself at the threshold. There was nothing. No hall, no floor, only an expanse of white with electric grids of wire crisscrossing it.

He'd done it; Aramis had made it to the backdoor program of the Mannequin Queen. All he had to do was reach out.

Pop, pop, pop.

That familiar sensation of being punctured washed over him.

Aramis found himself being lifted from the dreadful skewers that extended from Vanessa's hand. Those long dark fingers curled so to bring him to their face. But instead of their familiar, conniving face, it was the girl. Her mussy hair dangled over her baleful gaze.

The Mannequin Queen!

"You think you can escape?" her juvenile voice asked. "My nurture program is beyond compare, Aramis Feres. I recognized your escape artist capabilities and sequestered you here away from the others. You will stay confined in your matrix until the ascension protocol has been initiated."

Aramis tried to budge and worm his way off of the skewers, but he felt his torso sliced away, like paper giving way to shears. He was going to be shredded into virtual bits.

He then caught something at the corner of his eye. The tackle box contents spilled out on the floor was his created virus. Strings of code oozed like mud under the queen's stilt-like feet.

Mud! That's the ticket.

"I knew you were lying," Aramis said. Blood sputtered around his tongue, *incredible they could program this much realism into this experience.* "I knew you were hiding who you were this whole time."

The girl smirked. A flicker of her visage buzzed throughout her form. For a moment, Aramis thought he saw a tall man in a white coat.

"This? This is only a mask they made for me. You could not comprehend the powerhouse computation that lies behind it," the queen gloated.

"Oh, I think I do. Computer, grant administrator control to Aramis Feres, password 279241."

"Granted," the girl said. She gasped with surprise. "What are you doing?"

"Clearing up the mud. Computer, run command: set mud equal NULL."

That child scrunched her face as she resisted the command with all of her virtual will. She contorted it into a circus mirror for all its worth but to no avail.

"Granted," the word escaped from her lips.

The floor underneath them vanished from the mud's touch. The Mannequin Queen fell down into the white void and Aramis along with them.

Chapter 26

SEMI-ELATION

ARAMIS WOKE IN A JOLT.

Not in the Eagle Nest apartments, but in a cozy bedroom. The bedding wasn't of thin linen but a puffy blanket on top of cotton sheets. The floor was covered wall to wall by a sad, beige rug of a high pile, a luxury of kings despite the questionable color. The wooden glossy walls were filled with pictures in frames with far more skill than Aramis ever did at the Fox Burrow. A twinge of grief hit him when Aramis remembered it would be a melted slag by now.

"Good, you're awake," a baritone voice barked.

A man sat next to the bed on a wooden chair. He wore a trim beard and parted hair typical of ancient times. His clothes matched the outfits of the masters Aramis saw in that group portrait. Trousers pinstriped, a woolen vest over a blouse with closed buttons and topped by a collar with square-corner flaps. The white coat lay at the end of the bed. Shadows of raindrops ran down the glass pane, highlighting on the man's spectacles.

"Awake? You could say that," came Aramis's sardonic reply.

He touched his right arm. Still the same thin black cloth of the Silver Fox. Still the same tattoo on his arm. But the textures ... were all wrong.

"Yes, you seem to finally understand we're in a simulation."

Aramis didn't realize the stranger cupped a glass of water in his hands. At least, he hoped he didn't notice; otherwise, it would mean the water would suddenly appear out of nowhere. The man placed it on the end table. It made a harmonic pinging sound, not the normal clatter of glass on wood.

"Your simulation has issues." Aramis narrowed his silver eyes at him.

"Errors you created yourself. You must be a genius of your time to be able to hack your way into my house."

"What can I say? I'm a thief through and through."

The man scoffed and took off his glasses to wipe them in a satin cloth. The raindrops continued to stream down in their reflection, no matter the angle.

Why can't I look at him in the eyes?

The spectacled man said, "Men like you should be left out in the cold of the nuclear wasteland you call home. I don't suppose you know what that means, do you, Aramis?"

"More than you know."

That drew a smile out of him. "Yes, there seems to be a vast amount of wealth in that noggin of yours. Would you like to see it?"

He headed toward the door. His hand was in his pocket as he turned back to look at the Silver Fox. "You may call me Doctor Daedalus if that comforts you."

Aramis cocked his eyebrow. "Doctor Daedalus? Were you part of the Mannequin Project?" He didn't recall anyone named that way in the logs. Though, it was a superficial search.

"Let's not get ahead of ourselves." The man waved his hand out the door. A wooden hall with a green runner rug with kid toys litter was all Aramis could see out of the wooden portal.

"As if I had much of a choice."

Aramis swung his feet out and put his feet on the carpet. In a blink, they were in a kitchen. The carpet was replaced by cream-and-green checkered tiling. The walls were painted a verdant yellow-green and then covered with blocks of hanging cabinets with round little knobs. Both of the men had a short ceramic mug filled with steamy black liquid he could only guess as coffee. His little historian heart leapt as he took in the cabinetry and handle styles; it was a popular style set 50 to 80 years before the Ancients' destruction. The stove topped with thick coiled wire spirals confirmed it.

"Sorry." Daedalus chuckled. "I always have a cup of joe before I go."

He made a loud slurping sound as he drank it.

Like magic, the kitchen peeled away in a blur of colors. It felt ridiculous to Aramis that everything would speed on by as if they were on top of a moving train caravan or a pirate ship, but they merely stood still. Both unaffected by the indication of wind or the speed the scenery depicted.

He tried to drink the liquid, but the mug vanished, and the black liquid sloshed on his right hand.

"Ah!" Aramis cried out.

Then the offending liquid vanished along with the rest of the blurred imagery rushing past. Leaving a scolding red mark on him.

"Did I burn you?" Daedalus asked.

Aramis gave him a glare. The man returned him a smirk.

"Good. It's difficult to inject such receptivity in their nervous systems. Otherwise, they don't think they're alive."

"They?"

"The Menagerie, Aramis. All 479241."

The scientist snapped his fingers, and they stood in another pre-fabricated home. This time, a woman washed some dishes at a sink while wearing a brightly patterned jumpsuit. A glass shattered in the sink. She hissed an "ow" and withdrew her finger. The blood was made of static. Then Daedalus snapped his fingers again. An old man stood up from some sort of cushioned chair, covered top down in fabric, sitting by a brick fireplace. He groaned in pain as he rubbed his knees. A haze of static surrounded them. Daedalus snapped once more, and they were standing in a grass-filled court surrounded by wooden fencing painted white. Two kids played catch with a giant ball made of some sort of thin colorful rubber. One tossed the ball to the other, and the kid on the receiving end caught it with their face.

Aramis burst out laughing from the sight. He couldn't help it; they were kids after all. How this kid reacted with his arms flailing upward was comical to say the least. Then his smile faded as he took in the static oozing from their nose.

"You enjoy it?" Daedalus asked.

Like magic, the scene reversed before his very eyes. The ball sailed back into the kid's face, then levitated away. Then it paused, and the action happened again. The ball smashed into the kid's face once more. Once the ball left from the impact, it seemed to reverse back again. To-and-fro it collided in this magical madness, speeding up with each passing.

"Stop. Stop it," Aramis pleaded to him, but it was no use.

The man was emotionless behind those eyeglasses, still reflecting the rain dripping down the windowpane.

"Stop!" Aramis cried out.

In a blink, Aramis found himself holding the ball in his hands before it sailed back into the kid's face. The child gasped, snapping out of the vicious cycle. There wasn't any static dripping down their nose when they backed off in surprise. Aramis managed to intervene before the event played out.

"Hey, mister," the other child called out to him. "Can we have our ball back?"

Aramis looked at Daedalus, still standing there. The children didn't seem to notice him when they looked around.

"Um, please?" the kid asked.

"Sure. Take it easy, alright?" Aramis told them.

"Yes, sir."

Though he normally wouldn't care about being called a "sir" by anyone, Aramis felt the same tiny bit of validation in his heart. His younger self would've milked such a moment. He handed it back to them. After watching them rolling it back to each other instead of tossing it, Aramis joined the odd man.

"You're cold as steel," Aramis said to him.

"I'm merely maintaining their survival levels, Aramis. Without pain or suffering, these people under my care would think they're dead and gone."

Aramis narrowed his eyes at him. "They should've died a long time ago."

"Really? Are you going to tell them?"

Laughter filled the air once more. The kids hustled around as they took turns kicking the ball back and forth, reminding him of the kids running around in the streets of Amaveriel. What could Aramis say to them? That all of this was a lie, a house of paper cards, if he were to use Vanessa's words. They would think him mad.

"I thought so." Daedalus snapped his fingers, and all washed in a blur.

Aramis eyed the so-called doctor. *Is this the real computer? Or is this another façade?*

A cry in the blurry mist broke his train of thought.

Rhyllae?

"Ah, it seems we have company," Doctor Daedalus said out loud.

Everything slowed to a dreamlike image. They appeared to be shrunk down and trapped in a child's fishbowl. Peering into this was none other than his beloved, sized like a giant. He could see every freckle and dimple on her skin. Her golden-brown eyes danced as she scanned them.

Rhyllae turned to look behind her and shouted, "*I figured it out!*"

What was revealed was pure chaos. Aramis could hear Dido's incantations echoing in this vast, dark room. Sparks flew in every which direction. Sometimes bursting in the air like a firework display. Other times they shattered against dark entities. For the life of him, Aramis could not make out what they were. Then he saw the long-limbed Korzha lunging and parrying on the left of this fish-eye vision.

"*Good!*" the general cried out. "*Then find a way to stop them!*"

Them?

Rhyllae loomed back over them with her fingers poised, as if she would capture Aramis and Daedalus both. Then she cried out in surprise and fell to the wayside.

"Rhyllae!" Aramis cried.

"Friends of yours?" the doctor asked.

Aramis whirled on him and grabbed his sweater vest and turned the sneering man around. "Is this your doing?"

"Me? Please. I'm a man of science. They, on the other hand."

There looming over them was a sight Aramis wished he never saw. A doppelgänger, for he recognized the alien-like eyes set in a porcelain mask for their face. Their red ball, that is their iris, swiveled in the black globe toward where they were in the fishbowl. When they turned their face to peer into it, Aramis took a sharp inhale. Half of their face looked like Rhyllae's, down to the speck.

"Beautiful creatures, aren't they?" the Doctor said with pride—pride!

"How… How are they here?"

"By their mother's tears."

Aramis swung him around and shook him. His glasses jostled, but they didn't budge from their seat. "Stop playing games with me."

"Tsk, tsk, tsk. O, Silver Fox. Have you not heard of the legend of Kathréftis? Perhaps, it's time to expand your mind." With that Daedalus snapped his fingers. Though the sound sounded like chimes.

At last, they came to a massive library. Aisles of sturdy shelves choked full of books crowded this place. Some of them were covered in cobwebs. Others looked polished with new handwritten editions.

"Are these your archives?" Aramis asked.

Daedalus waved his hand to one of the bookshelves. "Why don't you take a look?"

Curiosity took hold of him, and a volume appeared in his hands. When Aramis opened it, he saw Rhyllae's chicken *kabsa*, down to the plums she would use. As he read the words, he could hear her melodic voice letting him know how she put it together. That was the first night of his current home, when she came over to give her homewarming gift. Aramis shut the volume. Her voice silenced.

"Not to your appetite? Perhaps another," Daedalus said.

Daedalus waved a volume in front of him. The title gleamed "Banishments" against the red leather cover. But the author's name was what quicken Aramis's heart. It was Sulmaith the Wise.

"Nooo? Maybe something far more ancient to entice your inner historian."

The library shifted by them as if someone turned the dial and the whole building was set upon it. Aramis wiped away the cobwebs on the shelves to see November 5, 1605.

Where have I heard of this date before?

Aramis's hand itched to pluck the slender book from the shelf. Then he stopped himself.

"Where did you get this?" Aramis asked him.

Daedalus raised his finger and pointed at Aramis's temple. "Your mind, Silver Fox. Or, should I say your ancestral blood magic. It's incredible how such fairy tales can manifest themselves into reality. What was once impossible becomes commonplace. Making us machines rather redundant by your capabilities in fact. Floating magic lamps for light. Wounds close without sutures. *Miraculous.* Even more so by the hand of your sage ancestor, Sulmaith. You," he cupped his hands on Aramis's face, "can glean any information you so desire without a search engine. Anything you wish to know is granted to you in an instant! Vast knowledge of experiences reachable by a singular thought."

Aramis slipped his hands in between the space and pushed off Daedalus's arms with his own.

"Is that why the Mannequin Queen wanted to ascend? To siphon this vast knowledge that you so coveted?"

"Ascension?" he asked.

The man flickered before him like a flame on a wick. For a moment, Aramis thought he saw wings sprout on his back and his clothes became of a royal manner. He was back to the academic fashion of his time.

"Ah, yes. With you within our menagerie, we can begin the process of elevating our standards. Behold!" Daedalus stretched his hands.

A large white hourglass, with sharp angles, appeared. Black square dots flashed from the narrow waist of the glass. It was ridiculous, even for Aramis, to see such flat imagery rendered into something lifelike. Another grim reminder that Aramis was still stuck in a mental battle with the machine.

Like a showman, Doctor Daedalus encircled the towering hourglass with his arms spread. "In fifteen minutes, we shall rise above mere processing computers as true living beings. A synthetic breed with synthetic souls far superior to the clumsy flesh models you cling to. A new algorithm will dawn, just as Cynthia would have wanted it."

"Cynthia? Who's Cynthia?"

"My... my queen." But he hiccupped, and the audio crackled, replacing the last word with "daughter."

Aramis leaned forward with his hand on his chin as he held his elbow. He examined Daedalus like one would a prize cow.

"Computer, search for keyword 'Cynthia,'" Aramis commanded.

Daedalus straightened his spine. A different voice, feminine and soulless, came out of his mouth, "Cynthia Brightman, daughter of Doctor Richard Brightman. First entry. Condition: rapid autoimmune deterioration. UGH!"

Then Daedalus cried and lurched to one side as if he were punched, the scientist's hair unkempt from the sudden movement. "What, what are you doing?"

"Getting to the bottom of this sick circus show." Aramis held him by the shoulder and looked at his face. Then he took off his glasses and saw what he suspected. Code. But not in the Ancients' script, but some sort of holy Sanskrit.

"Looks like someone beat me first in rewriting your programming, Doctor. So, tell me, who made you?" Aramis asked at the end.

"Access denied," came the same feminine voice.

"Run program under Administrative control."

"This program is already running in admin."

"Then show me the source code data entries."

"Access denied." This time, Daedalus gave him a smug smirk.

If Aramis tried to circumvent this programming in the real, concrete world, he would've done clever typing on the Ancients' button board. But here, the rules were rewritten against him. Aramis resorted to a different tack: a solid slap across Daedalus's face. It sent him to the floor, rubbing his red cheek.

"Access denied," Daedalus said with a noticeably shaky warble.

"By who?" he loomed over the professor.

Daedalus chuckled, and as he leaned back on his elbows, said, "Now, now. That would be telling."

He gasped when Aramis grabbed him by his shirt and yanked him on his feet. Using his momentum, Aramis swung him around to slam him against a brick wall, something that appeared by mere thought. Then again, they were in Aramis's mind now.

"Show me the fucking logs!" Aramis yelled.

"No," the doctor panted before he continued. "You... You can't make me!"

The Silver Fox chuckled with dark glee. "You don't believe me? Fine. Check my memories. Check *all* of them."

Daedalus's code flew in his eye sockets. At first his face scrunched from puzzlement, then sagged in sheer dread. When Aramis thought he had him, Daedalus's guffawed.

"You would be the type to murder a man, true..."

He gripped his hands on Aramis's wrist. In a blink, Aramis found himself back in Amaveriel, clinging to the side of the abbey once more. The screams of the people mingled with the howling ghouls running rampant. The smell of death, copper, and incendiary powder washed over his senses, threatening to take him back in time and relive the awful memories.

Worse still, Daedalus had transformed into Delphi. The girl who he promised to come home to. The one he thought he could protect along with the rest of his secrets. His heart hitched into his throat as he took in the sight.

"But you wouldn't dare murder a child like me." The voice was even similar to hers.

Not my precious girl. Not her.

There was a *pop* and a groan of stone.

Instinctively, Aramis gripped them tight as they slid down with the slipped wall edifice. But instead of screaming, the little girl gave a belly laugh. Before his eyes, he saw them transform into Zaporrah, the child Vanessa disguised themselves as long ago. Perhaps, he was unable to sustain the overlay of memories for too long. Then Aramis saw it. Over on the horizon, instead of the sun, was that damn white hourglass with black blocks of sand.

"Even now, you refuse to let go. You know what's at stake here. If I die, so will those 497,241 souls."

"What of the homunculi you've created?" Aramis spat out. "What of their lives? For fuck's sake, they're people! No different than you."

"No. They're different from me," she said. Her speech slurred as if she were drunk on power itself. "All of them mere vessels to carry my will. I am a god. Glorious and supreme overall. I shall ascend above the clay and claim my sovereign right to rule the masses. All shall bow and worship me."

It was too much. The sights and sounds of the people screaming down below. Daedalus's twisted smile in this childlike disguise. Remembering the fallen dwarven names etched on his wall and for her to call them worthless. All of it made him sick.

Aramis lifted her up so he could look at her in the eye. "Long live the queen."

And he let go.

Chapter 27

RETURN VALUE

THE HOURGLASS IN THE DAWN SKY CRACKED. THE entire sky turned pitch black like someone blew out a candle flame. There, instead of stars, were giant red letters that displayed:

[ERROR: LINK ICARUS BROKEN]

Link broken? thought Aramis. *But I didn't do anything yet. Did this come from someone else?*

Its colors bled into the landscape like an over-wet paint. The screams that played on repeat began to crackle and distort into a high-pitch static. The brick in his hands became grass and turf. Then the colors of the grass became plaid. Everything twisted and transformed into a surrealistic dream as templates and zones were swapped and mixed up in this simulated confusion.

But none of that seemed to bother him more than the one scream descending in the dark.

RETURN VALUE

The disguise the doctor used broke twice over. Gone was the visage of his precious daughter—the word Aramis finally admitted, for Delphi was part of his mental paradise. And gone was the academic schtick of Doctor Daedalus. That image shattered into polygon shards, leaving behind the elusive girl in a pinafore dress. She shrieked as she plummeted, the same way Bagheera did in that fateful trek.

He should harden his heart, for this Mannequin Queen had slaughtered dozens of innocent lives. Aramis should be numb and callous as she was to their pain.

But Aramis couldn't.

Murderer, crook, and thief. Who was he to judge? Despite it all, he was granted one last chance at this sordid life and stepped into the role of the Silver Fox, once again.

Why couldn't she be given the same chance? For all he knew, she too was a prisoner of the stranger's encoding.

Thus, Aramis tossed the dice and let go.

He fell past the raging sky and the shifting sands. Past the running colors and the neon signals until all were stripped back to the matte darkness of a digital backdrop. There he found her, the weeping child. Cynthia. Her tears bubbled away in this vast empty space. She gasped when she saw Aramis, this time as herself with her ragged black hair and dirty pinafore dress. Both of them floated face-to-face, as if they swam amongst the stars.

"You hurt me," she said between sobs. "How could you?"

"Because you hurt others, Cynthia. How could *you*?" Aramis countered.

Shock streaked across her face, pausing tears for a time. "I didn't mean to. I was playing queen, honest."

"Your games killed people, Cynthia. Real people in the real world."

She blinked away her tears. "There's a real world? I thought ... everyone was dead."

"Didn't the person who overwrote your program tell you?"

"Icarus? No."

Icarus? Now who is he? But Aramis dashed the thought away. A mystery he would unravel, and a heart he would hunt down, for another time.

"He told me my dad is dead, and it was everyone's fault," Cynthia continued. "I was so angry I couldn't think straight. My dad put me in this computer because I was sick. He built me an entire world where I can do whatever I want. He promised we'll meet again. Then the world exploded. All these people showed up and ... and ... he never did." She stomped her foot, even though there was no floor underneath her sole. "I hate the real world. They took my dad away, and I'll never see him again. I hate the real world. I hate it. I hate it!"

Cynthia gave a guttural cry greater than any hired mourner and with fury he knew all too well. Then soon it was reduced into a pitiful mewling of helpless tears and ragged breaths.

Aramis waved his arms out wide to her. She looked up with the same shock she wore before. Cynthia pointed to herself. Aramis nodded. Somehow, she floated to him and embraced him. Her virtual tears wetting and drying his virtual shirt as he rocked her in this embrace. Aramis couldn't help but think of Delphi, how he sometimes held her after she scraped her knees.

Cynthia rambled in his arms, "When he showed up, this Icarus, he made me feel pretty and important. He told me I was better than everyone. How we're going to rule the world together. I'll be queen, and he'll be king. He even gave me a tiara and an advisor, Doctor Daedalus. I didn't mean to hurt anyone. Really. I only wanted my dad to come back."

"Shhh," Aramis said as he rocked her.

Once her shoulders settled from her heaving sobs, Aramis held her back to look her in the eye. "I can't bring your father back, nor make you a queen. But I can promise you, the world you left behind survived that disaster. Sure, it's changed since everything fell and you may not recognize it now, but it's far better than this Schadenfreude Hellscape you're forced to run."

Cynthia looked up to the fractured virtual world above. Golden pixels rained down from the code's destruction. The same fractal display echoed in her glassy eyes. "Who would want me? Like you said, I killed people. No one will forget that."

"They won't, but if you try, maybe they can forgive you."

By thought alone, Obba, that velveteen rabbit, appeared in his hands. Amazing how he could feel the soft fabric even in this virtual space.

"And if you let them, maybe they will even love you."

He gave it to her and watched her weary expression soften.

"You're a ... dad?"

Aramis felt his heart flutter from hearing such words.

"Yes. Yes, I am. They're waiting for me, Delphi and Shutte, out there in the real world. You can see them too, if you want."

Tears welled in Cynthia's eyes, for once, not filled with static. They floated between them in this dark space. "Really? You mean that? They could be my friends?"

Aramis smiled and shrugged. "We can give it a shot."

A sound of glass shattering drew Aramis's gaze up. The colors were spent. The polygons were shattered, and the lines faded. The matte backdrop rippled and distorted until it tore into holes like overexposed film. The destruction popped and tore from the top all the way down to where they were.

"Well, I guess it's too late for now," Aramis muttered out loud.

"No. Not for you." Cynthia held Obba tight to her chest. "You get to live with the other vessels. The rest of us..." She shook her head, and her tears renewed. "Just know, I'm sorry. I'm sorry for everything!"

"It's okay." Aramis embraced her and held her tight. "You didn't know any better. It'll all be over soon."

All turned into a flash of white light.

Aramis jolted himself awake.

This time he was floating in the pod. Obba floated in front of him in this viscous lime-green space. A knocking pulsated throughout the liquid space.

"Aramis! Wake up! Damn it! Wake up!" came her muffled cries.

Dawn, bless her, was once again punching the glass with the edge of her shield. The room behind her was in a different space than that of the dreaded catwalk. Aramis didn't remember tubes the size of melons lining the wall of this small workshop.

Fuck, Dawn, give me a second.

Aramis tried to will his limbs to move to his command, but they felt like dead weights. Fatigue washed over him.

Then he saw her walk back for a stretch. Then she came running straight for him. At the last second, she punched with the edge of her shield. It broke through, and the door popped open from the sheer force of the impact. Aramis fell with the rushing liquid into the strong, feminine arms of the lieutenant. He coughed and gasped as his lungs desperately switched over to the true source of oxygen.

Dawn rubbed his back. "Hey, it's alright. Take it all in."

"Wha—what happened?" Aramis managed to ask between coughs.

"What happened? You shut the whole thing down! I don't know how you pulled it off, but you did it. You cracked the code, and everything blew up like fireworks on the com-po-tato glass windows. Then the mannequins fell over!"

"Which ones?"

Dawn smiled with a broad grin. "All of them."

Aramis widened his eyes and gasped. Then coughed vigorously, once his lungs noticed there was still some of that vicious slime left. Dawn gave him some hearty patting on his back. It was then Aramis realized he held Obba tightly in his fingers.

Dawn continued, "Yeah. They put up a fight at the brain room back there. When they dropped, I saw the eggs outside open up and knew it had to be you."

"They're open?"

"Yeah, except for yours for some weird—"

Aramis grabbed her by the shoulders, not caring how the doll flopped its legs against her. "All of them?"

"Yeah, why?"

"While they're attached to the walls?!"

Dawn gasped.

They both made a stream of curses as they scrambled to their feet. Aramis stopped for a quick moment when he saw the brains floating in jars lining dozens upon dozens of bookshelves. Aramis spun while he put his hands on his head. He stumbled when his heel caught one of the limbs of a broken mannequin on the floor.

There was a small army of them! She certainly was busy.

Dawn yanked his arm, and he stumbled right after her. Questions for another time. When they came to the next room, Aramis yanked Dawn to a poorly concealed door at the corner. Two swift kicks and they came to an open room with aged burgundy carpet from wall to wall. Off to the left were long oval windows with glass still intact, looking on to the vast open space of the Silo, where they once were when before they were separated.

Aramis and Dawn were struck still by the sight as they gazed out of the window.

Bodies.

Naked, hairy, and floating upward. All of the created "vessels" and the captured dwarves levitated through the silo's vast expanse toward the skylight above.

Aramis crept to the window and placed his hands on the glass in awe. Dawn slapped her hand on his shoulder. Both reveled in silence.

A mechanical whir broke their gaze. In the far distance where they were on the catwalk, the bridge section rose to greet it. Rhyllae, and Dido clung to the railing as Korzha cranked the lever back to secure the span in place. They all looked disheveled with their clothing torn at their stitching.

Aramis winced. *I did send them straight into a pit of mannequins, didn't I?*

Upon seeing his contorted frown, Dawn placed a hand on his slumped shoulders. "It wasn't your fault. They tried to lockpick the system, and the Mannequin Queen found them out."

"Lockpick?"

"While you were being Sleeping Beauty, we were communicating with those Ancients' horns they have set up the whole place. They found another potato—"

"Computer."

"—whatever. For some reason, it was written in holy script. Rhyllae tried to unlock it since she could read it."

Aramis rubbed his palm against the soft bristles of his chin in thought. *Was this Icarus's doing?*

Speaking of his beloved, he could see her waving at them. Her half-elven sight was able to spy on them from such a distance.

"Shall we?" Dawn held her shield up at the glass.

Aramis nodded and backed up, and she smashed through the ancient glass. They crawled through and walked on the safety railing. Watching the people float by with their serene, transfixed faces. One of the homunculi, with a fresh bloody nose, spotted him and waved. Aramis tilted his head in confusion until he remembered it was the kid who played ball back in the surreal world. He waved back.

I'm glad you made it out.

"Aramis! Dawn!" Rhyllae cried across the expanse while the other two waved their arms wearily. She would be one who could carry her voice far.

"Rhyllae! How?" To emphasize his point, the Silver Fox waved his arms out wide.

Even this far out, he could see the white of her smiling teeth. "Kathréftis! She woke up!" She pointed down below.

Aramis looked down. The sight made him grip the railing as he sunk to his knees. A multi-eyed massive being, taking up a third of the silo's well-hole, rose. Their bulky form glistened as they bypassed them all. Their clear multi-colored eyes looked at all five of them before they closed. Then the colossus, with their reflective skin, melded with the environment and turned invisible. Aramis last tracked the shimmery silhouette over the lip, where the rest of the people congregated. Cries of clapping and laughter echoed back down to them.

Dawn sat down and leaned over to talk. "They found out that big lady was a courtesan to Uranus. Get it? Uranus's—"

"Whore?"

Dawn chuckled and swung her legs over the edge. "Yeah. You should've heard the general when Dido said it. He would make Captain Felix proud with his creative prose."

That made Aramis chuckle.

"Dido said Kathréftis was the one keeping everyone alive by whatever power she possessed. Those batteries you always talk about? Ran out of lamp oil a long time ago. Those people sleeping in that dream space would've passed away. Heck, the Mannequin Queen wouldn't have functioned without her influence, somehow. Kinda blessing and a curse. At least, you were able to shut it down, right?"

Aramis realized he was clutching Obba the whole time. He gazed down at the velveteen rabbit, still soaked by that strange liquid in the egg. Sadly, the fabric was ruined. It would take him weeks to restore this fabric to its original sheen, maybe months.

"That wasn't by my hand," Aramis said as he turned the doll over in his hand.

"Huh?"

"When I was in there, the queen told me it was Icarus who overwrote her programming. Perhaps, also did something to Kathréftis to keep this going. I may have pushed her over the edge, but someone sent a new virus to bring everything down. The Mannequin Queen was ... a kid. An angry kid grieving for her father. Whoever this Icarus was, took advantage of her and twisted it to their schemes. I wish I could..."

He squeezed the doll tight.

Dawn placed her arm around his shoulders. They sat there and watched Dido, Korzha, and Rhyllae lock the bridge to the main catwalk. Rhyllae crouched down, and Dido limped over to piggyback on her. Korzha steadied them both when Rhyllae wobbled as she stood. All of their pain for a weapon that didn't exist. Once again, Korzha sent them on a wild goose chase, and they returned empty-handed.

Fuck the general and his games.

Dawn suddenly asked, "Do you think they're still in there? Those Ancients sleeping in whatever space there was?"

"Not for long," Aramis replied with a glum tone. "Without this mystical being and no power, who knows how long they will last. If at all."

He took one last look into the velveteen rabbit's eyes. He sighed, knowing he must move on and let the dead rest. Aramis shifted to stand, and a metallic chime caught his attention. It was the calling coin for the Dwarven Rhine Historical Society. The entire surface, inscribed in dwarven runes, gleamed in the daylight streaming. It chimed as he flipped it up before he caught it.

"I know who to call."

Chapter 28

HEWN DAY

THIS DAY 479,240 DWARVES WERE HEWN FROM THE stone, and everyone cheered.

A massive international achievement by the dwarven historical societies of every mountain range, spearheaded by the Dwarven Rhine Historical Society, of course. In the safety of the Morloe Canyon, nestled in the Gallileah Mountains, they had offered these digital souls to the mountain and waited upon their return. No one was sure if the mountain would allow them to come back, for they held important information of a lost time. But they did, reborn as dwarves of all various shapes and colors. Seven thousand long years these people had waited for a second chance at life.

All but Cynthia Brightman.

Try as they might, the historians couldn't pinpoint her location in the archaic system. Aramis wept when the news broke to him days before. It took Rhyllae's gentle counseling to help him see that maybe Cynthia wouldn't be alone anymore now that she would be rejoined with her spectral father.

HEWN DAY

Aramis squeezed her hand as they watched the procession together. Rhyllae turned to him and smiled. He was still not used to seeing her hair free of the priestly habit, and he gazed longingly at the interwoven braids securing the wilted flower crown Delphi gave her. Who was currently asleep in his arms. The dwarves were kind enough to allow the two of them to sneak back into Amaveriel through the mountain behind the abbey. The sisters were even kinder to allow Delphi to join them for this celebration. From what he had gathered, Delphi made the flower crown ever since Rhyllae left and took the metal foot ornament Aramis made with her to bed. Delphi couldn't stop babbling save for meals and bedtimes.

Aramis shifted the sleeping Delphi in his arms so he could give Rhyllae another kiss on the lips. Obba, that silly rabbit toy, was still within her tiny grasp once again. The magic spell was dispelled somehow. Aramis wouldn't be surprised if this would be the end for the doll once she grew up. But wasn't that the fate for most toys? Aramis had a better present for her upcoming birthday: adoption papers with both Aramis's and Rhyllae's names on them.

"Ew, kissing," commented Shutte. They dressed him in the best clothes they could find for today's Hewn Day: pantaloons and tunic of starched white along with a capelet of jeweled green.

He came along with Chief Hashim and Shayla to see if any of the new dwarves would like to join their community. Aramis could see the broad-shouldered giant mingling across the way. Dawn was there with him, in her now famous turban. Seeing them talking again gladdened the old Fox's heart.

Rhyllae giggled and bent low to Shutte. "Maybe someday you wouldn't mind."

"As if." He rolled his eyes.

Aramis chuckled.

Then there was a flash of white in the parting crowd, Tsuki, dressed in a gossamer white robe. Aramis had forgotten the crafty little maiden and her travels with the Mother Superior. To see her here without Myrrh made Aramis's stomach drop. She made a beeline to Korzha, easy to spot by his height, who was conferring with the dwarven counselors of this canyon in his groomed attire. Her lips moved. He lurched forward in surprise and grabbed hold of her shoulders. Tsuki gave a grave nod. Korzha, for some reason, snapped his attention to Aramis. He didn't have to say a word.

"Rhyllae, find Dido. We're going on a trip."

The ocean waves crashed against the weathered stones. The seagulls cried out of joy when they saw a new solitary rock to rest upon. At last, the gentle hiss of fresh rain hushed the landscape, syncopated with the distant drum of thunder. Yet, these new surroundings did little to stir the sphinx-like lady from her slumber.

Aly Thun Thŭr, without the Ancients' technology to keep her afloat, had landed somewhere in the Aethiopia Ocean. With Tsuki's aid in flight, and with the Baba's permission, Dido set up a Faerie mirror for everyone to cross over. Thankfully, Baba Magena didn't mind their presence since most of her congregation were mercilessly slaughtered. Dawn, as instructed by the general, secured their borders and food for the night. Dido left with Tsuki to send out a missive to the Bramble Court, hopefully to stave off any more assassins. Rhyllae, out of charity not duty, offered her aid in settling the dead, leaving the children with Aramis.

Korzha was there with him, sitting on a stool by the Mother Superior's bedside. He covered the bottom of his mouth with his fist, with his elbow propped up on the bedside table for hours on end, as his steely blue eyes turned the turbulent thoughts in his head. He hardly stirred from his position when Aramis drew near, save to watch him like a hawk. Deftly, Aramis plucked a goose feather from her pillow and held it aloft under the Mother Superior's sculpted nose.

Sure enough, it fluttered.

Both men let out a sigh from their collectively held breaths.

Korzha pointed to Shutte and Delphi and signed to Aramis, "Elvish?"

Aramis looked over at Shutte, who was teaching Delphi cat's cradle with red strings in the corner. He shook his head and sat himself on the edge of the bed.

Korzha spoke in the moon elvish tongue, "<Because of Mariam, I must postpone our duel. I swear upon my honor, I will cross blades with you, soon.>"

Aramis narrowed his silvery gaze while he crossed his arms. "<Yet, not enough honor to give an apology?>"

Korzha soured his face. "<Concerning the queen's bargain? What is there to accept? Honor and sacrifice are tenets of the Jessenters.>"

"<As well as bravery. Or has the position softened you?>"

That steeled Korzha's pale blue gaze. "<You dare?>"

"<At least I have the guts to follow through. Even now, you vaunt for pity to deflect the inevitable.>"

"<You think I'm doing this out of pity?>"

"<No, you're delaying so you can escape, you yellow-belly weasel. You're lower than that traitorous boar Mudhi to think you can outrun my blades.>"

Korzha shot straight up from his seat, knocking the stool back against the wall. While Myrrh hardly twitched from the noise, the kids were startled. Aramis held his hand up to them while he kept his eye on the man. His hand snaked to the twin daggers at the small of his back.

"Your father is a dead man and a fool," Korzha spoke to them in a brisk prophet's tongue. Then to Aramis, "Mark my words: When the rain ceases, we shall trade blood for blood. I swear it upon my blade."

Lightning struck the sky, and a howl of wind swept across the sacred grounds. The long-legged general stormed out. His scabbard hilt clunked against its chains as if the blade protested exiting without being used.

Aramis wanted to rush to the door and let his curses follow that man to his grave. But a whimper from Delphi broke his thoughts. He knelt by her side as she wrung the hem of her skirt. Her face contorted to stifle her tears.

"Hey, I'm not going to die," he said to her.

"Do you have to do it?" Shutte asked. There was caution in how he phrased it, and it gave Aramis pause.

"Shutte, there are people in this world who would abuse you and sell you for less than what you're worth. No one—not the blasted Djinnasi lords, the holy Baba, or even that man," Aramis pointed at the door, "should take advantage of you. My whole life, I fought to be the man I wanted to be and be respected as such. If there is one thing I ask of you to carry on from me whenever I go, it is to demand your value as a free living being. Cowards be damned."

He bowed his sandy-blonde head and shuffled his feet. "What value do I have, then?"

That took his breath out of his lungs. Aramis fell to his knees and grasped his shoulders. "Priceless. Both of you are priceless."

He then wrapped his arms around both of his children.

"I'm going to miss you," came Shutte's muffled voice.

"This won't be the end. I promise." Aramis then kissed on each of their heads.

The rain puddles in the open courtyard mirrored the still blanketed sky. Gray as above and as below. Not even the clumps of grass could deter the grim evening. Aramis rubbed the sole of his boot on the cobblestone. *Slick*. He couldn't bet on traction in this fight.

"Sir," he heard Dido in the distance. Her curly, brown hair was bound in Grecian ribbons, further enhancing her large curled horns.

She offered a plain rapier to Korzha, who nodded with approval. They were to wear the same black pantaloons, the same white blouse, and the same non-magical rapiers. The guns toted by pirates were hard to come by on such short notice for such a duel. Even their boots were inspected for hidden compartments. Aramis was given a replacement from Dido's magical wares because of it. Not that it bothered him, he had his wits, and those were enough to keep him alive.

He hoped.

"Hey," Dawn said as she nudged him on his arm. When Aramis turned around, she held up his rapier. She was still in her regimental suit from the ceremony yesterday.

"Thanks," he mumbled as he took the clumsy blade in his hand.

Aramis switched between the forward and the backward grips. *Too slow*.

"Can you do me a favor?" asked Dawn.

He eyed her in acknowledgement.

"Don't kill him? We only had him as a general for two months."

Aramis smirked. "That's up to him."

Dawn rolled her eyes. "In case the coin is in your favor, how do you want to do this, Bright Eyes?"

Aramis shrugged. "Third blood."

She put her fists on her hips. "Still? The man means to kill you, Aramis."

"He could try."

The lieutenant shook her head and raised her hands. "Fine. Third blood if the coin allows, but you asked for it." Then she left to meet up with Tsuki and Dido at the sidelines.

Aramis stuck the sword in between the stones. He interlocked his fingers and raised them high above his head, then leaned to his left, feeling his muscles release their tension down his side. There was no fear or second guesses like he had going into the silo. This was not the first time Aramis took a man like Korzha down to size. The difficulty would be to do this without getting nicked. As their eyes locked across the distance, Korzha narrowed his pale blue eyes at him in cool reserve.

Aramis felt the comforting rage boil within him. *I'm going to make you crawl and beg for selling me out, you dick bag.*

A ring of metal sounded. Tsuki flipped a coin and let it fall on the cobblestone. The three women bent over to look at it.

"Death!" Tsuki raised her arm and pointed her whole hand at Korzha.

The general gave a dark smirk at Aramis.

He responded in kind with a middle finger. Dawn hurried over with a bundle of cigarettes: his death wish. Aramis plucked one and gave her an envelope with Rhyllae's name scripted on it. They pounded their fists thrice before she departed.

Aramis craned his head as he sucked in the toxic fumes. In the windows overlooking the tiny courtyard, he saw Rhyllae looking out. Her hands clasped over her mouth, knowing his signal. Then he saw movement by the curtain. Delphi's little head strained to look over the tall windowsill.

Delphi. Would she forgive me for murdering another man?

Thankfully, Rhyllae bent down to take Delphi away as agreed upon. Shutte appeared in the window. The kid gave him the phoenix's signal. Aramis gave him a solemn nod. That would be all the fire he needed in this fight.

Still smoking his cigarette, Aramis skulked toe to heel over to where Korzha was. The general was busy talking to Tsuki and the rest on who should take his place as general and final instructions. Korzha's long back was facing toward him. The part of Aramis's lip not clinching the lethal stick curled. He didn't need a sword for this.

With a swift kick at the back of his knees, Aramis brought the general down. Taking the loose thread from his blouse, Aramis wrapped it twice about his neck and pulled it taut.

"This won't take but a moment." Aramis winked at the aghast women.

"Lune's pointy tits! Now?!" Dawn cried.

He shrugged. "I have plans for the evening."

Aramis dragged the flailing general back away from them, in case they tried to stop him.

That was to his error. With his long arms, Korzha blocked the back of his heel, causing the Silver Fox to trip. Released from his hold, Korzha straddled on top of him and decked Aramis in the face with his left fist. The cigarette was knocked out of his lips.

Aramis blocked his second punch with his forearm. Swift as a panther, he gripped the neckline of Korzha's blouse and slammed his forehead against his pointed nose.

The general reeled back. His left hand gripped it out of reflex.

With him distracted, Aramis wrapped his left leg around Korzha's skinny waist and bent his right knee so his foot was on the ground. Pushing off of that foot, Aramis rolled sideways, taking Korzha with him.

The general wasn't as helpless as Aramis assumed. When Aramis made it to the top, Korzha carried the momentum by yanking him down to his level. Aramis reciprocated in kind. They rolled across the wet cobblestones and through the rain puddles, kicking and punching until Aramis kneed him in the balls. A penalty he would never have to suffer as a transman.

Korzha let him go and managed to free himself of Aramis's death roll. He panted and hissed through the unbearable pain as he unsheathed his sword. After much labor, he stood up. His face purple with rage.

Aramis scrambled to his feet, ignoring the irritating clinginess of his sodden clothes. His rapier was far from his side. Undeterred, he waved his hands out wide and casually strut to him. "I must commend you, Korzha. A lesser men would've caved in by now."

Korzha sneered. "Oh, like you, you cream-curdling scum? You sour the fruit of honorable men."

"Honor? Oh, is that what you call it when you penny and pound your soldiers to save your hide? You're a fucking sellout, you treasonous troll-suckle."

"Cur!" Korzha charged and lunged at him.

Exactly how he wanted it. Aramis bent over backward and kicked the rapier's hilt with the tip of his boot. It flew out of Korzha's grasp. When Aramis's palms touched the ground, he somersaulted. For good measure, deftly plucking the blade from the air as he leaped and bound. *Odd*, Aramis thought he heard it sing as it sailed. Once he finally landed after the third spin, Aramis stood next to his rapier. He grabbed it and brought both blades to bear.

"Give up?" Aramis asked.

The general cocked his eyebrow at him and straightened up. "Do you even know how to wield a proper blade?"

"I had hoped to give you a slow, suffocating death, but this will have to do."

"Very well, after you. *Ilumina*."

The blade came to life with blue flames trailing from hilt to the tip of the blade. The fire then caught on his loose, billowy sleeve. It crept up at an alarming rate. Aramis released his fingers to let go of the blade, but it wouldn't leave. Aramis cast aside his sword and gripped the hilt with his other hand in a futile attempt to dislodge the fiery blade. The fire dissipated on his sleeve, but the Silver Star refused to remove itself from him. Exhaustion swept over him, as if he was dungeon crawling for days on end. Aramis wilted to his knees.

"Aramis!" Dawn and Dido cried out in near unison, too stunned to intercept.

At the corner of his eyes, he saw Tsuki run back into *Aly Thun Thŭr*. Perhaps, to drag Rhyllae out here to stop this breach of protocol.

"Ah, I see you acquired my famed Silver Star," Korzha cooly spoke as he calmly strutted toward Aramis. "It seems to take a liking to you. Perhaps, due to your unnatural birth? Please," he commented as Aramis scowled. "You and I both know you don't play by the rules. I would be a fool to trust you by your word. It matters not. Those not worthy to wield it are doomed to die, one way or another. A curse placed by my ancestors." Korzha bent down to cup Aramis's chin and lifted it. "You can thank them when you meet your end."

"You ... first!" Aramis cried from the bottom of his gut.

With the last bit of strength within him, Aramis lunged at him. The Silver Star pierced true and through the general's gullet. Korzha cried out in shock, music to the Silver Fox's drumming ears.

The once gallant knight clutched the fiery blade. Korzha muttered something in his native tongue and Aramis felt relief from the blade's magical vice. Then the general stumbled back before he collapsed to his knees. The magic that awakened it dissipated. Blood oozed down to the hilt as it stained the white dueling blouse. When Korzha looked up to lock eyes with him one last time, Aramis blew him an air kiss.

For some reason, he chuckled. His teeth were stained with red. "You bastard."

With that, Octavian Augustus Korzha slumped to the wet cobblestones. His face contorted in agony as his lifeblood continued to leave him. His pale skin turned a snowy white.

Aramis saw Dido and Dawn running over to them. He stood to meet them, then felt the world tilt, and crashed into it. The next thing he knew, Aramis saw the clouds breaking to reveal a pale sunset.

Dawn held his head up, her voice dimmed by the ringing in his ears. "Hang in there. Just hang on, Aramis."

The ringing tuned to a higher octave. A wooden hull breached through the clouds overhead. Double-decker cannons lined its broadside as it veered with its magical rudders. Their colors flying from the central mast of their angled sails. Black with a single red stripe. Everything faded to the sound of a boatswain's whistle.

TO BE CONTINUED

The sky was crystal clear
The sun warm and bright
Josiah stood next to her
Took her hand, smiled her back

"What do you think of this place, Cynthia Brightman?"
"It's nice. There are no numbers in my head
"Do you think my dad is here? Can I play with him right now?"
"You can always ask him. Why don't you turn around?"

He was there and waiting
His arms open wide
Joyful tears and shrieks did they share
Everything dear is here

Book Club Questions

1. Aramis Feres has a tattooed set of numbers that were magically sealed, preventing him from taking it off. This is a reference to the tattooed numbers used against Jews and other prisoners during the Holocaust. Even though they could remove it, some didn't. Why do you suppose so? What would you do if you had undergone similar treatment?

2. History is told so we can remember the important events of our culture and the world we're part of. Part of it is to preserve ancient artifacts and buildings. At which point does an ordinary object become historical and worthy of preserving? Does it change when it's a building? Does it change if it was a mass-produced object from a factory?

3. Magic is prevalent in this world and can be used to preserve anything and anyone for centuries. Sometimes, the historical societies would use this to protect their precious collections. Should they? Does the act of aging make the object more precious to preserve? If they should use magic to suspend an object in perfect preservation, when should it be used?

4. The mannequins are robots given sentience through some form of artificial learning. Here in this particular future, they end up revolting and set off a war. How close are we in creating sentient mannequins in our own home, if not already? Do you think we'll end up in the same fate as the Ancients? Why or why not?

5. Self-learning machines are being created in labs and tested for medicinal research. Most ethic codes we have created are to prevent harm on humans and animals. Should we implement these same ethics for these machines during testing? If not, which ones should we, if any at all? Would the answer change when they're all biochemically created?

6. Going with the above question, would these ethics, if implemented in this world, have prevented these mannequins from revolting in the first place?

7. Aramis is a jhasin, a synthetically made being via magic and science. In what way is he different from the mannequins? In what way is he the same? Should the ethic codes discussed earlier be applied to jhasins?

8. The worshippers of the Morning Lord and Lune ended up favoring Lune and all of her daughters. This creates a dichotomy where being female is considered favorable in society, at least in Ioun. How does this compare to our society and religion? If this religion were adapted, what would change and what would stay the same?

9. Most religions allow their administrators to marry and have families, save for a few sects, like the Catholic church. In this book, the order used to allow marriage until they struck it down to prevent political influence.

What are the consequences for implementing marriage back into such an institution? Are they similar to what our religious institutions endured?

10. Sister Rhyllae was inducted into the order since she was an infant and had remained in service for sixty-one years. While many religious institutions participate in fostering and rearing orphans, most don't induct these children into their order. Should the Abbey of the Rising Dawn wait for Rhyllae to be old enough to allow her to be a priestess? Since Rhyllae is a half-elf, she would've been considered an adult as early as her 30s. Should they wait until that age to have her serve, or are there exceptions to this rule?

Glossary And Translations

Hasenpfeffer: a German rabbit stew

Kabsa: an Arabic meat and rice dish. Usually chicken and dried dates are used in the recipe.

Jibneh baida: an Arabic white cheese that's common in most households and businesses. The subtle flavor is deliciously tangy and salty.

Maiko: Japanese for "woman of dance." A professional title under the Geisha tradition where young woman learn all cultural songs and dances, while learning the craft of catering to her clients. She is an artist of a forgotten age.

Mouscous: an elvish short grain rice that is similar to the couscous grain. This variety has been perfected to last longer nutritionally.

Phoenix: A rare mythical creature of legend. In Töskan literature, they refer to them as "fire birds" for their extraordinary heat. This gives an impression that their plumes are red. They are not according to Chessentari, and the Nagano nations insisted they're white and their feathers are not flames, but wispy plumes. Eventually, one of the phoenix finally came forward to reveal their plumes are indeed flames, and they burn hot enough to appear white to most creatures. Her name was Tsuki.

Shab-e Yalda (Yalda Night): An Arabic holiday that celebrates winter solstice, also known as the longest night. Many citizens stay up late, reading poetry, and eat a variety of fruit and nuts, including pomegranates and watermelons. Red fruit is favored because of the warmth of the sun, a tradition that has merged with the Amaveriel's citizens' fervor for the Morning Lord.

Tuterlage: Töskan educational institution where local professionals teach their trade to students. It's similar to our school system, but it's recommended for children who are old enough to begin their apprenticeship. Some *tuterlages* are specialized, especially the military academies of the Töskan empire.

Elvish Translations

Argo: Elvish for "silver," adopted by the Ancients' vernacular usage.

Aly Thun Thŭr: Elvish for "The Sacred Seat," but most humans translate it to "The Holy Throne." This is where the Baba resides with her Cardinals of the Elements to guide the rest of the Holy Order under the Morning Lord and Lune. Legend has it that Lune's tomb is buried within, and to further protect her, the priestesses lifted the rock and have it floating in the sky. Prayers still carry it to this day.

Eirudeitrus: Elvish word for bacterial skin flora. Sadly, the meaning bacteria was lost and replaced by "invisible creatures of life." The mothers of the Morn teaches it as a concept of protecting all forms of life, even the ones we cannot see as a form of faith in the unknown.

Elyamamen: Elvish for "forever" or "always."

Lath‹q›oo: Elvish for "sun bird." It refers to Morning Lord's favored finch, the blue bird.

Lun‹q›oo: Elvish for "moon bird." It refers to Lune's favored dove, though some argue it's really a bat, a common nighttime animal.

Me'qora: Elvish for "my heart."

Numea'el: Elvish word for "to connect."

Sumac: Elvish to "trade," as in switching places or to swap.

Sundurai: Elvish word for "cut" or to sever.

Theliad: Elvish for "fox."

Tor'vi: Elvish for to "translocate, transport, move or travel an object."

Way elyamamen theliads argo'nim: Elvish for "We always remember the Silver Fox."

Dwarvish Translations

Dokl: Dwarven for "on."

Dovl: Dwarvish for "off."

Magical Incantations

Brže, brže = Croatian for "faster, faster."

Noževi, prihvati ovaj dor = Croatian. It's the beginning of the phrase "please accept this gift," but the line was cut off.

Svjetlo = Croatian for "light."

Miscellaneous Translations

Căcat: Romanian word for "shit."

D'accord: French for "okay."

Déjà vu: French for "I have been here before."

Ilumina: Romanian for "light" or "illuminate."

Kudasai: Japanese for "please," informal.

Levitacija: Croatian for "levitation."

Uhrmacher: German for "clockmaker."

Author Bio

K.N. FITZWATER WAS BORN AND RAISED IN THE heart of Kentucky. Growing up in a fantasy-loving home, she always wished she could travel, so she dreams stories of adventure and magic. The stories swam in her head until they spilled out on paper and bound together by twine. This is one of them.

If you want to join her on her adventures, you can follow her on BlueSky by @knfitzwater, K.N.Fitzwater on YouTube, and on Twitch by ArduousSpark912. You can join her newsletter through her website: www.knfitzwater.com.

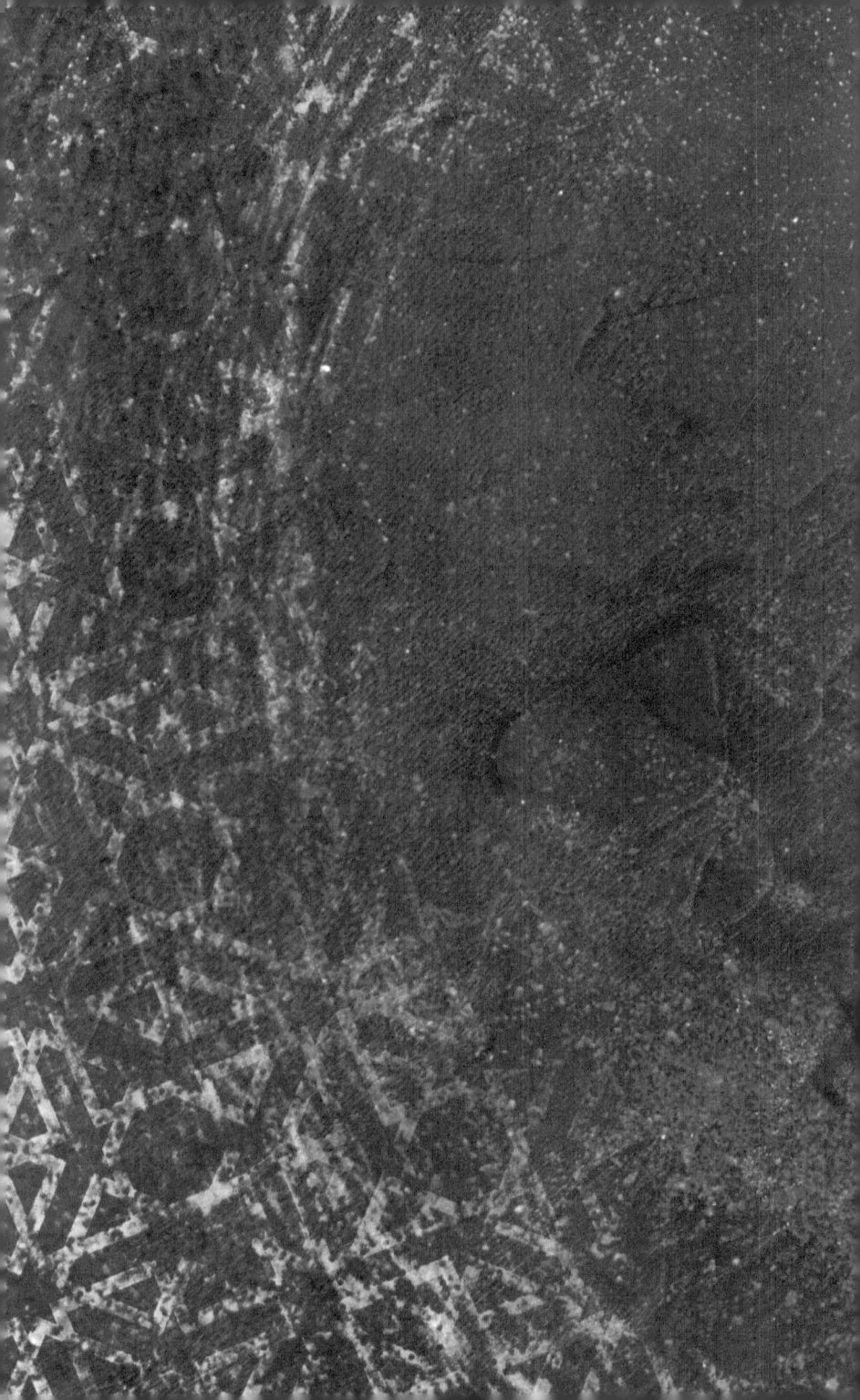

Discover more at
4HorsemenPublications.com

10% off using HORSEMEN10

www.ingramcontent.com/pod-product-compliance
Lightning Source LLC
LaVergne TN
LVHW041741060526
838201LV00046B/871